THE
WHITE SHIP

NICHOLAS SALAMAN

For Lyndsay

I

I opened the huge oak door of the barn, stepped quickly inside, and looked back to check that no one was watching.

The only thing that moved was the barn-smell which danced in the dust as I shut out the early sunlight behind me.

If you are interested in smells (and who cannot be), I can tell you it was a complex one. It was a dark, fusty, slightly gingery odour in which you could distinguish hay, rust, damp, horse, old wood, fungus, mouse droppings, rats, axle grease, and (if you sniffed very carefully) sex – and oranges. Oranges? I questioned my sense of the faint aroma – rare in these parts – but put it aside, distracted by a further aromatic seasoning from the moat, stirred by the morning breeze.

The oranges should have alerted me. Everything else was as usual, but I was tired that morning. It seemed anyway that I was safe; there was nobody about, not even a groom or a scullion. Everyone was late rising after the revels of last night.

The barn was a huge wooden affair on the other side of the grassy bailey from the castle itself, over against the marshalsea where they kept the horses. It was one of the favourite places for those wishing to make what the French call the beast with two backs – though usually not before dinnertime. Normally, I would not have been there at all (well, only after dinner and then hardly ever), but it is almost impossible to find a quiet place in a castle. Everyone's on top of you everywhere, even when you're having a piss.

All I wanted, intensely, that morning was somewhere to snatch a bit of sleep. There had been this great Feast of Easter celebration the night before, rejoicing at the princely presence and of course Jesus's Resurrection. After dinner, there was foolery, drollery, buffoonery, revelry and rudery.

You know how it is. The feasting went on late, there was too much wine, the Prince's fool told too many good jokes, and what with one thing and another and little Marianne, one of the

1

Comtesse's maids, I didn't get to sleep in my own bed until well past midnight, the hour when the Brothers at the abbey would be saying Matins. I had a bed in one of the knights' wooden halls that had sprouted in the bailey next to the stone of the castle, but my father, the Comte, had developed a habit of summoning me at all hours just to see if I was behaving myself, or out of sheer malice. Last night was no problem because he was drunk and wouldn't stir; but this morning it would be a different matter, and I knew he would be coming for me, rooting me out of bed and on parade before I was ready.

I had contrived to wake early because I knew that I still needed a good long sleep, undisturbed, somewhere my father wouldn't immediately find me. That was the first essential, to keep out of his reach – because he's a crusty old bugger, to be honest, especially after a night's carousing. He thinks he can still carouse, but if you ask me he's well past it, even if he has got a young wife. A man should stop carousing after forty and fix his mind on prayer and sweetmeats. Carousing is for younger men like myself – when we can get it.

So I had dragged on my clothes as soon as I woke, thought immediately of the barn as a suitable location, and sidled across the bailey, not for a moment imagining that I would stumble on a secret that, if divulged, would probably cost me my life. I entered, quiet as a harvest mouse in case a sneaking groom was skulking somewhere, and made my way towards the stacks of hay piled up like a house against the back wall.

Oranges! That was where it came from. The scent filled the corridor between the hay stacks. It was then that I heard them; a low whisper, a little cry. I crept nearer because there is a pleasure in secret discovery.

'Darling,' I heard a voice cry, a man's voice. 'Darling, darling.'

What I saw made me choke with surprise. It was the English Prince and he was embracing – I like to use that word because anything else would be gross and although I am a bastard, at least I am the bastard of a Comte – he was embracing the Comtesse, my father's second wife, bastard daughter of the

2

Duke who was also King Henry of England; the most beautiful woman you ever saw; blonde as an angel, middle to tall, with a skin the colour of late spring honey infused with a drop or two of very pale medlar jelly. Her mother had been a beauty before her, a lady called Ede, daughter of an English lord, it was said...

No, I have to tell you this in riper words, the situation is too strong for delicacy. The Prince William, known as 'the Atheling', in whom resided the hopes of all the English, son of King Henry and of the half-Scots, half-Saxon Queen Matilda, was fornicating with his half-sister, two years older than he was. He was fucking my stepmother and because this was not the sort of thing you do in public with your host's wife, they had found a quiet place removed from the hubbub of the castle, just as I had done, to make the beast with eight legs, as we say in Normandy. Of course, I had noticed before now my stepmother's predilection for the oils of orange that she used about her body, and here it was, heating up nicely.

I tell you, men have lost their lives for witnessing less. Do you think I gave a discreet cough and a 'good morning, Prince'? The hell I did. I moved out so quietly God himself didn't notice.

But perhaps I should explain myself and my life, which was precious to me at the time.

II

I am the son of Rotrou, Lord of Mortagne and Comte de Perche, a small county but important because of its central position towards the southern end of the Duchy of Normandy. My name is Bertold. I am a good-looking bastard, though I say it myself, or I was in those days, but the emphasis is very much on bastard. I am illegitimate. I don't mind making jokes about bastards, but I would rather you didn't.

Duke Henry is master of Normandy, or most of it – the Normans are a troublesome lot. It is the season of spring, in the year of Our Lord 1118.

A fortnight or so before, on my twenty-first birthday, I had been summoned to my father's castle. I had been in an abbey for eight years, learning Latin (it is the *lingua franca* of advancement) and other useful things, like avoiding the groping hands of certain monks. I had almost, but not quite, become accustomed to thinking that a monastic life was for me. It had its advantages, and there was no other comfortable alternative. I could become a soldier, but that was a desperate calling and I was ambitious. I wanted to turn my learning to some use; but what, and how?

The summons, which solved my problem, had surprised me. I had had no idea that the old Comte thought of me in any way at all, least of all remembered my birthday, since I was his bastard, not his legal son. It soon turned out that it was my dead mother's husband, my stepfather, the castle cellarer, who had put him up to it. He had urged the Comte to summon me home. At Mortagne, the cellarer was more important than in many such places because here the butler was old and infirm, and leant on him heavily. My stepfather was, in fact, his deputy and aspired to that title, but he needed someone to help him with his duties, and thought he could use me and pay me nothing. He was a mean man and never forgot a debt of any kind, and he considered that I owed him something for having been given his shelter as a child. No wonder my mother had succumbed to the temporary advances of the Comte de Perche who – though he, God knows, was no great shakes – at least appreciated a beautiful woman.

On my return to the castle, I had found the place in a state of some excitement, as sometimes happens when Lent draws to a close and the girls and boys start looking at each other in that way they have. It was particularly the case this year, however, because William, son of Duke Henry, was due to arrive with his retinue on Easter Saturday. The sixteen-year-old Prince was accompanying his father for the first time at the start of the year's campaigning in Normandy, knocking the barons' heads together, but he had taken leave from his military duties to celebrate the feast of Easter with his half-sister, my little stepmother the Comtesse Matilda, my father's bride of a couple of years. The Prince had been very close to her, apparently, when they were in England, but until today I had had no idea quite how close they had been.

The old Comte, my father, had married this Matilda, Duke Henry's illegitimate daughter, when she was just sixteen because his first wife had died. The Comte was feeling cold in bed, and the Duke wanted an ally, so it suited them both. Admittedly the girl was a bastard but still a daughter of a Duke – a Duke who was also King of England. It was an honour of a kind, even though Henry has more bastards than any King of England before him, and that is saying something. I don't blame him. If I were a king and a duke, I would have plenty myself, but somehow the same opportunities do not come my way. Lovely blonde Saxon girls are not two a penny in the county of Perche, where the local specialities are big handsome draught horses, sometimes dapple-grey, or thick-waisted Norman girls with hair like a rope-trick and a laugh like a saw-blade.

So it was a marriage of convenience, the Duke wanted powerful allies in Normandy, and the Comte de Perche, who was not universally popular – though who is in Normandy? – could bask in the ducal favour and all it entailed. Perche was useful to the Duke, who had given another beautiful daughter in marriage to the neighbouring Comte de Breteuil, a man with a face like a suet pudding whose favourite occupations were fighting and drink. The Comte de Breteuil and his Comtesse, half-sister to our Matilda, were also guests at Mortagne this Easter, on the occasion of the Prince, their half-brother's, visit.

No one had asked either of the girls whether they wanted to be married to these Norman gargoyles. The Pope had now declared it sinful for anyone to force a girl to marry, but when you are a princess there are other considerations, and the Pope was always ready to listen to reason from a king. When I think of what it must be like to be married to the Comte de Breteuil or to my father, I am pleased to be an unimportant bastard. Not that I think bastards are unimportant, please don't get that idea. As bastards go, I give a pretty good account of myself.

I am just under six foot tall (six foot on a good day). I have dark hair (with a Norman tendency to unruliness), clean features, a fresh face, clear, blue eye, and a ready smile. Too ready, my father – who values seriousness – would say, but I would rather disarm with a smile than fight. However, if it comes to fighting, then I am the man for it. In Normandy all the barons have their own little armies and love to use them. And one thing I learned at the monastery – well, I learned many things, but one thing I learned which may surprise you – was wrestling. I don't want you to think of me as a pale shrimp of a clerk. The monks loved a wrestle, a useful art in those dangerous days, though they would not necessarily have liked the world to know it, and some of them were very proficient at it, but I was abbey champion. The other thing we were good at was music. The Abbot saw no contradiction in that. *Mens sana in corpore sano* was his creed – or one of them.

Back to the barn, then, and on with the bastard's tale – a better one, you may find, than many a story told by a man born between lawful sheets.

III

I walked back across the bailey in some confusion; shocked, yes – not at the act of fucking, but at the enormous danger I had put myself in, and at them too. From what I had seen of him, I thought the Prince not a bad sort for an Englishman: arrogant of course; spoilt – that goes without saying – but you couldn't blame him because the whole world treated him as if the sun rose out of his arse and never set. And as for the Comtesse, I had been half in love with her myself.

My concerns must have made me careless, because a voice boomed out:

'You.'

I knew immediately that it was I who was being addressed. I really don't think my father knew my name. 'You' was what he habitually called me.

I stopped and adopted a low, subservient, watchful expression. I had found that usually worked best with my father.

'Where do you think you're sneaking off to?'

It was a shame, really, being a bastard. For one thing, you weren't called Comte like your father, you were called 'bastard' by your equals or 'you' by your father. You didn't inherit the castle, or anything at all if you were unlucky or didn't look appreciative when you were called 'you'. There was no dignity in bastardy (unless you were called William the Conqueror). That's why I say I am a nobody even though my father is a powerful man. I am nothing to him and nothing to the world, but quite a lot to myself, as you may have gathered.

Ever since I can remember I have had the peculiar sensation that I am an onlooker, not exactly part of the life that I am leading. It is like being accompanied always by your image in a glass that follows you everywhere. Perhaps other people feel like this. I do not know. There is nothing I can do about it. Once or twice, I feel I have been warned by my shadow self about something, and the warning has usually been right. Sometimes I seem to know things that I should not know and people look at me strangely, so I have learned to keep such things to myself. Someone is looking after me and, I tell you, we bastards can do with all the help we can get. Perhaps it is an angel and God really does look after us.

Of course, it depends whose bastard you are. Duke Henry or, as the English call him, King Henry, made many with those fair Saxon girls, sometimes high-born, sometimes little villeinesses. And, to be fair to him – which one should be because he has sharp ears and a long memory – he made sure that all his children married well, mostly (as I say) to powerful Norman barons whose allegiance or loyalty he wanted. That was why the daughter of his lovely blonde English mistress, Ede, had been made to marry the crabbed old Comte de Perche, my father.

My God, Matilda was a lovely girl: the sun seemed to have spun the strands of her hair. How she could endure mottled old father Perche was a mystery. He looked like one of his old dappled Percheron horses, only less shapely and bigger round the girth. But then it turned out she found comfort with her sweet half-brother; a bit of a prick maybe, but there was no doubt he loved her. I picked up a lot of gossip at the bottom of my lord's table because I always kept my ears open, though the discovery of just how much sweet William loved his half-sister was my own. If I valued my life (which I did), I would have to keep it to myself, because princes – even princes as young and spoilt as William – have a long reach.

'I was just going to put in some practice at the quintain.'

I knew my father approved of that kind of thing. The quintain was a sort of swivelling-iron device which presented you, as you approached, with a heavy image of a man with a helmet on. It swivelled towards you, and you were supposed to hit it with your mace in order to send it round again. Sometimes it had a sort of flailing attachment which sneaked round with an erratic motion and caught you on the head if you weren't

10

looking, very painful too. My father's quintain had that attachment.

'Don't give me that shit, boy.'

Being a bastard was much better than being a serf, I suppose, never knowing where you stood and liable to be sold along with the fields you worked on. In fact, quite a lot of respectable people were bastards these days. Making them was an honourable trade long before the reign of King Henry, but he had made it more fashionable than before, almost de rigueur as you might say, among those at court.

'It isn't shit, sir.'

It is actually. I dislike all that hacking and hewing. My father's fault, in point of fact. When my mother, who was a nice woman – a reeve's daughter, nicely brought up – came to him to tell him she was with child, he told her, if I were a boy I would never be a knight. He wanted to punish her because her news made him feel inconvenienced, embarrassed, guilty or maybe he just had a bad hangover. At any rate, she was pleased because she didn't want me to be a knight. She wanted me to be a priest. Priests had much better lives, were safer and better fed. My mother never wanted glory for me, only a soft bed, a full belly, and a nice little girl to cuddle, all of which a priest could have in those days.

The upshot was I was sent to an abbey to pray and learn Latin. It struck me as unfair that my father should expect me to be proficient with shield and mace on my return.

'You are a disgrace to the Perches.'

'Yes, sir. What would you like me to do, sir?'

'Get out of my sight.'

Bastard children, if they are men, are called 'fils' or 'son' of whoever the lucky father might be: Fils Robert, or Fils William, or Fils Gerald, but the English, who find it hard to say 'fils', call them Fitz. Almost every other person you meet in England is called FitzSomething, I am told. It's because the English drink so much – always have done, something to do with the weather – and the English women are promiscuous, the lot of them, as we have just seen (something to do with the weather). I

11

met a Dane once and the only thing he would say about England was 'English women have dirty feet'. So there you have it. Anyway, if we were in England, I would be called FitzRotrou because that is my father's name.

'I came to tell you how I was doing in the world, sir.'

But he had turned away to talk to his falconer. This was more like it. Perhaps I could get some shut-eye somewhere now.

My mother died of a fever when I was away at the monastery. She had caught a chill and had not looked after herself – as I would have made her do – but she was never one for being ill. Indeed she wasn't ill for long, and she died before they could fetch me to say goodbye to her. My father had thought it wasn't worth disturbing my education. She was a good mother and I was stricken with grief, but when you are fourteen years old and already half a man, nothing lasts for long, not even sorrow. I knew now that whatever life held for me, it was up to me to make it happen. I could depend on no one else. That is the bastard creed. Use or be used – and do both with a smile.

Mother had left me very little, only some old Norman silver. (Her father, the reeve, had a son to whom he had left his house and what little money he had.) But what she had done for me was to make me tall and well-featured, with eyes the colour of a speedwell flower (so they were described by the maid of my stepmother the Comtesse, and why argue?), and an expression that defaulted to a smile even when I didn't feel like it. This smile disconcerted my enemies and enraptured my lovers. It was more valuable than money in many ways, though it was about to lead me into one hell of a lot of trouble.

The trouble showed itself as I slouched away from that encounter with my father, hugging the walls in case he should suddenly reappear. Hugging them so tight in fact that I almost bumped into someone coming from the opposite direction, someone who looked like a slightly more imperious version of my own father's lovely Comtesse.

I was immediately assailed by her fragrance: rose, deep and passionate, a light touch of spice with something more troubling, the heart-quickening smell of wallflowers, with that appley-almondy smell of her skin …

I judged her to be some twenty-four years of age. She clutched at her bosom to draw breath. It struck me that she too had been anxious not to be seen.

'My apologies!' I gasped, thinking what a wonderful clutch that bosom made.

I had learned courtesy from my mother whose politeness had indeed, along with her beauty, so charmed the Comte my father that he had taken her into his bed, although alas she had not been able to teach him any. I had been furthered in the art of civilised conduct by an old Spanish Jew at my monastery, Saul Alfonsi. He had converted to Christianity and the monks called him Brother Paul because the apostle Paul was a Jew made good. His brother, a physician at court, had written *Disciplina Clericalis* drawing on the Mahomedan tradition of *adab* or courtesy.

'One might almost have thought you did not want to be seen, coming round a corner like that,' the beautiful girl remarked.

'It is true,' I said, feeling that honesty might be the most amusing course. 'I was trying to escape my father.'

Now that I had a little time to compose my mind and observe the girl's distinguishing features rather than her general impression, I saw that she was a tall young woman with a splendid head of red-gold hair, a fine full figure, green eyes and a flawlessly pale skin. That was how it struck me at the time, and I have not revised the impression since.

'Your father? Who is he?' she asked.

'He is Comte Rotrou of Perche.'

She laughed.

'There's more to him than meets the eye,' she said. 'And your name?'

'I am his bastard Bertold. May I ask who I had the honour of nearly knocking over?'

'I am the Duke's bastard daughter Juliana, Comtesse de Breteuil.'

I knew that the Duke was also the King of England, and another of the Duke's daughters was here to visit her sister at the castle, but I had not listened properly to any details. There were many pretty women at dinner last night, but I must have been blind or drunk – or both – not to notice this lady. The King's daughter! A phrase from the Psalms swam into my mind: 'Kings' daughters shall be among thy honourable women.' Oh yes, indeed, she could be among my honourable women any time. I was a lusty scoundrel in those days.

'We bastards must stick together,' I said, rather cheekily.

It seemed to me in my impudence that this encounter might offer opportunities for Bertold's advancement. I could see that the idea amused her.

'Oh yes,' she said, 'perhaps we should ...'

There was the tiniest pause between 'perhaps' and 'we should', as I believe she intended. She was too much a lady to say anything more obvious, but I noticed it. All you want when you are young is a fuck and a furtherance. Better and better, Bertold.

She prepared to move on. I thought I could not let her go without some furthering; we must pick apples when we see them ripe and there was a smell of apples about her – and an airy spice, and the faint smell of a spark just after the flint has been struck.

'When shall I see you again...?' I started to blurt in a desperate manner that my old Jewish mentor at the monastery would have deplored.

'Not so fast, my young Fitz. All in good time.'

She was almost gone, poised on that soft little bit of foot behind the toes.

'Who were *you* hiding from?' I asked.

'My husband, of course.'

And then she walked on. I stood, deep in thought because I had met a wonderful girl who might just, conceivably, be the way ahead for a young man without prospects. The next moment, a bucket of water was poured over me. I looked round, somewhat irritated, not wanting to appear ridiculous in case the Comtesse should come back, and ready to put the blame roundly on my father because it was just the sort of thing he would do. But it was not the Comte, it was that prick of a son of his, Robert, the son and heir legitimate. Fifteen years old and already a complete arsehole.

'Thought you were getting a bit hot,' he smirked. 'Thought you needed to cool down.'

'I'm going to kill you,' I said.

But he kept his distance and snivelled.

'Bastard,' he said. 'You bastard. You touch me and I'll tell my father. Anyway, you shouldn't go talking like that to your betters. I can talk to a comtesse because I am going to be a comte. But you're always going to be a bastard.'

I wasn't going to take this, Comte or no Comte. I made a grab for Robert and he ran off like the cowardly little twerp he was, and I couldn't be bothered to chase him. Instead I fixed my mind on Juliana. She was hardly older than me and I could sense that she liked me. She was a spirited girl that was for sure. She wasn't going to hide from me the way she hid from her husband. But why was she hiding from him?

I watched the man in hall that evening and the reasons were all too clear. He was another boring old fart. He picked his nose, which is absolutely counter to the advice in *Divina Clericalis* which Brother Paul had shown me, and when this Comte belched he did not look up at the ceiling which everyone knows is the thing to do. He was simply beyond the bounds of custom and duty.

IV

I hope you will bear with me if I take you again for a little ride into my past, because it has some bearing on the extraordinary tale that I am going to unfold for you, and also because I have an affection for what has been. I am not the only one. Does it not say in Ecclesiastes 3.15: 'For that which is past is now, and that which is to be hath already been, and God requireth that which is past'? It seems to me the past is the only thing that assures you that you really do exist. The present is all too self-consuming. It eats time and never gets any fatter.

I could recite nearly the whole of the Bible once, in Latin. When I was sent away to the monastery I wanted to go because I had an interest in medicine at the time, still have to some extent, and I had a mind to learn. I had heard that an abbey beyond L'Aigle on the road to Montreuil, about thirty miles from my home, was a place where the new teaching brought by the Jews from Spain had filtered through. It was the best place in Normandy for mathematics as well as doctoring and had a strong connection with the medical school in Montpellier. These were the weapons – mathematics and medicine, rather than the sword and the lance – that were going to make my fortune, and of course there was Latin to be learned, the language of scholars and men on the make. I was precocious in those days. Now my future is all behind me.

I was persistent enough to bring the Abbey of Saint-Sulpice to my mother's attention. She brought it to my father's, so in the end they sent me there, though my mother wept when I left, as did I. It was a hard place in many ways. The endless round of services – from Lauds starting before first light, to Matins at midnight, said as we kneeled in front of our beds in the dormitory – seemed designed to put a boy off a life of holiness rather than encourage it. Not that I was interested in a life of holiness at the time; the blood ran warm in those cold days.

The food for novices was anything the Brothers didn't want to eat themselves, often gristle and slops. Later, I made friends with Brother Gilbert, the cook, who also came from my county of Perche and didn't need bribing with a feel up my tunic. I don't pretend to be perfect. I would have let him have a grope for a loaf and a slice of bacon. It isn't so bad if you don't make a habit of it. That is a monk joke. We used to have a number of those. The trouble with masturbation is that it can get out of hand. And so on, and so on.

The bone-chipping cold in my stone cell, the beatings when I transgressed or was idle, the advances of some of the too-friendly brothers (especially Brother Thomas), were all tribulations, but on the positive side, I was taught to read. And what made my stay at Saint-Sulpice even more useful than literacy and Latin, music and medicine, was the new mathematics.

The old Jew, who taught me good manners, had brought knowledge up from the south, and was also a mathematician. It was he who showed me the new numerals of the Arabs which he had learnt in Castile and which made the Roman numbers seem cumbersome and slow – and what's more he taught me how to use them. Brother Paul made me put one set of the old Roman numbers on top of a lesser one, told me to take away the lesser from the larger, and then when I had juggled all those Vs and Xs and Cs and Ds and Ms, he showed how much simpler it was to do it with the new Arabic numbers. After that we did addition, and I discovered how to put the Arab numbers together to make a larger sum in half the time. And so on with multiplication and division. Multiplication I had previously found a graveyard littered with those Roman letters which passed for numbers. And division had been even worse.

Best of all, since I was acquiring a strong persuasion that the way to be happy was to be rich, Brother Paul showed me how these new numerals made tallying much easier. I could see a future in that.

'Do not call it tallying, that is for peasants and those who still use the abacus,' said the old Jew. 'You keep these figures on a slate or, if you are rich, on vellum. You write everything down. One side of beef ... three silver pennies. You must have a record of transactions if you are to control your trade and your life. And when you are rich don't forget old Saul who taught you that.'

'I shall not forget you, Brother,' I told him, and I meant it.

My head was astir with the possibilities of these new numbers which were so strange and yet so simple compared with the old Roman way. He talked about using these new numbers in a science the Greeks know as geometry and in an even stranger invention of the Arabs, a science hardly known in this country, called *al-gebra* which in time he would show me.

That said, he looked me solemnly in the eye.

'And now,' he said, 'I am going to show you a wonder.'

'What is it?' I asked him. 'Is it a trick with powder and fire? Or a way to turn iron into gold?

He took a piece of charcoal and drew a circle on the table.

'There,' he said. 'This is what you need to make the heavens themselves seem small.'

'A circle?' I exclaimed. 'Is it a magic circle into which you can lure spirits?'

'It is a magic circle, certainly, though I cannot speak for the spirits. But you yourself can perform miracles with it.'

'What is it?' I asked again, wishing to be great very soon.

'It is nothing,' he told me, gravely. 'It is naught. It is zero. It is the greatest invention of the Arabs. But it is truly not even theirs – they borrowed it from the Indians.'

'Nothing? I can't see what use nothing can be. You are joking. Or perhaps you have been hoodwinked. I have heard naught like it.'

'Naught with an a is a word but nought with an o is a figure – a circle with nothing inside it,' he told me. 'It is not just nothing – though it is the *symbol* for nothing which neither the Romans nor the Greeks had thought of. It is also the symbol of magnitude, of increasing any given figure by the power of ten if it is written behind it. Thus 6, the new Arabic number for the Roman VI, becomes 60 if we put a zero after it.'

I began to see what he was driving at.

'And 3 becomes 30…' I said, writing the figures down as he had shown me.

'And what if I put a nought after the nought?' he asked.

I was puzzled by that. I had never seen figures of this kind.

'If these were Roman numerals,' he said, 'it would be like multiplying by X every time you put 0 behind a number.'

'Why,' I exclaimed, '30 multiplied by ten becomes 300. And 300 times ten is 3000. And…'

My head was spinning with the size of these figures.

'He drew a few random figures to show me, announcing their quantities as he went.

'Copy these new numbers out,' he continued '1 to 9, and play with them, sprinkle the noughts around and see what figures you make! And the only one you cannot make is infinity. That is God's number.'

We had been able to calculate before but never with such simple means! I felt the power of the new knowledge surging through me; I was sure it had been looking for me as its vessel, not this scrawny old Jew, decent man and scholar that he was. Where would I be without him? But if I wasn't careful, he would go and blurt it out to the world.

'Don't tell anyone about this,' I urged him. 'We should keep it to ourselves. Magic stops being magic if everyone knows it.'

'You cannot hold back the spread of knowledge,' the old man told me, gravely. 'You might as well try to stop the Eure with a shrimping net. With these Arab numbers and the Hindu one for zero, any number can be written and the universe is within man's grasp. Keep it to yourself? It would be like keeping the secret of perfect proportion. No, no. This method is for mankind, not just for you.

'And do not be condescending or proud about nothing, for nothing is an absence of something and pregnant with possibility. Something itself can be dull, boring, flat and lumpen, but nothing is the creative state from which all things arose. Try to get back to it sometimes.'

Eccentric as I thought he was, I promised that I would do so if I could, and he went on to tell me more about the Arabs, how they had built castles all over Spain, in stone, when the French were still building with wood and earth. It was said that they had learned the art from the Byzantines.

'I hope you are not going to ask me to build a castle with you,' I asked him.

He chuckled. 'I would do it,' he said, 'if we had the time and the implements. I have an idea about rounding off the edges of castle towers to make them less vulnerable, but we will have to sit on that for a while. The Normans love their square towers ... Oh, and there is another thing I have to show you. Something the Arabs do with wine. They heat it and distil it in a retort over fire until a pure essence comes out of it which they call alcohol. See! Smell this.'

He reached across and put a small glass bottle into my hand. I took the stopper out and sniffed. A sweet and volatile aroma came out unlike anything I had smelt before.

'Taste it,' he said.

I put a little on my finger which I raised to my mouth. It stung my tongue and lips, and tasted fiery.

'Ouch. Mmm. What do they use it for?' I asked.

'For fragrant attars and essences of flowers; for anything that needs to be perfectly clean; for medicine; for preserving small animals or anything that is to be kept; and of course it can make you, very quickly, perfectly inebriated.'

'But you told me the Mussulmen do not drink wine...'

'They use this liquor for other purposes.'

'Did you make it yourself?' I asked. 'Is this the fire-water?'

'Yes, but you must not talk about it yet. There is a time for things. I have used it several times on injuries in the sickroom, to clean the wounds. It is a powerful thing, and needs to be kept carefully.'

'But you told me knowledge was to be shared?' I said, impertinently.

'Not if it can also do harm and make men sick,' he told me, reprovingly.

21

I promised him that I would not speak of any of this unless he wished it. He was a good man and a good friend to me, and he had given me much to think about. Time passed pleasantly enough in the abbey infirmary where I worked with Brother Paul. We were excused everything but the major services which usually amounted to three a day, and those during the hours of daylight and evening, not in the shivering midnight of Matins and the early morning Lauds. While we were not tending the ill or infirm, we spoke of mathematics and medicine and distillation and siege engines but never of women, which was a subject I also wanted to investigate. I managed to find a girl in the village when I was sent out to take a nostrum to the sick. She showed me the rudiments – and very rudiment they were – but I could see that Brother Paul disapproved. I was ready for the world, chafing at the predictability of abbey life, but there seemed to be no way out of it, until the message from my father arrived on the eve of my twenty-first birthday.

The Abbot wished me well and gave me a little silver for my journey, and some useful precepts which I am sorry to say I have forgotten. Then I went to say goodbye to Brother Paul. He embraced me and presented me with a portable chest into which he had placed sundry dried herbs and several unguents in sealed bottles, along with a leather-bound missal he had made and inscribed. I quickly established it to be a medicinal missal not a religious one: notes, ingredients and decoctions in *al-cohol* to help cure common ailments and one or two more complicated ones.

'Pray God you never have to bore into a man's skull,' he said, 'but if you do, you will find instructions here. It is an operation more frequently needed than you might think in these days of war.'

Enclosed among its pages was a single piece of vellum on which he had written various calculations – everything I needed to practise the new mathematics. I embraced the old man and thanked him for his teaching and his friendship. I believe I may have noticed a tear in his eye for we had grown close in the last months and I had come to look forward to his conversation, and his wisdom drawn from a long life and from encountering many hazards in lands whose names I did not even know. All this I had now to put behind me, and it pained us both that it should be so.

'Look after yourself,' the old Jew told me. 'You have a rare quality. That is, you see too much. What is good is that you have already learned to be careful with it. Don't seem too clever, or speak too much. Listen and watch, and all will become clear – if you are lucky.'

'And if I am not?'

'Then you will have to go forward in a fog like the rest of us,' he said with a twinkle, although he was the least foggy man I have ever met.

I embraced him and he gave me a small silver object which he said was an amulet. He told me always to keep it about my person and in the last resort to pray to the gods on it.

'The gods?' I looked at him in astonishment.

'Did I say that?'

There was a twinkle in his lizardy old eyes.

'Remember, if you ever have to tally, use the Arab numerals for money-in and money-out. They are worth more than a bag of gold,' he told me, 'or even a bright sword to hang by your side.'

'You have given me so much,' I told him, 'and I have given you so little.'

'More than you think,' he said.

I embraced him again, and took a last walk round the abbey, saying goodbye to my friends. I think the Brothers, though they lamented my departure and begged me to change my mind, were quite relieved to see the back of me – perhaps I was becoming a little wild. Brother Hubert who looked after the stables lent me a little black palfrey which I promised to send back to him, though he said I need not and it was a parting gift from the abbey.

So, in borrowed clothes from the abbey's charity-chest, armed with a curious old sword which Brother Paul had saved

23

from a dying veteran (for the roads were full of those who wished you no good whether you were English, French or Norman), and bolstered by the power of nought, I made my way on the little black nag which I named Blackberry. We ambled down daffodil lanes, through Rugles, L'Aigle and Notre-Dame D'Après, back towards the place where I had been born. It was the Ides of March.

And now I have brought us back to where I started and I can pick up the tale.

V

After my meeting with Juliana, Comtesse de Breteuil, by the curtain wall, I lived in a ferment of anxiety to see her again. My experience of women might have been slim, but instinct is everything, and sometimes you know that you have met the right person, one of the people in the world who carries a special secret only you can understand.

The feasting at the castle went on for days during which I glimpsed her several more times. I even spoke to her when I happened to brush past her in hall, formally and with a low voice as befitted my station, but there was no opportunity to rekindle the candour of our conversation by the castle wall. Perhaps it was best forgotten. There were many cautionary tales concerning young men who entertained thoughts of love towards high-born women, and they all ended disastrously.

Once Easter was over, the cellarman (my stepfather) began with all his customary charmlessness to instruct me in the mysteries of the wine trade which, I have to say, he knew backwards: the different types of wine, the best way to store the barrels, how to tell a bad wine from a good one (my untutored taste was for the sweeter wines like Malvasia), how long to keep a good one, what kind of bottle to use, how to veil flavour and add taste with herbs and how to mask a bad wine with spices, how much to pay and when to buy, how to account for every drop of wine drunk in the castle …

I liked wine but found little opportunity to drink much of it. Small instructive sips were all the old red-nose would allow. He guarded his barrels jealously, sometimes even sleeping down in the fragrant vaults. I think it was because of this tendency that the Comte was able to steal into the nuptial bed.

I have to confess that my stepfather was a sound teacher. If I had had six months of his tuition instead of several weeks I would have been able to take his place when he journeyed in October to the vineyards of Anjou – and give a good account of myself with my tally of wine out and in when he returned. I had already devised a way of using the Arabic numbers that was far quicker than the cumbersome method the old man used. In his tight-fisted and begrudging way he was almost grateful for my work, but I was careful to copy everything I wrote into the old tally system of notches on a stick. I was not going to give up my secret numbers and my nought yet.

However, my future in the wine trade was not to be. I was crossing the castle bailey one day, a couple of weeks after Easter, feeling sorry for myself because the excitements were over, the mood in the castle was flat, and I was in love. The Prince had already returned to his father, and the Comtesse Juliana and her husband had gone back to the castle of Breteuil. I was crossing, as I say, like a lovesick lamprey, when I felt a terrific blow between the shoulders. I staggered and nearly dropped the small firkin I was carrying. Brother Paul had taught me that it is dangerous to strike in that place unless it is in battle, for it can incapacitate a man.

'Ha!'

It was my father, the Comte, smiling like an alchemist's crocodile.

'What are you doing carrying wine, boy?'

'Helping the cellarer, sir.'

'Is this what we educated you for? Did you learn Latin to carry wine?'

'No, sir.'

'My wife's sister, the Comtesse de Breteuil, wants you to tutor her two girls. Is that rather more your *métier*, do you think?'

My heart leapt, this was the summit of all my wishes, something I had not even dared hope for, but I had to be careful not to show excitement or gratification. These things were so easily stamped upon.

'I should think so, sir.'

I adjusted my face to resignation. A thought had struck me.

'Sir?'

'Try not to waste my time. I have a great deal on my mind.'

26

All he had on his mind was humping one of the laundrywomen – sturdy girls like the one who was William the Conqueror's mother. Word was that my father's Comtesse wouldn't have him near the bedroom.

The favourite pastimes for a baron like my father were whoring, hunting and soldiering. Father enjoyed the hunt but wasn't much of a one for soldiering, although occasionally he had to send a few knights with some Percheron cavalry to march with Duke Henry for his various struggles. The Duke was always struggling with someone – the King of France, for instance – and on the whole he seemed to win. Then again, at other times, he seemed to lose. He had friends and, then again, he had many enemies (including his brother, the previous Duke, a hopeless case, whom he had fought and imprisoned for life).

I became aware that my father was waiting for me to say something.

'Your wife's sister, sir?' I asked, feigning stupidity.

'The Comtesse de Breteuil. Try not to be as simple as you look. She met you and formed a good impression of you, God knows how, when she was here for the Prince's feast. She is the Comtesse de Breteuil. Saddle up. Take a horse but not one of the big ones. That nag you brought from the abbey will do. Pack some decent clothes if you have any, and take the road to Verneuil and then on to Breteuil itself. Play it right and you may come back a better man.'

'Right, sir.'

'Don't disappoint me now. She is not to be crossed.'

I was beside myself with joy. The beautiful Comtesse had asked for me. Of course, I was young in those days and easily excited. My arrogance at that time still takes my breath away.

'I will do my best not to cross her, my lord. Nothing shall stand in the way.'

His face softened momentarily. Perhaps he was remembering my mother. Anyway, he threw me a purse with some silver in it.

'Don't spend it all on women, boy. It was your father's little weakness, but he could afford it.'

It was the first time he had ever referred to his paternity, and I was too surprised to speak, but before I could recover myself he had turned and was gone.

Before I left, I looked for the pretty Comtesse, my stepmother, to say goodbye to her out of courtesy, but she could not be found. Probably she was hiding in a quiet corner of the castle, not easy to locate, thinking about her prince. I had always found the cheese-house another good place for a quiet cuddle, but it was scullion's stuff and not suitable for the king's daughter, although I did look in there too because I thought Matilde might have a message for her sister Juliana.

Juliana. A lovely name, don't you think? A lady's name. One not to be trifled with and smacking of Imperial Rome, about which I had learned at the monastery. Brother Paul had managed to find copies of Ovid and Virgil and even Horace and Livy in the library. And Sallust's *History of Rome*, mustn't forget Sallust, he said, and Suetonius. I had steeped myself in the grandeur of the eternal city and the foibles of its inhabitants. There was nothing they could not teach us about treachery, brutality, glory, honour and the game of love.

When I told the cellarer, my stepfather, of the Comte's command, though he could not very well argue with it, he was considerably put out. I did not explain that, ever since I had come back to the castle, I had been intent on leaving it again. A world was out there full of new things, new ideas coming up from the Pays d'Oc, things I wanted to see. Now, though I would actually be going twenty miles to the north-east, it was a start; anywhere away from Mortagne seemed like a gate to the south.

As I was saddling up Blackberry, my little black nag – who greeted me with a whicker and a wag of the head as if to say 'What? More trouble?' – two people in succession came to see me off. The first was my half-brother Robert, who suggested that I had been sent away because no one wanted me around.

'Be sure not to come back too soon, if at all,' he said, and slunk off towards the kitchen (where they would give him cakes because he was the lord's son) before I could kick his arse.

The second was the Comtesse Matilda with one of her maids, who was instructed to stand a little apart from us.

'You are going to Breteuil?'

'Yes, my lady.'

'Tell my sister, the Comtesse, how much I miss her. I feel quite dead without my family. Will you tell her that? She will understand.'

I understood, too, having seen something of her particular involvement with her family. I felt a little mouse of sympathy, scuttling away somewhere at the back of my mind, for my oaf of a father who could not know about her unsisterly interest in the prince. She held out her hand, and I kissed it.

Every window in the castle seemed to have someone watching as I pricked out on Blackberry towards the gatehouse and the road to adventure …

VI

My journey to Verneuil, the first stop on my itinerary, was comparatively uneventful, though nothing is completely uneventful for a young man on a fine spring day. The may blossom was out early, my horse was healthy and I was going to see the beautiful Comtesse Juliana. Along the track the trees were putting out leaves of astonishing, almost impudent, greenness, and larks were singing high overhead. Sometimes I would pass a shepherd leading sheep towards the pasture or a serf taking cows out to a water meadow. Once, near the village of St Anne, a pretty milkmaid crossed the road, carrying her pails from the farmyard to the dairy, and I gave her good day. I was tempted to stop and ask her for a bowl of milk, and tell her how beautiful she was, but I remembered my Comtesse who was waiting for me, and I kept myself from straying, though it pained me to feel the girl's eyes following me down the road.

There is nothing wrong with admiring a pretty girl, just in case you think I was being disloyal. According to Plato, beauty in all its forms composes the spirit. And there is something fascinating about girls. Not just what you are thinking I'm thinking, but their entire otherness. You'd think the same if you'd been a mewed-up lad in a monastery from the age of fourteen to twenty-one.

I had to keep going because Verneuil was sixteen miles away, and I did not want to be late into town. I had been given the name of an inn there where I could pass the night, but I wanted to locate it by daylight and see the place. Everything was new that spring in 1118 anno Domini.

The road entered a forest, but it was fine and open, neither witches' wood nor robbers'. There were other travellers on the road. It was a little early for the Duke's campaigning season, but already there were signs of activities to come: supplies being moved and soldiers deployed to mount sieges on tactical castles. Occasionally I passed groups of men plodding along behind mounted knights bearing the colours of the Duke's allies, although there was one band of crossbowmen – a better class of soldier, so it was said – who sported the crest of Bellême and who stopped me and asked me my business.

'I am a Latiner,' I told them.

This was the briefing I had had from Brother Paul when I questioned him about life on the road.

'When in doubt, say you're a Latiner. People respect that. It means you are more or less a priest.'

It seemed to work now, though they asked me to say something in Latin.

'*Timeo Danaos et dona ferentes*,' I said, falling back on good old Virgil.

'What does that mean?' asked a burly archer who seemed to be their leader.

'I fear the Greeks even when they bring gifts,' I said.

The monks had been mad about Virgil. They needed some alternative excitement in their lives – more than an occasional visit of the bishop could provide. They secretly loved Ovid and his *Amores* too but always said they preferred Virgil.

'I don't know about Greeks, but I do know about gifts. Got any?'

I was all at once very conscious of the purse which lay hidden under the sack containing my clothes and paltry possessions.

'I certainly have,' I told him, 'the gift of benediction and God's grace. Bless you, my sons. *Deus vobiscum.*'

I made the sign of the Cross at him. I would have made a good monk.

'Hm,' he said, not totally convinced. 'Let's see what's in that sack of yours, Latiner.'

'Look,' I shouted, pointing back down the road, 'My lord Perche's soldiers!'

They all turned to look, and I spurred Blackberry in the opposite direction. She sprang forward like a trebuchet stone. I half expected a volley of arrows up our backsides, but I was told later by one of the castle guard at Breteuil that archers

32

never shoot unless it is to kill. They do not waste arrows, nor do they like to waste time having to retrieve them – which they must do since arrows cost money and are made with skill and craft. Breteuil and Bellême were not officially enemies. They might have had some explaining to do to William Talvas (Bellême's son and, like his father, a thorn in the Duke's side) if they had killed a Latiner belonging to his neighbour. Besides, the road was a little too public for a daylight murder. You never knew who might come round the corner.

I was lucky. These were funny times: soldiers on the road and no one quite knew who was on which side.

I reached Verneuil as the church bell was tolling Vespers. I was sure I had been told to take the left fork of the road as I neared Verneuil but, as it turned out, that was the road to L'Aigle and I wasted half an hour before I discovered my mistake. I have a tendency to muddle left and right at moments of decision. Anyway, I still had an hour or so to spare before dark.

It seemed a prosperous little place as I rode into the square, larger than Mortagne, with a big church. The usual after-Easter fair was going on with stalls, swings, jugglers, fire-eaters, feats of strength and so forth. The place smelt clean, and was without much rubbish in the gutters considering the fair was on. It was good air with a tang of woodsmoke and baking and, yes, *bacon* as we neared the inn, which we found without great difficulty since the smell drew us there – or drew me at any rate.

The tavern was well frequented. Men sitting on the benches outside the inn drinking cider gazed at us curiously as I took Blackberry round to the stables at the back. I found an ostler who gave her a stall and some hay. He had a full stable, he said, for there were many in town for the fair. I went back to the front of the inn, and a red-headed, buxom girl in a smock shook her head when I asked for lodging, but finally showed me upstairs to a room with a large bed in it.

'You'll have to share,' she told me. 'Lucky we have a room at all.'

'Share with you?' I asked.

33

'Go on,' she said. 'You can buy me a drink later if you like. No, your room-mate is Eliphas. He's a player. In town for the fair.'

They had an Easter fair too in Mortagne when people, especially farming folk, let their hair down and look forward to May Day. I had been sorry to miss it.

'Eliphas?'

'Yes. You know. A jongleur.'

There was a bellow from downstairs. The girl made a sort of shooing motion in its direction.

'Can't stand here gossiping all day. Some people have work to do. There's a fair on, you know.'

She made off down the stairs. Obviously this fair was a big event in the life of Verneuil. I learned later that they held a fair twice a year, spring and autumn, most important at the season when they celebrated the Feast of St George. The town's name was supposed to have come from Ver meaning worm or dragon, and St George was the man, of course, who had slain the dragon. Any excuse for a feast! The priests latch onto it and the people grab it.

You will have observed by now that, though I spent some years as a novice in the abbey, my views of God and his Church are not always favourable. I preferred God to his Church because it seemed to me that, left alone, he had done an estimable job in creating the world (although there are areas of question, like the problem of pain which you might like to put to him if you met him at the inn). But the Church was always muddying the waters. The Kingdom of God was not of this earth, but the Church was very happy to stake its claim here and jump all over you. There was always a priest waiting round the corner, spying on you, checking that you had or had not been to the castle chapel at least twice a day and sometimes more, hearing your confession and then whispering to my lady about your tendencies whatever they might be, and that bastards were not to be trusted. The Church was everywhere and made its presence felt. My own view was that the God of the New

34

Testament – in other words Jesus – was everywhere, but he was much more discreet. He didn't condemn my sloth or my envy or my greed or my wrath, or even my lust which was considerable and at times insupportable. Sometimes he would give a little cough which I could almost hear, and I would know that I had failed him, and I would be sorry. Call me a bastard, but that was the kind of God I thought I could get on with, though I keep this kind of thought to myself. There are spies everywhere.

But enough of that. Back to the little room under the eaves of the inn, a great ramshackle bed, an ewer on a table, a broken chair, and a smell of old beer and piss coming all the way up from the bar. I lingered awhile, looking at the bed and deciding which side I was going to sleep on. I hoped that Eliphas, whatever he did, didn't have brotherly inclinations like some of my previous monastic colleagues.

By now I was both thirsty and considerably hungry, and I went downstairs again, clutching my bag close to my side, in search of cider and a stew of some kind. It was a long while since I had stopped by a grassy bank in the sun and eaten my cold pie washed down with a draught of water from my bottle. I found my red-head friend, serving ale and cider in a long, low room where twenty or so people sat drinking and shouting at each other. Some were already eating; bowls of some kind of bacon and lentil stew were appearing and it smelt good to me. I asked her – for she came over and gave me a smile – if she would bring a flagon of ale and bowl of stew, whatever it was, with some bread.

'Whatever stew it is, it's not just bacon,' I said. 'There's something more in there.'

'It's bacon with a bit of venison, but don't tell the Comte.'

I knew that poaching deer was punishable by death; better not to ask questions. It was a sign of the times, though, that barons and their followers and servants had other things – like fighting and pillaging – to take them away from strictly guarding their forests.

'You all right upstairs?'

'Fine, thank you. Is my room-mate here?'

'He'll be in later. He's getting ready for the show.'

'I'll go and see him after supper.'

She was a cheerful girl, and I would have liked to have given her a cuddle, but she was busy and I was curious to see Eliphas at work, so when I had demolished the steaming bowl of stew, the rough bread, and the beaker of goat's piss she called ale, I went out into the town square to see the show. Eliphas turned out to be a long, thin man with an amused, mobile countenance, a face on which expressions came and went like clouds on a windy day. He was sitting at the back of his covered wagon, his legs dangling over the side, addressing a small crowd of townees and visitors. I added myself to their number.

'Why are you all here tonight?' he asked us. 'Not because of the fair, not because of the food, not because of the drink, but because of me. You have never seen anything like the things I am going to show you. And because we are celebrating a holy day today, I am going to show you something which concerns us all – the Fall of Adam.'

'We have enough of all that in church,' grumbled one swarthy bystander.

'But it is not going to be all that,' retorted Eliphas. 'Here you are going to see the hero and the villain. The most beautiful woman in the world, and the vilest creature ever created. It is a story that concerns us all. But if you feel you have seen it all, I won't show it to you.'

'No, no,' the crowd protested. 'We want to see it. Show it to us.'

'Very well,' the man continued smoothly, 'but you have to do some of the work. Imagine that this, where I am standing now, is Paradise. Look up at it. Isn't it wonderful? Strange trees and groves, delicious woods and copses, sweet odours of flowers and ripening fruit. Look at me, now! That's more like it. You are with me now in Paradise. You are surrounded by sweet-smelling flowers, and twined with leaves and soft tendrils. You are sitting on a grassy bank, and little creatures – hares and voles and little birds – are with you watching ...'

The man seemed to have the people in a sort of trance. They were feeling Paradise inside themselves. They were there.

'I am Adam,' he continued, 'and in here...' He gestured towards the wagon's canvas opening, just ajar, beside him . 'This is my wife Eve. Isn't she the most beautiful woman you ever saw in your life?'

We waited for this vision of loveliness to emerge, but nothing happened.

'Come on, then,' shouted someone in the crowd. 'Show us your fucking wife.'

'She's shy,' said Eliphas, reprovingly. 'Do you think Eve, our mother, wants to show herself to a crowd of pot-swillers and pissheads like you, who can't be patient for one minute without cackling like geese and shouting filth? No. She wants you to think of her. Your mother Eve ... Yes, it is hard to think some of you had a beautiful mother, but you did. Be nice to her. Think of her. Imagine her when she was young and lovely, graceful, slender, nubile, coming out of a grove, adorned for her husband. There, yes, you can see her now. "Adam," she says, "husband, how shall we spend the day? Shall we walk? Shall we feast on fruit? Shall we drink the sweet liquors of the flowers and the trees? Shall we talk to the birds and the beasts and converse with the fishes ...? Shall we ...?" and she shows herself to me in all her glorious, innocent nakedness, rejoicing in her body, "Shall we make love?"'

'Oh yes,' shouted the crowd, swollen now to a considerable size like Adam's original member.

'But it isn't enough for you, is it? The loveliness of Eve, the perfect pleasures of Paradise? Oh no. Now I want you to imagine something unutterably loathsome, something so vile that you are going to have nightmares about it. What is it? Sssssssssssss. Long, sinuous, scaly, oozing, corrupt, with a vile stench coming out of its mouth and its eyes weeping foetor, like a grotesque and interminable penis, it has taken the opportunity provided by Adam's exertions – he has fallen asleep – to address his wife and wind himself grossly about her, filling her with a strange and unfamiliar sense of ... What? Excitement

37

and … could it be curiosity? What is that foul thing saying to her? Listen. Can you hear it? "What are you doing, Eve?" "I am living here with great pleasure." "Is all well with you?" "I know of nothing that troubles me." "You could be even better." "I don't know how." "Do you want to know?" "Yes. But I don't think I should." "Why not? You are the most beautiful creature in the garden, more beautiful than your husband, and cleverer too. Why does the Creator always speak to him first? You should have precedence, everyone thinks so …" "Everyone?" "I was speaking to the tiger only yesterday and he was saying exactly that." "What should I do?" "Well now, my dear…"

And so Eliphas went on, with the audience hanging on his lips and the old familiar tale rendered completely new in his telling of it. He performed the parts of the Devil and Eve with a wonderful dexterity of voices: the Devil deep and foul and insidious; Eve so voluptuously, so gladsomely innocent, and yet slightly silly, but very human; and Adam mulish, stuffy, worthy but uxorious and biddable. All these, he performed, and more: a parrot for instance, which repeated the serpent's sly reasonableness, and an owl, which urged Adam to refuse.

I swear the man was a magician or necromancer for he seemed to me to turn before my eyes into the most delectable naked woman you ever saw. Then he materialised again into the most revoltingly attractive and colossal serpent; before he appeared as Adam, muscular, honest and simple; and at last – huge, mighty, omnipotent and omnipresent – in the person of God.

I was hooked to that stage from beginning to end, but as he finished, admonishing us to attend tomorrow evening (for the fair was a two-day matter) when he would perform the mystery of St George and the Turkish Knight, I was overwhelmed with fatigue and could barely make my way to the inn. I had to brush off the red-haired girl who was waiting for the drink of ale I had promised her. I gave her a penny or two to buy it for herself – yes, it was ungracious, but I only just managed to clamber up to my chamber and throw myself on the bed where I expired (well, not literally, I am glad to say) into the sleep of the dead, and slept so soundly I might as well have been a corpse. I was woken, almost as into another dream, by an angel singing, very softly, 'Come hither to me, my pretty dove' in a high melodious voice.

'You must have been in a monastery to sing like that,' I said as I woke, expecting heaven.

But it wasn't heaven at all, it was a small shuttered bedroom with a huge rank bed which took up almost the whole space, a bed into which I now perceived the man who played God as well as the Devil was proposing to introduce himself. I realized that at some point in my torpor, my legs must have strayed across the invisible dividing line, and they were now in his portion.

He picked up my legs and put them back where they belonged. I was suddenly wide awake.

'By your leave,' he said.

'I am sorry my legs have strayed – like Mother Eve. They crossed the line,' I told him.

'So you have been in a monastery, my fine bedfellow,' said the man.

'Yes, for eight years, learning Latin and the meaning of cold,' I said. 'And other things.'

'I too have been in a monastery … and other things,' he said. 'It is one of those necessary stages one has to go through, like circumcision.'

'Circumcision? You are a Jew?' I asked.

'No, I was just using it as an example. There is much to be learnt from the Jews, as they have learnt from the Arabs. They both love a good story, for instance.'

'Where did you learn to make a performance like that?'

'Oh, here and there. The south. Italy. Spain. Moving around, keeping my eyes wide and my ears open.'

He was some kind of foreigner but he spoke French very well, almost faultlessly but with a slight accent that made his speech particularly attractive. He seemed indeed like a vital spark.

39

There are a few people we meet who seem for some reason to be intrinsic to our life and whom we remember for ever.

'I am Bertold FitzRotrou,' I said.

I had never called myself that before. It sounded good. He reached over and grasped my hand.

'So you are a bastard'

I was not offended. It seemed the most natural thing in the world.

'Yes.'

'I bet your parents had a better time making you than they'd have done if they'd been married.'

'I hadn't thought of that.'

'And tomorrow you are on the road again?'

'Yes. To Breteuil. The Comtesse is my father's sister-in-law.'

'I have been there. It is a new castle with a fine moat. I did a Christmas show there. She is a beautiful woman, the Duke's daughter, I hear. But Monsieur le Comte is a boor, a dangerous oaf. You want to watch out for him.'

'Ah.'

I didn't want to say too much to this magic man who could transform himself like Proteus, for fear I would tell him everything about me, and there would be nothing left.

'And now we must sleep,' he said. 'Enough for one night. We shall speak again tomorrow if we are spared.'

'If we are spared?'

'Death is just a hair's breadth away. I am always surprised to find I am still here in the morning. Good night,' he said.

'Good luck.'

'To you too. And here's a thought to go to sleep with.'

He sang in a soft, sweet high voice a song in Latin which I translate loosely:

Snake in the grass
She looked quite harmless
Virtually charmless
Until I made a pass
Doing her a favour –
Slinky little raver
Bit me on the arse.

He gave a little laugh, and in a minute he was gently, almost companionably, snoring.

VII

It had clouded over in the night and I woke to a grey dawn. It was later than I had planned. Eliphas was gone. I went downstairs to the pump and splashed water over my face and chest, and asked the girl for bread and meat. She didn't look good in the morning, but who does? She brought me ale and the remains of a bird of some kind, and I picked it over moodily. The magic of the night before had vanished; there was no sign of Eliphas or of his cart outside. I asked for bread and water for my journey, was given a crust and found the water muddy. I asked for small ale and filled a bottle with it, paid the bill, collected my sack with its few belongings, rescued Blackberry from the stables where she was contentedly chewing hay from her nosebag, and threw a coin or two to the ostler. I was disappointed not to have said goodbye to the showman.

Verneuil was getting ready for the second and (I had been told) less respectable day of the fair. Two peasants were already lurching around in a sort of warming-up way under the disapproving eye of a priest who stood at the side of the square. As I rode slowly past, I caught sight of the player's cart being impounded by a reeve and a constable, while the man himself argued with a priest who was standing by.

'You mistake, sir priest,' the player was saying. 'I am showing the triumph of good over evil. The fact that I do it by showing people not telling them is rather to the good, don't you think? They learn more. Perhaps you should profit by the technique yourselves.'

'Don't be impertinent,' snapped the priest. 'You are clearly nothing better than a vagabond. I have a good mind to have you impounded along with your cart.'

It was time for me to step in. I knew how to talk to clerical people.

'I know this man,' I said to the priest. 'He is a good Christian and friend of the Comte de Breteuil.'

'And who are you, sir?'

'I am the Comte's …' I did a quick calculation '… nephew by marriage'.

It was near enough to be impressive though too complicated to be easily checkable. Even so, he had a stab at checking it.

'Marriage to whom?' he enquired.

'My father is the Comte de Perche,' I replied. 'His wife the Comtesse is the Comtesse de Breteuil's sister. They are both daughters of the Duke.'

There was rather a lot of illegitimacy in the roll-call, but enough comtes and comtesses to make him shut up. He would have known they were daughters of the Duke, but I thought it better to throw everything into the equation.

'Oh, very well,' he grumbled to Eliphas, 'you may go and your cart too. But try not to cause a commotion.'

I waited while Eliphas retrieved his property and set it up again in the square.

'They make a token appearance and then they make themselves scarce for fear the peasants will revolt,' he said. 'Last year one of the Brothers got thrown in the duck pond. Thank you for your help, though. Good connections!'

'Not quite as good as they sound, actually.'

'What is? Anyway, remind the Breteuils of my visit last year. Maybe I'll turn up again and give them a new play.'

'I'd like that.'

'You're an unusual traveller. Educated, I can tell, but not a priest, nor yet a knight nor a nobleman. You don't quite fit in, do you?'

'I suppose not.'

'That is why I like you. If you can't find anything that fits you, you can join me and become a jongleur.'

'I should like that, too. But first I have to go to Breteuil and see my Comtesse. She is wonderful.'

'Take care of yourself, little brother bastard. I am sure we shall meet again. At least I shall know where to find you.'

He embraced me warmly. I swung up into the saddle, gave Blackberry a little prod with my heels, and we were off. As I left the square and took the street at the end to the right (or should I have gone left?), I turned and waved, and the magician, walking away from me, seemed to know what I had done for he too paused, and turned as if I had tapped him on the shoulder, and waved back.

VIII

After a grey start, the sun came out as I left the town and it turned out to be another fine spring day. There's something about spring, isn't there? Horace has it somewhere: *Diffugere nives* and all that ... When you are young and in good health, every day seems like an excitement, and as I rode out on little Blackberry, my palfrey, I felt like a knight riding forth on high commission, and Blackberry a great destrier, a true knight's steed.

Verneuil straddled the main route to Paris from the west, but the road to Breteuil was only used regularly by farmers and peasants. Doubtless there would sometimes be other comings and goings – knights and castle folk, messengers on the Duke's business or that of his enemies, strolling players – but there were none that day. Indeed, even the farmers and peasants were in short supply. There were sheep in the fields, deer and pigs foraging in the woods, and on the lakes and ponds I passed – for this was a country full of rivers and streams – there were duck, geese and swans for company.

I have always been fond of swans. It is said they only sing once in their lives, before they die. How useful it would be if we were only allowed to speak – once – at such a crucial time, and how pregnant our message to our friends and family would be. A lifetime of experience expressed in a sudden, brief outpouring of sense and melody. I made a mental note to tell Eliphas next time I saw him.

As I rode on my solitary way, I occupied my mind with these fancies, and with the thought of my lady Juliana, whose pretended favour – a sprig of cherry blossom – I wore now with the pride of one entering a tournament. The result was that I crossed a bridge and came upon Breteuil sooner than I had anticipated, while the sun was still high and only just beginning to decline towards the west. Breteuil appeared to be an undistinguished little town with an air of neglect about it that spoke of an indifferent lord or castellan. It was said you could always tell a town by its lord. Mortagne, for instance, was well maintained, its burgesses kept up to the mark by my father who, though I thought him decrepit and coarse, had old-fashioned views on keeping things in order, like the old soldier he was, which he transmitted to his tenants and leaseholders.

Little touches betrayed the neglect in this place. Grass or moss on too many roofs, doors and gates hung athwart, a gutter clogged in the middle of the street...

I needed no directions on the way to the castle because it stood on an eminence above a lake just beyond the little town, and was plain to see from five miles away. This was water country. The river Iton had split into two a couple of miles back, it bifurcated and the land within it became what was almost a huge island. The town was built on the northern side of this divided Iton, and all around were ponds and lakes, and streams that fed into the river.

On closer inspection, the château was a larger and newer building than many so-called castles of the time, which were little more than towers on an earthen mound with a wall around a bailey below. This was a modern stone castle such as ours at Mortagne with a moat and a drawbridge, a gatehouse, and an extensive curtain wall suggesting a substantial keep inside it. The Comtes de Breteuil – the FitzOsberns, and indeed the Comtes de Perche – had been important figures for more than a century and required the latest castles for the protection of their families and followers – which was why the King of England and Duke of Normandy had allowed his daughters to marry them. It may be said that Eustace, the current Comte de Breteuil, was a bastard too, though it was a black mark and a kicking at Breteuil for anyone who raised the little matter of the back stairs and the bar sinister. It was all right for him to be a bastard, apparently, because his father, William of Breteuil, was a bigwig, and his grandfather was a famous warrior and right-hand man of the Conqueror.

The fact is, the Comte de Breteuil was a true bastard in the broadest sense of the word, but the Duke did not care about that. All he cared for was keeping the barons on a tight rein, and establishing his line, or so it seemed to me.

The Duke wouldn't allow his sons-in-law to put his daughters in a duff castle with a wooden tower planted on an earthwork, because all Normandy was watching. Prestige, power, publicity – the three Ps that guided much of what Duke Henry was about. Not for nothing did they nickname him Beauclerc: the man who gets things done. You could dislike him, you could hate him, you could fear him; but you had to respect him.

New though it was, even this castle of Breteuil, rather like the little town, seemed to me to show signs of inattention. Not more than thirty years old, it already had patches of weed on the outer curtain walls, and the roof of a barn which showed above the wall had lost some of its tiles. There was more weed than there should have been in the moat which was deep and wide – the bailiffs should have had that cleared every month.

Blackberry and I walked round the castle giving it our inspection before finally crossing the drawbridge and addressing ourselves to the gatehouse. Well, I addressed it; Blackberry simply munched the grass and had a piss, but I felt she would like to be included. It was a new place for both of us.

There was no sign that anyone had noticed our arrival, so after waiting five minutes or so for some kind of hospitable gesture such as a salutation or the opening of the gate, or even the barking of a slavering mastiff, I dismounted and knocked on the small postern door some way from the great gate itself. I realised that all this knocking involved a certain loss of dignity, but Blackberry didn't seem to mind, and contentedly munched more grass, and pissed again. Getting no response from this door either, (I later discovered that it was a false door, merely wood laid upon stone, a stupid ruse to deceive even more stupid besiegers on whom to pour boiling oil) I returned to the main gate and beat on it anew, indignation lending force to application.

'Hello,' I shouted, and then 'Oi.'

This went on for several minutes and I was growing increasingly conscious of the spectacle I must be making. What was wrong with this place? And then I remembered. Of course: it was dinner-time. At last I heard bolts slowly sliding back, and then the door opened an arrow's breadth.

'What do you want?'

It was an irritable voice, thick with mutton stew, not at all apologetic.

'I want you to bloody well open the door and let me in. What do you think I want?'

'Ooh. Hark at him. Who might you be, young master? The Duke's court jester? We don't let anyone in here unless we're expecting them.'

'But you are expecting me.'

'No we're not.'

'Yes you are.'

'No we're not.'

I could tell he was going to play this game all day. It was his way of jousting.

'This is ridiculous. I am the Comtesse's nephew,' I told him. 'She is going to give you such stick if you don't let me in.'

That seemed to loosen him a little.

The door opened, revealing an ill-favoured little man in a chain-mail shirt over a leather tunic; any smaller and you would have called him diminutive. He had rotten teeth, little brown stumps, and his breath smelt bad enough to repel an army of invaders.

'They said nothing about a nephew,' he told me.

'She is expecting me. I have come with a message from my stepmother, the Comtesse de Perche.'

'Comtesse this and Comtesse that,' he grumbled. 'Nobody tells me anything.'

'Now open the gate and let me bring my horse in.'

He could think of no reason for not doing what I asked – I could see he racked his brains for one, but he wasn't up to it – and soon enough Blackberry and I were inside the castle grounds and making towards the stables and marshalsea, which lay over to the right part of the curtain wall. At least I could make Blackberry comfortable, even if my own reception might be frosty. I handed her over to a stable boy who seemed unexpectedly helpful, and I gave him a little silver coin to encourage him to be kind to her which cheered him up no end. I said goodbye to my little horse and promised to be back later to see how she was, and then I set my steps to the central tower of the castle itself around which a varied array of wooden buildings had been erected. It was in fact less a tower than a massive square building, six floors high with a watch-tower at each corner. I had to cross a substantial moat, deep and wide, over a small drawbridge to reach the front entrance which was guarded by a stout portcullis.

This time my approach was monitored through a grille, and before I could knock, the portcullis was raised and I walked through to the guardroom where I was interviewed by a whiskery sergeant – or some kind of official – in a leather jerkin beneath a surcoat with the raven of Breteuil embroidered upon it.

'Here to see the Comtesse, are you?' he asked when I had explained myself.

Somehow I had been expecting everyone to know about me.

'Yes. I shall be tutoring her daughters.'

'Tutoring the young ladies, are you?'

At least someone had got the message.

'Yes. I shall be staying here.'

'Staying in the castle, then?'

He was repeating everything I had told him as if it were school Latin. He had hairs sprouting out of every orifice except his mouth, although maybe some were in there too. His voice was curiously muffled as if he were speaking through his cheek not his lips, like a bad travelling player.

'Where shall I go to find the Comtesse?'

'She is not at home.'

'Not at home?'

What was this? I had come all this way to find a new life and my benefactress was not even here to greet me or introduce me to my charges.

'When shall she be back?'

'I dunno when she'll be back.'

'So what shall I do?'

'You can go and fuck yourself for all I care,' said the sergeant, suddenly galvanising himself out of repetitive mode. 'Piss off and talk to the nurse up yonder. She'll know where the young ladies are.'

He jerked his head in the direction of a door behind him so I took the hint and opened it. A short, covered way led to a flight of broad steps which ended in a substantial door in the side of the castle wall. I climbed, knocked on the door and, receiving no answer, flung it open.

The smell that hit me was of unwashed bodies, dirty platters, old food, fouled rushes, stale beer and wine, sweet marjoram and other herbs (too few and too old), woodsmoke, and an overlying tincture of unhappiness and animosity. It was not the best introduction.

I saw a great hall full of noise in which some knights were discussing jousting and other knightly matters and wrestling with one another. They took no notice of me, and there was no sign of herald or harker who could announce me to the temporary castellan, in charge of the castle while the lord was away. Eventually, I spied a stairway which looked promising. Mounting it, I found myself at last in a smaller hall or solar where several ladies were seated, sewing and gossiping and discussing the matters of the day. They all shrieked with laughter when I arrived clearing my throat noisily in case they were contemplating anything indiscreet.

'You can't come up here,' said one red-headed matron. 'What do you want?'

This woman's hair was very dark red-gold, unlike Juliana's golden-blonde. Normandy is full of this colour hair, and I know it. It has a particular fragrance, the way red earth does. It is the quality of redness that infuses the matter. I suppose blueness would have a quality you could smell too but we don't see blue girls in Normandy, except perhaps in winter. It is a cool smell, I daresay.

'I would like some water if you have any,' I said.

A little, fair woman ran to a closet and poured me a cupful. I drained it gratefully. The ride had not been as long as the day before, but it had been long enough on a hot day.

'I am looking for the Comtesse,' I told them.

That set them twittering like starlings.

'Ooo, the Comtesse …'

'Fancy that …' and so on.

'What do you want her for?' the redhead asked. She seemed to be the interrogator of the group – they called her Angeline.

'She has asked me to tutor her daughters,' I told them.

Again there was more twittering.

'She and the Comte are away at the moment. They return in two days. You should be talking to the Chamberlain downstairs about this. Men are not allowed here. If the Comte knew there would be a terrible scene; you would probably be castrated,' said Angeline, pleasantly.

That made them laugh as though they would piss themselves.

'Don't worry,' said a lovely, dark-haired girl, coming forward – I noted that the others seemed to defer to her – 'he usually only blinds people and cuts off their hands.'

More laughter; quite hysterical, really.

'Hush,' someone said. 'You'll make the poor man nervous.'

'They told me to come up,' I said, reddening.

'Well they would, wouldn't they?' said the dark-haired girl.

She smelt very slightly of fresh coriander and almond milk. I wondered whether she rubbed herself with it. It was a charming thought, but one not to be pursued.

'Can you tell me where I can find the little ones?'

'They are in the nursery upstairs.'

'Do they not come down and talk with you?'

'It is not allowed.'

'Who by?'

53

'The Comte. He says children should be kept upstairs, out of the way. The world is a dangerous place, the Comte says. He would like the women to be kept upstairs too, but Madame the Comtesse drew the line at that. There was a terrible row, but she won that time. So they can come down when the Comtesse is at home.'

'I am glad to hear it. How old are the girls?'

'Marie is eight and Philippine is six.'

'I will go and see them now.'

'You can't do that.'

'What is your name?' I asked her.

'Alice. What is yours?'

'Bertold FitzRotrou.'

'You are the Comte de Perche's son?'

'Yes, of course.'

'But you are not his heir?'

'Not that it is your business, but no I am not. I am here to teach Madame's daughters Latin, Alice. I must go to them.'

'It is unheard of to teach girls Latin,' broke in the redhead. 'What use is it to a girl? Teach them to sing. Teach them embroidery. But for Jesu's sake don't teach them Latin. No one will want to marry them if they speak Latin. Leave that to the priests.'

'They will be able to read the great writers of the past. They will be able to see beyond the walls of a castle. There is life beyond embroidery, Angeline. And marriage, for that matter. I shall also teach them the art of medicinal herbs, so they can cure you of piles.'

All the women laughed, and the red-headed woman's cheeks burned as red as her hair at my indelicacy. Perhaps she was a martyr to them.

'Take the second door and go up the stairs,' said dark-haired Alice, pointing towards the corner of the room and the rounded wall where the south tower lay. 'We are pleased you are here. I think it is good for the girls to learn Latin. Take no notice of Angeline. She means well.'

I left the women chattering and squeaking like a nest of field-mice, and followed the stairs upwards to the nursery. A stout door at the top barred the way. I knocked at it firmly.

'Who's there?' asked a gruff voice whose sex was not evident.

'The new tutor for the girls. My name is Bertold.'

'I don't know nothing about a new tutor,' said the voice, as the door opened an inch or two, revealing its owner to be a little, portly old woman with a substantial moustache. 'What did you say your name was?'

'Bertold.'

'Is that a Christian name? I never heard of a Bertold.'

'It is a Christian name because where I come from the town priest is called Bertold. What is your name?'

'I am called Catrine. That is a Christian name. Saint Catrine was put on the wheel and is the patron saint of aches and pains, which is funny because that's what I got. You'd better come in, Master Bertold. I looked after the girls' father when he was a lad. A right handful, I can tell you. Little demon, he was. Not much better now, but I had to wallop him sometimes, and these girls take after him. Little demons. Where are you, girls? Marie ... Philippine...'

She clapped her hands, and two of the prettiest little, blonde girls you ever saw appeared from an inner room.

'This is your new tutor, girls. He is going to teach you ... What are you going to teach them?' she asked, turning to me.

'The language of the birds ... what the bees say ... how to cure a boil and charm an apple tree,' I said. 'How to put a fairy back in his foxglove. Things like that. What do you say, girls?'

They giggled together a little and said 'Yes!'

'I am going to teach them a little Latin so they will become wise and be able to speak to wise and clever men. I will teach them a little medicine so that they can look after themselves and other people. I will teach them how to sing. I will teach them a little calculation, so they can understand the nature of the universe and the movement of the stars around the world. I will

teach them about nothing which can always become
something ...'

'Nothing?'

'Well maybe not nothing ...'

I thought perhaps Saul's concept might be too abstruse for
little girls.

'I want to know about nothing,' said little Philippine.

'But you don't know what it is,' I ventured.

'That's why I want to know about it.'

'What is it anyway?' asked Marie.

I put my finger to my mouth and looked alchemical.

'Wait and see,' I said. 'And now I must go and find
somewhere to put my things and, with any luck, a bed.'

'Can't you sleep with us?' asked Philippine.

'Certainly not,' interjected the old woman. 'It wouldn't be
right.'

'I will find somewhere for now,' I told them, 'and when the
Comtesse returns we will speak of it again. She may have a
view as to where she wants me.'

'I warrant she will,' said the old woman.

'Then that is settled,' I told them. 'And now I will say
goodbye until tomorrow.'

'Until tomorrow,' cried the little girls.

'Don't forget,' said Marie.

'I want to start with the stars,' said Philippine.

'And then the medicine,' said Marie.

'And then nothing,' said Philippine.

'You've got them all excited now,' said Catrine. 'How am I
going to get them off to sleep tonight?'

It was a question I was shortly asking myself. There was
little chance of getting any sleep if I had nowhere to lay my
head. In the end, the castle Chamberlain, Renouf – a large,
untidy, hopeless-looking man with vague hands – found me,
with great misgiving, a temporary place to doss down in the
corner of an auxiliary guardroom under one of the towers. It
was where the guards slept while not on duty so there was a
great deal of waking up and bedding down in the night which

did not contribute to a quiet repose, but it was better than nothing. I was sure the Comtesse, when she came back, would want me to have suitable accommodation.

IX

I woke early and went downstairs before all but the bakers and scullions were stirring. A stomach-rumbling smell of fresh bread hung over the hall, and I begged a crust from a charitable cook. I carried it outside and savoured it as I made my first proper exploration of my new surroundings. Once down the steps outside hall, I crossed the drawbridge. Of weathered grey wood, solid as the tree it came from, it registered my passing with the faintest of shivers. The great contrivance that lowered and raised it was housed just behind me in a stone extension to the castle wall. Underneath, the moat was deep and dark, weedy in too many places, though a family of ducks busied about, pecking at the weed, and diving for fish. Beyond the bridge lay a vast green bailey. Nearer to the castle walls were a number of big timber extensions, where the knights slept and stores were held, along with all the other services that a small town might require for its daily needs and survival under threat (for what is a castle but a small town encased in stone). I passed beyond these and on towards the marshalsea where the horses were kept. I thought I might perhaps see my Blackberry and say hello to her.

I found an early groom and he led me to her. She had a little stable to herself and was contentedly munching at some hay. She whickered when she saw me and came up and pushed me with her nose. It was good to have her company in this strange place, and I think she felt the same. I gave her a little bread, which I probably should not have done, and wished I had an apple. We spoke together for a while, and then I let her go back to her munching, thanked the groom, and continued on my tour. The sun was now fully risen above the horizon; the air was fresh but not cold, with a light breeze from the south; the sky was blue, with a few small ineffectual clouds. It was going to be a fine spring day.

There were gardens to the south and west of the castle – a walled garden for produce, a flower garden that was hardly in bloom yet, though some primroses and cowslips were evident, a little orchard of apple trees in blossom and cherry trees full of frothy white snow, and a herb garden which already proclaimed itself with the sweet pungency of thyme, rosemary and lavender. This part of the garden was a little higher than the rest, so I could see out over the wall to the countryside beyond. To the left was the town which looked its best, almost snug, in the clean morning light, and to which the road led having crossed a wide meadow traversed by the river. In front of me was a wide lake, sparkling in the sun, which on its further bank seemed to show a boat-house, with a forest beyond it stretching as far as the eye could see. Behind me, there were low wooded hills, and to my right was the castle.

I was well pleased with what I had seen of my new home. There were many worse places to live in, I concluded – and of course there was the presence of Juliana to look forward to. Oh yes, that would convert a shambles into a paradise!

At that point, my stomach began to suggest that one small loaf was not enough to sustain a man on his first full day in a strange place, so I turned my steps back to hall. My mood of exhilaration and optimism was not exactly confirmed when I found stale bread (where was the fresh?), small beer and fatty bacon on the table, and ill-nature surrounding it. Indeed, it helped me to form a more complete opinion of the castle of Breteuil.

Though blessed by nature and by its builders, there was an air of discord and neglect about the place. Neglect in the look of the hall, in the unchanged rushes on the floor, the dogs pissing where they liked, and discord in the surly or lazy servants, the bad manners among the pages and the squires, the indifference and lack of proper pride among the knights. My fellow trenchermen were raucous oafs who seemed to find a Latiner in their midst amusing. They kept challenging me to jousting duels and wrestling matches. Finally, it irritated me so much that I agreed to go outside and wrestle after breakfast.

Quite a crowd gathered. My opponent was a large, red-faced fellow called Fulk with spots and a low forehead and evil in his mind. He seemed to me one of those inevitable bullies who by their size and conspicuous nastiness seem to emerge and thrive in closed institutions, like foot-rot in a barracks. He had kept addressing me as darling Bertoldia in a high falsetto voice until I told him that if he did that any more I would cut his testicles off and stuff them in his mouth, and then he really would have something to squeak about.

We formed up outside in the bailey, a generous extent of three or four acres enclosed by the curtain wall of the castle, that also served as a parade ground. Fulk's cap was thrown into the ring and I picked it up, signifying my taking up of the challenge. Two sticklers were appointed to see fair play, not that they would since they were obviously Fulk's cronies.

'Best of three throws,' said the sticklers. 'No holds barred.'

We stripped to our drawers, and warily circled each other. The monks in my monastery had been much given to wrestling. The Abbot, known for his strong views, thought it honest, brotherly exercise such as Christ's disciples might have engaged in but also considered it highly practical in those days of violence and pillage – when the Church's own properties were no longer sacrosanct – that the monks should have at least some grounding in self-defence. I had learned much from Brother Sebastian, the almoner, but it was Saul again who taught me some of the arabesque or guile tricks that the Arabs had learned from the Indians. I never used them against the other monks on the advice of Saul; I believe he thought it might engender hard feelings or jealousy. He had learned the hard way, as a Jew, when to keep his head down; but he had also learned, like the Jews, when to fight and to fight well.

Norman wrestling, Saul said, was different from that taught elsewhere in northern France, and different for instance from the German style. It was more in keeping with the kind of wrestling common in northern countries. It was said the style stemmed from the Norse invaders of old. We allowed stamping (on the feet) but not kicking, whereas in the West of England, in

61

Devonshire, according to Saul, kicking is encouraged, though not in Cornouaille.

All this was speculative. I did not expect Fulk to employ anything more than strength along with whatever meanness and trickery came into his head. I was wrong. He was quite a good wrestler. A little slow on his feet but with a firm grip and a fighter's instinct for what the opposition will do next. He actually caught me with a grip under the arms and managed to throw me, holding on firmly while both hips and a shoulder were seen to touch the ground.

'First throw to Sir Fulk,' they cried, even though he was a mere squire and not a knight.

Fulk extended a hand to me and I pulled myself up, only for him to release his hand, letting me fall to the floor again. There was a general laughter, though some of it was sympathetic. It is part of the knightly code to be hospitable to newcomers and at least some of the spectators were aware of it.

I rose and continued the bout much more warily. The man I was wrestling was at least as good as Brother Martin, and he had been champion of the abbey. Brother Martin had beaten me in the end – though, as I say, I had never used guile on him.

I circled the loathsome Fulk, containing my rage at the mannerless lout, tempting him to come for me, and in the end he did. He was overweening and arrogant – a bad thing to be in the wrestling ring.

'Come here,' he called in falsetto. 'Come hither, Bertoldia my princess. Don't be shy.'

There were gales of laughter from his supporters. I pretended to be nervous, dodging and weaving, and then he came for me. He half caught me by the arm, but not enough, so that I was able to twist round and stamp hard on his foot. He doubled up with pain, and I caught him by the shoulder and rammed him with a thump down to the ground so that both shoulders and a hip were solidly on the earth for all to see.

'A throw!' the fairer portion of the crowd called out, but the sticklers shook their heads.

'A throw!' the shout was louder and angrier.

The sticklers looked nervous.

'A THROW!'

'All right. A throw,' they said. 'Just.'

I extended my hand to Fulk where he lay winded, but he shook his head, fearing a trick.

'You should not impute to others your own lack of good manners,' I told him, amid much laughter. Now the laughter was on my side. 'You'll never make a knight at this rate. I'll give you some lessons later if you like.'

He was now in a rage, dangerous if he caught me because he would want to do me real mischief, and I circled him warily again. He too was trying to be cautious and we moved round each other, but he was too cross and mortified, and he could not restrain himself for long. He made his move – a good one – catching me by the knee and doing his best to tip me over, but I chopped him on the funny bone and he gave a grunt of pain, though he succeeded in ramming a foot down agonisingly on my toes, which brought tears to my eyes. We circled again, and I feigned inattention, half turning away – indeed I became aware of something happening at the gate-house – and he lunged forward, catching me under the arms with his hands locked behind my neck. This is a position you never want to find yourself in when you wrestle. Time for a little guile, I thought. He expected me to struggle, but I did not. Instead I fell backward, suddenly and violently, twisting slightly to the right so that my shoulder and hip, the hard parts of me, fell onto him, knocking the breath out and making him easy prey to my hands, freed now to pin him down and achieve my winning throw of two hips and a shoulder.

The crowd, for some reason, seemed strangely silent. It was nothing to do with the match: more some exterior event of which I was ignorant. And then a voice I recognised addressed me, speaking from a height as I crouched there looking upwards, dazzled by the sun.

'Ah, Master Bertold, I am glad to see you taking exercise. I hope you have made yourself comfortable while I have been away. I was sorry not to have been here to receive you.'

It was the Comtesse Juliana who had arrived in my moment of triumph. I dusted myself down and bowed in my semi-naked state. It seemed to be the courtly thing to do. She told me to wait upon her in the hall when I had made myself presentable.

X

I limped my way to the pump in the bailey – my toe was hurting where Fulk had trodden on it – and washed myself down as best I could. A kindly servant girl brought some old linen to serve as a towel. Then I struggled back into my clothes (always harder when you're half-wet) and, watched now with surly intransigence by the defeated Fulk, I mounted the outside stairs to the hall, as the Comtesse had instructed, taking care not to limp any more.

I found her standing before the fire in the centre of the room, while a couple of greyhounds writhed about behind her, fawning for her attention.

'Come,' she said, and repeated my title. 'You are welcome, Master Bertold.'

She held out her hand and led me up a broad flight of stairs to the second floor of the castle. When we reached the solar where her women were sitting, it was like a fox entering a chicken run. They all leapt up and started running about and twittering at her.

'Oh, Madam, we weren't expecting you.'

'You wouldn't believe what happened at dinner yesterday!'

'Do you bring good news?'

'We were hoping to finish the rose-garden pattern, but you have come back too soon …'

The Comtesse clapped her hands.

'Quiet, everyone. This is Bertold FitzRotrou, son of our neighbour at Mortagne. I know you have met him, but I thought I would introduce him again. He has come to teach my daughters Latin, singing, storytelling – and embroidery.'

'Embroidery!'

They all started twittering and screeching in dismay. They were like birds in a cage, poor things.

'Oh my faith!'

'Sweet Jesu!'

'Whatever next?'

'A man!'

'That was my little joke,' the Comtesse told them.

There was a gasp of relief.

'Wicked Comtesse.'

'You lay such tricks on us!'

'And now,' said the Comtesse, 'we go to see my little angels. Have you been playing with them? I told them to look to their lessons and give you no trouble.'

The women exchanged glances.

'Well,' the red-headed woman, Angeline, stepped forward and smiled. 'Maybe just a little.'

'You mean just a lot, I'll be bound,' said the Comtesse.

'Just a little bit of a lot.'

Everyone started laughing. I was impressed by Juliana's good humour and her handling of the women, some of whom seemed quite simple. I later learned of the Comte's attempted depredations and raids on the solar women in the days before his grievous wound, but I was glad not to know about it then. It had been the subject of furious altercations between the Comtesse and her lord.

I noticed now that the dark-haired girl, Alice, whom I had spoken to before, held herself back from the rest, and then quietly came over and stood behind the Comtesse as if in a privileged position. She was a beautiful creature – white skin, straight nose, observant grey eyes, and an expression of gravity that gave way, at unexpected intervals, to almost instantly suppressed amusement. She gave me a certain look now with her big grey eyes as though she knew more about me than I knew about her. It was all over so quickly, I could almost have imagined it.

'Alice, this is Bertold,' Juliana said, introducing us. 'Bertold, this is Alice. She is my personal companion and attends me when I travel.'

I exchanged greetings again with the girl, who looked at me gravely yet with a sudden little smile.

Juliana now held out her hand to me, which I took. The women widened their eyes as she led me upstairs. I thought she was leading me to the children's room, of course, but instead she took me into a chamber adjoining the bedroom which she unlocked. It had a small bed in it, and a great deal of clothing as well as some gold and silver plate. A delicious, smoky, orangey smell proclaimed the presence of spices. It was the room they call the wardrobe. She locked the door behind us. I thought for a moment she was going to order me to make love to her, and I was almost relieved that she didn't. I needed to get the measure of all these people, this woman, this place. I was nervous, I was on edge, I wanted to make a good impression, but at the same time, I was desperately disappointed. I wanted her more than anything in the world.

She walked around the little room, dipping her hands in spice.

'I am glad you have come, Bertold FitzRotrou,' she said to me. 'The girls are glad too, and Alice likes you. I look forward to knowing you better.'

'And I you,' I said.

She turned and kissed me. It was a long kiss. I had never really kissed someone I loved before. What a wonderful moment it is! Then she really did surprise me. She started to take her clothes off.

Has anything happened to you, so quickly, so unexpectedly? It was like a dream, but I would find it was typical of Juliana. That was the kind of woman she was, full of fun, full of surprises; they say the Saxons are like that. You felt that you were alive when you were with Juliana. Even I, hardly more than a youth, crass and full of myself like a randy badger, could see that she was a prize beyond a prince's treasure. And so does a needle feel when it is pulled towards a magnet.

She wriggled out of her clothes like one of the Breteuil eels – the castle moat was full of them – and for the second time that day, but to rather better purpose, I struggled out of mine. I was young, I was inexpert, but she was patient with me as well as instructive, and I hope I gave a good account of myself. My heart was in it, and that she must have known. How slender her waist was, how high and firm her breasts were – as commended for the ideal lady in the new troubadour songs (she said they were not quite as high and firm as before she had had two children, but they seemed fine to me) – how sweetly slippery she was between the legs, and how cleverly we joined ourselves together.

When it was over, I lay with my head on her breast and told her that I loved her. She stroked me and murmured an endearment in a strange tongue which she told me was English.

'My leman,' she said. 'My sweet leman.'

'Why am I *limon*?' I enquired. 'A bitter fruit?'

'Leman is sweetheart in English. Swete heort. That is the way they talk where I grew up. My mother was English. She was called Ansfrida.'

We bathed in those few minutes as if the bed were a wooden tub and the maids were pouring warm water over us. But why me? I thought. Why me? It was a question that I knew a lover should not ask, even then. I was suddenly, shamefully, conscious that if her lord found us I would probably be castrated, and blinded for good measure. He would enjoy it.

She had the trick of reading my mind.

'He never comes up here, night or day, and nor will anyone. The Comte will be arriving back at the castle in an hour or two. But now we perhaps should meet the children. I want you to make them clever but not too clever, and certainly the happiest little girls this side of the Channel. Their father doesn't want them. He thinks they should have been boys so they could have grown into knights. I will not have more of his children. He cannot. He was injured in a tournament. I will not have him anyway in my bed.'

'I will love the girls all the more,' I said. 'There are better things to be than knights.'

'That's my bastard,' she said, kissing me.

I was only young but I thought: this is the thing. You don't feel that often in life, do you?

She started to get up and I lay and watched her as if I had known her all my life, as if we did this every afternoon.

'You are beautiful,' I said, 'beyond the dreams of little boys in monasteries.'

'My father betrothed me to the Comte when I was ten years old,' she said. 'It was none of my wishing. He said he needed Eustace on his side, and that is what kings' daughters have to do. My father put a number of noses out of joint by appointing Eustace Comte, because he was not the only one up for it. He was a cousin of the old Comte who died, and there was another man who believed he had better claim. He still makes trouble. A de Montfort, of course.'

'When did you marry the Comte?'

'When I was fourteen, and what a bad day that was! I cried all through the service. He never made any attempt to make a friend of me, let alone be my lover. I had Marie when I was sixteen and Philippine when I was seventeen, and then I refused to have him in my bed any more. If he came to my bed, I threw up. That stopped him. Soon after, he was wounded. That stopped him even more. And then he discovered drinking.'

'You are a woman of spirit, Juliana,' I said.

A spirited woman with a spirited name, and a king's daughter, too. What a lucky boy I was that day! There was just one little cloud: I had the feeling you sometimes get when you are being watched by someone who doesn't want you to know they are watching. Strange, wasn't it? I put it down to guilt, there was no one in the room, I was sure of it, and anyone foolish enough to disobey the instructions of the Comtesse would have had to have had a very considerable, even suicidal, quotient of rashness. In spite of all her charms, she was a formidable young woman whom you would never want to cross. I put it down to conscience in the end. Nevertheless, the thought of being watched made me uneasy. I mentioned it to Juliana, but she dismissed it as newcomer's nerves. Had she done this before? I must admit the notion scampered across my mind like a small rodent before I sent it scurrying back to its hole. I could not help feeling that we were taking an appalling risk making love in a room which was – at least in theory – open to the cooks for access to the spices, but I didn't want to make too much of it because it seemed weak and fearful. You don't want to look weak and fearful in the eyes of the beloved. The new *chansons* of the troubadours which the ladies so dote upon are full of the virtues of strength and bravery, but I cannot deny that the thought of the punishment that could be meted out to the trustless knave who ravished the lady of the castle – especially when she was a king's daughter – made my scrotum curl.

'Come,' she told me and my brave face, 'I have kept you too long. When you meet my husband you will understand. Now we must wash and dress and meet the girls. They tell me they have met you already.'

The daughters were playing in their room just on the other side of the castle. They had arranged a series of jumps around the room and they were playing ponies. I will always remember that moment when Juliana opened the door just a fraction so we could see through, and there Philippine and Marie were playing, full of life and innocence and hopefulness, while the old nurse dozed in a great chair in the corner.

'Come on, Pippi, your turn...'

And then they saw their mother.

'Maman!'

They ran towards her and hugged her. My heart went out to them. They looked so happy together, a little circle of warmth in this bleak place surrounded by dark waters. Juliana turned towards me.

'Girls, say hello to your tutor, Master Bertold.'

'Hello, Master Bertold,' they chorused.

'You'd better be nice to him or he will read you some terrible Latin curses and turn you into woodlice.'

The girls giggled.

'I would too,' I said. 'Or centipedes. Which would you prefer?'

The girls thought about it for a bit.

'A woodlouse, I think,' said Philippine. ''Cos I could curl into a ball.'

'You had better be good, and then you won't have to decide,' said Juliana. 'Lessons can start tomorrow. Master Bertold is going to teach you some songs as well, and polite conversation, and storytelling. It is all going to be wonderful. Come along now, Master Bertold, and we will find somewhere for you to sleep.'

The girls held their faces up for their mother to kiss them, and I gave each of them a kiss as well. They seemed to expect it.

'I can see you're going to get along very well,' said Juliana as we left.

She found me a little room upstairs just over the girls' room, more of an extended cupboard, which had been used as a storeroom and had subsequently been abandoned. It was just about big enough for a bed and a chair. Juliana accompanied me as I collected my belongings from my temporary quarters and stowed them inside. As we passed among the twittering women and through the solar on the way downstairs, I noticed the pale, dark-haired girl with big grey eyes. She gave me a look, holding my eyes for a moment, which I could not at that time interpret. It was not unfriendly; more speculative.

'Come along,' said Juliana. 'You are going to meet the person I hate most in the world.'

'Who is that?' I asked, surprised.

'My husband. And watch out for the steward who sits by him, not to mention the Chaplain if he is there.'

And so began the strangest, happiest days of my life.

71

XI

Juliana was a beautiful woman in the full bloom of that lovely thing called young womanhood. Her head came up to my shoulder, which has always seemed to me a comfortable height for a woman. Her hair was not red like some of our Norman girls, as I say, but combined that redness with blondeness to provide a quality that almost beggared the word 'hair'. It was not hair but a rich golden commodity spun out of grace and truth with a seasoning of joy and a pinch of desire.

But I run ahead of myself. I just mean to say that, callow though I was and priding myself on having been taken up by a Comtesse and anticipating all manner of worldly advantages, I fell in love with her. Her skin had that colour upon it and smoothness about it that tells you the person who lives inside it is healthy and blessed by God with a sound constitution. There was nothing but delight and enticement about that thing which Horace denigrates when he says '*Ut turpitur atrum desinat in piscem mulier formosa superne*', and yet, say what he will, he seems to love it.

Her complexion was white and it was also pink, like one of those peaches that, once bitten into, gives you both colours at once, the white blushing into the red. The woman who wears these colours on her face is going to have soft, firm lips, a tongue like Cupid's own quivering dart, and a mouth that tastes of roses and Falernian wine. (I have never actually tasted Falernian wine but Ovid speaks highly of it, or Brother Paul did, and that's good enough for me. It doesn't go down your throat like a liquid fretsaw and make you fart.)

Her nose was straight, her eyes a very light green like a chrysoprase: piercingly and strangely bright, as if they were able to see things beyond normal capability. Just to look at her made me feel I must pay court to her and at the same time it made me realise my essential unworthiness. Well, I knew anyway that I was not good enough. I was a comte's bastard

73

and she was a king's daughter. I had been brought up by a cellarer and she had been raised at court. I was a smelly male nobody and she was a fragrant princess.

But I must not write myself off, as my mother used to say. Women are strange feeders, and I am only giving you first impressions. It was the character of the woman herself that finally bowled me over. It is quite something to be a king's daughter, a grand-daughter of William the Conqueror. There is a quality that makes you hold your head up; she inherited that from her father. The monks of Abingdon – where her mother came from – had taught her to read and write at her father's insistence, exceptional in a woman, so she was a Beauclerc too, indeed a belle clerk. From her mother – who had been a great beauty – she had inherited a ready smile, a sense of the absurd, and a quick and affectionate nature. This could have made her vulnerable, but there was always her father's Beauclerc practicality – you could say ruthlessness – like a keel underneath it, rarely showing, but holding the lovely ship together and on course. That ruthless side was one you didn't want to see too much of; it was alarming, but the alarm was part of the attraction. This lovely, graceful, intelligent girl could turn into a dragon if she was wronged – or if her children were at risk – and that of course was the other thing about her. Once women are mothers, something about them changes completely. There is the steeliness of the lioness always there.

Who, I thought, would wish to wrong her? Why would anyone want to play discords on such a lovely instrument?

The answer was of course her husband, Eustace. It had not been a happy marriage. In fact, you could not think of a worse husband for her. It was bad luck on him too. For a start, she was an educated person; he was not. She was intelligent; he was not so much stupid as endlessly mistaken. She was peace-loving; all he seemed to want to do was fight. She loved a calm, well-ordered life; he loved to drink and carouse. She was confident; Eustace at bottom nursed a kind of corrosive dissatisfaction. He felt ill-used.

It was true that he was a bastard like me, but he was, as I say, descended from one of the great lords of Normandy, the Comtes de Breteuil, if from the backstairs of that noble house. There were other claimants, including the difficult and resentful Amaury de Montfort who you will meet later, but Duke Henry had decided that Eustace should inherit – on condition that he married his daughter Juliana. Good for him, you might think.

Juliana had been furious but Henry had explained with his customary steely firmness that unless she did, she could expect no further help from him; indeed the only thing for her to do would be to go and live in a nunnery. She was plainly not nunnery material, so there it was. The idea of Breteuil was good. It was one of the premier lordships of Normandy. She would be a great lady. There was only one snag. The man himself.

I was to get to know him well in the next few months. Large, shambling, older than Juliana by twelve years and already middle-aged, Eustace could still have won her affection if not her love, but he was, as I say, an unhappy man.

He hated the fact that he had had to marry Juliana in order to become the Comte. He could not forgive her for that. It undermined his position, so he decided to thwart her whenever the opportunity arose. What he had not bargained for was the grief that this would give him. She was better at thwarting than he was, and in much more subtle ways. She slept with him, with some disgust, and produced two daughters. That was enough, she said, and refused to sleep with him again. Naturally his great ambition was to re-found the Breteuil dynasty, and for that he needed a male heir, which was not to be forthcoming. He lived in a state of frustration and impotence; no wonder he liked a drink, he said, married to such a woman. Why could not the Duke have presented him with a nice, pliable Norman girl like that Angeline de Montgomerie who had once given him a handkerchief? She would have played with her maids while he played with his soldiers; she would have meekly done his bidding as they investigated in the baronial bed the possibilities of founding a dynasty – but then he would not have been Comte de Breteuil, but a sad nobody like this Latiner his wife had got in to teach the children. It was an impasse from which the only escape was wine.

The Comte de Breteuil was indeed descended from the famous FitzOsbern, Steward to William of England, the first English earl created by the Conqueror after his victory at Hastings – he told me so several times. Yes, the doltish, arrogant sot I met that day in hall, was the great-grandson (albeit by the back stairs) of the very great Earl of Hereford, a lion among men.

To look at, the Comte might not originally have been an unworthy example of a man of good lineage. He was tall with a mass of red hair, which was greying now, and a great red beard. He might once have been impressive, but the hair was now lank, the face reddened from too much sun and wine, the eyes reddened (there was a stupidly cunning, furtive look in them), the cheeks puffy, the stomach corpulent and too big for the thin legs, the beard besmirched and at mealtimes crumby – the overall impression was of a great sunflower gone to seed.

This man, Eustace, was a disgrace to the whole idea of nobility. Indeed, if I may say so – and it is not original – he was more cont than Comte. You may think me biased, of course, because I was in love with his wife, but it would be hard to find a man more undeserving of a beautiful and generous lady than he. Though you scoured the castles of Normandy and of England too, and carefully combed through the canon of bad, weak, stupid, drunken, oafish, ponderous, vainglorious, self-satisfied, short-sighted, brutal, loud-mouthed, bullying, mercenary, mouth-maggoty barons, you would be hard put to come up with a candidate who even came close. You may consider my view to have been partial, but we can still admit that Eustace was not a clever nor a likeable man. He was not a successful strategist, nor a clever tactician. He was impulsive and short-sighted, but his greatest mistake was not to cherish his wife. He found her threatening in some way which he would never admit. So there you have it. I have gone on about him enough. Now you will meet the man.

XII

The Comte was sitting at table in the hall, waiting for dinner, when we came down, the inevitable mug of wine at his hand, with a pasty, devious-looking fellow with lank, mouldy straw-coloured hair beside him talking in his ear, and a cluster of favoured knights around him; sorry-looking thugs, I thought.

The Comte was apparently dealing with some local dispute, for the first thing I heard him say was:

'Well, there's only one thing to do. Throw him in the moat and see if he floats.'

There was a burst of laughter around him.

'Ah, there's my wife with her Latiner,' he said, contemptuously.

'He is not my Latiner, Eustace. He is our daughters'. It is time they learned,' said Juliana.

'You want a Latiner, my dear, you have a Latiner. So long as you don't want me to learn *amo amas amat* and all that cant. It doesn't get you very far when you're charging a line of enemy infantry without covering fire from the archers.'

'No,' said his wife, evenly. 'I don't think we will ever expect those words to cross your lips.'

He completely failed to catch the irony, and now he addressed himself to me.

'Well, Latiner, I hear you are the bastard of that old whore-chaser up at Mortagne.'

He was being deliberately offensive with a side-swipe at my mother. I thought it better to meet this head-on. I had not had eight years at one of Normandy's biggest abbeys for nothing. It is surprising what bullies and intemperate teases God-people can be.

'My mother is dead and she was not a whore,' I told him. 'And chivalry, I am sure, is not dead at the castle of Breteuil.'

Juliana shot me a warning glance. It said: don't get him completely riled if you want us to have an easy time. The

Comte obviously felt that he had gone too far for the moment. The steward whispered in his ear again, and then spoke to me.

'I hear you wrestle well,' he said. 'That is unusual for Latiners.'

'I have not had the honour of an introduction,' I told him.

'You don't need an introduction. You just need to know who he is,' said the Comte, brusquely.

'The name is Odo, I am the steward of Breteuil,' said the man, pouring wine into the Comte's beaker. 'So where did you learn to wrestle?'

'I learnt a few tricks from the monks when I was at the Abbey of Saint-Sulpice,' I told him.

'I bet you did – escaping from those old bugger monks,' said the Comte.

His sycophants erupted with laughter which seemed to mollify him. He stared at me with his piggy little eyes.

'Very well,' he said. 'Welcome to Breteuil. You may sit in hall below the knights and squires, but above the pages.'

'Don't you think ...'Juliana began, obviously concerned at this lowly ranking for her appointee.

'You're right,' he told her, 'it is too high. He should be below the pages but above the messengers.'

There was much guffawing among the squires and pages – especially, I noticed, from Fulk – although I was glad to see there were one or two knights whose faces expressed shame at their lord's default on politeness. Some of the new poems and books of chivalry had started to circulate at Mortagne, and had no doubt also reached Breteuil.

The Comte made a sign, indicating that he was now ready, and a sly, obsequious-looking chaplain with a face like a pale raisin said grace.

I took my place beside the youngest of the pages. The first course with several removes appeared – a watery broth, a sallet and some fish not in its first flush of freshness. We sipped and supped and fiddled with the fish, and waited for the next course during which time – it was rather long – I had an opportunity to

78

look at my fellow diners. I noted that the ill manners of the head had reached most parts of the body. At length, the next course was brought on: some sticky gammon, a tough old capon or two and some fatty mutton. The best thing about it was the stale bread we were each given as a trencher. My companions belched, they farted, the dogs pissed under the table, and my next-door neighbour – a verdurer – who was my partner in the bowl of carrots, had such dirty fingernails that I swear I ate more dirt than food when he had dipped his hand in. The wine was thin and bleak. My other neighbour, the lowest page, a friendly-looking downtrodden youth of some fifteen years, pointed to the steward and told me he was responsible for turning out such a pig's dinner. The weasel-faced rascal kept himself busy pouring wine from a private flagon which he shared with the Comte, and whispering in the man's ear.

After dinner came the entertainment. A harpist performed a melancholy piece, before, to my delight, Eliphas my jongleur appeared. He told three good jokes (I only remember one – the worst – a story about the sieve who got a hernia through too much straining), and then performed a small piece about a cuckold and his wife, an idiot and a hangman, and a crocodile who stole ladies' clothes, which had the hall in fits.

'How glad I am to see you!' I said to my friend afterwards when the Comte had been carried off to bed. 'This is a strange, unhappy place – at least it was until you came along.'

He smiled. There was something elfin and elusive about him, as if at any moment he could disappear.

'Even a good wife can't manage a bad man,' he said.

'Can't or won't,' I suggested. 'That is the truth of it. She won't because there are no thanks for it. In the end, the bastards get you down. And I'm a bastard so I should know.'

'I think you are the sort of bastard she would like,' he said. 'But don't go getting yourself into trouble. And let me know if you do.'

'How would I do that?'

'Go to the sign of The Bear in the town. The innkeeper is part of the brotherhood.'

'The brotherhood?'

'Innkeepers mostly. They just keep in touch with each other. Armies coming, sickness, bad men, strolling players ...' the man smiled. 'You will remember that?'

'The Bear.'

'That's the one. This is not a good place to be. I have to leave early in the morning. I do not normally do entertainments at Breteuil. I came to see how you were getting on.'

I was touched.

'Thank you, Eliphas.'

'The Comte should know that he is not clever enough to play politics and be disloyal, but he doesn't. Look after yourself.'

'I will.'

We clasped each other, and he was gone, out beyond the bailey to his pony and his cart. I was overcome with weariness. The hall was clearing now; the Comtesse had gone. I had been aware of fatigue for some time, it had been a day of considerable event, but I had been buoyed up by the sizzle of love in my veins. Now, all at once, my tiredness hit me and I could barely drag myself up the stairs to the top of the castle. I fell asleep against the stone wall in my little cupboard, smiling at the thought of the lady Juliana whom I knew in my young heedlessness to be mine.

I dreamt that I was awakened some time later (one of those funny dreams when you wake up but are still dreaming) – just how much later I could not tell – by an instinct that told me someone was watching me. I turned over and sat up in the darkness.

'Who is it?' I said, in some alarm.

'I know what you did up there with my lady,' said a voice I half recognised, not unfriendly. 'I don't expect you would like me to tell anyone, would you?'

'Tell the Comtesse and see what she says,' I replied, with some misgiving.

'Oh no, that would never do. Much better to tell the Comte, and then we would be rid of you, lording it with your Latin and taking the Comtesse away from us. What would you give me not to tell?'

The words, though discomforting, were mitigated by the laughter in the voice. I recognised it now. It belonged to Alice, the dark-haired girl I had spoken with in the solar. She had had, I thought, an ironic, even mischievous look in those big, grey eyes. Everyone else in this castle seemed to be teeming with malice, but not this one.

'I have little money,' I said, 'though you are welcome to that. But that's not what you want, is it?'

'Oh,' she said, carelessly, 'as for that … why don't you give me what you were giving to the Comtesse? That would be much more valuable.'

'Not now,' I said, playing for time, although I must confess I felt a sudden disloyal lurch in my loins. 'I am exhausted.'

'Look at your face,' she said. 'Just testing.'

She lowered herself beside me, almost on top of me, and gave me a kiss on the mouth. Then she got up, straightened her shift, and turned to go.

'Say nothing,' she said, and slid off into the darkness. 'I love you.'

At least, I thought I heard her say that. It was not real, of course, any of it. How could it be? I confess I felt a pang of disloyalty to the Comtesse, even though the whole thing had been a dream. There was no question that I had been put in a difficult position: one has a duty to a lady, even in a dream, to be gallant, loyal and hospitable; it is a rule of chivalry. One cannot, with honour, refuse a lady, even in a dream. And, of course, as a bastard, one must take what one can. Even in a dream.

In the morning, I believed that I had been visited by a succubus, but as old Saul used to say in the monastery, aren't we all sometimes? But, yes, I did feel shame as well as excitement.

XIII

Next morning I witnessed for the first time a tendency in Eustace that I was to see many times in the two and half years or so I knew him. He could not leave well alone, nor evil either. He was always plotting. It was to him like the act of love that he had lost. News came with breakfast and, quite apart from what it did to Eustace, it served to put the succubus and other idle fancies out of my head. Indeed, it was of sufficient importance to cause a stir throughout the castle and set a hundred tongues wagging. I bent my ear to the general tattle and was soon rewarded.

The Comte d'Évreux, a powerful neighbour of the Breteuils, had died. It was unexpected – a sudden seizure – and he had died without any direct legitimate heir. His closest male relative was a known troublemaker, Amaury de Montfort. They were a fiery Breton family, the de Montforts, and Amaury was no exception. He had some property in Normandy but felt no loyalty to the Duke because he was a Breton. He had fought against Henry previously, and the consensus at the table was that no one could see why he should be rewarded with the title of Comte which was the Duke's to give or remove. The rumour was that he was *not* going to be rewarded, and serve him right.

The general feeling was that this supposed slight was going to lead to a great deal of trouble but, if the rumour was correct, that the Duke had done the right thing in a difficult situation. Indeed, he was more or less obliged to do the right thing, having removed his brother from the dukedom for misrule and for not being fair and even-handed in all his dealings.

The rumour was shortly afterwards confirmed by a visit I made to The Bear. De Montfort was not to be the new Comte d'Évreux.

I learned from Juliana later that she loathed de Montfort. He was always egging Eustace on, and then had a habit of quietly disappearing when things got hot. She was happy that her father had slapped the man down.

Eustace turned the news of his neighbour's demise and Amaury's disappointment into his first move for making trouble for his father-in-law, Duke Henry. He immediately started planning a tour of inspection of his knights, soldiers and castles at Glos, Lire and Pont-Saint-Pierre. (In fact, he had only just returned from doing the same thing at his castle of Pacy.)

I began to sense that I was going to have to do some ingenious wriggling if I was not to be drafted into Eustace's private army as an auxiliary squire. He had his eye on me, if only to thwart his wife.

I looked in vain for Juliana. I was eager to see her but nervous that she would have changed her mind about us and would be disgusted with me – and perhaps herself – for our abandoned lovemaking. Women can be funny like that, and I agree with them: we should be ashamed of ourselves, but that is half the fun.

In the end, I could risk being down in the hall or in the bailey no more. Eustace was on the prowl. The very wardrobe was not safe. The best place that morning was the solar, so I looked in upon the ladies who were all a-twitter. There was no sign of dark-haired Alice.

'Oooh,' they shrieked, 'you shouldn't come in here. Madame doesn't let the Comte himself come in.'

'Please,' I implored, and they immediately softened, 'the Comte is looking for me to join up as a squire for his wars, and I really don't want to serve him. I serve Madame.'

'Serve?' they shrieked again. 'You can't say that! Whatever next!'

'I am her true knight,' I told them, and they looked at me with some respect, and quietened down.

Just at that moment, what should I hear but the heavy tread and wheezing grunts of the Comte himself outside the solar door which stood ajar. He had decided to come and find me. He paused for a moment to catch his breath – more grunting and puffing *ad libitum* – and then burst open the door to stand on the threshold in his coat of mail like a bit-part player in the comedy of Hercules. Happily, by then I was crouching in the middle of a circle of ladies where they closed ranks around me, so that he could not see me, and began to sing something ridiculous. The Comte did not enter further, which showed that Juliana had taught him some respect.

'Where is my wife?' he shouted at the ladies.

They stopped singing, quailed and twittered.

'Oh, my Lord, she is gone.'

'Gone?'

'She is gone with the nurse and the children.'

'Gone where?'

'To the farm to see the darling new lambs.'

'Hnpphh,' he snorted.

It was a most disagreeable noise.

'And where is *hic haec hoc*?'

'Who?'

'The Latiner.'

'Maybe he has gone with her.'

'He has no right to go with her when there is a call to arms. I am sure I have seen him around.'

'Oh, sweet Jesu. Is there a call to arms? Are we in danger?'

'No of course you are not in danger. But he bloody well is if I catch him. He's around somewhere.'

His piggy eyes narrowed.

'Why are you all standing like that, huddled together?'

'We are practising a carole to the spring which Madame has written? Would you care to hear it?'

'No, I bloody well wouldn't.'

'I think I saw him heading towards the herb garden,' said red-headed Angeline.

That set him off again for the stairs.

'Get on with your caterwauling, then,' he shouted over his shoulder. 'But tell me if you see the bugger. We ride within the hour.'

When he had gone, they all screeched and tittered and called me *hic haec hoc*, and I thanked them for their presence of mind.

'We are well practised,' Angeline laughed.

'Please do not think badly of me,' I asked them. 'I am as willing to draw my sword as the next man if the cause is just and the leader knows what he is doing.'

'You need say no more,' Angeline assured me. 'That man is our lady's bane.'

I stayed upstairs with them until the Comte was finally ready to leave, wondering in a lover's panic whether Juliana would be constrained to join her appalling husband on his tour of inspection.

Happily, Alice told me there was no question of that. The Comtesse, who had returned to Breteuil the previous day, had only accompanied the Comte to Pacy to see a woman who was skilled in needlework about a much-loved tapestry repair. She normally held the fort during the Comte's travels, using his absence as an opportunity to tidy the place up, undo his worst decisions, and instil some sense of order and discipline into steward, butler, pantler, cellarer, dispenser, fruiterer, poulterer, baker, brewer, slaughterer, and the huge retinue of mostly male servants – some in the castle, some from the town – whom Eustace seemed content to let fall into a state of slovenliness while he was around.

Alice was quite impassioned. All he used to care about, she said, was melees, war-making and the instruments of war: lances, swords, crossbows, quarrels, quintains, destriers, battering rams, trebuchets and siege engines. It had been whore-mongering too until he had had the accident. One could understand that, at least – that is what men did – but all that serious martial tendency had also faded. His great solace and delight these days – his fuel, his goad, his spur and his master – was brother-bottle, while he dabbled in politics and merely played at soldiering.

I thanked Alice for her help, opinions and advice. She was a clever and spirited girl, but she worried me a little. I wondered whether she was being too frank, and whether there might not be a snake in that grass: a lady who was not what she seemed, who would pass messages on.

They all looked perfectly charming, but I was not so young or so new to castle life as not to know that we cannot judge a traitor, especially a woman, by her looks. It is a mistake the painters make when depicting Judas. He is always made to look such an obvious traitor. I mean, you would never take someone who looked so underhand into your innermost circle, or invite him to your last supper. Judas, in reality, was a handsome man with an honest face, and you would trust him with anything, with your life. The one I wouldn't trust would be a disciple who looked like a girl.

It was a relief when Eustace was yanked up onto his enormous charger and set off across the bailey with his forty knights. The castle seemed to exhale as he disappeared with his troop, riding out through the gatehouse and across the bridge that spanned a tributary of the Iton river, flanking the outer rim of the curtain wall. Away he went, clattering down the lake road away from the town towards Pont-Saint-Pierre and the route to Rouen, leaving the castle quiet again.

XIV

Juliana reappeared next day, neither studiously avoiding me, nor seeming anxious to pursue familiarity. I worshipped her discreetly. I saw that she was instantly busy, taking the place by the scruff of the neck, as Alice had foretold, and gingering up the servants. It was not the lady's place to run the household: that was down to the chamberlain, the butler and finally the steward, who answered to the lord. Juliana's money and her dowry all belonged to Eustace so she had no power beyond the force of her own will. Now (I like to think invigorated by my presence) she set about ordering new rushes for the floor and having the disgusting residue underneath the old ones swept, dug up, and removed. This was her first priority before she turned her attention to the kitchen.

It was clear that I was not going to see much of Juliana that day or the next. It was just as well, since my young pupils kept me busy and indeed exercised.

I tried to avoid the solar, and did not even notice whether the dark-haired Alice was present. At one point when I met Juliana on the stairs I spoke to her but she turned her head away as if she had been thinking deeply and was unaware of me. This threw me into a fit of pique, but I was sensible enough to recover.

It was almost impossible, anyway, for us to be alone together and there were as many spies as there were eyes in that place. It was her game, not mine. I had been favoured for an hour, but now I must wait to see what the next move might be, if there were to be one. I was not the first young man, I told myself, to be a Comtesse's plaything. Meanwhile there was much for me to learn and do.

Ten days or so after the Comte's departure, while I was in the kitchen garden with the girls, teaching them the names of herbs – for I had good training in that art from the abbey – an unexpected visitor appeared. Evidently he was a great man since he rode in with a party of his own knights. There is always a frisson when a man turns up unexpectedly with soldiers in tow, especially when the head of the house is absent, so I watched their progress with interest and some concern, motioning to the girls to keep out of sight.

As a couple of squires saw to the horses, tying them up near the stables, the leader of the troop strode across the bailey to the drawbridge, mounted the steps to the hall door and presented himself to the castle steward. He seemed very full of himself, and there was a swagger to his step. I led the girls by a postern door to the back stairway and put them in the charge of their nurse, somewhat to their annoyance. It was best to keep them out of harm's way. I knew enough about the world to distrust strutting coxcombs with a troop of knights at their beck and call. The next thing that happens is they're riding off with you as hostage, and laughing while you yell blue murder.

I nipped down from the nursery and watched at a discreet distance as the steward announced the visitor to Juliana – who had come down the great stairs, not too hurriedly, to greet him – as the Lord Amaury de Montfort. Her face tightened slightly when she saw him. He had not wasted much time. There was ill omen about the man. He was dapper and dangerous.

He bowed low to her.

'Your servant, Comtesse,' he said. 'Or may I call you cousin?'

'Are we cousins?' she asked.

'Sooner or later everyone's a cousin to the de Montforts,' he said airily and, I could see Juliana thought, rather cheekily.

'In that case I think Comtesse will be sufficient,' she said, putting the little bugger in his place. 'What brings you to Breteuil, sire? It is not often we have the pleasure.'

'I am sure your lord would not like to hear you say that.'

'You presume too much, sir.'

'Is your lord at home?'

'I fear not.'

'When will he be back?'

'Several days. Could be more.'

'Ah.'

The man had an almost permanent smile on his face, but it was not a smile I liked. It spoke of duplicity. He was a good-looking man but with a very slightly rodent quality. Yes, he was a very handsome rat.

'Will you and your men take some refreshment? Some wine? Or water from our well, which is good?'

'That would be kind. My men are thirsty and we have to go north now to speak with Baldwin of Flanders who has thought fit to come into Normandy with his army.'

Wine and good well-water were brought, and the seated knights drank thirstily. Juliana and Amaury continued their conversation. I recalled having once heard my father at Mortagne speak about the de Montfort family, whose head was the Duke of Brittany. They were prolific. 'Never trust a de Montfort,' he told me, 'they spread like mould on an apple-rack.'

'So what was it you wanted to tell my husband?' asked Juliana.

I hovered around, trying to look useful, in case she needed support, though she was more than capable of dealing with this fellow. Having seen his men refreshed, he took a cup of wine, swept his eyes round the hall, and at last settled his eyes on me, with scarcely veiled condescension.

'Who is this?' he asked, as if I were a species of beetle.

'My daughters' tutor, Bertold,' Juliana told him. 'He is the son of the Comte de Perche.'

'Indeed?'

I could see him wanting to say 'and who is his mother?' but he was just a little nervous of Juliana's response, which was sensible of him. She did not tolerate that kind of rudeness.

'What is Baldwin thinking of?' demanded Juliana. 'He is surely wasting his time.'

'There are some who think your father rules unjustly – not of course that I would be of their party. But you must know it is true. They have spoken to Baldwin of their dissatisfaction.'

'In that case, why are you going to speak with him?' she asked.

'To dissuade him, of course. I hear he is in league with King Louis and means no good to our Duke.'

'He who sups with the devil needs a long spoon. Have a care, Amaury, or you will be caught up in affairs that do you no good.'

'Oh, I shall, Comtesse. And now I must be on my way. Perhaps I shall meet your husband as he comes from Rouen…'

'How did you know he had gone that way? You are well informed, Amaury.'

'Indeed, I try to be. They say that knowledge is power.'

'So what was it you wanted to tell my husband?' asked Juliana.

'It will keep, dear lady.'

'It is warm for the time of year. I trust it will not go off.'

He laughed, unamused, and she laughed back at him. I tried a little laugh too, but she shot a look at me that said don't be so bloody stupid.

He bowed, summoned his men, and they were off towards the marshalsea where their horses were tethered.

'God, what a shit that man is!' Juliana exclaimed.

As I was the only person in the vicinity, I assumed she was talking to me. It was the first thing she had said to me since we had lain together in the wardrobe, and I was happy.

I would have followed her upstairs as she went. I was burning to have converse with her, to ask what she was thinking, to know that she had forgiven me for taking advantage of her moment of weakness or whatever it was she was holding against me, but now was not a good time. She did not want to speak. She knew the castle and its people better than I; perhaps something was up. I desperately wanted to talk to her, though, to tell her about the girl with dark eyes who seemed to me to have something of the night about her – though, here again, there were limits as to what I could say. I could hardly tell Juliana that I had dreamt I had been visited by one of her ladies, the very night after I had declared my passion and made love to the mistress. It would have been rude as well as impolitic. After all, I comforted myself, it had only been only a dream; although Saul had sometimes suggested that dreams are the truth and what we consciously think is error.

As I walked up and down in the bailey that evening, brooding on these events, I did not notice a dark figure waiting near the postern gate until I had practically stumbled on his shoe. I saw him then well enough: a man with a pale face, fleshy lips and hard little eyes, only a few years older than myself. It was the sly, whey-faced Chaplain, Crispin de Laval – another Breton – who had said grace before dinner that afternoon.

'What is on your mind, my son?' he said. 'You seem troubled.'

'Not troubled,' I told him, 'just exhausted in my mind. There has been so much to take in for a newcomer.'

'Yes, indeed. You have previously been in an abbey, I understand.'

'In an abbey and then at my father's château at Breteuil.'

I did not want him to think I was fresh out of school.

'I too was at a monastery as a boy. We must get together and talk about it. Perhaps I can encourage you to join the priesthood yourself. It seems a pity to waste your good learning.'

'I am not wasting my learning if I am teaching.'

'Quite so. But anyway, we must meet and talk about the old days. There is much that I miss about them. The camaraderie. The closeness with some of the Brothers. Do you know what I mean?'

He was very close to me now, almost brushing me with his hand, frisking it down my doublet. His weird breath was all over me. I knew exactly what he meant.

'No, no.' I said hurriedly, 'I've left all that behind.'

It was the wrong thing to say, and he got quite the wrong idea.

'Tell me more,' he cried. 'What secrets have you left behind that trouble you so much? Come to my study after Matins tomorrow. The Comte is very particular about attendance, and likes to see my Book. My door is always open.'

'Thank you, Father. So kind.'

'I feel we are going to be good friends.'

It was an uncomfortable thought.

The word around hall when I asked next morning was that the Comte was not in the least interested in the Chaplain's Book. The Chaplain, I learned, was famous for having little favourites among the pages who served as his spies. It was said that he reported to the Archbishop of Rouen who reported to the Pope's legate, Cardinal Cuno (a right little cuno, it was said, always sticking his nose in and causing trouble), who reported to the Pope who reported to God.

The Chaplain's door was always open but it shut pretty quick when he got you inside. He liked Malvasia wine and blond boys who liked Malvasia wine.

XV

Days passed and turned into weeks in that slippery way they have. The Comte came back, tossed some pots, and went away again.

My lessons with the girls were going well. They were bright and had aptitude for learning. Marie was a little more serious as so often happens with elder daughters, the younger more skittish, but both of them were delightful, and I loved them as much for themselves as for their mother.

It was by no means all lessons. We played Blind Man's Buff with the nurse and Juliana, and Are You There, Chanticlere?, that game where you blindfold someone who is called Mr Bones and give him a rolled-up 'stick' of cloth, and the 'victim' has to lie face down on the floor. Mr Bones says 'Are you there, Chanticlere? And the victim has to crow like a cock and then roll sideways, left or right, up or down, without moving his or her hips. Then Mr Bones strikes and, if he doesn't hit the victim on the head, Mr Bones becomes the next victim. This game was a great success. I taught them to play hide and seek and, in quieter moments, chess and draughts and fiddlesticks.

What fun we had when the Comte was away and Juliana was running the house! She was talking to me more now and had apologised for our indiscretion. It had shocked her, she told me, as had her feelings after it. This was why she had avoided me in those early days. She had decided that it must never happen again, it was far too dangerous, but that we could still be friends.

Of course it was not what I wanted to hear, but I understood life (to say women would have been arrogant) well enough to think this might not be her final word on the subject. I knew myself and Ovid well enough to know that once I had tasted the spring of knowledge, I had to drink deeper. But I could wait. It seemed to me then that we had all the time in the world, and I told myself what Catullus used to say, that a pleasure deferred is a pleasure increased.

She loved me, I was sure of it. I walked, bouncing on air, as if I had inflated bladders under my feet.

The Comte was away longer than expected, as it happened. Juliana said he had probably found a small war. I hoped I could take her to the greenwood the night before May Day to go a-maying, to make our bed in the forest and bring home green boughs with the girls and boys in the morning. But it was not possible. It was too soon, there were too many people watching, she said (proving indeed that my intimations were right). We were able to snatch a little bit of May madness in the wardrobe when they were all away though. Even the girl Alice with her big grey eyes and dark hair didn't notice. At any rate, she didn't let on that she had. That girl was a portent of something waiting to happen, but at least it was waiting not happening, and when you are young the happening is the thing that matters, in spite of what Catullus says. The present is like a siege projectile shattering into fragments of possibility as it hits the walls of the future, but I didn't know that then or, if I did know, I did not care. To be honest, I don't think Juliana cared either.

'Perfect love doth not cast out fear,' Brother Paul told me once, 'it just numbs it like an infusion of poppy.'

And then came the news that the English Queen, Matilda – the Duke's wife and Juliana's stepmother – had died.

XVI

The death had happened a few days back, in England. Matilda's real name was Edith but the Normans couldn't pronounce it so she was called Queen Matilda. Being descended from the old English kings, Edith Matilda was the sister of the King of Scotland as well, and an altogether important person.

Eustace, who happened to be plotting nearby, returned to Breteuil on hearing the news. There was immediately some question as to whether Eustace and Juliana were expected to go over to London for the funeral. The Queen certainly deserved due honour. She had done her duty by providing Henry with a son as well as a daughter, and he had trusted her enough to make her Regent in England when he was away in Normandy. He might even have loved her. But the news we received in Breteuil – news from my father in Mortagne, swiftly confirmed by the landlord of The Bear in town – was that the Duke preferred not to go back to England: the situation in Normandy was grave enough for his continued presence to be necessary.

The morning after his return to Breteuil, the Comte was making a hearty breakfast of capon's leg, bread and ale, even though he had been carried out insensible the night before. He cursed the Queen roundly for being a nuisance and interfering with his political alliances and declared that he, at any rate, was not going to England, a miserable country at the best of times.

'That will hardly upset her since she did not know you,' said Juliana. 'Nor will it upset the Duke since he is not going either. As for myself, much though it dismays me to agree with you, I feel it is an English affair, and I must be a Norman now.'

'She was a good lady and endowed monasteries, I understand,' said the Chaplain, always looking round corners and nicknamed (I discovered from my neighbour at table) Snooping Jesus. Luckily, it was said, he had very large feet so you could see the feet coming before the rest of him appeared.

'I shall pray for her,' said Juliana.

'Oh no, Comtesse. We must have a Mass. It would be an insult not to. Imagine what would happen if word reached the Duke that we had insulted his dead wife by not having a Mass. Brickbats would fly, Comtesse. I personally know the Archbishop of Rouen.'

'Very well, Father Crispin. If you insist. A Mass it shall be.'

'*I* do not insist, Comtesse. The Queen's bones cry out for it.'

They get these orotund phrases from the Apocrypha.

The Comte himself, though never at his best at breakfast, saw the Queen's death as an excuse for making trouble for the Duke once again. His next step, he decided – after sending a rambling letter of condolence to the Duke – was to arrange a series of consultations with his dubious friends, most of them disaffected enemies of the Duke, chief of whom was of course Amaury de Montfort, with whom he could plot further mischief.

We had the Mass in the château's chapel, a cold thin place with a high ceiling and hard seats. The boys from the town sang as best they could, but their best was not good enough. In fact, one of them was so bad that I saw him coming out of the Chaplain's room later quite red in the face.

Several days later, we saw the Comte clatter off with the knights of his bodyguard, this time in the direction of Évreux where de Montfort had various interests.

XVII

The hours passed happily when Eustace was away. May was graduating into June and Juliana was happy. The château worked properly, there was no discord, and indeed there was love.

There was something of fire about that girl. She was a Scorpio, I discovered – an Egyptian, versed in these things, came one day and read her fortune. She was tenacious and dangerous to cross – a water sign – but she had a strong Taurus in her character, which made her sensual and beautiful, and her moon was in Leo which was where the fire came in. The man was doubtless skilful enough, but I knew all these things from the first, though not to call them by the right names. I was a raw youth before I met Juliana, but she cooked my rawness and made me comestible. I never quite knew what I did for her because she was clever enough to keep it secret. She kept me simmering away at the back of the fire, until suddenly she was hungry, and she moved me back to the flame. I was content just to be near her and I believe that she loved me too, but she (I mean we) had to be careful. One indiscretion and all could be lost. There was no end to the list of punishments and humiliations that a wronged husband could mete out. It fairly curled the sphincter to think of them.

Over the past few weeks I had instituted a regime of lessons for the girls which was not too onerous but which included an hour or two of Latin every day. I intended that they should enjoy their Latin and not dread it as I had in the monastery. I began by teaching it as a Roman child would learn it – with words rather than declensions. 'Milk', 'bread', 'meat', 'fish', 'water', then adding adjectives and only then starting on declension. The verbs would follow in due course. It was not the academic way I learned it – but I had learned declensions and conjugations slowly and painfully. My new way appeared to work; the girls really seemed to be interested. They were so proud of themselves when they could ask for 'panis' and 'aqua' at table, impressing the knights and squires with their learning.

Saint-Sulpice had given me other useful skills beyond Latin, however. Medicine was one of them and illustration was another. Both of these came in very useful with the girls, since they were boisterous little things – endlessly falling over and cutting themselves – and they also loved drawing and painting, Marie especially.

Beyond these, there was a further art that the monastery at Saint-Sulpice had been famous for – its teaching of music and the making of it. I managed to borrow a little psaltery from one of the castle's musicians, a small harp-like instrument on which I started to give the girls lessons. Music was Pippi's especial forte.

They were both good at singing, and had a good ear. I taught them some of the new songs called caroles that were coming out of Provence, and songs for little ones that my mother used to sing, and a May song for the merry month that was so nearly over.

Pippi, six years old, had a voice like a high recorder; sweet and high, it quite caught at the heart. Marie's voice was just a little more alto, so they made a lovely duet together. Sometimes I would chime in with my tenor, and I swear people would have paid to hear us sing 'Sweet sorrow fills my heart' and 'All the birds of the morning'.

'Do you think people would pay to hear us?' asked Pippi.

'Without a doubt,' I replied. 'Such a beautiful sound was never heard in the whole of Normandy.'

I told them that we should have travelled on the road with my friend Eliphas the Player, and we would have drawn the crowds in every town we stopped in, so sweet and high we would have been. We would have drawn the birds from the trees and the beasts from the forest like Orpheus, I told the girls, and they wanted to go out on the road that very day.

'I think we would have to make preparations,' I said. 'The thing to do when people are going on their travels is to get a longish stick and a big wide handkerchief, put all the things you

100

need to take in it, then gather up the corners of the handkerchief, tie them to the end of your stick, put it over your shoulder and there you are, ready to go.'

Then of course we had to go and cut the sticks and find handkerchiefs that were big enough to hold what they considered important, which meant large quantities of sweetmeats and a big shawl in case they were cold at night. Juliana came in while we were tying the bundles to our sticks and wanted to know what was going on.

'We are going on the road,' Marie told her, 'to find Eliphant the Player, with Mr FitzR.'

'And then we will sing to the people wherever we stop and they will come to his cart to hear us,' chimed in Pippi.

'And what have you got in your bundles?' she asked, smiling.

'We have sweetmeats and a warm shawl,' said Marie.

'That sounds very sensible. And what does Mr FitzR have in his?'

'Sweetmeats,' I replied.

'And a warm cloak,' added Pippi.

'And I will take a sword in case of trouble,' I added. 'You never know in High Normandy.'

'And where will you sleep when you are on the road?' Juliana asked them. 'When it gets dark and the wolves start to howl and the rain starts to fall?'

'That will be a problem,' said Pippi.

'Mr FitzR will beat the wolves away,' said Marie.

'But even Mr FitzR, who is second to none in my regard, even Mr FitzR cannot keep the rain off two little girls on a soggy night.'

'We want to go, we want to go,' the girls shouted.

It was clear that the prospect of the adventure had really taken hold.

'We will go for a little walk with our bundles and see how it feels. They may be too heavy,' I said. 'It is essential to get everything in trim and properly sorted out.'

101

Juliana seemed to think that this was a good idea so, after an early meal, we put our sticks over our shoulders, I buckled on a sword, and we strode up to the gatehouse and I beat upon the stout oak with my stick, Juliana observing us from a discreet distance.

'Open up,' we shouted.

The old First Gatekeeper wheezed himself out of the lodge. I was happy to note that his surly colleague with whom I had crossed swords on my arrival at the château was not on duty that day.

'Whassup?'

'We are going to seek our fortunes, and beguile the world with the sweetness of our voices,' I said.

'Oh all right then, if m'lady says it's all right. It's a hard world out there,' he said to the girls, who began to look slightly uncertain.

We marched out, turning to wave to Juliana, who waved back at us.

'Isn't Mummy coming too?' asked Pippi.

'No, silly, or it wouldn't be an adventure,' her elder sister told her.

We walked on. Soon we were passing down a close avenue of trees, and slowly the forest closed in on us.

'Do you think we should sing like Orpheus to draw the beasts out?' I asked.

The little girls looked dubious.

'I think they might eat us instead,' said Pippi. 'We would be singing away with our top half sticking out of their mouths.'

'They might be enchanted with our music,' I said.

'But what if they're not?' said Marie.

'Good point,' I said, 'perhaps we should go back for now. I will send a message to Eliphas and see what he thinks.'

Just at the moment, who should come round the corner but a jingling-jangling body of knights with our old friend Eustace at the front.

'Halt!' he roared, and they all stopped and looked at me.

His wicked little black eyes bulged and looked ready to shoot out at me like vindictive olives.

'You,' he bellowed at me, 'what are you doing with my daughters, fellow? Are you absconding with them? Are you taking them hostage? My God and by Saint Elmo's beard, I believe you are. Arrest that man, sergeant.'

A large man leapt from his horse and advanced towards me, but my dear little Marie came to the rescue. She stood her ground and spoke to her father in a loud, clear voice.

'No, Father, he is not taking us hostage. He is teaching us the way of the road and how hard it can be and how poor men fare upon it. We were about to turn back at the very moment you appeared. My mother has given us permission.'

She was a true grandchild of the Duke at that moment. Even her father looked startled. Pippi joined in.

'That's right, Father. We are not going to be a hot … a hot … a hotsage.'

Some of the men smiled, even those iron hearts.

'Hmph. Oh. Very well,' said Eustace to the girls. Turning to me, he said gruffly, 'Take them back at once and teach them some Latin if that's what you do. You are a Latiner, teach them Latin. You are not paid to tramp around the forest like a mad monk getting up to God knows what.'

And so he rode on, and I followed after with the girls, sick at heart for my part, because kill-joy had come back.

The little girls were going to sing their May song in hall at dinner time; they had practised really hard. But then Eustace spoilt it all. He became intoxicated with the decent wine that Juliana had made the butler get in, and didn't want to hear his daughters. He declared he would hear it tomorrow. Now he wanted to talk about war and machination, and taking sides against the Duke whose vassal he was. De Montfort had got at him as we had feared.

'Eustace sees himself as some kind of king-maker,' Juliana told me when we met on the stairs later. 'But he is in truth only a pawn to be moved by his friends and removed by his enemies. It would be sad if he weren't such an ox.'

She never used ugly words about him because she was well brought up. That made the 'ox' sound really horrible. As of course he was.

There were scenes over the next few days. My little charges wept bitter tears at their father's behaviour over the May song. Their mother became moody herself, living in a quiet fury against the oaf her husband. He was a sort of angry, ugly monster whom nobody liked, maybe not even he himself.

The only good to come out of it was that he was soon out on his conspiracy trail again.

XVIII

I have never much cared about political intrigue and even less about war. Knowing that the Comte found them fascinating, I rated them even lower. My only care was my passion for the Comtesse who was good enough to treat me kindly and very occasionally let me make love to her.

No, that sounds far too passive on my part. I was impatient, sometimes I sulked because I wanted all of her attention, I was prepared to face the worst and be found out *in flagrante delicto* with her, so that the Comte would know I had cuckolded him, and his wife and I could leave and live in happiness and poverty together. But of course that was ridiculous. The Duke, her father, would never allow it. She had children; disgrace was not an option. She pointed this out to me when I mentioned it one day as we walked in the bailey while the children played around us.

'My father would have you poisoned, even if my husband did not. Or he would send someone to cut your throat one dark night on the way to the tavern. You must not even think that way. The only hope for us is that my husband will go too far, and he will be disgraced or imprisoned, or killed in some futile skirmish. But for the moment, we must be secret, always watching the corners and looking backwards, guarding our tongues ... We have been lucky so far. A castle is no place to hide things.'

Lucky? I was in torment, a torment from which I could not bear to be separated. I wondered now whether she did really love me. She was a passionate woman and an ardent lover, and I was a convenient boy who happened to be around. She found me amusing. I gave her a new interest and perspective. I showed her how desirable she was, but what did she care about me?

Like a gauche boy, I raised these questions with her, and her eyes flashed. I saw a tear of anger on her cheek, and her lip trembled, and she turned away and said nothing to me for a week. In the castle there were eyes and ears everywhere, waiting to betray us, and I saw, to my shame, what a fool I had been and how I had underestimated my lovely Juliana. I was low and unworthy.

Since we could talk if we could not make love, I began to see Normandy and the Duke's predicament in a new light. As Juliana explained it to me in our many conversations, the to and fro of baronial loyalty and disaffection started to make more sense. My journeys to The Bear in town were now undertaken more for information than refreshment. Each time I heard news that was in some way detrimental or adverse to the Duke I rejoiced, because it might take the Comte away from Breteuil again. And in that summer of 1118 there was plenty to feed the Comte's feverish ambitions.

The Duke was encountering trouble from every side. Even Hugh de Gournay, who had been brought up by Henry, was rising against him. Henry had encouraged him to marry off his pretty sister to a trusted courtier, Nigel d'Aubigny. But this made de Gournay petulant, so he left the wedding party, killed a castellan loyal to the Duke, and gave the castle to a friend of his. I mean, how crass can you get? Normandy was full of people like that in those days. Brutish people to whom life was a knacker's yard.

Of course it meant that Eustace was off again, and the castle was left free of the brooding presence. It was nearly midsummer and there had been not a drop of rain for three weeks. The farmers complained, but the town and castle had better things to think about.

We were gathering together for the midsummer pageant when almost anything went, and the château was supposed to roast an ox in the meadow outside the walls for the townsfolk to enjoy.

The steward wanted to conserve resources because of the wars (despite siphoning off much for himself) but the Comtesse gave him a dressing-down and told him not to be so miserable. Of course the ox should be roasted on Midsummer Night; the stars would fall from the heavens, the trees would leave the forest, if we did not celebrate. The Chaplain clasped his hands together unctuously and talked about heathen practices and dangerous beliefs in fairies and goodfellows, but Juliana pounced on him too and told him about the importance of not being serious about everything. The children were excited because there would be swings and booths and jugglers and three-legged races. Even better for me, three days earlier Baldwin, Count of Flanders had advanced further into Normandy with his army and thereby guaranteed that Eustace would not be at home.

I watched Juliana moving among these people like a swan among ducks, unaware in their ducky way of the enormous favour she was granting with her presence. She was born to command and yet she was at ease with the world. She made you feel easy even if you were a scullion or the lowest kind of scroyle. Only with the dishonest or the vile did she show her iron.

Juliana had hinted to me that on Midsummer Night, after the race round the lake and the tug of war and the ox-roast and the conjuring man and the fattest woman in the world and the fire-eater and the dancing to a consort of lyras, and after the little girls were safely in bed, watched over by their old nurse, we might be able to steal away to a little summerhouse beside the lake. She knew a way we could escape without being seen and then we could spend part of this most magical of nights together.

There was a breathless expectation about the great day, as much in the castle as the town. The ox had been killed, the great fire built, tents and stalls started to go up, people spoke of nothing else, and I thought of nothing but Juliana and what she had promised me.

XIX

There were no lessons when the day finally arrived. The little girls were on tiptoe, dizzy with excitement – and, I have to admit, so was I, for I had had no opportunity to be alone with Juliana for two weeks, which seemed to me like a lustrum, a decade, a quintillion, an aeon. I was obsessed with her, consumed, un-made and re-created. I seemed to have lost what it was I had thought myself to be.

It was a hot day. The little girls ran me, their mother, and the old nurse ragged, visiting all the stalls, trying the cakes, throwing the hoops, knocking down the skittles, peeping at the world's fattest woman, and becoming hopelessly entangled in the three-legged race. Juliana was in great demand as a judge and arbiter. It was she who was asked to cut the first slice from the ox, and what a fine animal it was! It fed the town to a perfect and chin-dripping fullness, and darkness was well fallen before the little girls started to droop. I scooped them up and returned them to the castle, and the old nurse gave me a wigging for keeping them up so late.

'It is true that it is late, Nanny,' said Marie, 'but it has been the best day ever and we didn't want it to finish.'

'It is true that it is late, Nanny ... but ...' echoed Pippi, and then her eyes closed and she would have fallen if I had not caught her.

'Dead on her feet,' the old girl grumbled, and then she winked, 'but, by Jesu, that ox was good. Steward says he never authorised it. Wash his mouth out with soap if he sneaks to the Comte. I'll box his ears, so I will.'

I told Juliana about it when we met at last at the postern door. She was wearing a gauzy veil which partially hid her face above her summer dress. I was reminded once again of the dangers we faced if anyone saw us together.

'The steward is a poisonous little rat. Let him do what he will,' she said. 'That ox was probably bought and fed with my dowry.'

She led me by the hand down to the dungeon, which of course she had emptied of prisoners. In truth, there were only two, both of whom had offended the Comte in some way or another.

'Eustace is away and the mice will play,' she said.

The gaoler was still at the feast, filling his knobbly face with beef dripping, and dancing grotesquely like a wodwo with anyone who would have him. The revels would continue until midnight and beyond. He would pass out in a tent and not wake up until somebody pissed on him.

Juliana led me down a passage in the very entrails of the castle to a door which looked, on cursory inspection, like part of the wall. It was locked but, conveniently, she carried a key. She opened the door and a long, low, damp, dark tunnel revealed itself.

'This tunnel was ordered by the Earl FitzOsbern, grandfather of my husband, who built the castle. For whatever reason – some said fear, others said prudence, others still said love – he liked the idea of escaping from the place without anyone knowing.'

'Sensible man,' I said.

'It stretches for fifty yards beyond the curtain wall to the shore of the lake.'

She produced a candle which she lit from the tallow lamp that provided the dungeon with its dim and eerie illumination.

'Come,' she said. 'No time for faint hearts. And watch out for puddles.'

She pushed me forward, closing the door behind her and locking it.

'We don't want any followers tonight,' she said.

She handed me the candle which I held aloft and, hand in hand, we made our way down that spooky little rat-hole, dodging the drips from the ceilings and the slime on the walls, until finally, just as I thought the tunnel must end in a rock fall,

110

we came to another locked door which responded raspingly to the key that she held, and we were out.

We were in a low cave scooped out of the side of the hill on which the castle sat. I had never noticed it before. Juliana locked the passage door and placed the key on a ledge hidden from inquisitive eyes. There was a little rowing boat drawn up upon the slope with the name *Perrine* written on its stern, and two oars resting against the wall. I checked to make sure that we were alone, but everyone was still up at the roast and its aftermath.

'So far so good,' she said. 'You know this is madness, don't you?'

'A divine madness, the Greeks would call it,' I said, immediately regretting my stilted pedagoguery.

My desire was making me nervous.

'I take it you can row.'

'I learned on the lake when I was at the abbey,' I told her, 'helping with the fishing. Also on the Risle when we needed rushes.'

I pushed the boat down to the edge of the lapping water, handed her in to the stern seat, passed her the oars to be stowed on either side, and stepped lightly in to take up position on the sculler's seat, facing her. There was a moment of precarious wobble as I did so, and she stifled a little cry of alarm.

The still surface of the lake shone like the newly polished armour of a prince. I dipped the oars in the water, and it was like paddling mercury.

'We are floating on metal,' I said.

She leant forward and kissed me.

'Head straight across the lake,' she told me. 'There is a place to land by the little summerhouse.'

I had walked past it many times, but I had never thought I would see the place in such a circumstance. That paddle across the lake was like a journey beyond time. So closely did the still water reflect the stars, I had a fancy that we were rowing across the sky. Juliana's eyes were fixed on me. I wished our journey could go on for ever.

But, yes, we arrived with a bump, and we climbed out of the boat and pulled it up near the wooden summerhouse with its tiny jetty.

'Shall we stay here?' I asked.

Decisions tonight rested with her.

'No', she said, 'we will go to the house in the woods.'

I was not so sure of that. The woods were very dark and visibility was close. I had never ventured far into these woods. There was something about them that kept you out. Probably it was just the Comte's gamekeeper, but you heard things that you could not see, and would not wish to. There was talk of wodwos, goodfellows and witches.

Juliana was confident enough. She knew the path, and I was glad she did for it led us a merry dance hither and thither, until I thought we were retracing our steps. We must have walked a mile and more. Perhaps she did it to confuse me. Finally we arrived at a tumbledown cottage, lost in the forest, as the moon glimmered above the trees, and distant cries in the wood sounded half-human in that way they do. The thought crossed my mind that we would have the devil of a time getting back, but I pushed it away. Juliana knew where and how and what this evening. I knew for sure that I did not.

Another thought came, completely unbidden, that maybe she had done this – with someone else – before. It did not worry me. Why should it?

'Hello,' she called at the cottage door. 'Mother Merle!'

There was an answering call from somewhere inside, and at length the door was opened by a pretty girl of seventeen or so. A cat with green eyes played around her legs.

'Good evening, Madame,' the girl said, curtseying charmingly. 'Everything is ready for you.'

She showed us into the kitchen where a table was spread with meats and cheese and bread, and a flagon of wine.

'You may leave us now, Merle,' said Juliana.

'The room is ready for you, Madame. Good night.'

'Thank you, Merle. You have done well. Good night.'

The girl went out into a room at the back.

'Eat,' said Juliana, pointing at the table. And indeed I found I was hungry after our wanderings in the forest.

I poured some wine for us both – an excellent Burgundy of which my father the cellarer would no doubt have approved. I was still nervous. The strangeness of the evening made me feel as if I were an actor in one of Eliphas's plays, but my apprehension began to leave me as we sat there. Was there something in the wine? Everything seemed to take on a dusky crimson shadowing. Things appeared to move more slowly and in a gliding motion which made me laugh.

I had never been so happy.

'Come,' said Juliana, and led me upstairs to a little room with a large bed.

She undressed so slowly that a disaster was nearly precipitated in my precipitous state. Just as slowly she undressed me so that we both stood there, in the moonlight, liquefying. I seemed to have become my penis.

At last she drew me onto her on the bed and we engaged in the longest, fiercest, most utter act of love I have ever experienced. I think my soul came out of my cock. And then we had another one; gentler, sweeter, calmer, caressing, like a long, liquid, slithery Amen. And then we fell asleep.

I woke once or twice to hear noises outside, the sound of voices that could barely be heard and creatures snuffling in the wood. Juliana was the only person I have ever known who could sleep with her eyes open. At least, that is what she told me.

Finally I woke up to early sunlight and an urgent tugging from a naked Juliana. She had been washing herself from the ewer in the corner.

'Wake up! We have to get back.'

I sprang up, not tired at all. That wine must have had a clever cordial in it. I felt I could do it all again, and put a hand up to her breast, but she pushed it away and started dressing.

'No time for that. He's coming back today.'

'How do you know?'

'I know.'

'Merle told you?'

She smiled.

'Who is she?' I asked.

'Get your clothes on.'

I bundled them on and we went downstairs. There was no sign of the girl, but an old crone was stirring a kind of pottage in a pot on the fire. She turned as we came down.

'There you are,' she croaked. 'Sleep well, did you?'

'Very well,' I said.

'You'll have some gruel?'

Juliana took some and lapped it like a cat.

'No thanks,' I said.

The woman took a bowl and thrust it into my hands.

'You'll have some gruel,' she said.

I took it reluctantly, but, on tasting it, felt an instant uplift and dash. If I had been feeling good before, this was an extra shot of the bolt.

'Thank you,' I told her, finishing the bowl and handing it back. 'I'd like that every morning.'

She and Juliana exchanged glances.

'You can't,' she told me, 'greedy pig.'

'That's telling him,' said Juliana. 'Come on, we must go.'

XX

We hurried back to the lake taking a path through the woods that seemed a much straighter route this time.

'The way changes,' was all Juliana would say.

At the little summerhouse on the shore, we found the boat *Perrine* waiting for us as we had left her. I took a good look round before we pushed off in case there was some peeping eye, but could discern nothing.

'Come on, scaredy-cat,' said Juliana. 'You find a threat round every corner.'

'And there usually is one,' I said. 'The question is whether it chooses to come out or not. I have lived a harder life perhaps than you.'

'You do not know what it is like to live under a conqueror,' she said, eyes blazing as only hers could. 'The English are abused at every turn. My mother had to be Prince Henry's whore before she could win back her land.'

'I am sorry,' I said, and felt so too.

'Row hard,' she told me, 'and we will not be missed. Eighteen castellans have now risen against my father; the Count of Anjou has joined the rebels and taken a castle. My husband will be stirring the pot. He will not be looking for me – or you – when he returns.'

How had she come by this news? I thought it better not to ask, and applied myself to the oars. The lake had a light morning mist around it, which mitigated our exposed position. The revels of the previous night had served us well and no one seemed to be stirring. We landed quickly, drew up the boat and hurried into the tunnel. At the far end, by the door to the keep, Juliana stopped.

'You go on,' she said. 'It is better that we enter the castle separately.'

I was distraught at having to leave her after all that had passed between us, and started to tell her so.

'I know,' she said. 'Go now, quickly.'

I was cast down, but she was right. She gave me a chaste kiss. I pushed the door ajar, saw no one around, and hurried up the stairs to the hall where a few squires lay propped against the wall, dead to the world. Noises from the kitchen proclaimed that others – scullions and bakers – were already up and at work. I flitted across the room and made for the stairs.

'And what have you been up to?'

It would have to be Fulk, of course.

'Sleeping in the forest on Midsummer Night. Waiting for enchantment. Something you wouldn't understand, Fulk.'

The only way with Fulk was attack. He was momentarily set back. He glared at me but frankly I was too tired. I just prayed that Juliana would not come up at that point. I turned and climbed the stairs up towards my cupboard.

'You wait till we have a melee,' he shouted. 'Then you can kiss my arse.'

What the hell was he talking about? I slept late that morning. Luckily my little pupils were also tired and played sluggard. Juliana told me later that she had climbed by a secret staircase to the postern gate, and walked in the herb garden before falling asleep sitting upon a bench and waking with dew upon her.

XXI

When I came downstairs the arrival of the Duke's messenger had brought a buzz of excitement. Henry had sent out a military summons to the whole of Normandy – whether it would be answered, least of all by Eustace, was moot to say the least. The messenger, a knight called Bourdet, had ridden in haste and had still further to go. He was refreshing himself in hall before leaving south for Mortagne. I approached him on hearing this last piece of news.

'My father is the Comte de Perche,' I told him. 'Will you please give him my salutations and tell him that I am well, and that I hope that he is?'

'I will do that willingly,' he replied. 'I too hope that he is well and the Duke wishes it also. We hear that there is trouble from the tenants of the Comte of Bellême, whom the Duke imprisoned for the trouble he caused. The Duke has transferred the Bellême lands to his own nephew, Theobald. Theobald is a good general, but he has made these same estates over to his brother Stephen who is less of a soldier. Stephen now has to defend the whole of the south of Normandy, and the Duke needs your father's support since Mortagne is but a day's ride from Bellême, and the whole of the south of Normandy is aflame.'

'I am sure that he will give it,' I replied, knowing that my father, if a bit of a duffer, was staunchly loyal to the Duke.

'I am relieved to hear it, as I am sure the Duke will be. These are difficult times and the bedrock of the duchy seems to be melting.'

'Melting, is it?' an all-too-familiar voice broke in.

It was Eustace, just arrived, clanking hot from his machinations with Amaury de Montfort and God knew who else, and smelling of horses, metal, sweat and drink. The news nexus had not let us down.

'My lord,' said Bourdet, rising from the table.

'Sit down, man,' cried Eustace, tempering minimal politeness with crassness. 'So to what do we owe the pleasure?'

Bourdet resumed his seat and repeated the details of his mission.

'A military summons,' growled Eustace, 'when all the duchy is at sixes and sevens. The Duke cannot keep order. He offends the barons, takes away their castles and gives them to his favourites.'

'I will not argue with you, Comte. I am here to deliver a message which I have done.'

'I have friends who have suffered from the Duke's foolishness and inattention. He forgets past favours and promises, and stirs up rancour from Alençon to Dieppe and from Vernon to Cherbourg.'

'He is your liege lord and therefore he can require your assistance.'

There now ensued the spectacle, fatuous if it had not been such bad form, of Eustace climbing onto his high horse.

'Do not you tell me, knight, what I can or cannot do. Who do you think you are? You come into my castle and throw your weight around. Get out of here.'

Bourdet put down his beaker of water, and rose to his feet.

'You forget, sir, whom I serve.'

'I forget nothing …'

Eustace's face was now registering a familiar shade of purple.

Bourdet held his hand up.

'I urge you, sir, to say nothing now that you might regret later. I will leave now since I have far to go, but I urge you to consider the Duke's summons. It may go ill with you if you ignore it. I am but the messenger. Please …' he lifted his hand as Eustace started to rumble and harrumph again, 'I will see myself out.'

The Duke's envoy left the room and we heard him and his attendant descending the steps outside the hall. The majority of those present had the grace to look ashamed; this was no way to treat a visitor let alone a royal envoy.

'Well done, Eustace,' Juliana's voice rang out from the foot of the stairs. 'You certainly know how to make enemies. Was it so necessary to insult the Duke's man?'

'It is necessary for a man of honour not to dissemble his true feelings,' spluttered Eustace. 'A man of honour nails his colours to the mast.'

'But they are not your colours; they are Amaury de Montfort's colours; they are Comte Baldwin's colours; they are the Comte of Maine's colours; they are Louis of France's colours. Troublemakers the lot of them.'

'You speak of matters you know not, madam. Kindly keep your opinions to yourself and we can laugh at them in private.'

With that, Eustace sat down, poured a goblet of wine and turned his back on Juliana. I thought she was going to pour the whole pitcher over him, but she controlled herself. Her parting shot, as she turned to mount the stairs, was much more lethal.

'God Almighty, Eustace, you do try my father's patience. It surprises me that you still have any castles left. But you won't have them for long, and then we shall see who is the ruler and who the ruled. Good evening to you.'

XXII

There was to be no respite for Duke Henry for whom – though I had not yet met him – I felt increasing sympathy (to be the father of Juliana he must have done something right).

July and August brought him more trouble while we at Breteuil picked strawberries and cherries and saw the harvest come in. Eustace and his merry men, some of whom were not so merry at being separated from their homes and loving families, were kept on the *qui vive* while he cantered around drumming up support for faction and strife, and offering his services to those too cynical to refuse. Juliana kept herself in touch with the news of her father's troubles, and I am convinced sent him details of her husband's activities and his foolish dealings with dangerous men.

Next came news that Gilbert de l'Aigle – head of a great family with estates in southern Normandy and England, and a faithful servant of Henry's who had fought for him at Tinchebrai – had died suddenly. His son Richer looked to succeed to his father's estates in England. The Duke, however, reckoned that Richer's brothers Geoffrey and Engenulf de l'Aigle had a superior claim since they had served the Duke as soldiers of his household. This infuriated Richer who sought the help of the French king, Louis, who was ever eager to press a little thorn into Henry's flesh. Soon Amaury de Montfort was offering soldiers and support, and along came all the rest of the plotters and malcontents.

The Duke decided to accede to Richer de l'Aigle's requests on the advice of none other than my father of Perche, but it was too late to stop the French king and his mischievous intervention. Louis – tall, pear-shaped – won the surrender of the Château of l'Aigle with a sudden pounce in spite of his corpulence.

We heard all about it not long after the events unfolded, as the grapes ripened on our vines, and the nodding wheat yielded to the scythe as it had always done, disturbing the dormice and unleashing the conies. The upheaval furnished Eustace with yet more material for his travels, especially as Amaury de Montfort was a key player in all the plotting and machination, but it all still seemed far away to me; someone else's business. Until, all at once, there it was knocking on my door.

Juliana was a favourite daughter of the Duke. Perhaps he was missing the reassuring company of his wife, perhaps he was feeling his age, but whatever the reason, it was all getting too much for him and he asked – requested, commanded – Juliana to make the journey to Rouen and stay with him in his castle. He could no longer trust his own circle, he told her. He was beginning to fear for his life, and he was usually a sanguine man. She had to go.

I said goodbye to her sorrowfully. It was late August, that wobbly time when you can feel summer coming to an end, and winter blowing its little distant horn. There is dampness in the air. Vapours cling to the grass, mists shroud the trees. Bread grows mouldy, and swine, if they have any sense (which they do), start to feel apprehensive about Michaelmas when good pigs turn into ham.

'It is the end of something good,' I told her.

'Rubbish,' she said. 'I will be back. Winter's a good time. Fires and hot ale and spiced wine, dancing and music, caroles and Christmas ...'

'There'll never be another summer like this one.'

She went the next day, and of course everything else started to go downhill. The little girls were sad and missed their mother. We talked about her every day and tried to imagine what she was doing far away in Rouen. I am afraid I was an inadequate substitute, but they clung to me. Their father, when he was there, simply frightened them. The running of the castle began to slide. The moat grew weed. The rushes grew foul and the steward cheated on the meat. The trenchers were served up with mould on them, the wine was like mule piss, the small ale sour, and the servants surly.

September came with a fine early harvest of apples and pears, and cider-making began. I received a short, hurried, secret note from Juliana telling me that her father feared for his life – there were indeed suggestions of a plot to kill him – and that she must stay at least until the beginning of October.

Michaelmas arrived and the pigs' worst fears were realised. Pork, left over from the salting, appeared in hall rather too often and indifferently presented by a listless cook. The steward had salted away the best cuts to be sold by himself, elsewhere.

The little girls were beginning to decline irregular verbs, and starting on the easiest bits of Ovid. I wrote them a series of stories in Latin featuring the exploits of two young witches called Case and Tense. It was pretty good rubbish, but they seemed to like it.

I had some conversations with the lovely, dark-eyed Alice in Juliana's absence. She told me a little of her past as daughter of a country knight and tenant of the Comte de Carentan, brought up in a remote manor house near Barfleur. She had led a life of excruciating boredom, tempered by reading, which her mother (who was related to the Carentans and had married beneath her) had insisted she was taught to do, and was relieved when her mother found her a position at the neighbouring Château de Bayeux. There she attracted the notice of the Duke – who sent her as companion to his daughter at Breteuil. That was how things happened in Normandy.

Alice was devoted to Juliana, hated Eustace, and had a mighty wish in due course to see more of the world. We spoke a great deal of Juliana, and any feelings I might have had for Alice (I could not help recalling the dream I had had on my first night in the château) were tempered by the respect we both had for the Comtesse. I did not ask Alice if she had any intimation of being part of my dream, or of me being part of hers. It would have been disloyal to Juliana to start such a hare, but I could not help feeling that there was more than connection between us.

Soon it was time to pick the grapes and make the thin liquid that sufficed for wine, served to the rank and file in hall, on which the steward made a profit. The left-over sourish grapes also added a quality of freshness to the drab diet that was our daily portion. The steward could not think what else to do with them. They were fit for us or the pigs, and the pigs had been slaughtered. Even the pages and messengers were starting to complain about the food. God knows what the scullions were saying.

I received a second, longer letter by secret devise from Juliana, which I can give you verbatim since I still have it with me.

Dearest leman mine,

I hope you are as well as I am, and thinking of me just as much as I think of you. There is much afoot here, most of it bad. There has been a conspiracy among some of the very closest of my father's companions, even those who sometimes eat with him, to remove him in favour of his nephew Stephen. We do not think Stephen knew of this, though it is possible. How they proposed to remove him, I cannot say, but it is more than possible it involves murder.

My father moves around, changes his room, his bed, increases the number of his guard, even sleeps with a shield and sword in his grasp. Who was behind the conspiracy we could not at first discover but finally it emerged. The culprit was none other than one of his trusted treasurers, a secret malcontent called Herbert, so smooth and affable on the surface you would not believe.

When my father found out, a dreadful punishment was inflicted on the man – he was blinded and then castrated like a dog. I heard the screams as I stood on the topmost tower to get away. It took place, as is customary, in the marketplace for the people to see. My father is not a bloodthirsty man but certain rituals have to be performed in Normandy, he says; justice must be seen to be done. Otherwise he will be considered no better than his brother Robert who could not or would not keep order, and whom he himself deposed on the urging of the Church.

Now for the good news. My father feels much safer now that the plot is uncovered and the chief architect put out of action. He says I can return to Breteuil after the first week of October when he has called a great council meeting at Rouen. Aren't you happy to hear that, little Latin leman? Only a few days to go! Give a close fart to my husband, not that you would do anything so unmannerly. Keep yourself clean of limb, pure of mind, and constant of heart, and forget about the first two so long as you cleave to the third.

All the love that a letter can contain before it runs over and spoils the ink.

Your true
J

So! She was coming back and I could live truly again instead of shadow-playing.

Before she returned, however, the castle was busy with the drolleries and shudders of All Hallows Eve when the spooks rise from their graves and haunt the living – very much in the guise of Bertold the Bastard who, wrapped in a sheet, made the little girls shriek with fearful giggles and shiver in their beds so that old Catrine, their nurse, became quite incandescent with reproach. I had to repeat the performance for Alice and the ladies. Alice had managed to obtain some of the better wine, kept for the Comtesse, and we all had much laughter playing games of forfeit including Kiss the Spook. I became aware that I was half in love with Alice, but there was no question either of my mentioning it or of my love for Juliana being in any way diminished.

Can one be in love with two women? That unreliable guide Catullus says that it is more than possible.

Next day, the Chaplain with the roving eye officiated at a Mass for All Saints, and I prayed to God for direction without any great sense that I would receive it, or that I even deserved his help.

XXIII

Six days later, Juliana returned. I had waited for this moment like a man dying of thirst in a wilderness, and it seemed that she felt the same for she took me without further ado to her wardrobe room and gave me all that I had dreamt of in her absence and more. When we had finished making love, we lay on the bed smelling of each other and perfumed with cinnamon, citron, verbena, orris root, southernwood, lavender, cloves, galangale, saffron, grains of paradise, attar of roses, bitter almond, dried orange peel, and the honeyed fruit of the strawberry tree …

'Let us lock the door, barricade ourselves in, and stay here always,' I said to her.

'That would be perfectly lovely,' she replied, 'though we might grow hungry. Spices are meant to provide flavour not nourishment.'

'Is that what we are to each other, do you think? Flavour not nourishment?'

'Very good flavour,' she smiled.

Stupidly, I took umbrage.

'You are not simply my food,' I told her. 'You are the air I breathe and the water that gives me life. I am sorry that I do not provide the same for you.'

'Don't be silly, Bertold,' she said. 'You know what you are for me, but I must have other considerations. You do not have children. My daughters are rooted in my life and I in theirs. My father is another such. They do not take me away from you; they co-exist. You, they, all of you are nourishment. I give myself entirely to you as a lover, but as a mother and a daughter I belong to others.'

My silly anger subsided.

'Of course, you are right,' I said.

'And it is because of these others that we cannot lock ourselves away. These are dangerous times, Bertold. My days with my father have taught me just how dangerous. We may yet be caught up in something – a web, a plot, a trap, an accident even – born of these evil days, which undoes us all.'

'I will protect you and the girls in all events,' I said. 'Or I shall die in the attempt.'

'I know you will, my Latiner. But let us hope that it does not come to that.'

I was unsettled by her forebodings, for I trusted her judgment, but I was young and still believed in the triumph of good in the tournament against evil.

XXIV

Juliana had more communications from her father now following her visit. Not a man who trusted many, he found it helpful to unburden to his daughter. Messengers appeared and delivered sealed letters which Eustace, when he was around, deeply resented. He felt they should have come to him – and of course he yearned to use their contents in his machinations against the Duke. But Henry took great care that his communications were handed only to Juliana, no one else, and that they were destroyed once read.

Juliana told me that, despite having solved his immediate domestic crisis, her father was now under pressure as never before from his enemies at large. I tried to meet her every day after the little girls' lessons, and when despatches arrived, she would discuss their contents with me. When you hear about political affairs from the protagonist's own daughter, they take on a much more immediate dimension, and I was caught up in these matters of state, almost as if the problems were my own.

The great council at Rouen had been a key strategy of her father's. He had invited the Archbishop of Rouen, four Norman bishops and a number of the principal abbots of the dukedom as well as Thurstan, Archbishop of York, who had been a long-term thorn in his side but was on occasion a useful ally. Also at this convocation was the papal legate, Cardinal Cuno, whose presence was something of a surprise. He was invited by Henry, although he was not always popular with the Duke, to lend greater weight to his efforts to secure calm and tranquility in Normandy. The Church was of course a central pillar in Henry's hold on the dukedom – and had been from the first. Any kind of message of peace would be in Cuno's best interest as well as Normandy's. Alas for Henry, it did not work out like that. From the very first day of the council, Juliana told me, things went terribly wrong.

Audoin, Bishop of Évreux, did not come to the council because his see was under sustained attack from – guess who? – Amaury de Montfort. The constable of the castle, a crony of de Montforts, held the view that Amaury was the victim of injustice and had been unfairly cheated of his inheritance. He came out in sympathy with Amaury and was promptly joined by other adjacent lords. Embarrassingly for Henry, the whole area was soon up in arms. The armed garrison of the castle proceeded to sack the town, a fairly standard though nonetheless melancholy event for the townsfolk, and the Bishop took to his heels, an absence that would last a year.

Henry wound up the council and in November marched with his army first to l'Aigle where the French king was waiting for him. By all accounts the king's soldiers were good. They emerged from the castle and attacked the attackers. One of the Duke's nephews and best generals was unhorsed. Henry himself and his other nephew Stephen had to come to the general's aid and, in the struggle that followed, Henry was struck on the head by a rock, which would have caused serious injury had he not been wearing a helmet.

Juliana turned pale as she read this report, and I know she implored him in her next letter to keep out of the line of battle himself. He was not a natural soldier, but he was brave and – more importantly – he was lucky.

'That is where my husband is now,' she told me. 'He is one of the self-same lords who are flocking to Amaury's banner. Eustace is better at the banquet than the melee, but our Marshal, who leads his soldiers, is good, though God knows how we manage to keep him. Our men are brutish but well trained. No wonder Amaury eggs him on. But it will all end badly. The Marshal himself does not like to take arms against my father but he has no choice for he serves my husband. It would be all much better if women ran the world.'

It was not the first time that I had heard that sentiment. My mother was ever fond of repeating it, as was the barmaid down at The Bear.

130

The next week brought new trouble for Henry when some experienced troops, led by an ally of King Louis, disguised themselves as English soldiers in order to gain entrance to the strategically important castle at Andelys. Once inside they swiftly sang out the French war cry, 'Montjoie'; the garrison collapsed and the French were soon in command of both castle and town.

'What a stupid war cry that is,' the Duke was heard to exclaim. 'Mount Joy? It sounds like a brothel. Perhaps that is why the French like it.'

Montjoie was what the French called the mound of corpses they built after a victory, an unpleasant habit which Henry thought barbarous. I heard of this battle at The Bear. Henry did not write of the small setback to his daughter, perhaps ashamed of it.

The citadel of Andely soon became host to a nest of vipers in league against the Duke. They controlled all the land from Andely to Pont-Saint-Pierre, and strutted about with their veteran soldiers, taunting Henry. Meanwhile in the south, at Alençon, disgruntled townsfolk took exception to the Duke's favourite nephew, Stephen. The taking of hostages was a normal part of a battle, but these townsfolk were indignant that Stephen had taken the wife of a rich burgess and put her in the charge of some bad characters who had humiliated and raped her. Henry, of course, would not hear a word against Stephen (inept soldier though he was), so the townsfolk complained to the Comte of Anjou, who never let slip an opportunity to discomfort the Duke. Anjou besieged the castle, and when Henry marched down to relieve it with Theobald and Stephen, he got a bloody nose. Anjou cut the castle's water supply and called in the help of the Comte de Maine, another reliable opportunist in the Henry-baiting stakes.

They fought a pitched battle and Henry lost. It was only a small battle, but apparently it hurt. He wasn't used to being beaten. Everywhere there seemed to be enemies. The only bright spot on the horizon was that Baldwin, Comte of Flanders, was dying – he had received a grievous wound in battle earlier in the year. Even so, as Henry remarked in a letter to Juliana, it was like the Hydra's head. You cut one off and ten grew in its place. He could never stay anywhere for long enough to mount a proper siege before there was trouble somewhere else, and he had to bustle off to deal with it. Everything was *ad hoc* and *quam celerrime*.

So the season of fighting ended miserably for Henry. We did not see so much of it at Breteuil because it was known that Eustace was a collaborator of the malcontents, so the malcontents left us alone. Henry himself was on good terms with his daughter even if he abhorred her husband, so he left us alone too. Eustace being away much of the time was an added bonus. Soon it was Martinmas, and we began to look forward to Christmas.

Breteuil was a cold castle but wine mulled with honey, cinnamon, grains of paradise and galangale started to appear in hall, and warmed us, thanks to Juliana's prompting, though it was officially the Advent fasting-time before the Christmas feast, and the Chaplain looked askance (while he drank the wine).

And then Eustace returned.

He was so full of himself that bits of him seemed to spill over. He had grown fat on his travels. His chin and his cheeks topped his jerkin like over-stuffed puddings. Nonetheless, his little, piggy eyes stared out with the same old malevolence.

'You have grown soft in my absence,' he shouted at us. 'In the new year, I shall be wanting every man jack of you out in the field, wearing my colours and fighting my fight. Yes, even you, Latiner. What we need, before Christmas weakens us and softens us, is a melee. What do you think of that?'

There was a deep, grumbling lowing noise from the majority, though I did hear someone shouting 'YES'.

I looked around and I think you can probably guess who it was. Yes, it was Fulk. And he had his eyes fixed on me. He really did hate me, that man. Later, that evening after dinner, he accosted me on the stairs.

'A word, Latiner,' he said.

'*Ingrediamur*,' I replied.

'What's that supposed to mean?'

'You asked for a word and I gave you one. In my role as Latiner, I felt I should give you one in Latin. *Ingrediamur*. It means let us go in.'

'Go in where?' his face showed a mixture of puzzlement and aggression.

'Let us go into what you want to say to me.'

'Oh. I see. Very clever. Well you won't feel so clever when you hear what I have to tell you.'

'What have you to tell me?'

'I know what you are up to.'

'Tell me.'

'You and the Comtesse.'

I felt the floor under my foot turn to quicksilver. I suppose somebody had to discover us one day, but that it had to be now – and that it should be Fulk – seemed unnecessarily brutal. What to do now? Denial was a possible course, but the man clearly had proof of some kind otherwise he would not have dared speak out. Juliana and I had had such good luck for so long that perhaps we had become careless. My mind raced and my scrotum contracted as I recollected what happens to courtiers of a castle who cuckold a comte.

'Not so high and mighty now, are you?' said Fulk, noticing my chagrin.

'On the contrary, Fulk,' I said, collecting myself. 'I am higher and mightier than ever. It is you who are the fool. You really feel the Comte would listen to you rather than to my lady who everyone knows is a virtuous wife. No, what would happen to you if you blabbed is what happens to tattle-mongers and slanderers everywhere. First you will be whipped and then you will have your tongue cut out.'

I was deeply worried, but I didn't like to show it to Fulk. It would give him enormous satisfaction.

'It's …'

'No, Fulk. It is the standard treatment meted out to those who break the seventh commandment. Thou shalt not bear false witness, you horrible piece of witless sediment.'

'I'm …'

'Yes, Fulk, you are. Convicted out of your own mouth. Say one word to anyone of what you have just mentioned to me, and that will be that last word of any kind that you will say. I personally will slice your tongue out and serve it at high table, jellied in aspic, with a piquant sauce, because otherwise it will taste of you and your rancid lies.'

He sidled away, cursing me roundly, and vowing to find me in the melee next day and beat my head in.

I managed to chance on Juliana upstairs, unaccompanied for a moment, and I told her the news. We looked at each other desperately. This could be the end, and yet we had hardly begun.

'You must kill him,' she said, 'in the melee. It's just the place. People get injured all the time. It's part of the sport.'

I thought she was joking, so I answered lightly.

'What if he kills me?'

'That would be unfortunate. But you're not going to let him. You have fought with sticks?'

'I have, it is a sport we novices practised at the abbey. We all had to have some training in military service in case we were attacked by people like de Montfort.'

'You were good at it?

'Quite good.'

'Well, there you are. Knock him down. Addle his wits. Kill him, if you must. He is a danger to us, Bertold.'

'I don't like to kill him,' I said. 'He's just an angry man.'

'Milksop.'

She took it for granted that I would do it for her and, alas, she was probably right.

XXV

The next day we were all drawn up and instructions on the melee were issued by the Marshal, who knew his stuff even though he did not always enjoy discharging his duties for Eustace. Juliana had told me she would not even peep through a window at the bloody struggle. She had told me I could cry off if I liked. She could get me excused, but of course I could not agree. We had an argument about it, but I would not budge. Even a bastard does not like to be kept. To be honest, I was keen to fight the fight. I was quick and strong and ready for Fulk any time he liked.

'You will be divided into two armies,' the Marshal told us. 'They will be called French and English.'

'Why not Norman?' someone asked.

'Because you are all Norman, and the last thing our Duke wants is to see Normans fighting each other.'

I could see Eustace chewing his beard at this, but he said nothing because he did not want to lose the best marshal in south-east Normandy. There were others who would take him as soon as look at him.

'You will be armed with a helmet, a stout stick and a shield. Each side will have a standard and a standard-bearer. The object of the exercise is to capture the enemy's standard. Once someone is down, there must be no further contact with him. Leave him alone. We do not want serious injuries. Anyone seen behaving dangerously will be disciplined. The melee is an exercise designed to show the realities of battle without the use of steel and the spilling of unnecessary blood. It is not an opportunity to settle scores. Is that understood?'

We stood there like oxen in the cold wind.

'Is that understood?' he shouted.

'Answer the Marshal, you dogs,' called a sergeant.

'YES, SIR,' we shouted.

'We will proceed, French first. The infantry – that is the squires – will be led by the knights who will position themselves at the front of their infantrymen at the left-hand end of the big field outside the castle wall. The English will follow the same procedure at the right-hand end of the field. When I sound the trumpet, the cavalry will charge each other. Foot soldiers may only intervene if the standard is in danger. When I sound the trumpet twice, the cavalry will withdraw. On trumpet call three, the infantry will advance and fall upon each other. On the last trumpet call of four, all fighting will cease completely. Anyone disobeying will be ...'

'Castrated,' called Eustace.

He thought that a huge joke. The Marshal started to divide us. I was careful to be English when I saw Fulk was French. We passed into the field, preceded by our steaming cavalry.

Some castles, I knew, had recently taken up a much more courtly form of ritual combat, charging at each other on their horses. Armed with bated lances, their object was to knock each other off their steeds. My father's dangling-iron was a new-fangled auxiliary to the sport. These new, so-called tournaments were all very well, the Marshal had told us, but as training in the matter of real fighting, the hard and shocking, reeking and dismembering actuality of the battlefield, there was nothing to beat the melee.

What would it be like to cut off a man's arm or his face? And what would it be like to have that done to the face that you thought of as you? It was impossible not to see men with terrible wounds these days: soldiers spewed out by the troubles in Normandy, peg-legs with just one ear or eye or half a mouth, and so on.

I was pondering this as we faced up to the villainous Frenchies on the other side. We started to mutter against them, whipping ourselves up into ferocity and group-courage, and next we were shouting obscenities and insults at people we had regarded as our comrades moments before. When the trumpet sounded, our knights thundered across the ten-acre field towards their adversaries. They were armed with wooden poles

136

with rounded ends and they wore their armour cap-a-pie, but as they clashed together, there were some who fell heavily and lay still for a while, and others who raised triumphant gloved fists into the air. Those who had failed to unhorse their opponents used their wooden staves to beat at the enemy. When the cavalry had fought itself to a standstill, the second trumpet sounded, and the riders withdrew. Servants hurried onto the field to carry the casualties with sore heads and broken bones away to the infirmary. Neither of the standards had been taken yet.

The third trumpet sounded.

The drums started beating. I had forgotten about them. It is a sound to instil both fear in the enemy and courage in the vanguard. It hits a certain nerve in the head and sets off a madness, which one needs on the battlefield. As we neared the French, the insults began to fly again, this time at close quarters, and they the same to us, and then we were upon them, raining blows with our sticks and trying to avoid their assaults. One large Frenchy came at me as I was thwacking a little eely fellow, and he caught me a blow on my helmet which made my ears ring, I turned, quick as lightning, and poked him hard in the midriff which took the breath out of him and then I kicked his knees away as he doubled up. I clouted another fellow who came at me from behind – I pretended not to see him – and then I turned, quick as a flash, and hit him squarely on the earpiece of his helmet. He sat down on his bottom as though his wits were addled. Then, out of the corner of my eye, I saw Fulk. He was fighting his way through my band of stout English warriors who were, I could see, beginning to taste victory. We were close to their standard now, but Fulk was having none of it, and was fighting like a wild man of the trees, a man possessed. He really wanted my head on his wall. I could taste blood on my mouth and the blood was hot, though I had no idea where it came from. And then he was upon me.

'There you are, Fulk,' I grunted. 'What took you so long?'

He didn't wait to reply, but swung his stick low and meanly at my manhood, which I only half escaped and felt a great low sickle of shrieking pain stabbing at my centrepiece. I was not going to let that stop me, though. I swung right and then feinted right again, but I caught him left with a kick to his knee, which he half avoided but which almost brought him down. He threw away his stick and drew a knife, which was strictly against the rules.

'You are a little fucker, aren't you, Fulk?' was all I could say before he was upon me with the blade, swinging it at me dangerously close to my stomach.

I caught him off-balance and thumped him across the top of his back, just below the neck, the place which numbs you and breaks your grasp, and his knife flew from his hand. He bent low to the ground to find it, and I crashed my stick on his helmet, making a noise like a gong, and turning his brain to syllabub, but he had the knife again, and I dropped my stick and closed with him, and we wrestled.

He stabbed me once, but weakly, in the chest, and then I had his arm and we fought over the weapon, twisting and turning as the struggle raged around us and the French standard was won. We rose, we fell and we dropped again. He had the strength of madness on him, and I feared that he would triumph and everything would be lost, so in desperation I used Saul's guile again, the trick where you fall and drag the opponent with you. Fulk must have forgotten it or at any rate been unprepared. It fooled him, though some instinct told him to drop the knife as he went down. My weight knocked the wind out of him, and he lay there for a while as I struggled up, grabbing the knife as I did so in case he struck again.

The fourth trumpet sounded, almost in my ear.

'What is this?' cried the Marshal, sternly.

He had walked over to see that the standard was handed over correctly without any chicanery from the defenders, and had spotted the knife in my hand.

'It is a knife, sir,' I said.

'I can see it's a bloody knife. But who does it belong to?'

'I don't know, sir,' I replied. 'It was on the ground and I picked it up, thinking to hand it in, sir.'

I could see Fulk sitting up, and looking at me with an expression of surprise. I was surprised at myself, to be honest. But in the abbey I learnt the universal lesson that you don't sneak on a colleague even if he is your worst enemy. This one wasn't just *my* worst enemy, though, he was also Juliana's and I very much doubted if she would be as lenient as I was. It was too late to retract, though.

'Well, well, well, what have we here?' wheezed Eustace, squeezing his shanks over towards us.

'This man has found a knife, sir.'

'*Found* a knife? *Used* it more like. Filthy coward's tricks. Who is the man?'

Eustace loved the prospect of a punishment.

'I found the knife, sir,' I told him.

The Marshal intervened.

'He seems to be the wounded party, sir. Look, he bleeds.'

'It is a scratch, sir,' I said.

'I might have guessed it would be the Latiner. Fights like a woman, as you might expect. Who was he fighting with the knife?'

'It was my fault, sir,' said Fulk, rising to his feet. 'The knife was on the ground. I saw him pick it up and start to take it to the Marshal. And in the heat of battle, sir, I attacked him. I don't know why. You know how it is when the blood's up. I must have twisted the knife around in the struggle, but I had no intention of stabbing him.'

'Well, well,' said the Marshal, 'no harm done. A melee is a melee.'

'I disagree, Marshal,' cried Eustace, his dander well up. 'The Latiner carried the knife, so he is the guilty party. He must be taught a lesson. I am not sure that taking a knife to a melee is not a capital offence. I will have to consult the rules.'

'But he did not take the knife to the melee, sir,' said the Marshal. 'We have a witness who saw it on the ground. It must have been left by some townsman.'

'Don't chop logic with me, Marshal. Have the man arrested and taken to the dungeon to cool his heels. Let him *amas amat* down there. Then we shall see what our purposes dictate.'

And so I was marched off by two Frenchmen back through the gatehouse, across the drawbridge under the gaze of my little pupils and their mother, and down the stairs into the dungeon where the gaoler put me in an iron cell and locked the gate. I had done what I had always been advised by Juliana not to do, put myself in Eustace's power. Worse still, Fulk was at large to spread whatever poison he chose about Juliana and me. It was a pretty pickle, but I still felt some exhilaration at having survived an exercise which was as close to a genuine battle as one could get. Every man must wonder sometimes what it feels like to fight at close quarters. I was not at all sure that I wanted to do it again, but to have done it at all was some kind of achievement.

It was cold in my cell, and growing colder, and the straw was none too clean. I tried to sleep and must have succeeded, tired after my exertions on the field.

I was woken sometime later by a voice softly calling my name, and a hand waving at me through the bars. I knew immediately it was not Juliana. The hand was large and hairy, and belonged to Fulk whose face now appeared, illuminated by a single candle.

'I have brought you some chicken and some bread and a flask of wine. I have been to see the Comtesse and told her it was my fault. But don't get the idea that I like you.'

I seized the food gratefully, and took a long draught of the wine.

'Did you tell her about your secret?' I asked. 'The one you spoke to me about?'

'I made an oath to her that I would never breathe another word of it.'

'So how did you discover it?'

'I made it my business to watch you. I saw you escaping on Midsummer Night. I hated you for it.'

'I know that we have not been friends, Fulk.'

'I hate you, Latiner. You see, I love the Lady Juliana, too, but you are luckier than I am, the son of a poor country priest. I can never be good enough for her.'

'You really love her?'

'Don't sound so surprised. A dog can look at the moon.'

'Of course it can. And howl.'

There was a faint hint of a smile.

'She commands me to like you,' he said.

'Can you do that?'

He paused for a while before answering.

'Not easily. I will try. I will speak up about the knife being on the ground. Even to the Comte. I will maintain it. Meanwhile, she commands me to give you this key, and you will know what to do with it. I have already unlocked your cell here. She advises you to absent yourself for two days, by which time the Comte will have gone. Things are astir in Andely. And now I must go before I am missed. I have already been too long.'

I held out my hand to him which he took.

'I am sorry that we quarrelled, Fulk,' I said.

'You fought well,' he told me. 'I respect that, Latiner.'

And then I said something that I regretted, both then and later.

'You know, you should tell the Comtesse how you feel about her. It can do no harm.'

What was I trying to achieve? Was I trying to encourage him or cheer him up? It could only be a source of embarrassment to her, and probably to him. Just occasionally you do something truly idiotic, and this was such a moment, but at the time he seemed to take it well.

'Maybe I'll do that,' he said, in that half-truculent, half-apologetic way.

And so he slipped away into the shadows of the dungeon while the gaoler slept. My heart had lifted. The danger had seemed imminent and my predicament uncomfortable to say the least. Now it seemed there was a way out and Fulk had played Ariadne to my Theseus.

I took the key and the candle Fulk had left me, stole past the snoring gaoler, and unlocked the door of the tunnel that led to the lake. Half an hour later, I was at The Bear, sleeping soundly in an upper room on a moth-eaten pillow.

XXVI

I returned to the castle after two days, as I had been advised, to find that Eustace had left on his travels again. Like love, plotting is addictive: it takes over the mind and seems to be what all of life is about, the end is lost in the delight of the means. Eustace had forgotten about me, and the gaoler had not even been chastised for my escape.

Juliana embraced me when we could be alone for a moment in the wardrobe, but no lovemaking, she told me, there was too much afoot, her mind was aflame. She was convinced that Eustace was going mad. Meanwhile, she had Christmas to think about, since it was almost upon us and there was much to be done.

'Eustace and the steward have organised nothing,' she said. 'No, that is not quite right. The steward has organised a cut for himself with Master Roger the cook, who is never here, and the town butcher Gascelin, in the event of there being a Christmas feast. It is left to me to pull the feast together, and give the children, the castle, the town – and, yes, you – a Christmas to remember.'

Traditionally the highlight of Christmas was a dinner for three hundred people. People had worked hard for a year, there had been fierce storms, floods, raids from rebel soldiery, lootings by deserters, crops destroyed, buildings burnt, and the people needed to let their hair down. This one had been an average kind of bad year, and now it was time for the castle to give back a little of what had been taken. This was the way loyalty was bred. Juliana knew this. Eustace had no conception of loyalty so could not understand that it mattered.

Alongside the feast there would be charades, games, caroles, dancing, mummery, forfeits, boars' heads, gifts for the servants, alms for the aged. There was frumenty to make and umble pies, swans to be caught, summonses to the feast to be sent out, and the whole solemn buffoonery of the season to be planned.

Of course, Juliana admitted that she didn't have to do all the work herself, but she had to oversee it and catch it before it went wrong. Last year there had been no feast, and noses had been put out of joint. This year one of the huge, brown robin pots which seethed whole carcasses was cracked owing to a careless kitchen boy not watching the cauldron. Another one would have to be bought and fetched from Verneuil. There were a hundred, no, two hundred, such considerations.

I found her one day temporarily overwhelmed with administration – the Steward was driving her mad – and I took her out for a while, the day being exceptionally mild, to walk in the winter sunshine around the bailey. She confessed to me some of her frustrations as we walked: the poor organisation in the kitchen, the waste of resources, the complete lack of records in the cellar, all of which should have been in Eustace's remit, at least to oversee. And then since she was on to Eustace, she told me that she had thought about killing him.

I looked around anxiously lest we be overheard, but the bailey near us was deserted. It was for much the same reason, she said, that her father had deposed his brother Robert: neither Robert nor Eustace was any good at his job. Eustace was an incompetent castellan and a poor leader, just as he wasn't any good as a husband – which was, she said, part of his job; and should be the best part, if he had had any sense.

'I never had a girlhood,' she said. 'My father betrothed me to Eustace when I was ten years old. I married him four years later. I told my father what a terrible thing he had done, and he said he was sorry, but we couldn't always do what we liked. You can imagine what Eustace was like in bed. No, please don't. I had my lovely daughters, and that was it, for me, as I've told you. I never wanted to see him again. I do not see the point of him any more. He keeps coming back here like a bad smell. Why don't I just kill him? Or … you?'

'You want to kill *me*?'

'I mean, you could kill him, stupid.'

'I don't think I'm clever enough for that,' I said, dubiously.

I was seeing a dark side of Juliana that I had only glimpsed before, but that was the thing about her. I kept seeing new Julianas. Twice in the last few weeks she had mentioned killing someone. First Fulk and now Eustace. It was not to say that they had not asked for it, but all the same. Many of us say to ourselves that we wish someone was dead, but to say it out loud, and mean it, that is something different. In view of what happened later, I should have taken more note of it – but at the time I felt sorry for her. To be so young and so imprisoned in a marriage that was forced on her; it was a terrible thing.

'There is definitely a Roman side to you, Juliana, and it isn't just your name,' I told her.

The joke covered my confusion. Eustace was appalling, but I couldn't wish him dead. Given enough rope, I thought, the man will kill himself anyway. Juliana laughed and said no more about it. If I saw danger then, I refused to accept it. I was addicted to her, you see, as Eustace was to plotting. I didn't like her in this mode, but I still loved her.

We had arrived back at the drawbridge and, as we mounted the steps to the hall, she turned to me.

'You will help me, won't you, Latiner,' she said.

It was not a question. We parted and she went back to her planning and ordering in the Comte and Comtesse's private rooms behind the hall. She had a meeting with the butler and steward (likely to be stormy). I returned upstairs to my pupils whom I had left with the ladies in the solar making decorations for the festivities.

XXVII

The twelve days of Christmas passed wonderfully, as I knew they would as soon as I saw Eustace return. He arrived back from Andely on Christmas Eve, pale, shivering, covered in snow, and starting a terrible feverish cold which laid him out for all twelve days of the celebrations.

He could do nothing except lie in bed like a great bottled sea-cow with a headache and a nose redder than ever, groaning and calling for wine. I did not get out my medical box as I could have done, for there are medicines there that will cure everything but death, and that too *in extremis*, but the man did not deserve it. Nor did I advise him that the wine would simply prolong the illness, for I wanted it prolonged. I wanted it infinitely extended.

The result was that from Midnight Mass in the castle chapel till the last crumb of the great feast of Twelfth Night, we had no Eustace. Never has a disease brought so much happiness. The castle overflowed with joy as never before and, *tristabile dictu*, never again. But the Twelve Days of Christmas 1118 became legendary.

It started snowing on Christmas Eve, which showed the castle in an admirable light. On the return from Midnight Mass, we lit the Yule log, cut from a cherry tree, specially felled, which reminded us of our Norse heritage (according to the chaplain). We drank mead, and embraced each other.

The chaplain said Mass again at dawn, and a further Mass was held again later in the morning. It coincided with a visit from the Bishop of Evreux, forced out of his bishopric by Amaury, and staying in the town with the rector who was an old friend of his. By staying in Breteuil, a royal estate, he was under the protection of the Duke. He gave us a fine sermon. I could see he did not take to the chaplain and kept interrupting him in conversation, which of course endeared him to Juliana and me. He and the rector stayed the rest of the day with us. The Lord of

Misrule held court in the afternoon, hitting us with his bladder, making suggestions to the ladies, and generally being insupportable.

We had an exchange of presents. I gave Juliana a subtle perfume of jasmine and wallflower that Brother Paul had put in my medicine box with instructions: 'to melt the heart of a young woman'. It did seem to have a remarkable effect.

She gave me a silver coin of great antiquity which had been in the possession of a crucified centurion. It showed the head of the Emperor Elagabalus, a particularly nasty individual, but the coin was said to have had great powers of protection. I keep it always about my person.

The little girls got everything a little girl could desire, including some wonderful new chalks for drawing, and some costumes for dressing-up

Before dinner, we had a walk in the snow to the lake, and the girls threw snowballs at us, one hitting the Bishop really quite hard on the nose, but he took it well. Then there came dinner. This was not the great Christmas feast which was planned for Epiphany but was still a considerable spread with at least four courses each with several removes, goose being the traditional pièce de résistance. Everyone was there: knights, squires, pages, messengers and grooms. The bishop threw himself into games with the children, and succeeded in downing a whole quart of burgundy. There were minstrels, and a gitterner, there was dancing and a game of forfeits with embarrassing questions and exchanges of clothing. Alice lost one of her garters. How we roared! Fulk was nearly naked by the time we had finished with the forfeits. We had to put the bishop on a sledge in the end, lying like a carved effigy, and then all of us, in procession by lantern light through the snow, took him back to his quarters in town. The sexton thought someone had died. We nearly died laughing.

Our happiness continued through eleven whole days of the Christmas Feast. What fun, what glory, what mystery, what joys we had: the visit from the Man in Red all the way from the North where the Normans came from, King Herod playing hide and seek with the children, clutching at draperies and cupboards with his long bony fingers ... the gypsy fiddlers and the story-tellers ... the Weird Woman and the fortune-tellers ... the dancing and jigging to a consort of vielles ... the great frost when we skated on the lake and roasted chestnuts on the fire built on ice ... the Mystery Plays performed with magical effects by none other than Eliphas who turned up with his troupe, or what seemed to be a troupe because with Eliphas you could never really tell...

I congratulated Eliphas after the performance, and suggested to him that perhaps he was the angel, because it was said that we might entertain angels unawares, to which he gave no answer but looked at me thoughtfully.

'Bertold, my friend, nothing happens in this world without a purpose, dark though it may seem to you,' he told me. 'Our meeting in Verneuil was inevitable. I should like to help you, for you have chosen a hard path. Juliana is a beautiful woman but her stars are afflicted. I fear that your feelings for her may lead you into danger. Have a care. The great are clumsy with lesser people.'

I thanked him for his kindness. 'But what do you mean?' I asked, 'Juliana loves me. We are happy.'

'It is good to be happy at Christmas. But we are insects on a leaf, drifting down the river. Listen hard, and you will hear the sound of the weir.'

'It may be so,' I told him. 'But Death will be swallowed up in victory.'

'*That* may be so,' he said. 'But Death is Death. And it is God's wish as well as mine that you stay alive as long as possible. I will help you to do that, as much as is in my power. I urge you to be careful.'

I had no idea what he was talking about but he was a good man, even a remarkable man, and he had my interests at heart which was good enough for me, so I thanked him and assured him I would look after my life as if it were my own. He laughed at that, and gave me a playful dig in the ribs.

'You really think it is, don't you? That's funny.'

And then Juliana came out and laughed with us and we kissed and danced and ate sweetmeats while the stars cartwheeled overhead into the Year of Our Lord 1119.

XXVIII

On the Twelfth Day of Christmas, the Feast of Epiphany when Christ was revealed to the Magi as the Son of God, we had a feast indeed. It seemed that the entire town had been invited, and we had to have a couple of extra cooks in from Verneuil: Master Hugh, and Gilbert Mimizan, the pastryman.

The steward had finally been told by Juliana that the game was up and he had better stop lining his pockets or he would be arraigned for theft at the next assizes, and likely strung up by his scrawny neck. He went white and buckled, and then he buckled to. Supplies for the feast came from as far away as Paris. The town bakers worked for us night and day on the eve of the feast.

The hall was ready: the minstrels were in the gallery and the wine, ale and bread were on the tables – apart from the top table where the wine was waiting in a huge, ornately worked silver jug. The jug featured, in relief, the fate of Acteon, who was turned into a deer and hunted by Artemis and her maidens and was a gift from the Duke to his daughter, to remind her of him, she told me later, being hunted by everyone.

Three hundred people now took their places. I have never seen so much food in all my life, not even at Mortagne where my father enjoyed the pleasures of the table, lusty old beggar. Juliana had surpassed herself. All the while, the minstrels played on their organistra and lyras, and a recorder came in from somewhere; and all the while we chattered away like the geese we were so busy eating. At the end, you would not have thought anyone would feel like dancing, but some did. Others simply slumped at the table. So there was more music, and then Eliphas did a magic show, extracting strings of sausages from the Chaplain's cassock. Juliana went upstairs with the little girls, who were happily exhausted, and I slipped out a little later to meet her, unnoticed except by Fulk. And then there were games of forfeit again, which we returned to, and at last a storyteller round the fire with ghost stories and tales of love and war. And then, all at once, in the middle of all this, there was an apparition.

It was a figure wild of eye, lank of hair, pasty of face, big of belly, bandy of leg, with a mouth that opened and shut like a gurnard's.

'What the devil's going on?' it said.

You've guessed it. It was Eustace, risen from his bed and looking worse than Lazarus.

'Who gave permission for all this?' he asked, groaning and holding his head.

'I did,' said Juliana.

He could not think of an answer to that.

'Well … well …' he said, and then he passed out.

'Take him back to bed,' she ordered. 'I know him. He'll be up tomorrow.'

And that was the end of the best Christmas we ever had at Breteuil or would ever have anywhere again.

XXIX

True to Juliana's prediction, Eustace was up next day, looking slightly better for his fortnight's illness, but having shed none of his unpleasantness. He hated the idea of our having had fun without him. He would see to it next year that *he* ran the revels. They would be a man's revels, none of this silly girls' stuff.

He was prodigiously hungry, and while he made a great breakfast out of some of the leavings of the feast, his mind was full of something new, to me at any rate, what he called the Ivry problem. He summoned me to sit with him while he stuffed his enormous jowls with capons and roast pork. It seemed that he had made up his mind to try and employ my skills on his behalf, to seduce me from Juliana. Fat chance, of course, but since he was so fat he had to give his chances a go.

The problem all stemmed from Amaury de Montfort who had, it seemed, been stirring Eustace up on the subject of the nearby castle of Ivry which belonged to the Duke. But it didn't really belong to the Duke, Amaury maintained, it belonged to Eustace. Why did it belong to Eustace? Because it had been granted by Duke Robert, Henry's brother, to William of Breteuil, Eustace's father.

I realised it was another Amaury plan to cause trouble for both Henry and Eustace; Juliana had told me that Amaury had his eyes on Breteuil to which he himself had a good claim. He hoped by rocking the boat that he might end up, after some cathartic brouhaha, stepping into the vacant castle himself. Besides, he loved rocking boats. If he saw so much as a wooden duck on the water, his instinct was to go up and pat its bottom.

After breakfast, Eustace took a walk in the bailey where a path had been cleared in the snow. At last he had a grievance of his own. He must have Ivry back. There would be trouble in eastern Normandy until he did. The Duke would know next time not to take Eustace of Breteuil for granted.

He invited me to walk with him and, though I pleaded my lesson with the children, he insisted. He wanted my counsel, and outlined his cause. He should have had a chancellor to do this kind of work but the last incumbent was infirm, and Eustace had not got round to appointing another. I think he thought that I might be able to do the work of scribe and accountant without the dignity of office or reward.

I tried to tell him that I thought his cause was futile. He was already a great baron, he had four other important castles, what need was there of more? Disappointed by my lack of enthusiasm, he even sought the opinion of his wife who also counselled against it. Her father would not be happy, she said. Had Eustace not made himself nuisance enough already? She told me later that she should have argued strongly in support of his plan, for Eustace had a habitual reflex of immediately rejecting anything that she suggested, but the die was cast.

Eustace thought about it some more, and the more he thought, the more convinced he became that Ivry should be his. A spell of milder weather prevailed, and he even rode over with a few knights to have a look at the place. What he saw entranced him. The knights liked it too – as they would.

'A fine place,' he announced on his return. 'I immediately felt I had come home when I saw it. The house of my fathers...'

So there it was. Inflamed by the weasel words of Amaury de Montfort, and against his wife's advice, Eustace sent what was tantamount to a challenge to the Duke, his father-in-law. He wanted his castle back or (reading between the lines) the Duke could look for his allegiance elsewhere. The Duke, of course, already knew about Eustace – it was better to have him as an unofficial enemy than an uncertain friend – but it was another thing to spell it out in a letter.

If Henry had been in a better position *vis à vis* his enemies – principally King Louis of France, the Comte of Flanders, the Comte of Mortain, Amaury de Montfort, Robert de Bellême 's son down in the south of the Duchy, and ex-Duke Robert's son, William Clito (wherever he was, always lurking away somewhere) – he would have told Eustace where to get off, indeed he would have put it more roundly since he was a man who didn't mince his words and had a proverbially robust temper.

But on this occasion he was sweetly reasonable. He was all affability indeed. He proposed, in a couple of weeks' time, to visit Eustace and the lovely Juliana, his beloved daughter, and to bring with him Harenc, the Castellan of Ivry himself, together with his young son. He sent Eustace a letter using these very words which the Comte received with considerable satisfaction.

'You see,' he said to Juliana that evening in hall, thrusting the unsealed parchment towards her as he mangled a capon wing, 'what a mistake you made in advising against tweaking the Duke's nose, and what sound judgment I displayed. As in war; so in peace. I am a leader in the tradition of my forebear Osbern who would never grovel for a favour.'

'The Duke my father is a clever man, they do not call him Beauclerc for nothing,' Juliana replied. 'It takes a clever man to depose a duke who would be king, and take both titles for himself. Be careful not to enrage him or it will be the worse for you and, I fear, for us. This letter says he will be with us in a week's time. We must prepare the castle to receive him. Bertold, you must also prepare since the Castellan's son is the same age as Marie, and he will need some entertaining.'

'He is just a castellan, a keeper of a castle, Lady Juliana,' said Eustace contemptuously. 'Just a caretaker, not even a vicomte. He and his son must take what they find.'

'And I suppose my father is just a duke and a king and must do the same?' retorted Juliana, with some spirit. 'You are like a mastiff, Eustace, only good for war and mauling people.'

The Comte took that as a compliment.

'Very good. Mastiff. I like that.'

There was a pause.

'You will heap misfortune upon this house and upon yourself. In no way do I understand you or wish to do so,' she said. 'I give up.'

'You had better,' he advised her, 'because you know I will win in the end.'

He was stupid enough to believe it, and a great misfortune was to fall on the house of Breteuil because of it.

XXX

The Castellan of Ivry Castle and his son appeared ahead of the Duke, with a modest body of men as befitted his custodial rank. Ralph Harenc was not a nobleman, but one of the new men who were coming up – my sort of man; an honorary bastard (he might even have been a real one). He was a good soldier, stern and brave it was said, but he was also a good administrator. Duke Henry liked that; he was a man after his own heart. 'More gets done by good administration than by any clash of arms' was a favourite maxim of his.

At any rate, Harenc, with his bristling black beard, seemed a good enough sort of man; straight as a die. I would not have liked to have got on the wrong side of him. You could see he could be severe even on his own men, and hard in battle. Yes, he was a hard man – not one to laugh much. I dwell on his character because much of the trouble that was to come was because of it. I should say, if it was a case of dishonour to him or his family, he would be implacable.

His little boy, Roger, was quiet and polite, a good-looking lad of some eight years old. He was introduced to the girls and led away to play. He was not the kind of boy who scorned to play with little girls; if he would have preferred to have gone off to look at the horses or play with some of the younger pages, he did not let on.

All in all, the Harencs made a good impression on me and on the Comtesse too, I discovered. She whispered a few words to me as I followed her upstairs after the children. We tried to avoid too many conversations in public.

The Comte had taken to calling me her lap-dog in her presence; luckily he did not know quite what a dog I was. I kept reminding myself of my good fortune. I was in love with her and she with me. She had told me so and I believed her, though I never really knew what went on in that lovely head under its cauldron of red-gold curls. We snatched moments together in the midst of all these plots and machinations, and I rather hoped this was going to be one of them. Going upstairs was always a good start, but I was still understandably anxious, as I think she was, that I should not lose my testicles through some careless indiscretion relayed to the explosive Eustace. There was always the dark-haired Alice to consider, but I knew that she looked at me favourably and without rancour, and I instinctively felt that she would not rat on us.

'If Amaury wants Harenc to trick us, I don't think that is going to happen,' Juliana said when we reached the top of the stairs and were safely out of sight of the hall. 'He is not that kind of person. So we must consider what it is that Amaury has up his sleeve. I suspect it will be some kind of agreement he makes with Eustace – behind my back, of course. My father arrives tomorrow. Amaury will keep out of the way.'

We left Roger to Marie and Pippi, and the girls, having shown him their room and their goldfish, kindly offered to take him round the castle and bailey. The old nurse was asleep so Juliana and I went into the wardrobe and locked the door.

We made love, but there was something troubling her and afterwards she wept a little. I had never seen her cry, and of course I asked what was the matter. At first she shook her head.

'Don't cry,' I told her.

'I cry because I love you, little Latiner.'

'And I love you too,' I told her eagerly. 'I want it to go on for ever.'

'That is just it. It can't.'

'But why? We can find a way. Eustace is bound to fall off his horse or be killed in battle...'

She shook her head again.

'I am married to a bad man, perhaps a mad man, certainly a fool. I am in love with you, but whatever is to come of that? I feel something bad is going to happen.'

'To me?' I thought, I'm afraid selfishly, of my testicles.

'I don't know. Perhaps to you. Perhaps ... I don't know. Something bad *is* going to happen. I feel it in my heart. It weighs *on* my heart. I dreamt of a ship on dry land, hauled up on the rocks. In England that means a death. I have the power, you know. My mother had it … she used to say she was a wicce. That is what you call a witch, but it is not quite the same. It means a sorceress.'

'Perhaps it was too much venison pie,' I said, foolishly.

'Don't joke, little Latiner. A cloud is drawing over this place. As long as Eustace does not turn Harenc against us. I could see he did not like him. He will start to call him Herring and make fun of him.'

All at once there was a beating at the door, and I panicked.

'Madame. Madame,' called a voice.

'Yes, who is it?'

I hid myself, as we had pre-arranged, behind the curtain covering the spices in the far corner. I tucked myself down below the boxes.

Juliana rearranged her long dress and opened the door. Peeping out, I saw Alice, standing outside in some agitation.

'The butler needs more grains of paradise for the spiced wine to greet the Duke tomorrow. The wine must be steeped overnight, he says.'

The girl made to come and get it, as if she knew that I was there, but she was stopped by a look from Juliana that would have halted a knight in full armour charging on a Percheron.

'You tell the butler from me, Alice, to use cinnamon and galangale, and that the King and Duke, my father, prefers good wine neat – unless of course the wine he buys for a king is not up to the job and he neither.'

The proud Alice looked abashed, unusual for her, and I felt a fleeting sense of sympathy for her.

Although besotted with Juliana, there was something about Alice that excited my interest – more than interest, if I'm to be honest. You must have sometimes passed someone in the street who smiled at you, and you sensed that a secret message passed between you, that you were both members of a society which until then you hadn't known existed. Alice was beautiful, and had almost lain with me, once, in my dreams. You can't get over a thing like that. My loyalty to Juliana was unshakeable: in terms of honour, since she was my lady; in terms of love, since I was bewitched by her; and, it pains me to say it, in terms of practicality, because the last thing I wanted to do was to find myself back at Mortagne, humping casks. Can a man be in love with two girls at once? I asked myself again. I think you know what the answer to that is.

And then Juliana said something which convinced me that she carried those powers of the English wicce which she had spoken of.

'I know what you're up to, Alice.'

'Me, my lady. I am not up to anything.'

'In that case I know you better than you know yourself. If you want to stay in the castle with me, I advise you to stop.'

'I am curious, my lady, that is all. I was taught by the Holy Sisters to be inquisitive. I would like to learn about spices and about everything in this castle.'

'That is all very well, Alice, and very good up to a point. But you know what happened to the cat in the story, don't you?'

'The cat, my lady?'

'It was so keen to see the bottom of the well, that in the end it fell down it. Or maybe it was pushed.'

The girl, for all her bravery, turned pale. There was no mistaking Juliana's threat, and I began to see my beloved in a new light. There was something of her father in her, people said, and indeed it had revealed itself now to Alice – and to me – as a streak of ruthlessness. It would not do to cross her, or I would find myself in a far less agreeable place than the wine cellars of the Comte de Perche. It increased my respect for Juliana, but I have always found that fear driveth out love. So it was that, from this day, my passion seemed to slacken a little. Lust is a different matter. We bastards know all about that; it sings to a different note on Pan's pipe, and is woefully hard to expunge. Please don't think too hardly of me. One has to make one's way in the world.

XXXI

Henry, King of England and Duke of Normandy, arrived at the castle in the afternoon a few days later, the fourth of February, with a flourish of trumpets and a compact force of men at arms, the King's own guard. They looked very spruce and grimly efficient. It had been a dry week, and their horses looked cleaner than most of the Comte's men.

Juliana had ordered the servants to tidy themselves up and wash under the pump, and had made them wear their best tunics, and even Eustace had agreed to take off his chain-mail and wear a passable tunic with his hose. His man had been ordered to comb the Comte's beard and generally cut and trim where necessary.

When Henry entered the hall we were all lined up for him. He paused in the doorway and surveyed the scene as a king should, hands on his hips and his head thrown back. I was eager to study him in the flesh and – having heard so much of his troubles and the machinations of his enemies – I felt I understood something of the tension that he lived with: the necessity of a finding an equilibrium in Normandy without which the place would degenerate into ruin and anarchy. That was the duty of the ruler of a turbulent kingdom full of restless barons with private armies – to strive endlessly to find the fair, middle course, and punish those who strayed from it. All very well to describe what you had to do, but still very hard to do it.

As I looked for the first time at this bright, hard, brave, clever man, father of the woman I loved, I found there was indeed a quality in him that I respected and felt sympathy for.

Henry cut a fine figure physically. He was around average height, with a good strong nose and mouth, his chin and upper lip concealed under a beard of thick, dark-brown hair with a reddish tinge to it, his head covered with a good thatch of the same. His black eyes were alert, needle-sharp, always on the move. It was an intelligent face, severe; not kind but, I thought, fair and just.

'Ha,' he exclaimed on seeing Juliana, 'my favourite daughter.'

'Now, Father,' she smiled as she curtseyed and came forward to kiss him, 'you say that to all your daughters.'

'You are quite right,' he smiled back, 'but to you I am not lying.'

'But you never lie, Father. I am not even sure that a king can. Just as he cannot commit treason.'

The Duke was amused, and tilted his head as if in agreement. Then he spotted Eustace looming like the unhappy giant he was.

'No more, I am sure, than our friend the Comte de Breteuil could.'

Eustace, of course, completely missed the hint of irony with which this was said. He knelt awkwardly, almost perfunctorily, and mumbled a few words of ritual greetings to his lord before Juliana led her father into the hall, introducing him to the Marshal, one or two of the senior knights and the steward, and then to his grand-daughters whom he kissed and made much of.

'So you are Marie?' he said to the eldest. 'You know what they call me? Beauclerc. Do you know what that means?'

'Yes, sir,' she said. 'Beau means handsome…'

'Yes,' Pippi burst in, 'and clerk means you speak Latin.'

'And we can speak Latin too,' said Marie. '*Amo, amas, amat…*'

'*Amumus, amutis, amunt,*' finished Pippi triumphantly.

I was somewhat mortified that they had not chosen a more distinguished way of showing their aptitude in Latin, but the excitement of the occasion had no doubt got the better of them.

'Well,' said their grandfather, 'you are very learned and will soon be talking to abbots and archbishops and writing letters to the Pope.'

'And you must meet our guest Roger,' said Marie, presenting Roger to him.

162

'He is the son of Ralph Harenc, your castellan at Ivry,' said Juliana.

'Of course. Greetings to you, Roger.'

He held out his hand and the little boy knelt and kissed it. The Castellan, his father, now stepped forward.

'And to you too, Castellan Harenc,' he said.

The Castellan did as his son had done. This seemed to satisfy the Duke. Little Marie and Pippi now took me by the hand and led me forward. I could not resist.

'This is Master Fitzrotroot,' Marie told her grandfather.

'He is a Latiner and he is our tutor,' said Pippi.

I fell to my knees before the Duke, it seemed the right thing to do, and so it turned out. He took my hand and raised me up.

'So. You are a son of my son-in-law the Comte de Perche.'

'Yes, sire.'

'So. We are almost related. Please do not tell my daughter the Comtesse de Perche what I have said about the Lady Juliana being my favourite daughter!'

His eyes twinkled as he spoke.

'I understand, sire.'

'Good. You are a Latiner, are you?'

'Yes, sire. I learned the language at the Abbey of Saint-Sulpice.'

'A fine place. I have visited the abbey, and granted them lands. What else did you learn there?'

I remembered his visit, which happened just after I arrived at the place, though he clearly did not remember me, and why should he? I had been a shivering novice missing my mother.

'Music, sire. Singing.'

'Yes, they are good at that.'

'Some medicine, learnt from one of their brothers who had learnt from the Arabs. And also some of the new mathematics.'

'So you are a man of parts. My daughter has chosen well. We must have better knowledge of you in future. Medicine, eh? Mathematics? These are useful things.'

At that point, Eustace burst in. He could not endure to be ignored, though his idea of being the centre of attention was to get drunk, horse around, utter the Breteuil battle-cry which was 'Osbern', touch up a wench, and belch or fart without looking up at the ceiling (which, as you know, is the polite thing to do).

'Come and be seated, my lord Duke,' he cried. 'We have some fine Rhenish wine in and nobody pours it better than my wife, your daughter.'

'Surely you have a butler to do that, Breteuil, do you not?'

'It is a custom here when there is a visitor of note. Go, Juliana, fetch the wine,' he commanded her as if she were a servant.

It was typical of the man to wish to show his superiority over his wife, but he obviously did not know his Duke very well.

'Stop. By the death of our Lord, sir, I do not wish my daughter to serve me wine. I would consider it a discourtesy if she did. Please allow me to be the arbiter of that. But, yes, I will drink a little wine with you.'

He laid a light emphasis on the word little. I looked at him with new respect. He had obviously done his homework on his son-in-law. They said the Duke was interested in everything that went on in Normandy, that he had people reporting to him, indeed that he had spies everywhere. I began to wonder who his spy was here. I even began to think it might have been the dark-haired Alice. She was hovering around in the hall even now. Sometimes one can suspect everyone.

'We have much to talk about,' the Duke said to Eustace as they sat down. 'I cannot stay long. There are outbreaks of disorder everywhere. Robert de Bellême and his son Talvas plot endlessly, and that man de Montfort stirs up trouble wherever he can find it. King Louis of France can't wait to nibble away at my duchy, and some of my barons swing around more readily than the wheels of a haycart. But they do not know their man. I will see to them all, believe me, but I do need you on my side.'

'You can trust me, sire. I am your daughter's husband.'

'I know that, Breteuil. But I did hear that the creature de Montfort was sniffing around here. Tell me that is not true.'

Here Juliana broke in.

'It is true, Father. But ...'

'But we sent him packing,' Eustace broke in.

The butler now served the wine, and it was excellent. The King drank like a man who was thirsty, and asked for water if it was good. I was now sitting further up the table near the Duke since even Eustace could not very well demote a Latiner who was in some way related to the royal visitor.

'We can talk over our meal later,' said Eustace. 'We ate at twelve, but will sit down again at six o'clock if that will suit you.'

'It will suit me well,' said the Duke. 'We have only one meal a day now, apart from breakfast. It was an idea of my good friend Robert, Comte de Meulan. Two meals wastes too much time when you are campaigning.'

Eustace's face fell – he liked his two meals a day – but still, there was dinner to look forward to. This prompted another thought that lobbed like a trebuchet's missile over the battlements of his mind and landed with a thud in his parched seat of reason.

'Would it not be better to discuss our differences in a private room?' he suggested. 'We don't want the whole rabble to get involved.'

'I hardly think your knights and your steward, to say nothing of my daughter, would take kindly to being called a rabble, Comte.'

'I meant those whose business it is not, my lord.'

'On the contrary, our business is everybody's business. They live here. Your interests are their interests. You are their lord. No, let us discuss the matter of my ...' the Duke corrected himself with even more than his usual tact ...'*the* castle of Ivry ... over a table laden with your excellent food and drink. Justice should always be seen to be done, not stitched up by clever men in secret rooms. We shall feel more contented and altogether more benign when we are eating. Besides, I have always believed that the process of chewing in some way encourages the mental processes.'

I could see that Juliana, who had been uncharacteristically withdrawn (her father had that effect on her), approved of this plan.

'Very well,' muttered Eustace. 'If that is your wish, sire.'

'It is indeed. And now I am sure my knights and I would like a little time to prepare ourselves for your hospitality.'

So the Duke went to the quarters that had been arranged for him. He had ridden hard that day and no doubt was glad of an hour or two to wash, rest and reflect on the difficult discussion ahead with the feckless Comte. The fact was that the Duke especially liked the château at Ivry and had placed his trusted castellan Harenc, one of his best captains, there as a mark of his esteem. At the same time, he needed to be able to rely on his daughter and her husband, or at least rely on his ability to put the squeeze on them, and at the moment he could not quite do that. I imagined the Duke stared at himself in the glass his man had brought, washing his face and hands, and hating being caught again in such a situation. It was hard being a king-duke (even though it would be harder still not to be) and he could surely be excused for having, at times, a temper that exploded like a Greek fire bomb. He must try to see that it did not happen tonight.

XXXII

The dinner that evening was to become famous at Breteuil among the pages, squires and knights, and the servants who served and stood in attendance – famous for the lavishness of the entertainment and for the sight of Comte Eustace trying to contain his temper until it swelled him up like a great red pumpkin. It all started well. Eustace had given in to his wife's requests for a show, and the place was full of colour and delightful odours. The rushes had been changed and the floor under them swept and scraped and swept again. Tunics, mantles and hose were bright with yellows and reds, magentas, purples and greens. Eustace wore a clean linen coif decorated with feathers and buttons and tied by strings under his great chin, which made him look like a booby. Juliana wore a gorgeous dress of wonderful green whose colour seemed to have been plucked fresh from the forest.

The whole castle smelt of good food.

The feast started with a course of fish – removes of carp and pike, boiled and stuffed with ingenious spices and served with curious sauces, scallops, eels and lampreys of which the Duke was known to be especially fond.

While this was being brought on, served and eaten, a group of musicians with harp, oliphant and four lyras started to make sweet music in the gallery, above the increasing din of the party.

The feast progressed to swan, duck, and capons stuffed with larks' tongues, and vegetables: new carrots and cabbage and leeks from the castle gardens. This was followed by a remove of venison and wild boar from the Comte's forests, you know the sort of thing, and then a great roast baron of beef which the Duke especially praised for its tenderness.

'If only some of my barons were as tender as this, how easy my life would be,' he remarked to Ralph Harenc who sat near him, though he meant it to be heard by Eustace as well. There was hearty laughter in which Eustace joined though he did not quite catch the joke. However, it encouraged him, now that the feast was well under way, to raise the topic which was nearest to his heart and upon which this whole occasion was contrived.

'How think you, my lord, perhaps we can now talk about …' he began, but the Duke cut him short.

'I can predict the future. Did you know that?' he spread out his arms, addressing the top table.

'Tell us,' the top table shouted.

'I know what the Comte Eustace here is going to say next.'

'What is he going to say next?'

The duke turned to Eustace and raised a questioning eyebrow.

Then, as if pulled by wires, they both spoke at once:

'Ivry.'

The top table erupted with laughter. Eustace laughed too although I could see that he wondered if he had been made to look a fool. He decided he had, which made him enraged with the Duke. It was too bad to be made to look a fool in his own hall.

'Yes, Ivry,' he went on. 'The castle is, by rights, mine. It belonged to the great William de Breteuil, my grandfather.'

'Yes,' said the Duke, 'who bestowed it upon William?'

'Why – the Duke of Normandy?'

'Precisely. That is why, when your uncle died, I decided to take it back. It was, and is, useful to me.'

'But a gift is a gift. It is not a loan.'

'Everything in Normandy belongs to me. I am the Duke. If I decide, on someone's death, to take back what is mine, that is … what I can do. The castle was granted to your cousin by my brother Duke Robert. When the Church and certain barons called on me, I took issue with my brother and defeated him in battle because he had let Normandy run to ruin. And part of the ruin, so far as I was concerned, was letting a castle like Ivry go from my possession when it was evidently so strategically important. So I took it back. It was all part of my plan to make Normandy secure again.'

168

'The castle is mine – mine, I tell you.'

Eustace was drunk by now, and angry. Juliana leant across and put a hand on his arm as if to restrain him, advising caution, but he shrugged her off.

'By the death of our Lord,' exclaimed the Duke, 'you had better be careful with your words, Comte Eustace. We were going to discuss the issue at dinner, not fight over it, or I would have brought my sword.'

Eustace saw he had gone too far. He was after all the host and there are obligations in such matters, leaving aside the fact that he was talking to his liege lord.

'Could there not be an agreement at least to look into our claim further?' Juliana suggested.

'Amaury thought it should be ours,' grumbled Eustace.

'Yes,' said the Duke, 'and a nasty little silver-tongue he is. He thought he could make trouble between us and then steal in and pick it for himself. He too has a claim to Ivry as good as yours, if not better. To Breteuil as well.'

The Duke paused meaningfully. I knew, of course, as Juliana had already told me, that Eustace was an illegitimate son of the old Comte de Breteuil and not a direct claimant to the title.

'I think what we need is a guarantee of honest dealing on both sides, Comte Eustace,' the Duke continued. 'You guarantee your support for my campaigns in Normandy and I will give close thought to rewarding you, one of my trusted captains, with one of the castles that you crave.'

'What guarantee would that be, Father?' asked Juliana.

'Well, let me see … What would be appropriate in these circumstances?'

The Duke stroked his luxuriant, dark-red beard.

The game seemed to be running away from Eustace. He had felt sure that the castle would be his by the time the croustardes came in – and they were coming in now, along with the fruits and the marchpane and the pastry cooks' *pièce de résistance* – an entire pastry castle filled with raisin soldiers, ladies of honeyed almonds, and horses made of marzipan drawing little carts full of sweetmeats across a drawbridge of burnt caramel.

'Come along, Comte Eustace, your suggestion. What do you offer when you are besieging a castle and both sides want to end the siege, but you don't quite trust each other?'

A beam of inspiration unfolded like a beautiful dawn across the ill-ploughed furrows of Eustace's face.

'You'd exchange hostages, of course.'

'Try the crustarde, Father. We made it especially for you,' said Juliana.

I could tell she didn't like the direction this was going. The Duke shook his head.

'I wouldn't mind some more of those lampreys, though,' he murmured.

'Bring back the lampreys!' shouted the steward.

The shouts could be heard going all the way back to the kitchen. There was a moment's silence in the hall as we listened to the echo.

'Lampreys…'

'Lampreys…'

'So who do you think the hostage should be?' mused the Duke.

There was a deathly silence. No one likes to be a hostage. The lampreys came back. The Duke helped himself. Finally, he spoke again.

'I think, Ralph,' he said, addressing his loyal castellan, 'I think that your son Roger could fill that part. He is a presentable and clever boy. He seems to like it here. My daughter and the Latiner will see that he is well looked after. He might even learn some Latin. Just for a very few weeks while we review the situation. Then he can be with you for the summer.'

The Castellan did not look happy. He loved his son in his soldierly way, but the Duke was his liege lord and he trusted him.

'Very well,' he said, 'though I do it with a heavy heart. I know that my wife would have had something to say about the deal – and of course I must explain it to the lad. But I also need surety. What can I have?'

170

I think Juliana knew at that moment what was going to be said and even what was finally going to happen.

'No,' she cried. 'No, no, no. It shall not be.'

The Duke looked saddened, upset, cross, sorry and all those things that rulers must feel when they are impotent, even though he was the master-builder of the situation. Eustace looked indifferent – he had wanted a son anyway.

'I want the Comte's two daughters as my hostages,' said Ralph. 'I know that he will look after my son, because I will have the girls as surety. We will look after them as if they were our own. My wife always wanted a girl though I never could understand why, saving your Comtesse's grace.'

Everyone looked at the Duke to see what he would say. He sat awhile in thought, as if suddenly alone. Then he stirred himself.

'No,' he said. 'They are my grandchildren and Ivry is too near the border with France. I am not having them taken hostage by the French king. I shall look after them in my castle at Caen where they will be well cared for. You, Mr Latiner, will remain here and entertain our young guest. If anything, Ralph, should happen to your son – which is scarcely likely in the circumstances – but, as I say, if anything should happen to him, I will send the girls direct to you upon my honour and my oath to be treated as the situation demands.'

The Castellan was clearly unhappy, but he could scarcely go against the honour and oath of his liege lord. I too was unhappy at the prospect of losing my little charges. The only person to seem pleased was Eustace himself who, against the earlier odds, appeared to have come out on top. Any fool could have seen that the future was full of traps and it only needed one of them to be sprung for the Duke's design to start whirring and revolving like the Arab water-clocks that Brother Paul used to speak of. We were all like little figures, bobbing and rotating in a predestined way at the mercy of the Beauclerc. What the end of the game would be, I had no premonition, but I would have been surprised if the Duke had a triumph for the Comte de Breteuil in mind.

171

XXXIII

Marie and Pippi wept bitterly when they awoke and heard the news. They loved their home and their mother, and they were experiencing for the first time that nasty feeling that gathers in the pit of the stomach at the end of something nice and the start of something unknown and quite possibly unpleasant, which assails the young when the grown-ups dictate the course of their future. My heart bled for them.

Their mother did her best to comfort them, and I did my best to comfort her. She wept and raged like a trapped tigress in the little wardrobe room behind the bedchamber.

'I will never forgive my father for doing this – nor Eustace either. He blunders into these things because he is such a fool, and he does not realise how dangerous these games are. Anything could go wrong. He gets so drunk, he does not know what he's doing or saying. And then anything can happen. He is a catastrophe on legs, that is why he is so dangerous. He will bring us all down.'

'I am sure he would not want to do something that might endanger his children.'

'He does not know what he wants or what he does. It was an evil day that my father betrothed mc to him.'

She would not be comforted, like Rachel weeping for her children, she said, but I told her that Rachel's children were dead; hers were very much alive. Poor Juliana! She had, she said, a feeling of impending disaster.

I busied myself as best I could, packing up little games and toys for the girls and helping them get their clothes together with the nurse who was to stay and help look after Roger. He was shortly to say goodbye to his father which must have been a distressing prospect for him, stern fellow that Harenc was notwithstanding.

After breakfast, Juliana confronted her father. I was not present at the interview but I understood that it became heated, indeed over-heated, and after the interview was ended and the couple emerged, we were treated to the spectacle of one of the Duke's famous rages.

'Don't bring that bitch-daughter near me again, Breteuil,' he snarled at Eustace. 'By the death of our Lord, I cannot be answerable if you do. I expect my barons to have control of their women. She is a liability, Breteuil. Chasten her or I will do it for you.'

Eustace would have been only too glad to do a bit of chastening, and even moved forward, but at that point Juliana whipped out a knife from under her shift and held it to his throat, and she seemed to include her father in her threat.

'Touch me and you die,' she said.

And she meant it. The Duke was impressed and his anger subsided. I was incredibly proud of her. Such a slender young woman, she was, with all that passion inside her.

'See what I mean,' he said, almost laughing. 'My daughter! Would you believe it?'

We were all impressed – the little girls and Ralph Harenc too – and it did take something off the mood of sorrow. It was almost an anti-climax when they all mounted up and moved off, the Duke first, with Ralph Harenc trotting up to ride beside him. Alice had offered to go with the girls and they had gladly accepted. I had lent her my little palfrey Blackberry who I now saw happily trotting beside Marie and Pippi on little steeds of their own. The Duke and Ralph were bound for the castle at Ivry, where they would be near to Paris and the forces of King Louis (which was of course why Henry valued it so much – a useful place and strong in defence). Six of his chosen men at arms would branch off after a mile or so, taking a different road westwards to escort the girls and Alice to Caen. The Castellan, Ralph, hardly glanced at his son as he rode away, whether out of sorrow or a soldier's discipline I could not say. His son remained with us. He did not weep because he was training to be a page, but I could tell his heart was heavy.

We waved and waved until the last horse was out of sight where the road turned into the avenue beyond the water meadows. Eustace turned blusteringly to Juliana.

'Ever heard of a wife's duty to her husband?' he blustered. 'Your father could see very well what a termagant you have grown up to be. Threaten me with a knife, would you? I'll have a whip on you soon enough. What sort of women do they make in England? She-wolves and mongrel bitches, I'll warrant.'

And so it went on. I took little Roger up to the nursery and talked to him about Latin and mathematics, but what he really wanted to do was go out with a little boy's bow we had found, and shoot it at a target, so that is what we did for much of the morning, and later we found him a pony, and he trotted and cantered round and round the bailey until it was dinner time.

As it turned out, he would not see his father again.

XXXIV

While Eustace drank himself stupid – no, what am I saying, his stupidity was already far advanced when sober – while Eustace drank himself insensible among his knights in the hall below, the Comtesse and I made love that evening in the little wardrobe room that had become a kind of second home to us. We indulged in make-believe that we were living in a cottage in the middle of a forest and indeed it seemed like that – a world of wildness, wickedness and the clang of steel outside, people on the move, soldiers, beggars, people dispossessed, madmen, witches and devils.

I was beginning to like the boy Roger. He was a brave little chap, only eight years old and never been away from home before; missing his mother, no doubt, but putting a brave face on it. He was sleeping in the girls' room, with the old nurse on a truckle bed in a tiny closet room outside. He had not been scared of the dark before, but this particular night he apparently woke shouting, frightened half out of his wits by a dream he'd had. This woke the nurse and she tried to comfort him, but it seemed to no avail. By this time we were awake, and I had time to slip on some clothes and come down to the bedroom.

'Now, now,' I said, 'what is the matter here? I thought it was a nest of owls hooting in the night.'

'The boy had a dream,' the old nurse told me.

He hardly seemed to be awake yet, and was staring ahead as if he had seen a ghost.

'Come, Roger,' I said, gently, 'what is the matter?'

'I couldn't see what it was my mother was telling me,' he said. 'There was something important she wanted to tell me, something bad that was coming in the dark, that I could not see. But it was coming. I knew it was. I had to get away.'

I realised that the boy had not seen a ghost. What was upsetting him was that, in his dream, he *couldn't* see whatever it was his mother was warning him about. That was the reason for the fixed stare and the haunted expression.

'Come,' I said to the boy, 'back to sleep. Very soon you'll see your room again at Ivry, but meanwhile you have me and Nanny to look after you, and I'm sure your dear mother will be cross with me if she thought I hadn't done a good job.'

The boy relaxed. He had a kind heart.

'Oh, but you have,' he said, looking first at me and then at the kindly old nurse. 'I would never say that you hadn't. I was frightened, that's all. And my father says a page must never show fear, especially in the face of the enemy or before a lady.'

'Quite right,' I replied, as the nurse smiled at his childish earnestness, 'but you can show fear in front of friends. That is what friends are for.'

'Do you think so?' said the boy.

'Very much so,' I said. 'What do you think, Nanny?'

'Certainly,' she said. 'You can show friends the truth. That is why we pray for them at night. It is a precious thing.'

The boy smiled. It was an enchanting smile with a touch of sadness in it, as though his life had been lonely in the castle of Ivry. We tucked the boy up and left a rush light in the room to drive away the spooks, and almost before we had left the room, he was asleep again.

Then the old nurse told me something that made me ashamed of my carelessness and manly talk. He was only a little boy.

'The boy does not have a mother,' she said. 'His mother died a year ago.'

XXXV

I told Juliana about the incident next day, because I was still a little worried about the child. I used to have the most dreadful dreams as a boy when my mother was alive, about being alone in the castle in the bailey with something coming for me through the gatehouse, something looking for me and half sensing where I was. I would rush up the stairs into the hall, knowing I would be safe if I could get there before the creature saw me, and reach the hall just in time, slamming the great door shut only to find the castle deserted. I would run up the stairs and search room after room, knowing that the creature had got in and was following me up to the very top. At this point I usually woke up to find my mother's arms around me and her soft hair in my face which almost made up for the horror of the dream. I knew what bad dreams were like.

Juliana too was upset when I told her about the boy's mother, and I knew she was thinking of her girls and whether they would be having dreams like that with no one to comfort them in the night.

'At least they will have each other,' I told her. 'And Alice, she will be there.'

She clasped my hand and I could see that she kept back the tears with difficulty.

'I should not have spoken harshly to Alice,' she said.

XXXVI

I felt now, as I watched the peasants bringing in logs from the forest in the rain, and the hours went from dark to grey to dark once more, that my position at the castle was becoming awkward if not impossible. Juliana was often cross and would hardly smile at me if her husband was around, which was too often the case, so there was little consolation in that direction. Without the two little girls to teach, I was beginning to seem to myself, and maybe to others, like one of those men that ladies keep in the manner of pet dogs – walkies, talkies, jokies, fuckies. Not that many ladies get fucked by their dogs, but I have heard it happens in Paris. I felt that I could hear odd remarks, little sniggers, as I ate at hall or walked around the castle.

I didn't have quite the same enthusiasm for tutoring the boy as I'd had for my former charges. He was a nice little chap, but since he would only be staying for a short while it was not worth starting to teach him Latin, better to keep him exercised and happy with the horses he loved. He had struck up a friendship with one of the grooms and that seemed to take care of it.

To combat my feelings of uselessness and unmanliness, I had taken Juliana up on the subject of the castle's accounts. She had complained to me that money poured out of the place as if someone was employed to stand on the roof and flick gold pieces down the gutters non-stop. She was convinced that she and the Comte were being cheated on a big scale, and she suspected the sly-faced steward, Odo, was the chief culprit. He certainly seemed to consider it his job to keep Eustace more or less permanently pissed, so the Comte himself was incapable of supervision. Odo had worked well enough for us at Christmas, after being kicked very hard up the arse, but now Eustace was back, he seemed to have reverted to his old ways.

I suggested to Juliana that I try my skill with Brother Paul's numerals to bring the castle accounts into some sort of order. Naturally, this was resisted by the steward and his staff, but Juliana and I were not to be rebuffed. I was able to teach Juliana the new symbols, and show her how much simpler it was using them to keep an eye on what came in and what went out. As we worked it grew clearer to us daily that someone was indeed robbing the castle and its estate on a substantial and well-organised basis. It was beginning to seem as though it was not just one person in on the act, but a group of them; perhaps the whole naughty retinue. But there had to be one mastermind.

Juliana concentrated admirably on the Arabic numerals, poring over the slates, checking the inventories, and interviewing those who made the orders for provisions: the cook, the pantler, the butler, the cellarman and, over all, the steward. He only attended our temporary office in the butler's room under duress, and sulking.

'How do you order meat, Odo?'

'I order what we need.'

'And how do you reckon what we need?'

'By what we needed in the past.'

'There seems to be too much waste.'

'No one has complained.'

'We are complaining now.'

'The Comte does not complain.'

'Last week you ordered ten barrels of Burgundy.'

'Did I?'

'Come, Odo, we shall find the truth anyway. And if we find you have concealed something, it will be the worse for you,' Juliana told him.

'The Comte does not complain.'

'The Comt*esse* does. Yesterday you ordered ten more barrels. Even the Comte cannot drink that much. Where did they go?'

We had a pretty good idea that the fellow was selling them on to a sleazy inn in the town. The butler, who had a sick wife and depended for his position on the steward, had broken ranks and told us of the latest delivery of Burgundy

'The Comte has a prodigious appetite,' said Odo with an impertinent look. 'And the Comtesse too, I think.'

The innuendo was unmistakable. I sprang up and was about to slap him into the next village, but Juliana put out a restraining hand.

'Leave him alone,' she told me. 'Let him work himself deeper into his own midden. It does not make him happy. Nor does it tell us how those two barrels reached the inn at Évreux when they should have been in our cellars.'

The steward blinked – I swear it was a confession of guilt – and glared at us both.

Juliana told me afterwards that her accusation was merely guesswork. What a creature she was! I had known she was intelligent and resourceful, but now I saw intuition and persistence too, and I admired her all the more for it. We sat huddled at a table, cheek by jowl, totting up the vast appetite of the castle, and all the while I was nourishing an appetite of my own, but our physical closeness appeared not to move Juliana at all. I might as well have been a scullion. She was intent on the job in hand, and of course I wanted to prove myself to her in this activity, but sometimes we touched accidentally, as when she put her hand out in restraint, and I burst into flame. It was agony. I burned while she froze. At least that is what I thought, though she told me later – when I taxed her – that a score of eyes were on us throughout our investigation even when we thought we were alone, and any sign of our affection would be used against us and reported. I think also that her thoughts and first care were ever with her little girls. She assured me though that there would be an opportunity for us to visit the wardrobe before long. It was a crumb, soon wolfed down.

'We don't need more castles,' she told me, 'we just need the estates we have to work better. Let my father keep Ivry. That place is nothing but trouble.'

Soon we would have enough evidence to show the scale of the steward's deceit, but would Eustace understand? And if he did, would he do anything about it? His normal response when difficulty arose was bluster and a flagon of red wine.

XXXVII

It was a bad time at Breteuil. It rained heavily for days on end. The logs were wet, the fires smoked, the long days of Lent stretched into the distance, there was fighting reported at Pacy and more fighting in the south. The knights were restive. They wanted action because that is what knights are about. Eustace's knights were not the courtly sort, interested in the new fashion for chansons and romans and lays of derring-do and dalliance. If a lady gave them a favour they would use it to wipe their arses. They would eat and sleep in their chain-mail if they could. But now there was much riding about and drilling, but no action.

Eustace was on tenterhooks for news about the Ivry inheritance; it had become an obsession with him. Duke Henry knew that and kept him waiting. Eustace was drinking heavily and picking quarrels with everyone, especially me if I came near him, so I avoided him. The only person he was wary of, even in his cups, was Juliana. Their contract was to leave each other alone.

In spite of my best efforts, Eustace found me one day as I was taking the boy Roger out in the bailey on the pony. Juliana had gone into the town on some local errand, and I rather hoped that Eustace would be asleep on his rank bed, snoring off his wine.

I had arranged some jumps for the boy at his particular request – I was surprised by the earnestness of it – made out of brushwood and bits of old barrels. Maybe he wanted to show off, who knows? All at once, there was Eustace, red in the face and swaying like an overloaded hulk in a Channel storm.

'And what exactly do you think you're doing, Mr Latiner?'

'As you see, sir, we are teaching the Castellan of Ivry's son how to jump. He is learning well.'

'Milksop stuff, Mr Latiner. Just the sort of thing a book reader would do. Go on, then, boy. Jump. Go on!'

And he smacked the pony hard on the rump, making him start and rush at the jump I had made so that the boy was almost thrown. I could see the lad was alarmed but he tried not to show it. He wheeled the pony round and took him over a couple of little obstacles – rather well, I thought.

'Call that a jump!' cried Eustace. 'The animal just walked over it. I'll make you a jump, boy.'

He walked up and put his big bloated face right up against Roger's.

'You'd like that, wouldn't you, boy? You want to be a knight one day, don't you?'

'Yes, sir.'

'Well, sir, knights don't just walk their way over obstacles. They have to learn to fly, boy. They have to leap ditches and charge over hedges while the sky is thick with arrows and heavy with the cries of dying men.'

While he was saying this, he was collecting the larger bits of wood I had discarded and building a veritable monument of a jump. He summoned a groom to help him. It was as tall as the boy by the time they had finished, and solid as a motte; not the sort of thing that would break up easily if you crashed into it.

I watched with misgiving. I was not keen to battle with Eustace because I knew that it would bring trouble to Juliana as well as myself. He saw me as her creature, although he did not know just what a creature I was – at least I believed he did not. However, I was not going to stand by and let the boy be bullied.

'There,' cried Eustace, 'that is what I call a jump. When I was your age, boy, I would take that with a foot or two to spare. Now, go on, jump that one, and then you can call yourself a chevalier. Take the pony up and let him have a look at it.'

I could see the boy was uncertain. The jump was too high, it was quite obvious even to the groom, and it seemed to me the pony thought so too. By now a little crowd was gathering. I had an inspiration.

'Why don't you show him how to do it, sir?'

The man was torn. Half of him wanted to show off, the other half warned him that it was quite a high fence for a rider with

186

three flagons of burgundy wine inside him. However, he seemed to think his honour was at stake, as indeed it was, and he ordered the groom to fetch him a horse.

'Now you'll see how to do it, boy,' Eustace told him earnestly, 'and this may prove useful for you when advancing in close order on the enemy. You have to grow up early in these days of war. Know your enemy, boy, because tomorrow he may be your friend. Or, like the Latiner here, know your friend because tomorrow he could be your enemy. Isn't that so, Latiner?'

I could smell the wine on the man's breath as he turned and swivelled his question at me, and I felt a great urge to punch his arrogant, truculent face in the mouth, but I thought of Juliana and the discomfort of the dungeon and stayed my hand.

'It is so, if you say so,' I told him, 'it is very much so, sire.'

'You don't know who the hell anyone is in these difficult days. The Duke's daughter is your bitch-wife and whose side is she on?'

It struck me that I had under-rated Eustace in the past. He was a sot, no two ways about it, but there was a kind of craftiness in there too. Perhaps he did suspect what Juliana and I got up to, and was just biding his time. The thought made me alarmed. I felt exposed out there in the bailey. There was violence in the man which could flicker up like a tongue and catch you if you didn't look sharp.

He paced about for a bit, thinking perhaps of something unpleasant to say, or some scrap of useless advice to give to the boy, while I gave Roger a reassuring smile and tightened his girth straps. Finally, the big horse arrived, and with much pushing and shoving, the Comte climbed into the saddle.

The horse snorted and reared a little and the Comte gave it a savage thwack with his whip, which did nothing to calm it. A great Percheron beast, it was, all the way from my home.

'Steady, Thunderbolt, damn you,' he said. 'Now, boy, watch carefully. We take the horse to the jump – if we have time – just to show him what he is facing. Then we turn around and go back, not too much, not too little. Of course, in battle, there is no time for this, I would be carrying a lance as well as wearing a sword, plenty to think about. Perfect control is the order of the day. You have to be part of your mount, you have to feel the beast, boy. Perfect control. Your horse is part of you while you are on it. Now, watch closely because you are going to do it next. Perfect control. Man and horse in perfect harmony, the perfect fighting engine, reins in hand, back erect, ready to charge the enemy ...'

We turned and watched the Comte as he trotted back and wheeled round to face us. I did not like to admit it, but the man was strangely impressive in his battle mode. It was the only time he was truly alive. He sat on his horse, poised, silent. Then he gave a curious cry, deep in the throat – doubtless something his forbears had learned at the side of Rolf the Ganger – and spurred his horse towards the enemy, which was represented in this instance by the jump he had made.

The horse cantered up to the jump – and stopped dead. The Comte slithered over its head, turned completely over, arse over tit, and landed painfully on his bottom.

'Oooooch!' he cried, and fell back as though dead.

There was an embarrassed pause. Even Fulk, my old adversary, opportunistically in the front row, had nothing to say. The silence was broken by Roger. What made him do it, I have no idea. Possibly the sheer embarrassment of the situation or perhaps something the castellan his father had taught him to do when he was down or in the face of adversity.

Whatever it was that had provoked it, the boy began to laugh.

The effect on the spectators was reflected on every face. Astonishment and almost awe. No one had ever laughed much at the Comte de Breteuil, not even his wife, and certainly not the Latiner. I looked at them. I looked at the Comte lying flat out on the grass, like a whale, beginning to stir. I looked at the boy laughing, a clear high joyful noise it was too. I wanted to laugh as well. I wanted him to stop. And then the worst thing happened. Everyone started laughing. Slowly the Comte sat up. To my amazement, he too was laughing. Oh well, I thought, I may as well laugh too. The groom advanced and helped the Comte to his feet.

The Comte suddenly stopped laughing, and everyone else stopped too, even the boy. You could have heard a dandelion clock drop. He seemed all at once to be stone cold sober.

'All right, show's over. Haven't you anything better to do than stand around gawping? There are butts over there waiting for the archers, and a dangling-iron yonder ready for the knights. Pages, go to the armoury and polish the hauberks and the fucking armour or I'll tell the sergeant to polish your backsides.'

There was a confused rush of men running to their various posts, eager not to be noticed by the glaring red eye of the master. I stood beside the boy with my hand on his shoulder. The Comte turned and regarded us with more than displeasure.

'You,' he said.

I gathered he was addressing me. I was used to that term of greeting from my days at Mortagne.

'Was it your idea?'

'My idea?'

'The jumping. Was it your idea?'

'Well … yes…'

I was about to say it was a good way to keep the boy happy. He did not seem to have much of an aptitude for Latin, when he went home he would soon forget it, and the games and pastimes we had in the nursery and schoolroom were more for little girls. Besides he was a good rider.

The boy surprised me by putting up his hand. He was brave, no doubt about it.

'Well?' asked the Comte.

'It was my idea. My father wishes me to become a good rider.'

'Oh, he does, does he?'

'Yes, he does.'

'And did he suggest this plot to make me look a fool? Put the jump up too high and make the bugger jump it?'

'No, sir. He said nothing of that.'

'But that is what he had in mind. He knows my passion for war and for the chase. I wouldn't put it past him. Cunning devil! He'd try anything to keep that castle.'

'It wasn't my father. It was my idea.'

'So you are the plotter. So young ... so wild...'

'No, sir. But ... Ivry ... it is my home, sir.'

'I'll speak no more of it. I will deal with you later. I am surrounded by plotters and enemies. They are using even children now ... they are disguised as boys but really they are devils...'

I feared he was going to harm the child, so I stood between them.

'Don't you want him to try the jump?' I asked.

'No,' he said.

I supposed he did not want to be beaten by a boy while there were still people around. It seemed to me an even chance that the boy would fall off and injure himself, but damage had already been done worse than a broken arm. The yeast was working now as I have seen it in the abbey brewery: swollen, alive and restless as sin.

'No,' the Comte said again. 'I have something else in mind.'

I did not like the sound of that at all. What on earth had possessed the boy to laugh? I had thought he was an intelligent little fellow. Perhaps they did things differently in Ivry.

I took Roger back to the castle and left him in the care of the nurse. Then I waited for Juliana to come back from the town.

XXXVIII

Juliana was a strange mixture. On the one hand she was made from the same mould as her father – clever, observant, brave – but essentially hard, the hardness so necessary in a king. She could be hot-headed like her father. She took what she wanted, for example me. One had to be careful not to draw the dragon out of her, her ladies could tell you that. But Juliana was not a bully; she had some of her Saxon mother's qualities too. Her mother's name was Ansfrida, a great beauty and widow of a leaseholder of the famous Abingdon Abbey, with properties near Oxford. She had come to Henry, then a prince, for help after her husband had been thrown into prison unjustly by Henry's brother, Rufus. She had been so 'radiant in her distress', that Henry could not resist her – and had not deserted her either, looking after her and her daughter until she had died – and even then he had prevailed on the abbey to let her be buried at the entrance to the cloisters. You did not win Henry's heart lightly. Well, her daughter had some of that radiance too, believe me, and that was why Henry was so fond of her. And that was why Eustace knew he could not go too far to annoy her, the Duke's favourite.

I told her about the afternoon's events when she returned from the town, and she looked thoughtful.

'He's getting one of his ideas,' she said. 'He thinks Ralph the castellan is using the boy to play a trick on him. That's typical mad Eustace. He completely loses sight of the main story, which is that Amaury de Montfort is pulling his strings. I keep telling him he doesn't really need Ivry. We have enough castles.'

'What about the boy?' I asked.

'Let's go upstairs and talk about it,' she said.

She smelt just a little of oranges and spice and sweet pepper. It was the smell of the wardrobe room. She must have slipped up there to make sure the coast was clear.

'We must take care of the child,' I told her. 'Eustace did not like the boy laughing at him today.'

'I am not sure I would have done either,' she said.

'It was unwise but rather wonderful. People don't laugh at Eustace enough.'

She drew herself up a little.

'He may be laughable, but he is still my husband. I do not want him publicly insulted.'

'It was not intended as an insult. I think now that the boy was laughing out of politeness. He believed that Eustace was trying to be funny.'

'Politeness would be lost on Eustace. At any rate, we must see that the boy is safe and well. Then I shall know that my girls are all right. The sooner this is over the better. My father plays with Normandy like a chess set.'

'But he is a good player,' I said. 'He has only ever lost one small battle, which is more than can be said for King Louis.'

It was fortunate that when we entered the wardrobe we were not holding hands, because Eustace was sitting on the bed eating raisins with, of all people, Amaury de Montfort, while the crafty steward Odo whispered in their ears. They rose as we entered: Eustace and the steward furtive, a little guilty, as though they had been conniving; Amaury as brazen as ever.

'What are you doing in my domain, husband?' said Juliana, coldly. 'You never penetrate to these heights normally. I cannot think of a time when you did.'

'I do not know about penetration, but I am sure there are others who do,' he said unpleasantly and, turning to me, 'Come for a little oil and spice to make an embrocation, Latiner?'

'As a matter of fact, I have. The boy complained of a sore back after his riding.'

'I hope you are not thinking of monkish practices.'

'Certainly not,' I replied. 'I hear that some of your knights are not so reluctant with the pages.'

The steward cast a side-long look at me. I did not like his dirty mop of straw-coloured hair which looked as if a horse had peed in it.

'Tell me who they are and I will castrate them,' Eustace said.

'And what are you doing here, Amaury?' questioned Juliana. 'I should have been told of your arrival. I fear you have not been properly entertained.'

It was a monstrous impoliteness to enter a castle's private rooms without being first welcomed by the châtelaine.

'Entertained well enough, Cousin Juliana. Nuts and raisins, feast fit for a king,' he smirked, and the other two giggled with him.

'And what plots are you hatching?' she enquired.

'Plots?' he arched his eyebrows.

'I know you well enough, my lord. It is always castles and lordships with you.'

'Well, my lady, since I am not in your best books, you will be relieved to know that my visit here is already over. I am gone. What you see before you now is a pale shadow, a wraith, a no thing, a memory. I have another appointment to keep, in Évreuil. No peace for the wicked.'

'And no wickedness for the peaceful. You should try it sometime.'

'I am gratified that you know me so well,' said Amaury, unabashed, 'and think of me so much. Farewell, Madame. Goodbye, Monsieur le Comte. And you too, Latiner. Not too much *amo, amas, amat* now…'

'I will see you out,' said Eustace.

'No need. I know this castle well. It was almost mine – until our gracious Duke decided you should have it.'

'I hope you don't think …' began Eustace.

'My dear Comte, of course not. No hard feelings. See me to the stairs and then you can go back to your lady. She needs to see more of you…'

He was the sort of person who cannot open his mouth without making an insinuation. They left together and I could hear them muttering to each other and laughing as they lingered on the landing outside. Eustace shouted for a page to see his visitor out, and returned to the room as Amaury tripped lightly down the stairs.

'Since you ask the reason why we're here,' said the steward Odo, still impertinent in the proximity of his master, 'the butler has run out of cloves and cinnamon. It's a cold evening and Lord Eustace thought we'd have some hot spiced wine. We seem to get through so much cinnamon and cloves, we never order enough. I don't know where it goes.'

This was an obvious dig at us and our investigation of his accounts, but Juliana was equal to it.

'Well, you should know where it goes, steward. It is your job. And the butler has plenty of cloves and cinnamon in his cupboard, as you should know too,' she said and turned her attention to Eustace. 'I don't like you snooping up here. I am the châtelaine and this is my domain. I cannot keep track of these stores which you know are costly if you keep sneaking in. And, talking of accounts, I have some problems with the steward's. We shall speak of it later.'

She made a little gesture with her head to indicate that the steward should leave. He looked at Eustace for assent, but the Comte was busy with another thought – you could almost see his head swelling with the effort. The steward bowed himself out. We three were left alone.

'I wondered why you smelt of spice, Latiner. My nose was ever sharp, and my mind runs after it,' said Eustace, delivering the sentence like a turd in the moat.

I thought quickly to try and deflect him from any suspicions he might have about me and the wardrobe.

'I learned of spice from Brother Paul in the abbey, sire. He came from Spain and had learned many things from the Arabs, mathematics … medicine … Some of these spices and herbs can work wondrous cures, properly used.'

The Comte was interested now.

'Cures, you say …? Can they heal wounds of battle?'

'Some of them, yes.'

I thought for a terrible moment he was going to ask me once more to heal the wound that had unmanned him. The idea of grappling around in that dark and unvisited portion quite set my teeth on edge. But his mind, it seemed, was on his favourite subject.

'Then you shall come with us when next we fight.'

You had to hand it to Eustace – there was no end to the unpleasant surprises he could spring on you. Going on campaign with Eustace was the last thing I wanted. I exchanged a glance with Juliana. Then I had a further thought. It seemed like a good idea at the time.

'There is an invention of the Arabs called alcohol. They distil wine to make a stronger aqua vitae. If I could obtain some of that from my old master, I am sure you would find it … exciting …'

'It is like strong wine?'

The man was interested now. I felt I had betrayed the confidence of my old friend Brother Paul, but I hoped he would forgive me.

'Very like strong wine … only stronger.'

'You must get me some of that, Latiner. It has a brave sound, does it not, Madame? Excellent, Latiner. Wheel it on. You are not as useless as you look.'

He left us on that note. It was the nearest Eustace ever got to a compliment. Evidently the steward had been waiting for him on the landing. We watched them go down the stairs together, the steward leaning over to talk in Eustace's ear.

'If they get any closer, his tongue will come out the other side,' I told her.

'I will not have Eustace coming up here,' Juliana said. 'He is becoming a nuisance. We may have to get rid of him.'

I looked at her again with a kind of admiring horror. Was this really the woman who melted in my arms as we made love to the scent of oranges and grains of paradise, and the swooning sounds that girls make?

'Would you really do that?' I asked. 'Get rid of him?'

'Keep your voice down, Latiner. Of course I would, if it were necessary. He knows that too.'

She was her father's daughter all right. Did she mean that I was to help her?

'But what if he bumped you off first?'

'I'd be ahead of him.'

'Shall I see if I can get him some of the distillation they call alcohol?'

'What will it do?'

'It will make him very drunk.'

'That will be good. It will keep him out of our way – out of everyone's way … The more he drinks, the quicker he will go, may God forgive me.'

'I will ride to Saint-Sulpice tomorrow.'

'No.' She put a hand on my arm. 'I need you here. You will only linger with your old friends at the abbey. And it would be too easy for Amaury to arrange to have you killed on the way. One of the pages shall go. There is a boy called Guyon. He can be trusted. I will summon him now.'

She went out and I wrote to my old friend Brother Paul, explaining the interest that Lady Juliana had expressed, requesting a small quantity of the liquid he distilled and enclosing a generous gift to pay for his further medical researches. I also asked for some advice as to how the spirit might be consumed. Juliana then returned with the lad Guyon, a strapping youth who looked as though he could take care of himself. What Juliana had said about it being easy for Amaury to have me killed, was beginning to sink in. It was difficult to imagine, but also terribly real. It is hard to believe when you are young that life is serious, and even harder to conceive that someone dislikes you sufficiently to have you bumped off. I found myself shaking. These were dangerous waters I was swimming in.

I managed to control myself sufficiently to give the lad instructions as to where to go – he came from the town of Bernay which was not far from the abbey – and I put the vellum in his hand saying that he should be sure to give it only to Brother Paul. Juliana gave him money for the journey, and he left forthwith. I sank down with relief into a chair. Stupid, wasn't it? I am not a coward but the thought of a stab in the back or a poisoned pastry at some low inn caught me unawares. I can face death only if I can look him in the eyes.

I did not think that Juliana had noticed my moment of weakness. I told her more about the alcohol, how I was confident Eustace was going to discover the most exquisite sensations which would render him even more insensible than usual more quickly. Frankly, insensible was the way she liked Eustace best.

'By the way,' said Juliana, smiling, 'what on earth persuaded you to encourage that boy Fulk to tell me that he was in love with me?'

I had forgotten about that.

'I thought it might help him,' I told her. 'He seems so depressed. And I thought it might keep him on our side. What did you do?'

'I'm afraid I laughed.'

'What did he say to that?'

'He said he was going to kill himself.'

'And what did you say?

'I told him not to be so silly, of course.'

Not for the first time, I wondered how such asperity and softness could co-exist in Juliana without inducing some kind of precipitation as in the dressing the cooks make with oil and eggs and vinegar to accompany a sallet. One little thing wrong and it curdles.

XXXIX

Four days later, Guyon returned carrying a half-firkin of alcohol and a letter from Brother Paul, full of kind thoughts. He was missing me, he said, and urged me to use the liquor sparingly. He reminded me he had obtained its recipe and means of production, not without difficulty, through a Jewish friend of his at the hospital in Salerno. In the right hands it could be a power of good. It had preservative strengths and was also sovereign for hardening the skin and for cleaning dirty wounds. It should only be consumed to revive the near-dead in cases of extreme exhaustion or to puff away ventosity or pounce the stone. I kept this good advice to myself, in my heedless way, and almost wept when I thought of my old friend and the chaste life I had led in the abbey, compared with the sinful and dangerous existence I had found at Breteuil. Brother Paul begged me to give up my sublunary life and return to the cheerful disciplines of Saint-Sulpice, but I knew I could not. Life was an adventure, the flesh was weak, and I was young. I debated with Juliana how best to introduce the alcoholic spirit to her husband's cup, and at what hour it should be.

'After his dinner,' she told me, 'tomorrow afternoon, that is surely the right time. He will have drunk wine and be ready to try the strong water. He is already excited about it. I heard him telling the steward to bring up cordials to mix with the alcohol. After that he will sleep where he sits with his head in a plate of cheese, if he wishes.'

We were stupidly excited about it, like giggling schoolchildren, but had we known what would follow, we would have saved the ill-begotten brew for the broken heads and wounds of the next tournament. It would at least have served the benign purpose for which it was made. As it was, it brought us nothing but disaster.

At first all seemed well. Indeed, I was pleased to be able to take Juliana's mind off her little hostage daughters far away in Caen. I approached the whey-faced steward, Odo, before dinner, and told him that his master wanted him to pour the clear fluid into a silver beaker, and give it to him at the end of the meal in the place of the Rhenish. I told the man, quite accurately, that it was a strong elixir drawn upwards by heat and collected in a coiled vessel from the sweat and steam of wine. The man looked dubious, but I told him that the Comte was counting on him; he would be angered if the potion was not presented as he had commanded. Odo sensed some kind of personal disadvantage in the scheme, but for the life of him he could not pinpoint it, and he finally agreed to do as I had bidden. His attitude towards me was a curious mixture of evasiveness and truculence. He knew that Juliana and I were aware of his dishonesty, but he wasn't altogether certain that it mattered since he was the Comte's man, although you could never quite tell in matters like this which way the Comte would jump. Eustace would naturally side with anyone whom his wife was against, but on the other hand cheats hate to be cheated.

The meal came to an end. Juliana and the ladies left the table, and in walked Odo carrying the silver goblet which he set down in front of Eustace.

'What is this, steward?' he enquired, fatuously. 'Some kind of potion to make me beautiful?'

The knights all convulsed with laughter.

'No, sir,' said the fawning little creature, 'you are handsome enough already.'

More laughter from the audience.

'Will it make me sleep a hundred years and be woken by a beautiful princess, and not my wife?'

I gritted my teeth at his oral infidelity to my mistress.

'Not woken, sir, no. But I am sure that any woman would be proud to keep you awake, sir.'

There was more raucous glee from the groundlings.

'So what will it make me do? Latiner,' and now he called down the table at me. 'What will happen when I drink this stuff?'

'Well, sir,' I tried to control the nervousness I felt for this was now the moment of truth.

'It will feel at first like a warm fire in the mouth,' I began. 'Then, as it starts to trickle down the throat, you will feel quickened, all your senses will seem sharper, for they will be trying to assess the meaning of this new sensation. Nothing like it has happened to them before. This will be followed by a cordial mellowness in the belly spreading to all the organs of the body. You will feel stronger, braver (if that were possible), more cheerful, more generous. Any doubts will disappear. Your companions will seem better fellows. Melancholy and choleric thoughts will dissipate like clouds before the sanguine breeze of the elixir. In short...'

'Enough, Latiner,' he cried, seizing the goblet, 'if it does even half of what you say, my life so far has been wasted. Alcool is the stuff for me. You can keep your Burgundy and your Rhenish...'

He made a clumsy sweep of his arm, knocking beakers in all directions. He was already drunk. And now we all watched as he emptied the goblet's contents into his capacious mouth. His expression as it did so followed very closely my description of the liquid's transit. His eyes rolled, his cheeks flushed, his stupid mouth widened in a fatuous grin, he rubbed his large stomach like a child and made a low sound like a cow being milked. He stood up – and then he sat down again, rather quickly.

'Where's the other one?' he asked me.

I had taken the liberty of ordering quite a generous stock from Brother Paul, not that I had told Eustace of it, but no doubt he assumed there would be a further supply. I handed a vial over, and it too was quickly despatched.

There was a pause.

'Mushic,' he commanded, and the old fiddler in the gallery responded with a jig.

Nobody moved. We were all watching the Comte as though he were in labour.

'I tell you what, Latiner, you're a good fellow ...' he started, fatuously, 'thish ish the finesht ...' but at that point he slumped forward on the table in a swound.

We thought that was the end of it for the moment, but then he raised his head again and spoke with the clarity of those at the limit of their powers, as those who are about to die deliver perceptions.

'I have had a message from my Lord de Montfort,' he said. 'The Castellan of Ivry is cheating us. Something must be done to change the game.'

A silence fell on the gathering. We looked at each other. And then Eustace slumped forward again.

'I hope it is not poison you have given him, Latiner,' said the steward, unpleasantly.

'Of course, it is not poison,' I told him. 'The Comte asked for the elixir himself. Its method and extraction is prescribed by the famous hospital in Salerno.'

'What nasty things occur in that evil mind of yours,' said Juliana to the steward, appearing quietly, as she so often did administering grace or reproof. 'You heard the Comte and now you have heard Bertold. See, I drink the dregs of this so-called poison. Watch while I turn black and vomit.'

She picked up both goblet and vial, and drained them.

'There is nothing there but what there is in strong wine – only stronger. It is a rare spirit and not to be taken lightly, but the Comte knew that. He will recover, but let him sleep now. Take him to his bed.'

'I say it is the devil's brew,' said the horrible little man, 'you had better pray that my lord wakes up.'

Juliana took a step towards him and the man cringed.

'You had better pray, Odo, that I never hear you uttering threats to me or my guests in this castle. That is, if you do not want to spend the rest of your days in a dungeon. You have already robbed us. If you call a constable, make it for yourself.'

The steward backed down immediately, of course.

'I hope you didn't think … I didn't mean any disrespect. It is just that in these lawless days, we begin to think that anything is possible.'

'Well, don't think, steward. You are not here to think. You are here to do your job – and that, it seems to me, you do not even passingly well and cause a great deal of trouble on the way. Take your master to his room and see that he is comfortable – put some water by his bedside, then leave him.'

He jerked a greasy thumb at four of the servitors, and they carried the unconscious Eustace up a further flight of stairs to the first floor of the castle where he had his bedchamber – a site as far away as possible from the Comtesse's, which she had personally selected for him. Juliana watched them for a while and then turned to the assembled knights in the hall. It was early evening, though darkness would not fall for another hour.

'The working day is not over,' she told them. 'It is the Comte's privilege to spend it as he will. But for you who have to fight and make a way in the world, there is plenty of work to be done. I am sure the Marshal will see to it that you are exercised before nightfall.'

The Marshal was a burly figure who ruled the parade ground between the stables and the main gate. He had a voice like Roland's horn.

'I will indeed, Madame Comtesse.'

He drew himself up, puffed out his chest, and shouted at the lolling soldiery.

'Come on, you idle knights. On your feet and try to look like soldiers, not like leftovers from the local pisshouse. Begging your pardon, Madame.'

'Go ahead, Marshal.'

He rounded them up and took them outside where he made them run, holding their swords over their heads, round and round the bailey. Juliana gave me a look that set my blood on fire as surely as any elixir.

She relaxed her usual rule, and we almost ran to the secret-scented chamber and made love.

'I don't know what it is you do to me, Latiner, but you should be careful that I do not have you named as a witch,' she told me.

I slept well that night in my own bed with the fragrance of her upon me. I was woken early by the sound of wailing from the nurse. I hurried out and found Juliana in her night robe holding the old woman by the shoulders.

'What in God's name is the matter? You have woken the whole castle.'

'Oh sir,' the nurse cried when she saw me. 'Oh madam ... the little boy...'

Juliana paled.

'What has happened to him?'

'He has disappeared. I have looked everywhere.'

Juliana looked stricken.

'Disappeared? It cannot be.'

She was doubtless thinking of the possible repercussions for her daughters. It did not do to lose a hostage.

'We must search immediately,' I cried.

We hurried downstairs and summoned the steward. To our astonishment, Eustace also appeared. He looked the worse for wear, his eyes were bloodshot, and he smelt of sweat and alcohol, but there was something about him that was new – he looked different, wilder, as if in love. Perhaps in alcohol he had discovered a sweetheart. Juliana, I could tell, did not like what she saw, but none of us had any inkling of the engine that had been put in motion, trundling along downhill, unstoppably, like a runaway siege piece.

Eustace lifted his hand as if in blessing.

'Not so fast,' he said. 'The child is not missing. I ... we ... have sent him back to his father.'

It was one of those moments that should have warned me that nothing, ever, was going to be the same again. And yet, at the time, it just seemed to be another piece of Eustace stupidity.

'You have done *what*?' cried Juliana.

She was not in any way panicking – panic wasn't her game – she was merely outraged that he should have acted without consulting her, because anything he did off his own initiative was bound to be a cock-up.

'I sent him back to his father,' repeated the Comte. 'It was the only thing to do. Amaury sent word that his father was plotting against us. He was strengthening the castle. That was against the terms of our agreement.'

'What agreement?' asked Juliana.

'Why the agreement that your father spelt out to us, of course! He would take our daughters as hostages and we would take the snivelling castellan's son. And during that term we would behave honourably and maintain the peace. When I heard from Amaury that the agreement had been broken, there was only one thing to do.'

'And what was that?'

'Send the boy back to his father as Amaury suggested.'

XL

The weather this year was more erratic than usual, and Normandy weather is erratic by its nature. We had had some hail which is unusual for late Spring. Now, right on cue, there was a loud peal of thunder.

'You did *what*?'

Juliana's face had gone white.

'I sent the boy back to his father.'

'But then we would be the losers, for our daughters are still hostages.'

'But only in the keeping of their grandfather. Do you have any more of that alcohol, Bertold? It is a brave juice.' he asked, turning to me, and using my name for the first time, for which I hardly felt better. 'They make it out of wine, you say? They could make it out of cider, I daresay. If I had but the secret, I could be as rich as the Great Sophy.'

I could feel the sinister unfolding of something that I was beginning to recognise as guilt. What had I done?

'You do not know my father,' Juliana told him. 'He will do anything to keep this kingdom and his inheritance together for his son.'

'That spoilt codling!' snorted Eustace, glad to shift attention away from himself.

'Don't let his father hear you say that. And don't let me hear it either. He is my brother.'

'Half-brother,' corrected Eustace.

'Half-brother is better than no brother. And who are you to talk anyway! Your mother was not married either,' she told him.

Eustace reddened. He did not like to be reminded of his bastardy. So that was how it was left, there was nothing we could do now, the bird had flown, the stable door was open.

'Nor was mine married either,' I said. 'God stand up for bastards because no one else does.'

'The al-çohol, Bertold,' Eustace mumbled.

I said nothing. Alarm was gathering in me like wind.

'We are getting away from the point,' said Juliana. 'With whom did you send the boy back? You must have given him an escort?'

'A couple of knights and a page to hold his hand. It is not far to Ivry.'

'Well, it is done now,' said Juliana. 'Heaven knows what my father will think of it.'

'I do not care what the Duke thinks,' cried Eustace, suddenly full of a kind of truculent bravado. 'There are soldiers and barons in plenty who can chase his arse all the way back to Winchester. Alcohol, Bertold!'

He gripped my arm urgently. Juliana answered for me; she had seen the damage the stuff had done.

'There is no more alcohol,' she told him.

'What do you know, woman?'

I decided step in.

'It is true. It can only be made in small quantities. You have drunk all we have.'

The Marshal, who had entered the hall and joined us as we stood around Eustace, now entered the lists.

'You have drunk enough strong waters, sire. Come, let us drink some wine. I am sure Odo can find us some.'

'That I can, sire,' said the fawning steward. 'There is Burgundy, newly brought in.'

Outside, the thunder grumbled away. Eustace would not give up.

'You must get more, Latiner, do you hear?'

'I will see what can be done.'

'I will chase your arse from here to Saint-Sulpice if you don't. Meanwhile, bring the wine to my chamber, Odo. And you too, Marshal. We will need to be prepared. The fire is laid, Odo. It just needs a torch and the whole of Normandy could be aflame. Here's what I need you to do...'

He launched into an extravagant scheme which involved a strategy to bribe a neighbouring castellan who controlled a small castle of no strategic importance. Juliana and I moved a little way off and continued to talk in undertones.

'That stuff you gave him has done something to his brain,' she complained. 'Imagine sending the hostage back! Even Eustace would never normally do that. It simply isn't done. Hostages must be exchanged. There's something he's not telling us...'

XLI

For a few more days, things continued as they were. I talked and walked with Juliana in the herb garden while Eustace marshalled his little army in the morning and drank his wits' ends away in the afternoon.

Perhaps I am being unfair to Eustace. I can admit the possibility at a distance. He was married to a remarkable woman who was his superior in every regard; he was overwhelmed. You can serve a woman like that, acquiesce to her peaceably, fight her, or fall by the wayside. You cannot simply ignore her, it would be like ignoring a volcano; you would be destroyed. Eustace adopted a combination of fighting and wine.

So things continued for a few days, as I say.

I was young, it was a remarkably fine spring, at last. I had a beautiful mistress and in the afternoon, when Eustace drank himself into oblivion with a few choice fellows, she revoked her rule that we must wait until her husband was absent from the castle, and let me pleasure her in the wardrobe while her ladies embroidered and fluttered in their canary cage below. Afterwards we walked and she pressed rosemary spikes on me for remembrance – which I thought at the time rather ominous, and I told her I didn't want to be a memory just yet – or ever. She looked at me sadly, touched my cheek, and we walked on. She wanted the girls back from her father, and though we made love again, she was not completely mine.

It was as well the chaplain ('my door is always open') was away. He had been taken sick with a fistula of the fundament, and sent to Saint-Sulpice of all places. God knows what he had been doing. I sent Brother Paul a note of sympathy that he would have to cure him. We had, for a week or two, a temporary substitute from Verneuil who was another poor advertisement for the Church. His door was always shut. He was in some way beholden to the steward, always creeping about, and tipping a cup of wine down his throat whenever he could. No wonder Eustace found him helpful at Confession.

In the mornings, Eustace would mount his great horse and survey the men at their exercise. Sometimes it would be the tilt and the quintain, at others he would ride down to the butts and watch them practise with the crossbow. Then out would come the swords and shields, and there would be parrying, clashing and slashing and a great deal of shouting. Inevitably blood would be shed. It was at this last stage that my limited medical knowledge came in useful. Rather than cleaning the wounds in water and then leaving them to heal – which was the usual recourse – I mixed the water with some of the alcohol I had kept back and tinctured with aloes so that Eustace could not drink it. Pure alcohol was too strong, Brother Paul told me, it almost cooked the flesh, but the mixture purified the wound and stopped the suppuration. It was fortunate that I had this skill or else Eustace and his sergeant would have had me enlisted as a crossbowman. Fighting for Eustace would land me inevitably on the wrong side. Juliana's father had a long memory as well as a quick temper. It didn't do to get on the wrong side of the Duke.

The steward whispered urgently in his master's ear one morning when Eustace descended from his horse. Some kind of message had arrived. Instructions were issued. Messengers came and went. Eustace seemed to be waiting for something that could go either way. His confidence waxed and waned. His swagger faltered and then picked up again with the next messenger. He looked for certainty in every cup of wine.

Juliana said things could not go on like this, but I saw no reason why they shouldn't. When you are young, uncertainty is invigorating; it is a challenge and keeps you on your toes. However, when you are a mother, it is different; Juliana fretted for her daughters, more now that the boy had gone. I tried to understand, but I was not at that time a father myself and even that is not the same as a mother who grows the rose in her own garden and feeds it with her blood.

And then one day, a horseman appeared – a messenger, wearing the Duke's livery. It was afternoon so Eustace was busy in his chamber where he drank with his cronies. I must confess I had given him some more alcohol, untinctured this time, which we now called *aqua vitae* because it made him feel better. It made me feel better too, because it kept him happy and allowed me more time with Juliana.

I would have been talking upstairs with her at that time, going over castle accounts or playing cards, but it had been a violent morning of mock fights, and I still had a couple of wounded soldiers to attend to, one of them was Fulk, feeling sorry for himself now and glad of my attention.

'I still think you are a prancing Latinising fuck-face,' he said.

'I have been called worse,' I told him, and carried on dressing his wound – it was a deep cut across the forearm. There was a silence for a while but I could sense that he wanted to say something.

'She laughed at me,' he said.

'She did not know what to say,' I told him. 'People laugh when that happens sometimes. She would not have meant it cruelly. It was my fault for suggesting you speak to her. I don't know why I did that.'

'There is nothing for me now. Just this and more of it. I should hate you. I did hate you, but now…'

He made a hopeless, waving gesture at the hall, the castle. I did not know what to say, but I didn't laugh.

'Do you know what happened to the boy?' he asked, after a while, as I applied a cloth bandage to the arm, and turned to pick up my medicine box.

'Which boy?'

'The son of the castellan from Ivry.'

'Monsieur le Comte sent him home,' I said. 'It was a couple of weeks ago.'

'The word is he blinded him first.'

The words hit me like a dagger, and I almost dropped the glass vial of alcohol with which I was treating him.

'*What?*'

I almost shouted, and others in the room, the chamberlain – friend of the steward – and two of the knights looked round to see the cause of the commotion.

'Keep your voice down,' Fulk urged. 'No one is supposed to know.'

'He can't have done,' I spluttered. 'Why would he have done that?'

'I had it from the groom. He told me to keep it quiet, but you looked after the lad so you should know. Keep it to yourself, eh?'

'You too, Fulk. Tell no one else – especially not the Comtesse.'

'I would die before bringing her ill news.'

I looked at him with surprise and some concern. The boy was too much in love, but of course where love is concerned there are no limits. Strange that I should ever have thought of him as uncouth.

Just at that moment, there was a commotion at the door, and the porter ushered in a messenger who wore the royal livery. Messengers love to make a commotion, it makes them feel important – unless of course they bear bad news in which case they creep in and creep out again like the cat who crapped in the crypt.

'Greetings,' said the man, entering the hall and approaching me. 'I am looking for Madame la Comtesse. I have a message from the Duke, her father.'

'I am the Comtesse,' said Juliana, appearing – as she so often seemed to – out of nowhere, floating down the stairs on air. She had eyes everywhere, that girl; nothing seemed to escape her. 'What is the message?'

'The Duke is on his way here. He sent me to warn you to prepare for his arrival. He will not stay long for he must go on to Ivry.'

'Is that it? All of the message? No greetings? No requests?'

'Only that he is coming, Madame. He will be here in two days.

214

The messenger bowed his farewell, and made his way out. I could see Juliana was troubled, but I could not tell her the terrible news I had just received. It might not be true, and it would surely better for her to face her father in ignorance. Her innocence would be better proclaimed without feigning and subterfuge.

'This does not bode well,' she told me. 'Why would he come here? And yet, perhaps he has heard of the return of the boy to the castellan, and is bringing my daughters home. That might be it.'

'Perhaps,' I told her. 'More than likely.'

My heart bled for her since an unpleasant suspicion was growing in me. The whole point of taking exchanging hostages was that it guaranteed the safety of both parties. If one was harmed, surely the other was in jeopardy? And yet the Duke who held the little girls hostage was their grandfather. It was inconceivable that he would allow any harm to come to them. That, at least, was comforting.

The next couple of days passed slowly; both Eustace and Juliana were preoccupied. Eustace did his best to subdue his dark thoughts with strong Burgundy, but Juliana, true to form, made no attempt to avoid hers, and paced about her chamber or in the garden alone, shunning me when I tried to make conversation. My own thoughts were gloomy; I had grown to love the little girls and I hated to think of them as pawns in this game of kings, knights, bishops and castles.

The Duke, with a face like thunder, duly arrived on a rainy morning. The wind madly twitched the knights' cloaks about and rattled the candles from the chestnut trees. Blossom fled across the land as if in awe of the Duke's approach. I said as much to him when he arrived, hoping to draw attention to myself, but he waved me away as if I were a gadfly. I am not a natural at sycophancy, but I like to give it a try now and then. I offered him a seat and some wine. He drank the cup down and asked for more. That was unusual. He was not a drinker.

'Where are the Comte and Comtesse de Breteuil?' he enquired, 'Did they not know I was coming?'

'They knew you were coming, sire, but they did not know when.' I told him. 'I have sent word that you are here now. They will not be long.'

'I expect you will be on your way soon,' he said to me. 'What do they call you? Latiner? You are Perche's bastard, aren't you?'

He had a fresh way of talking, but he had a good memory.

'Yes, sire. I am here to teach the little girls Latin.'

'You will be on your way soon. You are no good here. They won't need Latin.'

'But your daughter, sire, Madame La Comtesse. She wishes me to stay and...'

'I know what she wishes, Latiner. Things are hard enough in Normandy without you putting horns on your host. He may not be up to much, he may be a fool and a trouble-maker, but he is my appointment.'

'I don't know what you mean,' I spluttered.

'By the blood of our Lord, you know very well what I mean. And I shall be watching you.'

I looked around the hall. There were young men everywhere, talking together, looking at us. I wondered which of them were the Duke's eyes, which one had sneaked on me. I felt sick at heart. He was telling me to leave Juliana.

'If I am to go, I would rather leave now,' I told him. 'It would be painful to linger on.'

'You will leave when I tell you to. You can at least be of some use to my daughter for a week or two.'

'Use?' I mumbled. 'I don't understand.'

There was a stirring in the hall behind me.

'Shut up and listen,' he said, and stood up.

Juliana had arrived. She stood and looked at us. There was a terrible look in her eyes that I had not seen before. The Duke walked towards her and embraced her; he might as well have embraced a standing-stone. There was no movement or

216

reciprocation in her, only a look of desolation. He returned to his seat and motioned her to sit down.

'Thank you, Father. I prefer to stand.'

'As you wish.'

'Where are my daughters?' she asked him. 'Why have you not brought them with you?'

'You remember, I am sure, the terms on which we parted last, concerning the matter of the castle of Ivry and your husband's interest. The Castellan, Ralph Harenc, was very much against the idea and opposed it violently. He did not see why, to use his own words, a stupid toss-pot who couldn't find a pot to toss in, should lay claim to *his* home and *my* castle.'

'Yes, yes, I know all that,' said Juliana, miserably.

'Well, you also know that I went through the motions of listening to Eustace and, more than that, tried to find some reason, any reason, why I might favour him over my own rights and over the rights of my good servant Ralph Harenc. I did *not* want to offend my lord of Breteuil so that Normandy might hear there was a division between us. These are difficult times, Juliana, and there are many like Amaury de Montfort and my Lord of Mortain, to say nothing of King Louis, who will snatch any excuse to take up arms and seize advantage. I have to be diplomatic, Juliana, for form's sake. And how important that is, especially to people like Eustace – ah, here he is now, coming down the stairs, oh dear, just a little slip, help him up, somebody. For form's sake, I had to go along with him, to humour him and not to turn him down out of hand.'

Eustace, having tripped on the shoes he only wore for special occasion, took a little while to adjust himself. He now advanced at last on the Duke and embraced him closely.

'Ah, Henry,' he said, 'good to see you, no one told me you were here. Are you staying? What about some hunting?'

The Duke disengaged himself. He hated to be called Henry by Eustace. Though technically as a member of his family it would be permitted, it was a privilege normally suggested by the Duke rather than grabbed by a less-than-favourite son-in-law. On this occasion he had bigger things on his mind.

'I was just reminding Juliana,' he said, 'of the agreement that we reached last time I was here. Because of the impasse over the castle of Ivry …'

Eustace put his hand up and lurched forward, tugging at the Duke's sleeve.

'Yes?' asked the Duke, dangerously.

He did not like to be touched.

'I don't want it,' said Eustace with that irritating over-emphasis of the inebriate. 'I don't wannit. You can have it. I don't wannit. Got enough castles. Castles are shit.'

This seemed to exasperate the Duke. He turned on Eustace and berated him.

'Don't interrupt. Do you know how much trouble you have caused? You are a very stupid man. You remember the agreement? You remember that we decided on an honourable exchange of hostages while we examined the various possibilities of ownership, so that there should be no cause for calls to arms or sieges or burnings of the Ivry township while deliberations took place. All these things can happen when men with hot heads get ideas into their skulls.'

'I remember that,' said Eustace. 'Good idea. Hossidges.'

'You remember the young son of Ralph Harenc coming here while I took custody of my grand-daughters, took them away to Rouen? Do you remember that?'

'Vaguely.'

'And then what?'

'You tell me.'

'For some reason that has not yet been explained to me, you saw fit to put the boy's eyes out and return him to his father.'

Juliana gasped. She went deathly white. The terrible news robbed her of speech, and she leant on the table for support.

'I did that?' asked Eustace, stupidly.

'Yes, you did.'

Eustace pulled himself together. Pissed as he was, he could see some kind of danger looming.

'He was plotting,' he shouted. 'You ask Amaury de Montfort. Harenc was planning to take over my castle of Pont-

218

Saint-Pierre. He was raising a substantial force. He broke the agreement. Was I to stand by and do nothing?'

'You are wrong, Eustace. For much of the time, I was at Ivry myself. There was no plot. You should have come over. You cannot trust Amaury. He is a serpent. He pours poison in the ear.'

From what I had seen of de Montfort, the Duke's verdict on the man was accurate, even verging on the benign.

'I have always seen him as an honest fellow.'

'He has tricked you into making a terrible mistake.'

'I put out the boy's eyes. So what? People are popping eyes out all the time.'

'You must see it puts me in a difficult position, Eustace.'

'The man's only a castellan. He's not even a vicomte, he's a Harenc – plenty of those in the sea. Something fishy about him...'

'Stop it!' Juliana had sprung up and was looking at her father with a kind of hopeless fury. 'What is it ... you propose to do?' she asked him, eyes flashing and fists clenched.

They were peas in a pod, those two.

'You must realise,' the Duke said slowly and carefully, still speaking to Eustace who sat there, red-faced, alternately blustering and somnolent, 'that you have put me in an impossible position. You have harmed a hostage who was in your keeping. His father, my castellan at Ivry, has complained in the strongest possible terms. By all the laws of hostage, you are in the wrong and you leave me no choice.'

'No! Don't say it,' Juliana said, very loudly. 'Don't ... you ... say ... it. Don't say it.'

She pushed a little wrinkle of her golden hair away from her eyes – a habit of hers – eyes that were dangerously full.

'I shall have to give up your two daughters to the Castellan to do with them as he wishes.'

'No,' Juliana shouted at him. 'No. You cannot do it.'

The Duke was plainly not comfortable, but he was resolute.

'I think you will find I can. If I fail in this, which is my duty, all Normandy will see that I do not uphold justice and the law.

That is the very point on which my brother Robert foundered. When he was Duke he could not keep control. Laws were broken and the perpetrators went unpunished. Local wars broke out. The whole country was in turmoil. The poor starved and the peaceful were beaten. Fire, rape, pillage and disease walked the land. Finally I was urged by the Church to come and bring order. I defeated Robert in battle on just this issue. Now do you see why I have to do it?'

'And what do you think the Castellan will do to them?'

The Duke, for such a choleric man, had gone very pale.

'He will do as the situation requires.'

'And what will that be?'

'He will do as he thinks fit.'

'These are your grand-daughters, your own flesh and blood. They are innocent in all this. This hostage business was your idea, yours and his...'

She cast a disgusted look at her husband who was slumped, red-faced, drooling slightly, in his chair. The Duke stood up.

'They will be blinded. It will ruin their lives. It will destroy them. Please, Father. I beg you...'

She fell on her knees, something I never thought to see her do, clasping at her father.

The Duke was moved, I could see it, but there was steel in the man.

'You cannot do this ...' she cried. 'I won't let you. It is too terrible ... You won't send them? Say you won't send them.'

The whole castle seemed to be in the hall now, not a sound among them. The Duke tried to free himself from her clasp by walking away but she followed him on her knees. Finally, he forced her hands apart and was free. She fell to the floor, sobbing. The Duke motioned to his marshal, and walked with him to the door, turning to speak to his daughter before he strode out. He looked like death.

'It is too late. Your daughters have already gone. I took them.'

We all stood stunned, the silence only broken by the sobbing of the Comtesse on the floor. Finally, I approached the prostrate form and raised her up a little.

'Leave me,' she said.

Dark-haired Alice appeared and stood on Juliana's other side. She had returned with the Duke.

'Let us take you to your chamber, my lady,' she said.

Juliana was a proud girl. For the first time, she appeared to notice the crowd gathered in the hall. She nodded agreement and rose slowly to her feet. Alice and I supported her as we crossed the hall and started to mount the stairs. Eustace, however, wasn't quite finished. Now the Duke had gone, he recovered some self-esteem, though God knows where he had found it.

'That's right, Latiner,' he called. 'And when you've finished with my wife, I'm sending you to bring my daughters home…'

There was some laughter in the hall from a few of his lackeys – though not as much as the Comte would have liked – and a growing murmur of comment as we turned the corner at the top of the stairs and made our way across the landing. I was wise enough not to intrude on Juliana's grief that night.

XLII

In the morning, she was up early, beating at my door to wake me up and commanding me to ride with her and Alice to Ivry.

I tried to reason with her: it was not a good idea; her father would be there; nothing good could come of it; she would only debase herself; it was not fitting; she would make an exhibition of herself; the story would get out. I said I could not bear to see her rejected – which I was convinced she would be. She cared for none of it. So Alice and I rode with her on that bonny April day, almost exactly a year since I had come to Breteuil.

I told her this, hoping stupidly to strike some conversation from her. She had ridden five miles in dead silence, and then at last she spoke of Breteuil.

'It is a pity you ever came to that benighted place,' she said. 'And you must leave as soon as we return.'

I felt deeply wounded by this, but there was nothing I could say. I looked at Alice and Alice looked at me. There was sympathy in her eyes. After twenty miles of almost continuous silence, we arrived at the gatehouse of Ivry Castle at sundown. The curtain wall seemed endless; the castle itself vast, proud and hostile. The Caen stone, in the setting sun, glowed with truculence.

The journey normally required an overnight stop, but Juliana had driven us to the point of exhaustion. The horses could scarcely lift another hoof. Of course, Juliana was the first to dismount, and we obediently followed suit while the beasts started cropping the grass. Approaching the massive gates, we beat at them until a porter let us in. He looked at us with disfavour. Evidently the fate of young Master Harenc had aroused considerable resentment around here. No surprise about that.

'The Comtesse of Breteuil wishes audience with the Castellan Harenc,' I told him.

He bowed stiffly and left. After half an hour or so, the porter returned.

'The Castellan regrets that he is detained.'

'Detained? He cannot be detained. I will give him detained,' Juliana cried, and ran past the porter into the bailey

We followed as best we could. Juliana arrived at the drawbridge, which was hastily pulled up, and screamed at the castle.

'Come out, Harenc. Come out and speak to me. Are you too weak to parley with a woman? Come out, I say.'

I tried to reason with her.

'He has had his son blinded. You cannot show him you have no pity, no sorrow for what has happened.'

She seemed to take something of this on board.

'I am sorry for what has happened, truly sorry,' she cried. 'It was none of my doing. I will do anything ... anything to make amends.'

The drawbridge slowly descended and the man Harenc emerged in chain-mail, crossed the moat, and stood in front of her as she knelt before him. I thought I could discern from the man's demeanour that whatever he was planning to do, he had not done yet.

'What will you do?' he asked her, sternly. 'What can you do? Can you make a blind boy see?'

'I will do anything ... everything ... if you would just give me back my daughters, safe and sound. Where are they? Bring them to me.'

She shouted their names.

'Marie! Pippi!'

'What will you do?' asked the man, coldly. 'Can you turn back time? That would be of interest.'

She could not contain the question that now burst from her.

'Have you done it? Have you put their eyes out?' she asked.

'The Duke has brought them here,' he replied, 'for me to do as I see fit.'

'I will give you land ... I will get a divorce and be your wife ... mistress ... you can have me, Castellan...'

She rose to her feet and ran her hands down her body, caressing her breasts.

'See? Am I not beautiful? You can do anything … anything you like…'

If the man did not know how much her offer had cost her, I certainly did.

He turned to walk back, and she tried to catch at him, throwing herself forward to hold on to his feet. He pushed her off roughly as her father had done, and she fell to the ground, weeping piteously. Alice and I ran to pick her up and comfort her.

'If ever I see you again, Castellan,' I shouted, 'I will kill you.'

He turned. 'In that case,' he said, 'you will be executed.'

I must say, even at that awful moment with Juliana humiliated in my arms, I was impressed. The man, like the Duke, believed in the rule of law.

Slowly, haltingly, we removed ourselves from the bailey of Ivry. No help was offered, nor would have been accepted. It was too late to return to Breteuil, so we took shelter at the sign of the Wheatsheaf in the town. We ate little and in silence, Juliana not at all. We slept in our clothes in an enormous bed in the only room left at the inn. The return journey to Breteuil is something I prefer to forget.

It takes an enormous act of will for a proud woman to humiliate herself deliberately, and I was impressed with Juliana as perhaps never before; but humiliation of the loved one does something inexorable to a lover, and it is not for the good. I felt physically sick.

All the while, my heart bled for the two little girls who were prisoners of the iron man, Castellan of Ivry. All we could do was wait for news.

XLIII

I could not talk to Juliana. She was in a world of anguish of her own. She would not eat, she could not sleep. My stomach felt as though I had eaten the leaden weight of a plumb-line. I had to go out, into the woods and fields. I walked distractedly for miles with no clear memory of where I had been.

Three days later, we had a new arrival at the castle – a tall, elderly, gaunt, kindly-looking priest called Father Geoffrey who had been a chaplain at Breteuil previously, but had gone into retreat at Lisieux Abbey, probably because he could take no more of Eustace. The Bishop of Évreux, our friend, had suggested him as a temporary replacement for My Door is Always Open. The Comte was in no state to make any decision, so Alice, acting for Juliana, had agreed that we should ask him over, and he had immediately answered the call. News of our distress had spread, and it was good to know that we still had those who wished us well.

From the frail look of Father Geoffrey, he would not be staying long. However, a sane and kindly addition to the castle's complement was a welcome arrival indeed. He took over the Chaplain's room, settled himself in and, a couple of days after his arrival, asked me to come and speak with him.

Father Geoffrey told me that he had been talking in private to the Comtesse, and offering her comfort. She had made her confession to him. This, I confess in my turn, made me nervous. I had the feeling that she might have mentioned my name in her distress among the litany of her sins. However, the old man did not appear to be viewing me with hostility, even though his next job was to give me the most dreadful commission.

Speaking for the Comte and Comtesse, he said, he must ask me to fetch the Lady Philippine and the Lady Marie from Ivry. Word had arrived that the Castellan was expecting us. I told the Chaplain that I was aware of the situation and must do as he asked, though it was a service I could not relish.

Normally, of course, it would have been the father who fulfilled such a painful duty, but Eustace was still in no condition to do anything. Whether Juliana had spoken to him privately, or the Duke had sent him some secret message, or the Chaplain had given him some godly stick, I did not know, but the stuffing seemed to have been knocked out of the man. He was inert, apathetic – and he was not even drinking quite as much. Perhaps the enormity of what he had done was finally sinking in. Whatever the reason, he kept to his room and gave me no instructions. Juliana was clearly not going to come; she was ill. Distraught and weakened by grief, she had come down with a fever that had settled on her chest.

I was given six knights and a couple of grooms to lead the ponies the girls would ride on, and God knows they would need leading. It was the most thankless and miserable task of my life, but I would have it no other way. If the girls were to come home like this, they needed someone who loved them. The old nurse was not up to it. Their mother was ill, and their father, the very instrument of their ruin. I reflected bitterly that Eustace would doubtless have been more careful of a son and not run him into such danger, humiliation and pain. At any rate, it was clear the Duke would not wish him to go. It was my duty, and I must admit that I did not feel up to it.

I was able to say goodbye to Juliana before I set off. She lay on her bed, helpless with the fever. Alice sat beside her, sponging her forehead and wiping her brow.

'Who … who is it?' Juliana asked her.

'It is Bertold come to say goodbye,' Alice told her.

'Goodbye?' Juliana looked startled and raised her head a little

I thought it better not to mention the girls. Maybe the fever, merciful at least in this, would have driven it from her mind.

'I am going away for a couple of days. I will be back,' I said.

'Oh,' she fell back.

I kissed her cheek. It burned like a turn-spit.

'Get well, dearest Juliana,' I said. 'I want to see you better when I get back.'

'I want to die,' she said, and I thought of Ovid and of the Sibyl hanging in the basket at Cumae, taunted by the boys, tormented by Apollo, unable to expire.

Juliana had not forgotten her girls. How could she?

'No, you don't,' I told her and turned away though it broke my heart to see her so.

'Look after her,' I told Alice, though the girl's devotion was plain to see.

'And you too, Bertold, look after yourself,' Alice said. 'It will not be easy. I will pray for you.'

For some reason, perhaps rashly, I leant down and kissed her on the cheek. It was cool and very slightly fragrant. She turned her face – she told me later that it was completely without thinking, and I am certain she spoke truly – and kissed me on the lips. We looked at each other for a moment, and then I broke off in some confusion and left the sickroom, heading down the stairs and out into the bailey where the men and the horses were waiting.

'All ready, sir,' said the grizzled Marshal, my friend from the melee.

'Are you coming?' I asked in some surprise.

I had always classed him as one of those who, though naturally friendly, was resolutely Eustace's military man, and considered me as some kind of clerical milkweed.

'I am for the house, sir, whatever may befall.'

'I shall be glad of your company on this occasion.'

'I thought I should come with you in case there's trouble. You never know with that lot at Ivry.'

'You've had trouble before?'

'Oh yes. They're a rough lot, tricky too.'

'There won't be any trouble,' I said. 'The Duke will be there.'

'Some say the Duke is the trouble. At any rate, I'll warrant the little girls will be pleased to see us…'

He saw the look on my face.

'In a manner of speaking,' he said.

'It is not going to be easy,' I said.

229

'Aye. I have daughters of my own. Who would have thought he could do that?'

I did not know if he was referring to Eustace, the Castellan Ralph or the Duke himself, or all three of them.

The Marshal and I led the little procession out through the gatehouse and into the town. Some of the townsfolk, going about their business, paused to watch us ride through. I thought I could detect sympathy in some of the faces. Many of the castle servants lived there, others were closely involved in supplying it, and life was closely bound up with it for good or ill.

We turned onto the road to Damville which lay some ten miles to the east, aiming to spend the night at St André which was another ten miles further on.

We rode along, companionably enough, but mostly in silence, our thoughts keeping us busy. The jingling of the harness, the song of the birds in the hedges, the smell of wood smoke, the barking of distant dogs and the measured strokes of an axe somewhere not far off as we passed – country noises speaking of peace and order – contrasted starkly, it seemed to me, with the purpose of our journey. When I thought of my little friends Marie and Pippi in pain and darkness, with their lives in pieces, and their mother's happiness destroyed, I could not help slipping into a profound dejection.

These roads were old, connecting ancient strongholds, now great castles, over ways trodden by travellers from the beginning of history, my mentor Saul had told me. The Romans had passed this way, the Gauls before them, and earlier still the giants who placed the great stones in the earth. Our way took us through open country, fields where peasants scratched an existence between serving their lord (who was Eustace around here) and eking out the short and grubby interval between birth and the grave. Yes, I was gloomy all right, and part of that gloom of course was the knowledge that nothing between Juliana and myself would ever be the same again.

Our companions talked in low voices, perhaps because they did not want us to hear what they were saying, or maybe in deference to the occasion. I gathered there was no love lost between the men of Breteuil and those of Ivry, some ancient quarrel which the insult to the two little girls did nothing to allay. I began to feel again that there would be trouble when we arrived, and questioned the Marshal about it.

'Yes,' he said, 'I was thinking the same myself, even if the Duke is there. We must take the little ladies away quickly before too many words can be said. I will tell the men that they must remain mounted and no one is to speak or gesture, whatever is said to us. We shall not give those Ivry churls the satisfaction.'

'Are you happy that we have palfreys for the girls rather than a wagon?'

'The wagon is not comfortable. Too many jolts and bumps. That would be worse for the little lasses than the easy action of a horse. We shall see when we take delivery of them, but I think they might prefer riding pillion with you and me than sitting alone.'

'You may be right,' I said, and gave him a grateful look.

I had had the same thought. The more I saw of this man the more I liked him. I was glad at least that this commission had given me the opportunity to get to know him. He had been a distant figure before, shouting at the soldiers and sorting out the pages. His office was at the marshalsea, down by the armoury, next to the parade ground, part of the world where I had not much strayed.

We came at length to Damville, a town without much to commend it: a main street, a church dedicated to Our Lady one or two richer houses made of stone, mainly peasant cottages, a forge, shops, nothing to write home about, though it did contain a large inn, where we planned to stay the night on the return journey. People looked at us warily as we rode through. It didn't do to be too curious about soldiers these days.

The men would have liked to have stopped, but the Marshal made us ride on for a couple of miles before finally pulling up at the edge of a wood. Here we ate some bread and cheese and drank from our water-bottles before moving on again half an hour later. The Marshal was keen to reach St André before dark. He wanted us to be well-rested before the rigours of the morrow; it was a stratagem that had served him well in battle.

'What is it like to be in battle?' I asked him that evening, when we were at last quartered at the sign of the Stricken Hart in St André, a pretty town with prosperous houses and a big church.

The Marshal and I had been shown a room, two beds in a garret which, though bare, was fine for our purposes; at least there were only two beds. The knights and pages dossed down in the barn behind the inn. We had come down and ordered ale and a supper of rabbit stew cooked in cider which turned out to be hearty, sustaining and even excellent. We ate and drank almost without speaking. It had been a long hard ride and we were tired.

The girl brought us two more flagons of ale and the Marshal paused to savour the first draught before answering me.

'It is like being in a butcher's shop, only you are the butcher and the meat, and the customers don't like you very much,' he said at last. 'It is a melee with knives and swords and axes from which you will be lucky to escape without some gaping wound. The unlucky die quickly. The unluckiest die long.'

'I think I get the idea,' I said. 'So why do you do it?'

'I was brought up in the business. My father was a knight. What else is there to do? I have no Latin.'

He looked at me and laughed.

'You must think me a strange sort of fellow,' I said.

'My lady does not think so,' he said thoughtfully. 'She thinks you are a good fellow – otherwise you would not be collecting her daughters tomorrow.'

'I think she is the most extraordinary woman,' I said.

He said nothing, but watched me shrewdly.

'You would be a good soldier,' he told me. 'You are tall and strong. You would take down a good few knights before your turn came.'

'You think your turn will come?'

'Of course. It doesn't do to brood on it, but every fight that passes makes it more likely.'

'Doesn't that depress you?'

'Not really. The priests say that we owe God a death. That doesn't mean I would like to be maimed. We like a nice clean death in this business.'

'Rather like a butcher.'

'Indeed. What you don't want is a leg or arm off, or a wound with bits of metal in it that turns into a festering sore. Or a thrust though your guts that slowly poisons your whole body and lets you die in agony. Or an arrow stuck in your eye that you will never get out. I have had a couple of wounds but, thank Jesu, nothing serious.'

I offered him another jug of ale, but he shook his head.

'No,' he said, 'we need to sleep early and wake betimes. We need to be fresh for whatever tomorrow brings.'

'You are right, Marshal. Thank you for your company today.'

We mounted the stairs, washed in the ewer that the girl had left on a table under the window, and composed ourselves for sleep.

'No,' the Marshal said suddenly. 'You should not be a soldier, but a general. You think well, Latiner. Anyone can charge and stab and slay. Not everyone is blessed with a brain to make stratagems, create ambushes, feign attacks, and encircle the cnemy where he least looks for it.'

'I will think about it,' I said, drowsily.

'It is a gift from God,' he told me.

I slept badly that night. My dreams were fractured and unpleasant, the girls were calling to me from an island in the middle of a lake but the island was sinking and I could not get to them. Then I arrived at a castle that I thought was Ivry, but I was alone and there was no one there. I knocked at the gatehouse and the door swung open. I went to the hall, but it was empty. Even in my sleep I recognised this as a version of the recurrent nightmare of my childhood about the deserted house. I went up the stairs ... and then I knew that someone

233

very dangerous was following me. If I could find someone in one of the rooms, I would be safe, but I came to the top and there was no one. And then the door opened and a huge figure in a suit of armour – who I knew was Eustace, but who turned into the Duke – unnaturally agile, danced across the floor and lifted his axe to strike my head off.

I woke and dawn was breaking. The Marshal was up and splashing water on his face.

'You're a lively room-mate and all,' he said. 'Muttering and moaning, thrashing about, I thought you were going to strangle your pillow…'

'Did I say anything?'

'Nothing I could understand. But there was a name you kept saying…'

'What was that?'

'Juliana.'

'Oh.'

'You poor fellow. Well, you wouldn't be the first.'

That put me in a bad mood, coming on top of my dreams. What did he mean – that Juliana had had lovers before me? The worst of it was I could not ask him. He was a good man, but I was cross with him as I dressed and followed him downstairs.

'What's the matter with you?' he asked, as I sat scowling at the gruel that the kitchen wench had served.

I had to ask him after all.

'What did you mean when you said I wouldn't be the first?' I said.

'You wouldn't be the first to fall for a great lady,' he laughed, and stopped. 'Oh no. You didn't think I was referring to her ladyship?'

I nodded glumly.

'There has been no one,' he assured me, 'at least as far as I know. Nothing's secret in a castle. God knows she deserves…'

He stopped himself out of loyalty to his lord but I knew his meaning. She deserved someone to love her and not treat her like a tiresome chattel, and worse.

'I'm sorry I was bad-tempered,' I said.

He laughed.

'Time we got going,' he said, 'though I have never been so loath to do so. I have fought in many battles, most of which I have entered with a certain misgiving – you can't help it. If you're not afraid you tend to get killed. But this is a different thing and I am full of dread at what we have to see and do this day.'

We saddled up in the stables and took the road for the river Eure and Ivry-le-Château. The men seemed restless, almost sullen, during the two-hour ride, and the horses seemed to have caught the mood. They started out sluggish and needed the spur. Then they became fractious. They shied at a mad old hag who burst out of a hedgerow and started prophesying at us. At least I supposed it was prophecy – there was a great deal of woe in it.

I threw her a coin because any diversion was better than the feeling in the pit of my stomach. I did not have the stomach for what we were about to see. The old woman had spooked the men, who now talked of curses and witches, and I too felt sick at heart.

Yet when I saw Ivry again that morning, its pale grey turrets, towers and battlements outlined against the morning sun, it seemed the very epitome of grace. I almost wanted to cross myself. I could understand now why it had caused so much division. We drew up and gazed at it.

The Marshal told us it had been the first stone castle in Normandy, built more than a hundred and fifty years ago, now with a number of later improvements. Sited on an important crossroads near the old stone bridge over the Eure, it was a very useful place to have a castle – much prized by the King of France, according to the Marshal.

'It's bigger than Breteuil,' said one of the knights. 'No wonder they're all squabbling over it.'

'They say de Montfort wanted it,' said another.

'It's not worth our two little ladies' eyes,' said the Marshal. 'Come on. Better finish what we came here to do.'

We moved on, descended a low hill and the whole majesty of the castle presented itself to us. It was built to be overwhelming.

'Wouldn't like to lay siege to that,' said one of the knights.

'It has never been taken,' said the Marshal.

We were just making sounds at each other.

We arrived at last at the gatehouse, dismounted, and gathered in a circle outside it. I was suddenly seized by an extraordinary paralysis. I was so appalled at the thought of what I was about to witness that I could not move; I could not speak. I looked at the Marshal for help and I am glad to say he was made of sterner stuff. He strode to the iron knocker on the vast oaken door and gave it good exercise. It seemed we were expected for the gate opened at once, and the same ill-featured man with lank, black hair and a lazy eye came out.

'You are to stay here,' he said. 'By order of the Duke.'

'What kind of hospitality is that?' demanded one of the knights, a forward young blade called Malet. 'No wonder Ivry has a bad smell about it.'

'You can ask the Duke if you like. He'll be here in a minute,' said the fellow, sneering. 'From what I heard, the moat at Breteuil smells bad enough to fumigate an ape house.'

Malet's hand flew to his sword, but the Marshal stepped forward.

'It would be good for us all, and the little girls who arc the reasons we are here, if we could all conduct ourselves quietly and with patience.'

The lank-haired gatekeeper seemed to take that as an apology.

'Wait here,' he said again, and disappeared into the gatehouse, closing the great door after him.

'Are they not going to even offer us refreshment?' asked Malet.

'Doesn't look like it,' said another of the knights, a tall fellow, good at the dangling-iron, I recalled. 'Better no refreshment than poison from Ivry.'

There was a murmur of assent. Then the gate opened and a small boy emerged. He had a dog with him on a lead. We could all see that he had been blinded. My heart bled for the boy, he had been a harmless and likeable little chap; now he looked totally bereft, dark saucers where his eyes had been, his life blighted, his future dark.

'Hello, Roger,' I said to him. 'It's Bertold.'

I was going to say I was so sorry about what had happened to him, but I realised it was too late for apology. Such a thing would have been bad manners. One has to look for manners at times like this; they hold one together.

It was clever of the Duke to send him out first. He had it well worked out, did Beauclerc. He knew that something of our resentment and antipathy would be allayed by the spectacle of the wronged boy, before we saw the two girls.

The next to emerge was Ralph Harenc, the Castellan of Ivry. I noticed now that he had a long scar from God knew what encounter on his face. It fitted well with his slightly hooked nose and dark eyes like bradawls.

'Aye,' he said. 'That is my son. That is the kind of hospitality we can now expect to receive at Breteuil. There is no need for me to say more. Your little ladies could have been well welcomed at Ivry, garlanded with roses. Instead we had to ask the Duke, whom we have served faithfully, to send us his grand-daughters, your hostages, to do with as we willed. It gives me no pleasure, but it is with a sense of justice performed, to deliver them to you today ... My lord the Duke says that if the laws are not followed, if the barons do not see justice done, Normandy will fall. He will not allow that to happen.'

As he said this, and I was thinking again how clever it was of the Duke to put his words in the Castellan's mouth, the door opened again and the Duke himself emerged, leading my two little pupils by the hand. I nearly collapsed. My knees went. I was in shock. My two pretty girls were almost unrecognizable, their wounds more dreadful than the boy's.

Something in my head said: of course, the wounds are more recent.

I had a strange thought, whose origin was a mystery to me. It seemed to come from far away, another world. I suppose we all have these experiences now and then. I thought: I cannot believe I am living at a time when such things happened.

What was most shocking about the treatment of the girls was not their eyes which, God knows, was bad enough. We had seen the boy, though, and knew what blinding was like, horrible though it was on a child. It was savage and painful, but you treated it with white of egg, and it healed. Afterwards you would need help for the rest of your life. You would be unlikely to marry. You would be a burden until you died, and life would be a burden to you. You would be thrust in on yourself, and it was to be hoped that you would get on well with yourself because, if you didn't, it was too bad. That was the way it was. Even so, the wounds were dreadful to see: recently scabbed and crusting; great oozing wells in which the tears mingled with the juices of healing, red and inflamed, where pieces of the connecting tissue had been broken and veins still tried to bleed.

The eyes were pitiful, but the noses were worse.

Each girl's nose had had its tip sliced off.

The wounds were raw and red and trying to scab despite the flow of tears and snot from the nostrils, but the humiliation inflicted on the little girls' was the worst part. They had been so pretty and now they had been rendered grotesque like two little pigs. Even the blind can perhaps find love and get married, but these two would surely never attract a husband. They had been condemned to shame and even ridicule as well as darkness.

'How could anyone do that?' I muttered to the Marshal.

He had seen everything that can happen to the human body when butchered with a sword, pierced with a lance or transfixed by an arrow, but still I could tell he was shocked.

The knights were moved – to anger. One of them, Malet again, uttered an oath and advanced on the Castellan, drawing his sword.

'You piece of hell-shite,' he cried. 'Is that all you are good for at Ivry? Maiming little girls. Let's see how you fare against a sword.'

'Yes,' cried another. 'Blinding was too good for them, was it? You had to add your own stroke of evil. Bravely done, Ivry.'

The Castellan's eyes blazed and he too drew his sword. His own men gathered about him, raising their weapons. It seemed there would be bloodshed at any moment.

'Put down your swords – now. All of you.'

The Duke's voice was harsh.

'Disobey me and I will see that you are executed. Justice has been done. You have nothing to complain about.'

'You set this ball rolling,' said the Castellan, aiming his words at the Marshal.

'Yes. And you went further than you need have done. What purpose did it serve?'

'My grand-daughters do not need to hear all this,' said the Duke, sternly.

'That is all very well,' I suddenly heard myself saying, 'but it was your hard will that brought them to this pass. You have saved yourself trouble, but you have willed it on the innocent. You have made an enemy of your daughter and appeased uncertain enemies and dubious friends. You have become a monster.'

'Who is that man? What is your name, fellow?'

'Bertold, sir. Bastard son of the Comte de Perche.'

'Well, bastard son. You are going to discover what it is like to feel the wrath of a king. Take him away.'

Two men advanced on me and fastened my hands behind me.

'You cannot do that. Your grand-daughters need me, sire.'

'My grand-daughters need rest and food. They need to heal. They need their mother and their home. That is all the need they want. And what I do not need is truculence and turbulence and impertinence from a nobody. You are nobody, bastard. You do not even exist. You are like something seen at dawn, out of the corner of an eye, that vanishes. Take him away and forget about him.'

They were just dragging me away, protesting loudly to the Duke, when an imperious voice rang out.

'No!'

We all turned in astonishment. The voice appeared to have come from the face of the girl who had been Marie.

'I wish my tutor to take us back to Breteuil.'

The Duke started to argue, but there was no arguing with his grand-daughter who had the Conqueror's blood in her veins.

'It is best he stays here. He is insubordinate and must be punished.'

'You have done enough punishing. Punish yourself.'

Yes, it did seem to us all that the great Duke suffered from some compunction. I think he was as impressed as we were by the courage of the girl. Her younger sister too had stopped weeping and stood proudly beside her.

'Very well. If that is what you wish. I will not stand in your way. You, bastard, FitzRotrou or whatever you call yourself, look after my grand-daughters and don't let me see you again. Keep out of my way. Do you understand? Next time you may not have such a good advocate.'

'Yes, sire,' I said. 'But may I say one last word?'

'No.'

'Please tell your castellan, sir, to keep out of *my* way. My sword has his name written on it.'

'You don't have a sword,' scoffed the Castellan.

It was perfectly true. You could hardly call what the Brothers at the abbey had given me a sword. I had never had much use for them.

'Well, if it comes to that,' said the Marshal, 'he can borrow mine.'

'And mine.'

'And mine.'

The air was full of swords being proffered.

'Thank you, sirs,' I said, bowing.

Then I turned to the girls.

'Do you want to ride your ponies or ride pillion with me and the Marshal?'

'Pillion,' they said together.

I am afraid to say they both wanted to ride with me, which made me feel sorry for the Marshal. We came to a compromise that they should change places at St André, and so without farewells, but with hearts lifted by the bravery of the young ladies, we rode off into the morning, back the way we had come.

'I never thought to see the Duke abashed,' the Marshal said to me as our horses plodded, side by side, up the hill away from the river. 'It does not come to him naturally.'

XLIV

The ride home was almost cheerful for the two little girls were so glad to be back among those who loved them, and to be coming home, that they bore their pain and indignity bravely and would not allow us to be saddened. Their wounds, thank the Lord, appeared to be healing well. I had examined them for any trace of unusual reddening or the gathering of evil matter. When we stopped at St André for the night, I applied some healing balm from Brother Paul that I had in my travelling bag, and let God do the rest.

It was only when we were approaching Breteuil that I began to be uneasy again. How was their mother going to bear up when she saw her lambs so wounded and disfigured? Knowing her as I did, I feared she would run mad and do something that would harm her and maybe harm us all. There was no doubt in my mind that she would hold her husband responsible. She would very likely want to kill him, and when there is discord of this kind in a house it affects all those who live in it.

I expressed something of this to the Marshal when we stopped near Damville for refreshment, just a few miles from home, and I could talk to him away from the girls and their sharp ears.

'It is a bad thing for all of us,' said the Marshal, 'when something like this happens, it is bound to affect morale. Our knights here will talk and when the word gets round that the Comte has been responsible for the maiming of his daughters. There will be shock and revulsion. It will spread to the town and the whole neighbourhood will know, the whole county. Our friends will feel sorry for us and our enemies will laugh. We can only hurt little girls, they will say. We need something to make us feel better.'

'What can I do?' I asked.

'You have influence with Lady Juliana. Stay with her and see that she does not do anything to make our house of Breteuil suffer further. Revenge must be close to her thoughts at the moment. Try to persuade her to do nothing immediate.'

'My old tutor used to work with Sicilians at the hospital in Salerno. He told me they have a saying that revenge is best eaten like *vitello tonnato*.'

'What is that?'

'Thinly sliced roast veal on a bed of cooked tuna fish beaten into little pieces, mixed with a sort of savoury cream.'

'It sounds disgusting.'

'He said it was rather good.'

'And what is that to do with revenge?'

'It is served cold.'

The Marshal smiled.

'You tell her that, Master Latiner. I think she'll like it. Meanwhile, what are you going to do now your charges are in this sad condition? Latin will not perhaps be possible now. If you should contemplate a change of employment in the future, I am sure we could offer you a job as a soldier. You ride a horse well, you are good at the melee, you fight better than that oaf Fulk, and you speak Latin – always useful on the battlefield...'

'Thank you,' I said. 'You certainly know how to compliment a man.'

He laughed for the first time since we had collected the little girls.

'You would make a good soldier. I am sure we could enlist you with the knights after a week or two. What do you think?'

I thought about it as we walked. It was true, the Comtesse might very well have no use for me now. If that were so, there would be nothing to keep me at Breteuil or any of the Comte's castles. What would I do? The last thing I wanted was to return to my father wearing a beggar's hat.

I turned to the Marshal, gratefully.

'I am honoured by the suggestion,' I said. 'But I am my lady's servant. She found me and brought me here. If she still needs me, I must remain. If not, of course, your offer would be very welcome, though I do not think I could serve in the Comte's army.'

'That is fair,' he smiled. 'But there are times when it is better to have some employment than none. We need good men. There are so many evil ones about.'

I walked on more cheerfully, as we rejoined the party. It is always good to make a friend. But when we finally arrived at the castle, there was little cheer to be had. The usher must have briefed to warn her, for no sooner had we walked into the hall, than Juliana appeared, pale but evidently recovering from her fever, and lovelier than ever in a fine blue dress.

She ran down the stairs to the girls, ignoring the rest of us completely, gathered them up without stopping to look at their poor little faces, and took them with her up to her quarters. She said not a word. We took no offence. We all looked at each other, and that was that. The Marshal indicated to me that I should go up, but I knew Juliana better than he did. When she wished to be alone, you intruded at your peril.

Finally, the Marshal and the knights went back to their quarters, and the crowd disbanded. There was no sign of Eustace. Later that night, after a supper of ale and cold meats, I went up to Juliana's chambers and knocked on the door. She had evidently washed the little girls with the help of the old nurse, dressed their wounds with some of the salve I had given her, and put them to sleep in her own room. It seemed that she was proposing to sit up beside them all night. I took her in my arms when the maid withdrew and found that she was shaking. I thought that she was weeping, but it was pure rage. I did not want to wakc the girls so I took her into an ante-chamber.

'It is not possible,' she kept saying. 'It cannot be. It could not be done. Whoever heard of it in the history of the world?'

'You must keep calm,' I said, stupidly.

'Why should I? Just wait till I catch him and then we shall see.'

'Who do you speak of, Juliana? Tell me. Speak to me. I am your friend.'

'The bugger,' she said, 'the shit turd of the devil's own arsehole.'

A string of worse expletives followed which, though I am no prude and have sworn with the best, I still cannot bring myself to write down. It would traduce her memory. Sufficient to say that they were ripe. The worst thing was hearing such foulness from a mouth that was sweeter than roses. Where had she learned such a repertoire? She must have been hanging round the stables on pay day.

'Who are you talking about? Eustace?'

She stopped ranting and looked at me intently.

'Who are you anyway?'

'I am Bertold, as you know.'

'Don't you see what they have done?'

I was afraid she was going mad.

'I see only too well,' I told her.

'How can you see only too well when my daughters are blind?' she said, combatively.

She had not thanked me for bringing her daughters home from the Castle of Despair, nor did I need thanks, but I thought I should mention it if only to distract her from her convulsion.

'I know they are blind because I collected them on your behalf from your father and his castellan.'

'Don't mention their names. I have no father.'

I thought it better to leave. I was evidently doing no good.

'Don't go,' she said. 'Hold me. I must not go mad. I must be strong. I feel my life has ended, just as theirs has. Whatever I can do for them, if I devote my whole life to them – as I will – I can never make up for what has happened.'

I embraced her, held her to me. Even or especially in her distress, I was almost undone by desire for her, but it would have been worse than discourtesy to show it at that moment.

'I love you,' I said, simply.

'Fuck me now,' she said. 'Take me. Do what you will.'

She started tearing off her clothes and lay down on the truckle-bed in the corner of the little room, spreading her legs.

How much I wanted to possess her now, in this whore mode of hers that had never been displayed before. In every mode she was delicious. But I would not do it; and indeed I could not. I saw her on the grass beside the Castellan's long legs.

'No,' I told her.

She cursed me.

'Fuck you,' she said. 'Bastard.'

She arranged her dress, folded in her legs, and stood up, defiantly, completely unabashed by her extraordinary invitation to me. She was reckless, extravagant, possessed.

'I will love you always,' I said.

'What are you talking about?' she asked, as if I had been offering her oranges. 'Don't you see? Everything is ruined. You'd better go. I shall be myself or something like it in the morning. We shall pretend to the girls that everything is normal, that to be blind and to look like a little pig is the most normal thing in the world. We shall pretend to be blind ourselves. You shall be a pig and teach them blind Latin.'

'I will teach them Latin,' I said, rather doubting that was what the girls would want to do. 'The drawing classes we will have to cancel, but we will play with words.'

'Thank you, dear Latiner,' she said, suddenly relenting. 'That is a good idea.'

She laid a hand on my arm.

'Who were you calling a shit just now?' I asked. 'Did you mean Eustace?'

'No, of course not. Eustace is a fool. He is a fool who thinks he is clever, and that's a real fool. The shit is my father. He is the one who's going to suffer.'

'It will be hard,' I said. 'He doesn't suffer easily.'

'I will surprise him. You can be sure of that.'

'The Sicilians have a thing they call vendetta,' I told her. 'I was speaking of it to the Marshal. It can be a long business, but they never forget an injury, and it has to be avenged.'

'That sounds good to me, Latiner. That is what I'll do. Vendetta. I will have some of that.'

I left her and went to my little room. I was tired as a dog after my travels, and my home-coming had tired me more. I fell asleep at once, but at some point of darkness, probably about

247

prime, I felt or dreamt again the presence of someone enter my little chamber and stand for a while, watching me pensively, before departing.

XLV

Next morning, I woke early again and walked in the bailey as the sun rose, meeting the Marshal about his business in the marshalsea as he talked to the head groom.

He greeted me and bade me good morning, and I asked him where the Comte was, since this was an issue uppermost in my mind. I rather dreaded meeting the man again. One's own anger is rather frightening; there is no knowing where it will go. The Marshall put my mind at rest.

'He has gone to his castle of Pacy with some of his men, thirty miles from here. We passed near it when we went to Ivry.'

'He did not think to stop and enquire after his daughters?'

'No.'

I expected no better of Eustace. A man would have stood and taken the blame for his dreadful mistake.

'Well,' I said, 'that at least will give you some peace.'

He surprised me by laughing.

'Peace is worse than war for the fighting man. It's like being a priest in heaven, no one has need of you.'

'There will be fighting soon enough,' I told him. 'Normandy is full of people like Amaury de Montfort who cannot wait to stir something up, sack a village, rape a maid, maim a hostage, lay siege to a castle, sell his soul to the King of France…'

'And the Comte has a mind to join him. So my men and I will now be fighting against the Duke instead of for him. I cannot make sense of this country … who I'm fighting or what I'm fighting for … When both sides are wrong, where is the right?'

'You are a soldier … I suppose that is what soldiers do. They fight for whoever it is that pays them,' I said.

'Some do – Italians, Swiss, Flemings,' he replied. 'But mostly we fight for our liege lord. He calls us out and we fight – to the death, if need be. I have thought more about it. I am the

Comte's man for better or for worse. At the moment, after what he has done to the young ladies, I would not mind so much fighting the Duke, but he is the Comte's lord which means it would be a great offence to fight him – an even greater offence for the Comte, so I should try to stop him – but he is my lord and commands me to fight … Do you see my problem?'

'It is a predicament,' I told him.

'You will remember my offer, won't you?' he said.

At this moment, I saw, over his shoulder, the Comtesse coming out of the hall and looking across towards me.

Asking the Marshal to excuse me, I turned and hurried over the grass to meet her. There was no knowing what sort of mood she was going to be in today, but I was anxious to know how the little girls might be feeling after a good night's sleep.

'Good morning, my lady,' I said, neutrally cheerful. 'The grass is wet. I fear for your feet in those shoes. You do not need to get another chill. Let me take you in.'

There was a mist on the lake, the cold dew lay on the grass and I saw that Juliana was only wearing little, delicate slippers.

'Please do not speak to me as though I am a madwoman,' she asked. 'I was distressed yesterday, and I did not thank you properly for collecting Marie and Pippi, and bringing them home.'

'It was nothing,' I said. 'I was honoured to do it, and I made friends with the Marshal who is a good man, though rather stretched in his loyalties.'

'As well he might be. He and some of the knights are leaving soon and going to my husband – that vile thing it pains me to name – at Pacy, where the household will be going and I too in due course.'

'You must be cold. Let me take you inside,' I urged, but she shook her head.

'Let us walk in the herb garden over by the wall. The sun is warm there.'

'What about me? Will I be going to Pacy?' I asked.

Her brow wrinkled a little.

'I don't know,' she said. 'We will not be going yet. I have more to do here.'

I realised then that it was over between us. Her father had spoken to her and – though she was on bad terms with him at the moment – she accepted the truth of what he had said. There was no future for us and, what was worse, it tarnished her name. It had to stop. My position was untenable..

'I understand,' I told her. 'There is no work here for me now.'

'It's not that,' she said. 'The little girls still want to learn Latin. They told me so this morning.'

'It will be hard for them if they cannot see.'

'Everything will be hard for them if they cannot see, but that does not mean it cannot be done. They can still have accomplishment. I want them to have accomplishment.'

'Is that what they want?'

'They do not know what they want. One thing they do not want is pity. They have a strange pact between them. They will not give in. The pain made them cry, but that is over now. Strange, is it not? You can take the eyes out, but they can still weep. But now the girls will not. They are, after all, of the Conqueror's blood.'

In spite of the effort she was making, I could see that she was crying now.

'They thought I could do anything. I was their mother. I could give them a party, make them a dolly, tell them a story, take them on a picnic, heal their cuts, soothe their bruises, kiss them better; they thought I could do anything, whatever happened. And then someone came and put their eyes out and sliced their noses off. And I could not do anything. Now they realise I cannot do anything. Nothing to make it better. Nothing I can do, nor ever will.'

She banged her head against the old stone wall. She turned to me again, her forehead bleeding.

'You do realise, don't you, Latiner? It's the end of everything.'

I was seriously worried for her. She was blown about like a leaf in the wind. You have never seen such hopelessness. I realised that she blamed herself for the whole sorry business. She had seen it coming from the moment that the Duke had suggested taking her daughters away. She should have fought her father over that, but she had been distracted. She must blame me now as much as anyone. I would not leave her alone. Madness walked in that castle, I tell you.

'Come inside, your forehead is bleeding,' I urged her again. 'Have you had breakfast yet? You must eat.'

'It would choke me.'

'The Marshal offered me a job,' I told her, as we walked on.

She looked at me incredulously.

'You're not going to take it? One of Eustace's knights? You could never do that. And, if you did, he would see to it that you were the first to be killed in battle.'

'Not before I slid a knife between his fat ribs.'

She gave a mirthless smile. I could see her considering the idea.

'No,' she said, 'you are not going to be a soldier. I see you on a ship, but not as a sailor. I see you as … a merchant. Learn to be a merchant, Latiner, one of the new money men. You can do anything with money. Buy land and people. Lend it to the Duke and become a comte. Then you can marry me and the girls can come with us and be happy.'

She looked almost joyful for a moment, and then her face fell again.

'No,' she said. 'Too much has happened. Let us talk later about it. I must go to the girls now and help them dress.'

'Their nurse can surely do that for you,' I said, foolishly.

I simply wanted her to stay, but she rounded on me.

'They will want their mother,' she blazed. 'And I will want them. Nothing will separate us now.'

XLVI

She was wrong about that, as it happened.

The castle returned to a semblance of normality. The staff were somewhat diminished as the usual retinue had gone with the Comte to Pacy. I was glad to note that the Marshal still remained with us, though it was inevitable that he too would be called.

I tried teaching the girls a little Latin, and reading them extracts in French from Ovid, little stories of the more repeatable kind from his *Metamorphoses*, and tales of ancient Rome, but I could see their hearts were not in it. They were thinking of something else. They were very polite and tried to be attentive, and it made my heart bleed. I read them other stories and made some up, and then there were fairy tales that my mother used to tell.

They liked those and their little blind piglet faces lit up in a way, but it was like talking to people who were moving on. They were already on the way. They did not complain, in fact they conducted themselves with the greatest dignity, so much so that it worried me.

I tried them on their ponies again which they had used to love, but that was not any good. They were just jogging around in the dark and getting nowhere. I took them to the herb garden where they could smell growing things, although it was late for the pungency of summer. They sniffed with their poor little noses, but some of the power of smell seemed to have gone too. They held my hands tightly and walked sedately on either side of me, or stood together, hands entwined.

In the castle, they took to explorations on their own, quite dangerously, when the old nurse dozed off. They fell down some steps on one occasion, quite a short flight, and told no one about it but me. They said I was not to tell anyone, it was their adventure. They had so little to amuse them that I did not have the heart to sneak on them.

I tried to interest them in music, getting one of the castle musicians, an old man from the Pays d'Oc, to play to them on his rebec and show them how it was done. They listened politely, but the exercise did not catch fire. They liked the sound but not the instruction.

I did not like to tell Juliana of my concern because I feared it would drive her further into despair. The very sight of her daughters brought on such a self-loathing in her now that it might have been better for her to stay away, but of course they needed her. I did mention to the Marshal that the guards should keep their eyes open for the girls on their strange little adventures around the place, holding the walls and feeling with their feet for the next step. When I was in charge of them, I kept a strict eye on them both which of course they did not notice – unless I happened to stop them tripping over a chair – but I could not do so all the time, nor could the old nurse herself. There were other girls, under-nurses who shared the duty.

'It is unnatural,' I said to Alice, who came to see me sometimes in my little room, or whom I met in a shack where hay was kept near the curtain wall where we could talk. I had not forgotten her kiss, and I began to love Alice, though in a different manner, a different key, from the way I felt about Juliana. Juliana was the adored, Alice was the friend. Juliana was the unattainable whom I somehow managed at times to attain; my coinage was worth less than hers. Alice and I lived in the same country, on equal terms. I had to be at my best with Juliana. With Alice, I could be myself.

Juliana had found Alice and liked the look of her. Perhaps it was the difference between them that attracted her. Alice was as dark as Juliana was fair. Alice was a sea-witch, with very white skin and luminous large eyes which kept sailors from the rocks … or not.

'It is not unnatural that the girls should want to explore their home,' she said. 'They knew it well when they could see, now they have to discover it all over again.'

'They seem to be intent on something.'

'They are intent on not falling over.'

I left it at that. Something about them troubled me; but of course everything about them troubled me. They had been such charming little girls. Now they did not want to share who they were. They did not want to come down to the hall, for instance. I could understand that; who wants to be gawped at by scullions and pantlers? But still it made their solitary life more solitary if they would not even eat one meal with the household.

The melancholy quality, which you sometimes feel in spring when the year seems to be going somewhere that you're not, made the girls' predicament seem all the worse to me. They sat by themselves whispering to each other, intent little pig princesses. Do not mistake me: my heart bled for them.

The half-emptied castle seemed to echo with whispers. Most of the musicians had gone, along with the dwarf-jester Serlo the Stupid, who made Eustace roar with laughter because he was even more stupid than Eustace himself. I almost missed Serlo, what with the cold and the echoes and Juliana preoccupied. I wanted his stupid jokes and his tumbling and tripping and his dreadful songs out of tune as he accompanied himself on a little toy vielle, 'my little veely' he called it.

'Like to feel my veely?' he would call to the ladies, and it was rumoured he had quite a number of pretty women feeling him all over.

It just shows you what a pretty pass we had got to, that I wanted the tiresome man back.

The wind had gone round to the north, and the castle was cold. I know quite a lot about cold places having been in that monastery for seven years. And at the castle of Mortagne, my father was not one to waste wood. It takes a hundred years to grow a decent oak, and a day to burn it, he used to say. The east wind would catch Mortagne and make its stones so cold even the gargoyles on the chapel would weep.

But this cold at Breteuil was something different. It was a bitter, damp, arse-clenching cold, coming off the expanse of water that lay around. Lovely in summer, fog-infested in autumn, an ice-field in winter, and a wind-catcher in spring –

the cold wreathed into the chinks and crannies of the castle, so that you could hear the very stones shiver in their places.

It was at this time that Juliana sent a message to her father, proposing that he should come for a little peace-making with her and her daughters. The message took the form of a letter which she insisted I myself (in spite of the bad terms on which I had parted from her father) should deliver to Ivry where Henry had made his base. He was engaged in some head-banging among the eastern marches of Normandy, keeping an eye on Évreux where de Montfort was still causing trouble, and Louis-baiting, with his soldiers rattling their lances under the battlement of certain castles and marching through towns which Louis doubtless thought were loyal to him.

'Bring him back with you, if you can,' Juliana told me. 'I shall be ready to receive him.'

I truly thought that she had subdued her maternal rage, had forgotten her thoughts of terrible revenge, and meant to seek rapprochement. How little I knew that magnificent creature! I assured her I would do my best.

I rode over quickly, glad of the action, and also glad because it would give me the chance of renewed acquaintanceship with the barmaid Yvette at St André, a pretty redhead who had smiled at me last time and let me kiss her before breakfast. I had needed cheering up on that sad journey, and sometimes sorrow, especially other people's, kindles a kind of desperate and regrettable lightness in the lover as if one is throwing off a cloud and behaving badly seems a kind of exorcism. That was how it was with me, and I record it with shame. This time it went even better with Yvette after supper, until a burly wagoner who thought he had a better claim started to call me names and push me about. I took him in one of those wrestling moves that Brother Paul had taught me and threw him down the stairs. It did not go down well with his friends – or the landlord. The result was that I had to sleep in the stables. Happily, Yvette brought me breakfast, let me kiss her again and allowed me a second course, so it was later than I meant when I took the road again, passing the wagoner on my way out of town who threw an apple at my head and made Blackberry (none the worse for her ride with Alice) shy and skitter sideways.

I started out feeling pretty good that morning because it was almost May, the sun had come up and the fog rolled away like smoke from a burning town, only it wasn't a burning town which made me feel even better. And then I thought of the little girls who wouldn't be feeling good at all, and I felt wretched because I had betrayed them as well as Juliana.

By the time I reached Ivry, my bonhomie was a distant memory. Castles were built to inspire dread and Ivry was the archetype; foreboding hung around it like its resident crows. I beat at the massive gate and there was no answer. I beat again, and still nothing. I beat a third time and a surly shout could be discerned through the huge oak frame.

'All right, all right, I'm coming.'

Finally the bolts were drawn and the door opened, revealing a blear-eyed rogue wiping his mouth on the sleeve of his leather jerkin. It was the same rascal porter we had noted before. He liked to keep people waiting.

'Oh, it's you,' he said. 'I thought it was the Duke's messenger. If I had known it was you, I wouldn't have hurried.'

I wasn't going to be riled, though. I had strict instructions to be graceful and obliging.

'You can't come in,' he continued. 'Instructions of the Castellan.'

'I have a message for the Duke from his daughter, the Comtesse de Breteuil.'

I showed him the letter I had brought.

'They don't want nothing to do with you lot.'

'That is surely for the Duke to say. Take the letter, please.'

He looked at the scroll as if it might bite him.

'I dunno about this,' he said.

I knew the trick, and handed him some money. The Marshal had told me I would find it useful.

'I'm not sure,' he said.

I handed over the second purse and the man seemed to cheer up fractionally.

'You can't come in,' he told me again. 'Not to the castle.'

'I don't want to come in. I just want the Duke's reply.'

'Wait here,' he said, admitting me to the gatekeeper's lodge which smelt bad, but at least it was warm.

The porter trudged off and I studied the view of the castle through the porter's window. It was a huge place, and in better order than Breteuil. The men who moved about the bailey had a certain air about them, and I thought the Castellan must deserve his high regard in the Duke's eyes if he could keep the place looking so chipper. I waited comfortably enough for half an hour, but then I grew impatient, and walked out into the bailey to have a look around.

The marshalsea and stables were well-maintained and clean, and the horses seemed to be in good order. I stroked a couple of the big Percheron beasts from home, told them I was from the same place, and finally moved on to the armoury when a voice called on me to stop.

It belonged to the Castellan who had appeared from nowhere.

'What do you think you're doing?' he asked. 'Come to spy, have you? We have a place for spies here. Men! Take him away.'

Before I could protest, two burly soldiers had pinned my arms and, while I feebly protested my innocence, started dragging me towards the castle.

I had heard about the dungeons of Ivry, and what I had heard did not endear them to me. There was a children's story about them. Once you got in, you never got out.

'The Duke's business,' I told them. 'That is why I am here. Your porter has just gone to the hall to deliver it. I need a reply.'

'Brought your sword with you?' he asked.

The Castellan walked beside me as I was half-lifted, half-hauled to the steps of the hall, and then dragged up them. The hall was empty. Where the porter had gone, God alone knew.

Soon I was being man handled down some more steps, this time to the dungeons.

They smelt bad, I can tell you. I would rather have the porter's lodge aroma a thousand times. These dungeons smelt of despair and pain. They smelt of hopelessness and cruelty. They were cold as death and clammy as the grave. The soldiers clamped shackles on my feet. A gaoler from one of the lower reaches of hell, bearing a lamp, appeared through an open doorway. The soldiers took their leave and tramped back up the stairs. I heard the door shut somewhere above me. The sound seemed to seal any hope I might have had of leaving this place.

'This way, my lord,' the gaoler said, as if reading my thoughts, 'I think we can make you comfortable here. How many nights was you thinking of staying?'

'There's been a mistake,' I told him. 'I gave the gatekeeper a letter for the Duke from his daughter. She would like a reply.'

The gaoler opened a door and thrust me inside. I fell on the floor, rather heavily. It is not easy to walk with shackles on, believe me.

'A likely tale,' said the gaoler, shining the lamp upon me. 'No, what you really wanted was to sample the hospitality of the Ivry dungeons. They are legendary. In a recent survey commissioned by none other than the Duke himself we came top for sheer dungeon quality. And now you have achieved your wish. Our beds are especially singled out for praise…'

He pointed to some dirty straw in the corner.

'And for food and drink there is nothing to compare with our stale bread and foul water. If you wish for anything further, do not hesitate to call. This is the key to your quarters. Do not worry about losing it because …' and here he let himself out, locking the iron grill after him, '…because I am throwing it away.'

With that, rather theatrically, he did so. I heard it tinkle away into an obscure corner and then I was alone. I was filled with a sort of incredulous alarm. This was absurd, unfair, but yet there was no law against it. I was in the keeping of the Duke. It was said that Henry kept his brother, the previous Duke, in similar circumstances. He was quite a man, our Henry.

I spent the rest of the day considering my fate and shouting for the gaoler. Neither activity led to any noticeable result. I had no way of marking the passage of time since my cell admitted no light. My stomach was my best clock and it began to tell me in no uncertain terms that it was dinner time. After a seeming eternity, the sound of shambling footsteps announced the approach of the gaoler, bearing a hunk of bread and a pitcher of water. The bread was, as promised, stale and the water was as cold as the Castellan's charity, but it was better than nothing. I ate and drank and, there being nothing better to do, I lay down on the straw in the corner, thanking God that I had brought a heavy cloak with me against the early morning chill at Breteuil, and addressed myself to sleep.

It seemed that I had only slept for half an hour when the gaoler appeared again bearing another crust and more cold water.

'Your early morning call, sir.'

'Ugh.'

'Brought you breakfast in bed,' he continued.

The thought crossed my mind that he was playing a trick on me and it was the middle of the night, but I had no option but to go along with him.

'I expect you would like a pen and ink and some parchment,' he said, 'so you can write home and tell them what a lovely time you are having. But they would be no good to you in the dark.'

'Well, bring me a light,' I said, rather too testily.

'There you have the problem,' he said. 'You've put your finger on it. Shortage of candles. King Louis, he's bought up all the candles so the Duke has to entertain his guests in the dark. That's the long and the short of it, sir, a typical Capet ruse. So I am afraid for the moment you will just have to twiddle your thumbs and listen to the music of the spheres which you can hear in this room of yours, if you listen hard enough, and many have come to do just that. Or wank yourself silly, another all-time favourite. But don't let it get out of hand...'

Another old chestnut. With that, he closed the door with a bang, and I was once more left with my crust and my jug – which I proceeded to knock over – and my thoughts, which were even darker than the prevailing black. Another infinitude passed as darkness chased its shadow round the day.

Half an age later, I judged it must be mid-afternoon, I heard different steps approaching. Fitter, more purposeful, steps that were used to having their own way.

'Come on, man, I do believe you have gout,' I could hear their owner say to the gaoler who rolled along behind.

'Gout, sir? No, sir?'

'You've been nipping across to the cellars and swigging my wine, you old devil. You've been feasting on pheasant and numbles. Come on, let's look at your big toe.'

'Oh no, sir, I wouldn't do that, sir.'

'Why not?'

'It'll blow your head off, sir.'

The Duke laughed. Yes, it was he. I could hear him poking the gaoler in the ribs. He even chuckled. It is a disgusting sound to hear in a dungeon. It sounds like a life sentence.

'You old devil,' he said.

The next thing I heard was the door being unlocked, and a bulky shadow showed itself against the lantern light.

'Oh dear,' boomed the now familiar voice, 'what have we here, gaoler? A fish? It doesn't smell too good.'

'It's a day and half old, sir. Imagine what it'll be like in three years.'

'Stand up and show yourself, Mr Pisces Latiner,' the Duke commanded.

'I must thank you for your hospitality, sir. I had no idea you had a jongleur looking after your cellars. He has kept me very well amused.'

The Duke laughed, rather brutally, I thought.

'You don't fool me, Latiner. You were shitting your pants. You thought you were here for good, didn't you? And you thought: what good will my Latin do me here? Or the pretty Comtesse's favours...?'

'It is true,' I said, 'that I was thinking of making a complaint to the Chamberlain about the quality of the bedrooms here. But after all, you only have an uncouth castellan to look after the décor, a man who is rather better at slitting children's noses than matching the wall-hangings with the rugs...'

I knew I had struck home because the amused smile vanished from the Duke's face, and a look almost of shame flitted across it, quickly to be replaced by severity. I was indeed shit-scared now.

'Well,' replied the Duke, 'you have a ready wit, Latiner, and no doubt the ladies will laugh at it, but I rather think it is going to get you into trouble one day, if it has not done so already. Don't you know ...' and here he became really alarming and my knees nearly gave way, 'don't you know that I can keep you here, without trial or recourse to escape, for as long as you are alive and longer. No one will know what has happened to you, you will simply vanish like mist before the sun and you will cease ever to have been. That will be the beginning of the end of clever Mr Latiner when this door next shuts. So keep a simple tongue in your head and listen to me. If you give me false answers, I shall know you lie, and you will never leave here. The letter you have brought says my daughter wishes to make peace with me. Is that so?'

'Yes, sir.'

'Does she really mean that, or is there more?'

This was difficult. Knowing Juliana, I suspected that there might be more, but she had not told me of it. I thought it best to tell him so. It seemed to please him.

'So you suspect that there might be a trap?'

'She is very upset, sire. As you might have been...'

'I see. The Comte is at Pacy, I understand.'

'I believe so, sire.'

'So why does she stay at Breteuil?'

'The girls apparently prefer it. And she is doing all she can to please them.'

'And she cannot stand the sight of him?'

'Yes, sire. That too.'

'You are doing well, Latiner. I am almost minded to release you and send you back.'

'That would be in the best traditions of Beauclerc, sire. It would be magnanimous and it would be well-considered.'

The Duke smiled.

'So you would be a courtier, Latiner?'

'Oh no, sire, not I. Far too dangerous.'

The Duke laughed.

'Very well. We will let you go. Take his shackles off, gaoler.'

The monster bent and released my feet from their prison, bowed and withdrew.

'But I want you on my side,' Henry continued. 'If there is something I should know, you must find a way to tell me. Otherwise I shall have you back here quicker than a tart's fart. Do you understand?'

'Yes, sire. And...'

'Yes, boy?'

'There's just one thing, sire. Why did you put me down here in the first place?'

'To teach you to have a care, boy. The Comte may be a fool, but it is not good manners to make a cuckold of your lord. My daughter is a strong woman. Make sure she doesn't cut your balls off. Or get someone to do it for her. Tell her that I will be with her in four days' time. I will not stay the night.'

I told him I would do as he asked and thanked him for his advice, but he was already halfway up the steps and barely heard me. I collected my cloak from the straw, and was about to start climbing back up the stairs towards the daylight when I remembered I had something else to do. Seeing me pause, the gaoler waddled out of his cubbyhole to say goodbye.

'Off so early? I'll warrant you'll be back. We'll have your old room ready for you...'

'You'll be inside it next time I come here,' I told him.

263

'And we'll have a fire lit for you … right up your arse …' he replied, wheezing with laughter. I turned on him then.

'Was it you?' I asked. 'Was it you who put the little girls' eyes out and cut off the tips of their noses? Made them look like little pigs? Was it you, you shithead?'

The man cringed back against his cubbyhole door.

'Little girls?' he whined. 'What would I be wanting with little girls – apart from the usual. No … don't do that…'

I caught him in a wrestling feint and twisted his arm so hard I thought it would break. He screamed with the pain. It was music to my ears, like a melody my mother used to sing.

'It was the Castellan Harenc. He always has to do the executions and eye-jobs and things. I just do the small stuff like thumbscrews and pilliwinks.'

I picked him up and dumped him on the floor which jarred him a bit, and there I left it. There was no point in taking it further. Besides, he did have a sense of humour of a kind.

When I reached the marshalsea, my horse was ready saddled and waiting for me. More good Beauclerc organisation, I thought, as I took the bridle from the page who held him. There was no sign of the Duke or his dark Castellan. I would leave the Castellan to another occasion. I rode off at a trot through the gate. There was a new porter on duty who saluted smartly, one of the Duke's men, no doubt.

If that was Ivry, the Duke was welcome to it. Never have I had more joy in leaving a place.

XLVII

When I reached Breteuil next day, I found the place in turmoil. The two little girls had got themselves lost. People were scurrying about and Juliana was at her wits' end.

'Where have you been?' she demanded. 'I suppose my father feasted you and made much of you and the Castellan let you ride his best horse and hit his dangling-iron, and a good time was had by all. Meanwhile, my daughters are missing and I am…'

She burst into tears and sank into my arms. Then she sprang rather sharply back.

'Ooof,' she said, 'you smell worse than a jouster's pommel.'

I had hardly had an opportunity to wash since I had been a guest of Castellan Harenc and the Duke, so I took her comment rather hard. And where had Juliana learned phrases like that?

'Your father had me flung into his dungeons for two days,' I told Juliana, 'without any hope of getting out, and then he came and told me it was all a joke, but if I didn't tell him what you are planning, he would put me back in the dungeon again forever. He can do that, can't he? There's no law against it.'

'The bastard!'

'That's what I thought.'

'Well, I was going to tell you what I've planned to do to my father, but now I won't because you'll pass it on next time they catch you.'

'Maybe later?'

'No.'

She was almost back to the old Juliana, I thought, yet it wasn't the same; perhaps it was too soon.

'What about the girls? Where are they?' I asked.

'They love playing hide and seek – and they are getting too good at it. This time, we've really lost them. I'm sure they're all right, but we can't find them. They love it when we lose them.'

I now saw the point of the girls' determination to explore the castle by touch. They knew the place inside out. They knew something we didn't.

'I'll find them,' I said. 'But first I'd better wash.'

'No,' she said. 'First find the girls, then wash, and then you can claim the reward.'

'What is the reward?'

'Better wait and see. It has the pages very excited.'

She wore a gown in the new fashion that showed her ankles. It had been preached against in Paris, apparently. I took it as a sign that she might be recovering her spirit after the last few dreadful weeks, and I could even imagine tasting the joys again that had been so long withheld. I am afraid lust is no respecter of sorrow; indeed it is sometimes inflamed by it.

Anyway, first I had to find Marie and Pippi. All the obvious places had been searched, but where would be the best place for those who judged by touch? Somewhere in the dark, of course! Now, where was the darkest place in the castle? Memories of my own childhood came back. My stepfather, the cellarer, looking for me, calling my name when I didn't want to run an errand for him. The cellars! That's where they would be hiding, in an alcove, behind a barrel where nobody but a child could find them.

And that, indeed, was where they were; concealed behind a hogshead of '07 Burgundy, and a very good choice they had made – an excellent year with a burst of berry fruits tickled with a hint of wild strawberry on a bed of sun-dried apricot, fresh nectarine and prune. My stepfather in Mortagne always prided himself on his taster's vocabulary.

'In the dark, we are the ones with eyes,' Marie told me gravely.

'We are like moles,' said Pippi. 'With our little snouts.'

It made me weep to see them so brave. I returned them to their mother who was quite overcome, hugged them both and scolded them at the same time for giving us all a fright. She gave me a look of such gratitude which I interpreted as love so all I could see was stars. But it was just gratitude after all because when I went to her chamber afterwards and hoped that we might retire to the wardrobe, whose wafts of spice I would ever afterwards associate with the act of love, she gently deflected my passion and spoke only of her sorrow and despair.

So it was then, suddenly, in an upper room, with my member half erect as it touched the golden thread of her gown, that I realised that this phase of my life – the Juliana time – was over, and that all her thoughts and care must now be for her daughters. I could no longer dream of being part of her body or her life; I was simply not important enough. It was a horrible moment, I can tell you.

However, it took only a few more days for me to understand that there was something more. It was not only a mother's feelings for her grievously wronged daughters that had robbed me of Juliana, but something of which I should have taken note before. It was her hatred of her father (and perhaps by implication all men) that burned brighter and fiercer as the days went by – it was this inferno that overwhelmed our love. Love, unlike obsession, depends on some kind of input. Without that balm, the wound made by Cupid's arrow dries up or turns black. Perfect hate driveth out love. Now I could only stand aside and watch – easy to say but harder to do, because there are days when resolution turns to jelly.

It did not take long for Juliana's war with her father to move into more dangerous territory. Henry was a brave man. He was not a natural soldier and took the field as a last resort, but he was only once defeated and that was in some minor Norman skirmish. He fought against recalcitrant barons and people like Amaury de Montfort who was half-mad and liked nothing more than stirring trouble. He fought against potentates like the Comte of Poitou, who had strategic interests in furthering their territories, but he had never fought against anyone who hated him so sincerely as his daughter. He was a hard man but a rational one. He found it hard to understand why anyone should so let their emotions rule their judgment. He considered it a weakness. But it was his weakness not to take it into account, and it would nearly cost him his life.

XLVIII

The Duke arrived three days later with a small retinue. It was raining heavily in a continuous downpour like the tears of God at human wickedness, and Henry was not in a good mood. Having opened the great gates to them, the porter asked Henry and his men to wait under the archway, where their horses steamed and chafed and the puddles spread, while he hurried across to tell the usher of the arrival of royalty.

The Duke was an impatient man, and of course there was never enough time to do all the things in Normandy that had to be done so it added fire to his natural tendency. At any rate, after a brief delay, the Duke dismounted, giving his horse to a page to hold. Leaving his party to steam awhile under the arches, he strode off towards the hall as if he owned the place. When you are Duke of Normandy the whole place is yours, you can do what you like, and Henry did. He strode in today, as I say, and presented himself in his authority to the small gathering of knights who were still stationed at Breteuil and who were having their two o'clock dinner. This gathering included myself, for I had now been informally admitted by the Marshal to their company, so I was able to see the drama of the Duke's coming as it unfolded.

Henry had not thought to warn the castle of his hour of arrival or, if he had thought about it, he had dismissed the idea. So now the usher was in full agitation. He had only just finished talking to the gatekeeper, Lady Juliana needed to be warned and here was the Duke himself needing to be lodged comfortably in some state. He could not be received while a meal was in progress; there was another chamber designed expressly for this purpose, a long room entered through a doorway at the far end of the hall where a table was ready prepared, only lacking a comtesse to preside. Pages were now despatched in various directions to alert cook, butler, pantler, and of course the

Comtesse herself, while others went to the gate to bring the Duke's knights in to the hall.

The Duke meanwhile, seeing a dinner in progress, and famously loving good food and drink – especially lampreys, and there were lampreys on the table (having but recently come into season) – stopped by one of the knights whom he flattered to recognise, sat down beside him, borrowed his knife, pronged a lamprey and wolfed it down with great satisfaction, taking a big draught of the wine from the fellow's beaker. His dark mood was dissipating fast.

'By the death of our Lord,' cried the Duke, 'this is as fine a welcome as a daughter could ever give to her father. I'll have another of those, and another still. Bring me wine, good fellow...'

'But sir,' cried the usher, 'we will serve you dinner with my lady in another chamber where you can talk at peace.'

'Talk my lady's talk? What kind of talk is that when I have these good fellows to speak with?'

'Madame la Comtesse will be disappointed, sire. She especially asked to see you as soon as you arrived.'

The Duke relented. He had come in peace, hoping to patch things up with his daughter who was a good-looking girl though she had a temper like a firecracker, and he had loved her mother even though she was mad English. It was of course regrettable about his grand-daughters, but it was the parents' fault. He could not allow family matters – and she was after all only half family, being a bastard, not the same thing as his son Prince William or The Atheling as they called him in England – he could not allow family matters to usurp the place of politics and power. Families were for lesser mortals. Kings were about countries and, for your country the first thing you had to do was have a son. The second was to leave him something worth inheriting.

While all this was no doubt turning over in the Duke's mind, the acting steward (a decent little man called Gerard, standing in for the slimy Odo who had gone with Eustace to Pacy) came through the door of the far chamber, had a whispered conversation with the Marshal who in turn rose from his seat and spoke in the Duke's ear. The Duke was about to help himself to another lamprey (I have never liked the fish, too rich and far too ugly, I do not like its sucking ways which remind me of certain people), but now, casting it aside, he too rose to his feet.

'We must do what the lady wants, eh?' he said with matey condescension, and strode towards the inner room and the feast that had been prepared for him. I followed in his wake, thinking that I might be of some service, since I am half knight now, though I am still the Comtesse's Latiner and of her household.

The Duke pushed open the door and entered the chamber, and I entered with him. It was then that everything happened very quickly.

I was able to take in a sight that to me was quite impossible. My brain refused to register it for a split second. Juliana was standing at the end of the room with a fully loaded crossbow.

I had never properly understood up to that moment how completely her life had been broken when her daughters were mutilated – perhaps not being a mother I could never completely understand – but now, like a thunderclap, an awareness of her intention broke in upon me. Regardless of any consequence she was exacting her revenge.

My overwhelming thought at this stage was that it must not happen. Do not ask me why. I had no great liking for Henry, Duke of Normandy, though I was beginning to respect him. I had loved those little girls and loved them still. I suppose it was instinct, the outcast bastard preserving the status quo because he can never belong to it, whatever it was I knew that the apple cart was about to be upset, and that only I could stop it.

I had closed the door after me, understanding that Juliana would prefer it not to be a public spectacle when she spoke to her father for the first time since the terrible event. Only the Marshal was with me.

I don't think Henry saw his daughter at first. His eyes had gone to the table where the lampreys were. Out of the corner of my eye, I saw Juliana take aim. She didn't seem to be totally at ease with the weapon, but I could tell she was going to fire it. The Marshal was too far behind me to do anything. It was my call.

At this stage, time – which had been spilling out so fast – went into slow motion as if it were running in treacle. My hand went up as if to halt her, but at the same time I flung myself on the Duke who went flying sideways with me on top of him. I could tell he was not well pleased. Then came the sound that will live with me all my life, the deadly thud of the crossbow releasing, and the almost simultaneous thwack of the bolt hitting something hard. A crossbow, shrewdly aimed, will penetrate an inch of steel armour. I could sense the vibration of the bolt and knew I must be hit though I could feel nothing.

We both lay on the floor for a while, momentarily winded and eclipsed, even the great Duke.

'Oh my God … are you all right, sire?' asked the Marshal.

He was mortally afraid. It was not good to kill a Duke of Normandy. I could feel the Duke under me examining himself as best he could. At the same time I could hear Juliana struggling with the weapon for a second shot. For some reason I could not move and thought myself struck.

'I'm alive,' he said at last, 'but tell this great lump of a Latiner to move so I can get up. And take that crossbow away from my daughter.'

It takes some time to load a crossbow, even for an experienced archer. Juliana was not going to do it in a hurry. It is near impossible for a woman.

'Are you all right, Latiner?' asked the Marshal.

'I … I'm not sure,' I replied. 'I can't move.'

He looked concerned and examined me more closely, then he laughed.

'That's not very nice,' I said, 'to laugh at a wounded man.'

'You are transfixed like a stag by your coat,' he said.

And so I was. There was no extracting the bolt from the floorboard, so my coat had to be torn. The bolt was left where it had penetrated, still imperceptibly quivering. The Marshal walked across to Juliana where she stood, still struggling to re-load, and reached over to take the crossbow from her.

'I don't think you will be needing this any more, my lady,' he said.

She let him take it, but shot instead a look of pure and furious hatred at her father who had struggled to his feet beside me. It was she who found words first.

'Get out,' she said, 'you and your men, before I find some more reliable way of killing you.'

No one had spoken to the Duke like that before.

'It is I who should be killing you, Juliana,' he said, breathing deeply and reddening in the face. 'You have offended against all the laws of nature, religion, and your country. You have tried to kill your father and liege lord, and would have done so were it not for your Latiner here.'

'A curse on him,' she cried. 'Had he left it a moment later, I would have rid our country of a monster. Basely done, Latiner. Do not speak to me again.'

I had acted instinctively, and now I was indeed regretting it.

'Marshal,' commanded the Duke, 'you see how things are and the depths to which loyalty is fallen here. I command you now to take the Comtesse prisoner and escort her to the dungeons.'

'No!' I exclaimed.

The Duke barely glanced at me; he had already forgotten that I had saved his life.

But the Marshal too had his loyalties. He shook his head.

'No, sire,' he said, 'that I cannot do for I would be betraying my loyalty to this house. The lady and her children have suffered grievously at the cruelty of your servants, and it is right that she should feel – as we all felt here – that you had gone too far. This is the castle of the Comte de Breteuil and his lady, and she shall not be arrested in her own home. You came with but few men. I advise you to leave. If you wish to return with your soldiers, so be it. You have seen the warlike spirit of the lady of the house. I promise you we shall show you what the rest of us can do.'

273

The Duke listened to the Marshal with growing impatience and anger.

'Traitor,' he cried. 'I have you marked now. When I return, which I shall, and take the castle back – for it was mine and will be mine – than I shall have you swinging from the battlements, and I shall tell all who ask that this was a marshal who forgot his duty.'

The Marshal listened to him and smiled.

'You mistake, my lord Duke,' he said. 'Had I been in front and not behind the Latiner, I would have done as he did. We do not wish you dead, but if I cannot show loyalty to my lady, how can you expect me to show loyalty to you?'

'Chop logic, chop logic,' said the Duke. 'By our Lord's death, you will see some disputation when I return.'

With that he turned on his heel and went back to the hall, calling his several knights around and bidding them leave their dinner and follow him outside. They rose mid-mouthful from the table and proceeded to the marshalsea where their horses waited, still saddled. Soon they could be seen riding at full gallop out of the gatehouse and on towards the road that led to Damville and Ivry.

Juliana turned and without a word or any sign walked into the hall and mounted the great stairs. I did not think it the right moment for me to join her. I smiled at the Marshal.

'That was brave of you,' I said.

'Or bloody stupid.'

'But you could not have got her beyond the hall. The knights would not have it. There would have been a fight and the Duke's men, perhaps the Duke himself, really would have been killed. The Duke has a fierce temper, but a little reflection will surely tell him that you did the right thing.'

'He will return' said the Marshal. 'He always wanted this castle back.'

'And what about Comte Eustace? Will he be back to defend Breteuil?'

'I do not think so immediately. He has Amaury de Montfort at Pacy, drinking and plotting and talking war. We shall be alone here and cannot match the Duke, but we will fight him while we can. Tomorrow I shall call a muster and we will prepare the castle for siege order.'

'He wouldn't really hang you from the battlements?'

'Oh yes, he would. I saw him do that to Luc de la Barre. Oh no. I mistake. He would have blinded him but Luc jumped from the battlements *without* a rope round his neck before it could be done. He'll string you up too, Latiner, if he finds you here when he attacks. You had better make yourself scarce.'

'I shall remain at Breteuil,' I assured the Marshal, 'as long as you and my lady are here.'

'But the two little girls must go,' he replied. 'We can't have them here, frightened by a little war and, if we are overpowered, at the mercy of the Castellan's thugs.'

'True enough. I will speak to the Comtesse and see what she thinks. It would be best if they joined their father for the moment at Pacy. He will see no harm comes to them even if he was the cause of their ruin.'

I left him and went up to Juliana's chamber. I found her sitting in a chair, still fiddling with the crossbow, and I told her what the Marshal had been saying.

'The die is cast,' she said. 'It is war now. I will not have finished with that man until I have killed him.'

'Come, Juliana,' I told her. 'You cannot kill the Duke. He is the King. If he were simply your father you might do it, but there are too many people, good people, who depend upon their Duke.'

'Good people like that castellan?' She laughed derisively.

'No, but people like my father and the Comtesse Matilda, and many more who are loyal to him, churchmen and yeomen, who value what he has done to bring peace to the country.'

'I will be revenged on my daughters.'

'You must first dig two graves. It is another Sicilian saying,' I said, recalling the words of Brother Paul.

'Well. So be it. I will die in the attempt if necessary. Who else is to fight their battle?'

'You should take the girls away to safety,' I told her, mindful of the Marshal's advice.

'I will not leave here until I have faced my father in battle.'

'It is a battle that you will lose. He has many more men.'

'I am ready for that.'

I saw that it would be futile to argue further.

'Let me at least take the girls to Pacy where they will have a nursery and their old nurse to look after them.'

'And their father to bully them.'

'He will not do that,' I told her. 'Not now.'

'Are you deserting me, then?'

Before I could answer this, perhaps the most difficult question ever put to me, there was a cry of consternation from somewhere below. Juliana went to the door, I ran to the window, opened it wide, and looked down.

Almost immediately beneath me, in the bailey below, lay two little figures spread-eagled on the ground. They were still holding each others' hands.

'What is it?'

Juliana finding no answer at the door was looking across at me, the intimation of what I was looking at spreading across her face like the shadow of a cloud racing across the landscape. She knew before I spoke.

'It's the girls,' I said.

I could have done nothing, said nothing, to soften the blow. She sprang to the window, thrusting me aside even as I moved, and took in the scene below. And then she let out a sound that I have only once ever heard since – the noise of a man being drawn, quartered and finally castrated. Half howl, half groan; a sound telling of the deepest pit into which the human animal can fall. I could not face her anguish. I turned and ran downstairs and out into the bailey

Servants were already gathering there. The Marshal's valet, a knight called Jasper, Ralf the page, a man I had seen before in hall distributing bread, a laundress who had come in from the town with some shirts. It was good to see a woman there among all the men in that place.

I knelt and examined the girls. They were both dead. A sentry appeared, distraught, from his guard duties on the roof.

'The little girls came up there often. I never thought they could do such a thing. I turned to look at a horseman on the road. And then suddenly they were up there. I ran to stop them, but they were too quick!'

'You let this happen?' It was Juliana, raving madly at him. She seized hold of him and beat at his face with her fists until the blood ran. The Marshal did nothing to defend him. Finally, I interposed myself as best I could.

'It is not his fault,' I told her. 'They were going to do it anyway.'

Of course, that was what they had had in mind all along. Their supposed games had all been about escape. They had traced the castle with their hands, and though they were blind, their plan was clear, so clear I should have seen it. I knew the girls. They were intelligent; they could see the life ahead of them. They had no future except sitting by the fire listening to small talk. Their lives had been snatched from them by cruel men, and there was no recourse. There was nothing anyone could do to give them back what they had lost.

So they had decided. They were not going to be pitied, they were not going to be a burden, or an irritation, or have children point at them in later years and talk about the two old piggies in the corner. They were going to go out, holding hands, while people could still remember who they were, the Ladies Marie and Philippine of Breteuil, almost as lovely (people said) as their lovely mother. They had found the place they wanted, the highest point of the battlements, and while the guard commander was handing over to the new squad – inspecting men, checking weapons, passing the time of day, looking at horsemen on the road – they jumped.

They were not held up tiresomely by angels or carried to safety on the back of the castle ravens. No, they plunged to earth, holding hands all the way, and died immediately they hit the Breteuil turf, not even twitching. They were dead, and the best was yet to come.

XLIX

Juliana refused to send news of the girls' death to her husband or to her father.

'They have killed my daughters,' she said. 'You don't send funeral invitations to murderers.'

There was something in what she said. We held a little private service in the chapel conducted by the aged temporary Chaplain, and the girls were buried quietly at the southern end of the bailey, in the herb garden, where Juliana put a rosemary bush on each little grave. I wept for them, hiding my tears behind the postern doorway, hoping that no one would come out and see my unmanly distress. Juliana maintained, throughout the funeral, a face as fixed and impervious as the Caen stone of Château Ivry.

Strangely, the girls' death seemed to lighten the mood within the castle. It was almost as if their presence, alive, was too much to bear. It wasn't of course. I would far rather they had lived; I know that we could have made their lives worthwhile and interesting. I think that is true.

Juliana did not mention the girls once in the following days but busied herself with the defence of the castle. She carried that crossbow everywhere she went and in her spare moments, primed it, unloaded and primed it again. Her thoughts were on her father and she had him in her sights. She was the equal of any Flemish mercenary.

'He will not wish to destroy or burn Breteuil,' she said. 'He is too greedy to own it again. It will be hard won. And I will wing him if he gets within bowshot this time.'

The Marshal and I exchanged thoughts about the coming siege when she was out of hearing.

'We cannot hope to hold the bailey,' he said. 'Even if we had our full complement, it would be hard, but if we go back beyond the moat to the castle itself, we have some chance of holding out. Sooner or later, the Comte and his friends must come to our aid.'

'And fight against the Duke?' I asked. It seemed like treason.

The Marshal laughed. 'Why not?' he said. 'Everyone else does.'

And then he looked serious. 'I think the women should go,' he said.

'Surely the Duke would not permit any outrage?' I asked.

'The Duke is in a fury, and the Castellan is not to be trusted. He hates the Comtesse who he thinks blinded his boy.'

'This feud will go on and on,' I said. 'How can we stop it?'

'It will only be stopped when the final thing happens.'

'What is the final thing?'

'The terrible thing that makes anything further pointless.'

'I will speak to her later about leaving,' I promised him.

I visited Juliana that evening in her chamber where she was attended by Alice. Seeing them together, one so dark and one so fair, I was reminded of the happy times I had had with them both, and I was unable to speak, because sometimes desire takes you like that. I wondered whether Juliana knew that I had kissed Alice; obviously Alice knew about me and Juliana. She was fiercely loyal to Juliana, but she saw something in me that she wanted, God knows why. She was a naughty girl, and ambitious in her way.

'The Marshal and I think you should take your women and leave,' I said. 'If the Duke's soldiers take the castle, it could be dangerous for you.'

Juliana raised her chin and looked at me haughtily.

'Who is going to rape the Duke's daughter?' she asked.

'The Castellan, for a start. I have been in the dungeon's there. Juliana. They are cruel men.'

'It may have scared you, little man, but nothing will move me out of here except six pieces of wood.'

'That was unjust, Juliana.'

'What do you think, Alice?' she asked. 'Am I unjust?'

280

'I am not the Duke's daughter,' Alice said, thoughtfully, 'and I would not like to be raped, but at the same time, you are my lady and I shall stay with you. Perhaps we should send the rest of the ladies away, though.'

'Very well. Tell the Marshal to make arrangements, Latiner. They can go to Pacy and twitter away at Eustace.'

It was a measure of the new Juliana that she should be so derogatory about her people. Once, she might have said it in private, but never in public. All the sensitive, perceptive, amiable parts of her seemed to have closed up. Her armour was on and her visor was down.

Alice gave me an amused, alarmed look. We would be besieged together. The bad news was that we would very likely be killed or worse. There was nothing we could do. The die was cast.

'What is the final thing?' I asked Juliana. 'Whatever you have in mind. Don't do it?'

I took my leave, and went in search of the Marshal. As I lay in bed that night I wept because I still loved Juliana, and somewhere underneath all that hatred and remorse, I knew she still loved me. Alice, now – she was another matter.

XLIX

Next day, I worked with the Marshal to put the castle into a state of defence. The cook was sent into the town to buy extra stores and the assistant-steward rode round the castle's farms collecting pigs and cattle. Inevitably, news travelled swiftly around the town that the castle was preparing for a siege.

A siege always alarmed the townsfolk because the visiting army would raid it for subsistence and there was always the chance that a raid would spin off into looting, rape, arbitrary punishments, and arson. I don't say it made the town hostile to us, but it tended to encourage them to hedge their bets.

Breteuil was at a crossroads where the road from Paris to the west crossed the route from the south, from Poitou and Anjou. There was passing trade and regular trade and money to be made from local lace and livestock.

A smokery had been set up in town at the instigation of Juliana, adding to the brewery, lacery, apothecary, tannery, bakeries, butchers and tallow-makers. There were five inns and a brothel. Wars and fighting spoilt the serious business of making money. I noticed little groups of burghers in the streets and marketplace, nervous but purposeful. In one group was the mayor, a fussy little man, but not without his following.

'We shall have to let them in,' I heard him say.

I didn't blame him. The town walls and gates were strong enough to keep out brigands and bogeymen, but it was only a strong castle that could hold out against a determined siege for long. I relayed the general drift of conversation back to the Marshal as we walked together round the bailey

'The Duke will use the town and the town will use the Duke. No doubt they will wring some concession out of him,' he said. 'We will fare better inside the castle itself, once the drawbridge has been pulled up. The moat is deep – all this water around here has its purposes.'

The shambles in a deep pit at the back of the bailey, downwind of the castle, was full of the residue of beasts – slaughtered, sliced and brined. It was shortly to be covered with earth; meanwhile, it smelt of death. There would be more of that shortly. We both held our breath for a few paces as we passed.

'My guess is, as the Comtesse said, that the Duke will want to do as little damage as possible,' he said. 'Not out of kindness, but because he wants the place for himself. We can use that to our advantage. Once he finds the drawbridge up, he will want to parley. He won't want to get too close to my lady unless he can find some way to overcome her, some secret stratagem…'

We paused in our circuit at the graves of the two little girls.

'They were the brave ones,' he said. 'I wish we had them fighting for us.'

'Perhaps they will be in their way,' I replied. 'Whatever the Duke may say, their treatment must weigh heavily on their grandfather.'

L

The Duke was as good as his word. He arrived outside the town on a Tuesday with a small force of a hundred men. He demanded to be let in. Of course the gates were opened and the mayor hurried up to greet his liege lord and offer him the freedom of the town. The Duke was pleased to accept, and dispositions were made for the men to be quartered and their horses fed. It was mid-May now, eleven hundred and nineteen years after the death of Our Lord. The weather fine but windy, tickling the waters of the lake.

Henry clearly did not think that the siege of the castle was going to be a grand affair. One hundred knights hardly counted as a skirmish, but it was twice as many as we had, and he did have the advantage of being Duke in his own country. We were technically revolting and could be hung from some battlement if he defeated us.

The Duke made no effort to contact the castle and stayed in the town overnight. Juliana kept to her room and brooded. The rest of us waited for we knew not what.

In the morning we were summoned to a parley by a trumpeter. Juliana emerged from her room, dressed regally in red. The trumpeter was dressed in all the trimmings; gold braided jerkin and hose, his trumpet draped with the royal crest. He delivered his message in that strange French they talk in England.

'The Duke comes in peace and requests his daughter the Comtesse de Breteuil to accompany him to Barfleur so that she may embark with all the company and spend Christmas with him in England.'

'That she will not do,' said a clear, proud voice, before any of the rest of us could reply.

It was Juliana, of course, looking every inch a princess. She had joined our little group, coming up behind us without our noticing as was her way.

'Is that the answer you wish me to give to the Duke?' asked the herald.

He would have to brave the Duke's famous temper if he came back with the wrong reply.

'Indeed it is,' said Juliana.

She was the mistress here. There was no point in any of the rest of us speaking.

'You can go back to the Duke and tell him that we will open our gates to him and ten knights, and we will parley with him at our drawbridge. We have already made plans, which I cannot break, to spend Christmas in Normandy.'

The herald took his leave, none too happily, and returned to the town.

'He comes in peace!' said Juliana, derisively. 'My arse!'

She had a ripe turn of phrase when she wished. But it was a lovely arse, and now it was gone from me forever. I felt diminished.

'What would you like me to do, Comtesse?' asked the Marshal as we walked across the bailey. 'I can keep our men in hall or round at the postern, out of sight. Or would you like them to surround you as you talk to your father across the moat with the drawbridge up?'

'What do you think?'

'Have the men around you. There is not a great deal of space around the bridge. We will look more than we are.'

'If they manage to gain entry we are finished,' said Juliana. 'They will take me prisoner, and take you away to fight in their wars.'

'Or cut off our heads,' said the Marshal.

'I hope not,' said Juliana. 'That would be a poor reward for your service. I shall make sure you keep your head on. And you too, Latiner.'

'Thank you,' I said.

'Just in case we are over-run, I have ordered your palfrey to be saddled up and ready, with a mounted knight attending, and the gate to be opened for you, so you can make your escape to Pacy,' the Marshal told her.

'Thank you, Marshal. I do not think it will come to that. We just have to see that no one lets down the drawbridge,' said Juliana. 'Simple enough.'

She turned and walked off with her head held high.

'Simple enough,' muttered the Marshal, 'but nothing is simple in war, and everything has the potential for cock-up.'

'I shall be sorry to leave Breteuil,' I told him.

He looked at me sharply.

'Have you given in already?'

'No,' I said. 'My pupils are dead and there is no more for me to do here. I must move on. I have to make my fortune.'

'We could use you as a knight.'

'Thank you, Marshal, but I don't think it's for me, though I am your man in the coming fight. I am drawn to the town for a change.'

'What? Breteuil town?'

'No, no. Some big place. Not Paris, it's French and not too friendly to a Norman. But somewhere like ... Caen ... or Rouen. Yes, a man could make money there and grow to be a lord, like my father. I shall go to Rouen, if I am able, when this is over.'

'Well, I shall miss you, Latiner.'

'And I you, Marshal. You shall come and visit me and eat a great deal of fish.'

He was an honest man, which counted for much in those days of half-war on the marches of eastern Normandy, with the French King Louis sniffing around for opportunity like a dog in a houseful of bitches.

I sneaked out of the castle that evening to talk, as Eliphas had urged me to do if trouble came, with the landlord of The Bear. He told me about a place in the woods that gave folk in need a bed for the night. He did not say 'folks on the run', but he meant it. I made note of his directions and thanked him heartily. I rather thought I had visited that place already with Juliana. It sounded like the house of Mother Merle.

LI

Duke Henry turned up the next day with his bristling company of knights and archers and infantrymen. They looked well trained and keen as mustard, but they stopped outside the castle gate. After a brief discussion with the porter, the Duke, ten of the knights and a herald, who blew a horn, rode up to the raised drawbridge. And there they stopped.

Juliana gave a signal to the Marshal and we all poured out onto the platform under the little arch housing the hoisting apparatus. Some of the scullions and even a laundrymaid from the town came out – against orders but you could hardly blame them – and stood behind us. There must have been fifty of us out there and we seemed quite a throng.

Juliana spoke first. She was wearing a dress of fine silver cloth and looked like a goddess, I thought, with her red-gold hair and pale determined face.

'What is it you want with us, sir?' she asked, knowing full well what it was.

'I am here to take you back to England where it may be that we can teach you some manners and indeed your duty. You seem to have forgotten both in your sojourn in Normandy.'

'Manners?' she retorted. 'I do not think you are the one to teach such a thing. Is it manners to put out your granddaughters' eyes and mutilate them? Strange manners they are in a grandfather. If those are manners, I would wish to be uncouth. And, if you talk about duties, perhaps you should examine the duties owed by a prince to his subjects. Are not children protected in your kingdom? Suffer the little children? Not in the Duchy of Normandy with Henry at the helm!'

The Duke reddened. He did not like his knights to hear of his recent trouble – the act had been forced on him as head of state, but it was hardly a good example of knightly conduct.

'It is your duty to obey me and accompany me back to England, if I command it. Your duty to your father and to your lord.'

'I see my duty as lying elsewhere,' she replied. 'Who knows, you may have some prison over there with its jaws wide open for me. You have done that to your brother, my uncle. Why not to me?'

'Why not indeed?' snarled the Duke, now beginning to rage.

'Pray do not lose that famous temper, Father. I am astonished that I can keep my own, which doubtless I inherit from you yourself. You come here, making accusations and bold claims, when I have hitherto been the most attentive and respectful of daughters. Then through no fault of mine, you decide to offer up my daughters to a monster who puts out their eyes and cuts off their noses, for which, through shame and the loss of all hope, they jump off the topmost turret of my castle since life has no joy or promise for them any more. I therefore accuse you of murder most foul and I am surprised – yes, astonished – that you dare show your face in my presence. Would I were a tigress and I could spring at you even now and tear you to pieces.'

At the end of this terrifying speech, delivered in the calmest voice, she made a little pouncing movement as if she would spring across the moat, and even the Duke, as brave as any man present, flinched a little and drew back. I could see he was shocked at the news that his grand-daughters had killed themselves, but he wasn't going to show it now.

'Very well,' he said, at last. 'It will have to be war.'

He held up his hand, and all his host who had waited outside the walls, charged through the opened gates (doubtless they had overpowered or suborned the gatekeeper in some way), streamed across the bailey and stopped in formation behind him. We all withdrew at that point into the hall and waited for instructions.

Juliana conferred with the Marshal, and then spoke to us.

'The Duke cannot get in. He does not want to stay long here as he is due to go south to Exmes and Courcy where there is trouble, and things in Verneusses and Anceins are starting to stir. The drawbridge is up. There is nowhere for the Duke's men to put planks or make a temporary bridge. I have sent a messenger to tell my husband what is happening here, that his castle is under siege, and he will arrive in due course with his army. I suggest we all go back to our duties and that the Marshal and his men keep a close watch on the situation.'

With that, she turned and mounted the stairs to her chamber. Alice was about to follow her, but I drew her aside.

'If anything goes wrong,' I said to her, 'meet me in the dungeon and we will escape by the tunnel.'

'Where does it come out?' she asked, not altogether happily. 'I hate tunnels.'

'Down by the boat-house,' I told her. 'We will escape by water.'

'Romantic,' she said, 'like King Arthur. Will there be bats in the tunnel?'

'Very likely.'

'Then I won't go.'

'Alice. It may not be necessary anyway. But I have to leave. Will you come with me?'

She smiled at me, that slow smile that was very much Alice.

'It will ruin my name.'

'What else is here for you?'

'Oh very well, then.'

'And look out some warm clothes. If the Duke breaks in, you'll need them in a hurry. Take them down to the dungeon just in case.'

'You're very sweet,' she told me. 'I'm not frightened if you are there.'

Oh my God, I thought, I think I'm falling in love.

LII

As it happened, the Duke did break in. Well, break is not the word. He or his marshal had twisted the arm (probably literally) of one of the little laundrymaids who came from the town every day to do the castle washing.

She didn't go home that night but hid away in the pantry cupboard, crept out at dawn and used the cook's best knife to cut the thick ropes holding up the drawbridge. Down it crashed with a bang that shook the very foundations of the castle, and woke us all to the imminence of disaster. May her treacherous little soul never be washed clean!

Henry and his men were waiting for it. They stormed across the bridge and were soon in possession of the castle. Not in total possession of course, not immediately anyway. There were still certain staircases and concealed doors, and Alice and I made use of one of them. We huddled in the corner of a tiny stairwell that led all the way from the top guard tower to the darkest dungeon down below. There then unfolded for us through the arrow-slit window, a sight that became the stuff of legend.

The beautiful Comtesse de Breteuil, daughter of the King of England and Duke of Normandy, was standing on a ledge above the dark moat, removing her outer garments. Soldiers stopped to look at her from castle windows and from the path on the castle side. They could not understand what she was doing. Then, all at once, she jumped. It seemed to take her a long time to hit the water. Her long shift acted as a kind of cushion for air, billowing up and holding her as she fell, exposing for all of us to see, her beautiful body with the long legs and the perfect firm and rounded bottom, and as she turned, that lovely little V of golden hair between the legs. We followed the vision down as the water opened round her like a glass flower and she disappeared into the depths. There was a profound silence, and then a great cheer. It was meant to be very shaming for a lady to show her buttocks, but it seemed to have done her no harm with the men; even the Duke's men cheered. Only the old Chaplain looked worried, and crossed himself.

I must say my heart was in my mouth as I feared that she would drown or the weeds would wind round her long legs and drag her down to the depths where frogs would couch between her thighs as she settled into the mud. I was glad for her that she had not used that part of the moat which received the deposits from the garderobes but, even so, the water was murky. Doubtless it was also very cold. We watched and watched for the next act of the drama. And then we saw her. She was out, scrambling up the side of the moat and running across the bailey to the marshalsea where her palfrey was kept and her groom had had the instructions to be prepared.

A voice, that I recognised as belonging to the Duke's marshal, rang out.

'She's getting away. Stop her, you fools.'

All was instant activity. Men were running downstairs, clattering across the drawbridge, haring across the keep, waving and shouting. But they were too late. Juliana was away, hair streaming in the wind, a veritable goddess of the chase. Through the open gatehouse she went with guards scattering as she rode through them. They would never catch her.

'That's no palfrey. That's an Arab,' said Alice. 'One of her little secrets. She usually keeps it in the town. Had it brought round yesterday.'

'Time for us to get going too…'

'Swims well, doesn't she?' said Alice.

I knew Juliana could swim. We had swum together and made love in a secret pool in the woods last summer. I was hit by a dart of sadness.

'We may have to too if the boat's not there …' I said.

I did mention that first we had to get out, but there was no point in alarming her further.

LIII

No one had been through the tunnel since Juliana and I had walked there last August. I knew because we had put a trick line of pebbles across the path to see if anyone was spying on us, and they were still in position.

I opened the secret door and raised the candle. It was all as it had been. There was slime on the wall and cobwebs on the ceiling. A little trickle of water felt its way like a blind worm down the edge of the path. The air smelt of mould and slippery, dark things. Alice was alarmed and I have to admit (though I did not admit it to Alice), so was I. There were obstacles enough I could see, further on where the tunnel led beyond the castle walls.

Without Juliana's lead I had less certainty and now I could see that since I had last been here pieces of earth, stone and little chunks of masonry, possibly occasioned by the falling drawbridge, had come loose and littered the path. William of Breteuil had been played false down here by his builders. They had done a poor job for him. I only hoped that Alice and I could reach the lake before the whole thing came down upon us.

The more I saw of Alice, the more I liked her. She was beautiful, but best of all, she was made of fine mettle; though she was afraid, she said nothing more of it.

Behind us I could hear footsteps clattering down the stairway to the dungeon.

I took her by the hand, feigning confidence, shut the door behind us – it looked from a few feet away like part of the wall – and walked forward. I was aware that, if we wished to turn back, there was no obvious way of avoiding capture. There had better be no one at the other end.

I said nothing of my trepidation; first we had to get out. The distance down that dismal passage seemed longer than before. I knew it had to pass right under the bailey and beyond the curtain wall – some two hundred yards. At various places there had been slight fractures in the ground and water oozing over the rough stone made it treacherous. Juliana had told me that in case of an enemy's penetration of the tunnel, there was a device in the dungeon that could flood the whole length of it with water from the lake.

It struck me now that someone inside the castle might have the idea of flushing it out in case there was anyone rash enough to think of escaping.

Again, I did not pass this thought on to Alice.

'Keep going,' I cried. 'Press on.'

At any moment I expected a raging torrent to come surging round the corner.

At last the tunnel's end came into view. I knew from my expedition with Juliana, that the passage ended in a cave, its exit just behind a concealing and seemingly impenetrable outcrop that hid it from prying eyes. I worried now that the door might have no key; that Juliana might have been down here and taken it before she escaped; or some oaf might have dropped it, or some meddling pisspot pocketed it, but there it was, still in the lock as we had left it. It was stiff but it turned, and I wondered as I applied myself to it why Juliana had not taken this exit rather than the cold plunge in to the moat. But, of course, she more than anyone was made for the grand gesture: a defiant leap was more her style, not slinking out like a rat down a mouldy tunnel, unobserved. What an extraordinary woman she was!

I was thankful, though, that Alice and I were of a more discreet persuasion. Valour isn't everything unless there's no alternative. That is the bastard's motto.

I now extracted the key from the lock, pulled the bolts back – they resisted sullenly – opened the door, and we stepped out. I concealed my relief from Alice because I wanted her to trust me. She was taking a big risk, leaving the service of a great family, losing her name as like as not, by throwing in her lot with a bastard who had no employment. I felt responsible for a woman for the first time in my life. (I had never been responsible for Juliana; she had been responsible for me.) It was a slightly weighty sensation, but again it had a certain warmth to it. I felt like Theseus taking Ariadne away.

'Come,' I said to my Ariadne. 'Your whole life is about to change.'

The evening air was bracing but welcome after the musty chill of the tunnel. I locked the door and placed the key carefully on a high ledge in the concealing wall of the cavern. Alice asked why I bothered to do it, seeing that we weren't coming back.

'You never know when a secret tunnel may come in handy,' I told her. 'If not for you, for somebody else.'

The boat, a trim craft, was drawn up in its usual place at the entrance to the cave, and it took some effort for us to drag it to the water's margin.

'Can you row?' asked Alice. 'Because if you can't, I can.'

'I was taught at the abbey,' I told her, 'and coached on the Risle by the brawny Brother Pierre, a chandler's son. There is no end to the things you can learn in a monastery and they have a way of coming in useful when you get outside. I was even given instructions in picking a lock when one of the Brothers had lost a key. There is much to be said for monastic life if you are in the right place.'

I was talking too much, probably to hide my nervousness. A little bit of me was wishing that I was back there in the quiet room with Old Saul instead of being on a cold lake with evening coming on, and no night's rest in sight.

However, I said nothing of this to dear Alice and we were soon embarked and traversing the lake, my oars dipping cleanly – nothing alerts like splashes on open water. How different was this journey from the one I had taken before with Juliana – and now here I was betraying her. I could plead a good excuse – she and fate had forced me out. And, after all, I was only rescuing Alice. The thoughts went back and forth in my head as if in rhythm with the dipping of the oars.

As I looked back, I saw something that filled me with alarm. There was a flood pouring out of the entrance to the tunnel; somebody had voided the cistern. Was it because they knew we were likely to be there? Or just on the off-chance of drowning a traitor? I said nothing.

We were soon out of sight of the castle and under the lee of the woods. I heard the shouting of soldiery, but no one immediately seemed to have noticed us; there were no figures running along the shore to intercept us. We were, at least for the moment, safe.

We disembarked alongside the little promontory that had served for a jetty when Juliana had landed there last summer. If anyone had questioned such an excursion at the time, we had agreed we would say we were looking for wild flowers and leaves for the little girls to draw. Yes, it was a thin excuse, but who was going to question the Comtesse except the Comte himself and he didn't count. At least I had thought he didn't, but he surprised his wife all right. And now the little girls were gone, and Juliana and I were sundered, and another tiny fault had formed in the fabric of the universe.

Alice shivered. She was wearing a thick travelling dress and heavy cloak, but the wind from the northwest had strengthened. It was an unsettled May, but everything was unsettled that year in Normandy.

'Out of the frying pan into the ice-house,' she said.

We had to find shelter for the night.

I heard at that moment movement in the wood, too near at hand for comfort. I had brought a short sword, more of a long knife really, but it was all I had been able to find in the hurry to leave the castle. My hand flew to it, and I called out.

'Who's there?'

There could be soldiers everywhere. If the Duke had known about the tunnel, he would doubtless have taken measures to intercept escapees. I resolved to die rather than serve a further term in the castle of Ivry. A roe deer sprang out of the bushes and ran across our path disappearing into the scrub beyond. Alice laughed at my alarm.

'Who's afraid of a big nasty deer?' she said.

'It's all very well, but this is not a good place to be,' I told her.

My goal was the suggestion of the innkeeper, that tumbledown cottage deep in the woods some distance from a track that ran westwards at the far end of the lake. How could I forget it? It had been midsummer night, when good people should be in their beds. There was either an old woman living there or a young girl or both, and magic of a kind I could never find again.

I told Alice about it; not all about it, but some of it. It seemed the thing to do. She took it calmly – after all, we were not lovers.

'I knew about you and Juliana,' she said.

She shivered again, sending me off on shivers of my own.

'Could we not go to the town?' she suggested.

'Full of the Duke's soldiers; we'd be arrested in no time if we went there.'

There was no alternative but to make for the cottage as fast as we could, if I could find it. It was not an easy track. It plunged into the forest among undergrowth that had turned into overgrowth, it branched out in ways that I had not remembered, and more than once we found ourselves back in places where we had already been. It was growing darker by the minute. I was completely lost – though again I did not tell Alice so. I began to have visions of us being found, like the children in the forest, covered with leaves and snow and completely dead – but by luck and a little instinct, and the memory of summer days with Juliana whispering in my head, I found the path again, and finally we saw the light among the trees. It was almost dark; the northwesterly blustered about the trees. I put my arm round Alice and gave her a hug, as we set off again. Rounding a corner, we came in full view of the light's source – a dark cottage, battered and decayed.

'There's our palace,' she said.

'It will seem so if you are there,' I replied.

She kissed me for an instant with lips cold as a mermaid's, her eyes shining out from under the thick hood of her cloak like carriage lights. I beat at the hovel door and listened intently, but there seemed no sound in reply, only the scrape and moan of the wind in the branches overhead. I beat again.

'You will break the door,' said Alice.

'If I have to,' I replied.

Finally, a small shuffling sound from within hinted at movement.

'Hello,' I cried. 'Two travellers lost in the forest.'

I suggested to Alice that she say something too. It might reassure the inhabitants if they heard a woman in distress.

'Please let us in,' Alice said to the door. 'We are tired and cold.'

Finally there came the sound of bolts being drawn back, and the door opened an inch or two.

'Who is it?'

It was a very old voice, which I recognised as that of Mother Merle.

'I am Bertold – we met last summer – and this is Alice.'

'I know who you are. What do you want?'

'We don't want to die in the forest and we will if you don't let us in,' said Alice.

The door opened a little more disclosing the big chin, the long nose, and the long grey hair of the hag I remembered. She peered at us both intently from rheumy old eyes whose pupils flickered like fish in a dark pond.

'She looks like a witch,' whispered Alice. 'She'll turn us into beetles.'

There was a moment of indecision, and then the witch opened the door wider.

'Well,' she said, 'you'd better come in.'

The cottage, I knew, was better than it looked from outside.

A fire glowed in the grate, a pot of what smelt like rabbit stew steamed beside it, and three chairs stood in front of it near a table which was laid for three.

'I been expectin' you,' the old crone said.

She said nothing of having met me before, Perhaps it was merely tact, though I didn't know witches exercised that art. At any rate, it made an odd situation easier.

'You can't have expected us!' I exclaimed. 'We didn't know we were coming until this afternoon.'

'Don't tell me what I can't do,' she said. 'I wouldn't ha' laid for three if I hadn't been. Take off your cloaks and warm yourselves, my lovers.'

We accepted her invitation, gratefully.

A jug full of strong cider was put in front of us, and we poured it into our mugs and drank happily, feeling the warm glow spreading in our bellies. I had no idea where all this was going to lead us, but for now I didn't care. Alice appeared happy. Her eyes sparkled and her skin bloomed in the heat. Dishes of pungent stew were put in front of us, not just rabbit, but game and herbs and the lord's venison no doubt, and bread to soak it in. It did not seem right to ask the old woman where she obtained such supplies. Eustace's steward would have been interested, but perhaps he knew about the witch and stayed well clear. Or perhaps she did him service and provided good fortune.

We ate without speaking as the old woman watched. When we had finished she drew up her chair and sat with us, still watching. Finally she rose, took the kettle from the fire and poured boiling water into a jug from which a fragrant smoky aroma rose. She gave each of us a cupful after she had let it stand for a few minutes. It was both refreshing and drowsy-making, like poppy.

Alice was tired; her head on her hand, supported by an elbow propped on the table, served her as a cushion, and she was falling asleep. All at once her elbow slipped, jolting her awake.

'Well,' the old witch said, 'can't sit here all night talking. You can tell me what you're doing wandering the woods in the morning. What you need is a good night's sleep, I daresay. Go on with you. Up the stairs and into bed. It's big enough.'

Alice and I looked at each other.

'What will you do?' I asked the witch. 'Where do you sleep?'

I had not asked her that before.

'Oh, I shall do very well,' she said. 'Don't you'm be worriting about me. Up you go. Here's a candle to light you to bed.'

We did as she told us. There was the same fair-sized room under the eaves with a little window that admitted the pale light of a waxing moon, the place almost dwarfed by the enormous bed, covered with rugs and furs. We took off our outer garments and tumbled into it, Alice on the far side, I on the nearer. It smelt of old animals, but not unpleasantly; feral but welcoming. We fell asleep in the shape of a couple of Ss, our contours perfectly adjacent, clutching each other for comfort. It was no time for love.

After a while, I woke up. Something was prodding me awake. It was the hag. It seemed she hadn't meant she would find somewhere else to sleep downstairs, she proposed to join us here. Why had I not thought of that? It was not really my place to protest, but I wasn't altogether happy. It had not happened when Juliana was here. Perhaps the Duke's daughter merited special treatment. Anyway, as a guest I was obliged to do what my host required of me. I was dimly reminded of fairy stories my mother used to tell me when I was little.

'Move up, monster,' said the old hag in the night, prodding me again.

But she wasn't the old hag. It seemed that she was a lovely girl.

I did what she asked, and then she put a hand on my *membrum virile*. Alice stirred in her sleep next to me, moaning slightly. I know it may sound hard to believe, but I found the experience arousing. How could I, you will ask? I should have been revolted, but the witch-girl knew what she was about. She extracted my prick from my hose and fondled it with cunning practice. I trembled, I quivered and in due course I came, it seemed, monumentally. Strangest of all, she gathered my seed and crammed it into her mouth.

I feared that Alice would wake, but she slept on, frowning, moving a little, a tiny trickle of moisture showing at the side of her mouth, which beguiled me.

The witch-girl patted me as if I had been a good horse, turned over and went to sleep. I comforted myself that at least I had not offended against the contract between host and guest. A rejection would have caused offence, or worse. It was all very strange, but at the same time it was completely matter of fact, as though it had all happened before. Then I too feel asleep. In the morning, I woke up beside a beautiful girl on my left but, on my right, an absence. The hag had disappeared. I could hear sounds of someone moving about in the kitchen. No doubt she was preparing some sort of breakfast for us. Alice woke and smiled at me sweetly.

I came to the conclusion that I had dreamt of the little matter between the hag and myself, a strange concurrence, but I put it all down to my mother's fairy stories. At least the hag had had the good grace to turn into a pretty girl, or so it seemed to me.

'In the night, I dreamt that the old woman was lying beside me,' Alice said. 'But it wasn't the old woman, it was a girl.'

'Did she … do anything?'

'No … I don't think so…'

There was a slight hesitation.

'What did she do?'

'Perhaps I dreamt it.'

She would say no more. The thought of what the old witch-girl might have done to Alice was both horrible and curiously arousing. The monks used to talk about these things, but more in speculation than from experience.

'Perhaps you did,' I said.

Alice would never have let anything like that happen. She was still drowsy. I was happy for her.

'I don't know how you found the way down that path last night,' she said.

'Nor do I. But she seemed to be expecting us.'

'We must pay her something. Have you any money?'

'We have paid her in our way. She is a witch,' I told her. 'Witches don't need money.'

'Of course they do. Money is power.'

'Get up,' I told her, gently pulling her arm. 'We must move on.'

She disengaged her hand and snuggled in to the bed.

'Or we could just stay here.'

'The Duke will find us if we stay. We must go. I must find work.'

'Where will you do that?' she asked.

'We need a big town. Somewhere like Rouen. We won't be noticed in Rouen.'

'It's miles away.'

I looked out of the window. The wind had freshened and the forest leaves showed the sheen of fallen rain. The sun appeared intermittently between the clouds. 'About three days if we had a horse.' I said.

'But we don't.'

'The witch will lend us one,' I told her.

Of course, I could go back to my father's chateau of Mortagne, but it seemed like a step backwards. You don't want to do that when you are twenty-two.

We dressed and went downstairs. I left Alice sitting there in the empty kitchen, and went out into the yard to wash. A pretty country girl was making a kind of porridge at the stove when I returned, shivering. She poured boiling water into a jug full of fragrant herbs, let it cool for a minute or two and then pushed it towards us.

'Drink that,' she said. 'It keeps out the cold and lifts the spirits.'

It had a strange herbal taste, but it certainly had lift in it and I could feel the warmth coursing through me.

'Where is old Mother Merle?' I asked the girl.

'Oh, she's off somewhere, gathering lichen or summat. Always on the go is Mother Merle.'

'Is she a relation of yours? Perhaps your mother?'

'That sort of thing.'

She didn't seem to want to expand on the subject so I applied myself to the bowl of porridge she put in front of me. She wasn't going to talk about the last time we had met, either.

'What is your name?' I asked her.

'Merle,' she said.

'Merle too?' Alice asked.

'Merle Two.'

She smiled at us in an amused sort of way.

'You'll be off to Rouen later,' she said, after a while.

'It's a long way to walk on a windy morning,' I told her.

I took another sip from my cup. The drink this morning was really quite different from last night's brew. It was aromatic and fresh, bracing and vigorous. It smelt of springy meadows and high woods where woodruff grows, and thyme.

'Do you know where we might find a palfrey or even a nag?' I asked.

'I don't have one myself. Got an old donkey, but she'd buckle under the weight of you two,' she said. 'But the Marshal from the castle, he's got some. I sent word to him, private-like, that we had visitors. There's a chance he'll have a palfrey with him if young miss don't mind riding pillion. I always liked a good pillion ride, joggling about behind a nice bum.'

'I bet you did,' I said. 'Not so easy to come by out in the woods.'

I was glad to hear that my friend the Marshal had managed to survive the fighting and maybe even the Duke's wrath.

'You'd be surprised, my duck,' she said. 'There's always someone passing through.'

Alice was trying hard not to laugh. At that moment there was a knock on the door. I thought for a moment it might be the Marshal but it was one of his grooms. The girl let him in and I glimpsed my palfrey Blackberry nudging the spring grass as she waited outside, tied to a post.

'Marshal said you might be needing a horse,' said the groom. 'Old Mother Merle sent word.'

My friend Eliphas had hinted at a communicating system between the inns but it clearly included other reference points. It was after all a wise woman's business to know everything that went on. A good name they had for her too: Mother Merle.

The old blackbird had more tricks up her sleeve than the French King's Arabian conjuror.

'Well, 'I said, 'thank you for bringing the palfrey, and please thank the Marshal too. I thought he might have been taken prisoner by the Duke.'

'The Duke has taken no prisoners. He blames his daughter the Comtesse for stirring up enmity against him while all he wants is accord.'

'Or so he says,' I suggested.

'Or so he says. At any rate, the Marshal is free. I think he is leaving Breteuil for Pacy tomorrow, and I with him. He sends his greetings and hopes that you will meet again ere long.'

'And please return the greeting, and say that we very much hope so. Thank him for the palfrey. We are off to…'

I paused, wondering whether it was wise to declare our whereabouts. The Duke had not looked friendly when I saw him last.

'Maybe to Paris,' I said. 'Or to Caen. Or to Chartres…'

But I had some compunction about Juliana. I did not wish her to think that I had totally deserted her. I might no longer be considered a lover, but at least I could be a friend.

'Or very possibly to Rouen,' I concluded.

'The Marshal asked me to say that he knows the chief butcher in Rouen. He supplies the Duke's army. The Marshal said if you go there, be sure to look him up and mention his name.'

I wasn't sure what we would do with a butcher – I had no experience of chopping up dead animals nor had ever had a wish to – but any introduction was better than none.

'Tell him I will, and please thank him again.'

The groom wished us well, and rode off back down the little path towards Breteuil. The girl meanwhile put some bread and cheese together for us which she wrapped in a cloth (clean, I was glad to notice) and gave us directions for the road to Rouen – where she had evidently decided we were going.

'You must go back to the path you left to come here,' she said. 'Turn right when you reach it and then take the third path to the right, easy to miss, so keep your wits about you. That will bring you out of the woods in half an hour or so, and you will see the road to Conches-en-Ouche in front of you, if it hasn't been moved.'

'Moved?' asked Alice.

'Oh, my duck, roads round here in the woods they move a lot. They get worn down or muddied out and then we move 'em. It helps to keep the soldiers guessing.'

'We'll find our way,' I said. 'There's always the sun. We just keep going north.'

I gestured at the morning. A spell of bright sunshine filled the clearing where the little cottage stood. A robin appeared and chattered at us. Speckled brown butterflies busied themselves on a bank of cowslips, near a trickle of stream.

'There's always the sun until it goes in,' she said.

'We'll manage,' I told her with as much assurance as I could muster.

I did not want to alarm Alice. The woods were very deep the further you went and, I heard, dangerous. I was afraid Mother Merle or Merle the girl or whoever she was, was going to start talking about wolves and wodwos.

We thanked her for her hospitality and I gave her two silver pennies. I mounted the palfrey and Alice stood on a convenient bench and jumped up behind me. Merle the girl waved with a crooked finger as we ambled off into the forest. Just before we turned the corner where the big holly tree obscured the view, she shouted something I did not quite hear.

'What did she say?' I asked Alice.

'Something about water,' she said. 'Death by water ... What does that mean?'

'Maybe the water's bad in Rouen?'

'Maybe.'

'Better stick to the wine,' I told her.

LIV

The journey to Rouen was, to my relief, uneventful after the alarms of the previous days. Alice and I ambled along on the palfrey, meeting few people on the road. The country folk had drawn in their horns these last cold days, unnaturally cold they said for May, the hay wasn't ready to cut, and it seemed even the soldiers had stayed at home. There were a few wounded stragglers, some English, limping along towards the coast.

At mid-day we stopped for refreshment in Conches-en-Ouche, a funny little place with a big stone castle, seat of Roger de Tosny, a friend of my father's. He was not at home, we were told – not that we wanted to meet a local lord, there was no knowing which side he might be on or what kind of ransom he might ask for our safe return. Happily, we were not questioned or molested, but we did not stay long – the inn had been ransacked the week before by English soldiers on their way to the port of Barfleur, and the innkeeper was still clearing up and telling us about it.

That afternoon the weather turned milder, and we enjoyed periods of sunshine and a softer wind from the south west. Coming out of Conches, as we passed the crossroads that led west towards my old abbey of Saint-Sulpice and east to the town of Évreux, I allowed my thoughts to wander back to the old Jew Saul, my mentor, and the quiet life of study that I could have had, and the many roads that lead to that single point of the present. But Alice's warm hands were about my waist and soon I looked ahead again.

We were making for the village of Le Neubourg, which was still some nine miles away, and we would be lucky to get there by nightfall. From time to time, Alice broke into my reverie by complaining of a sore arse, and her arse was such a pleasant conjecture, sore or otherwise, that I abandoned my regrets for lost monasticism. She wasn't used to riding, she told me. I assured her that I would rub the afflicted part with one of my unguents that every evening, if she would just hold on for a few more miles. She grumbled, but held me tighter. We rode on, companionably, still with no sign of pursuit.

The light was just beginning to fail when we finally reached Le Neubourg, and tied up our palfrey at the sign of The Falcon.

It looked a promising place – a good fire and a friendly landlord called Hugues who told us Neubourg was in fact a very old bourg indeed with five roads fanning out from it, and that the manor belonged to Henry de Beaumont, Earl of Leicester. Hugues had got rid of the English soldiery by telling them about the English Earl and his legendary temper when people damaged his property.

The smells from the kitchen were encouraging. Alice and I had a jug of wine and a pigeon pie, and when we had finished the wine, we went upstairs to a room we had all to ourselves. I unpacked my medicine chest and found some liniment that Saul always recommended for bruising: arnica, witch hazel, elecampane root and *grani paradisii* mixed in sage oil. Alice's bottom, I'm sure, would have looked perfect to me, but she went behind a screen and doubtless massaged the oil into both cheeks and maybe one or two other places, and declared herself somewhat reconciled to riding.

There was still this little distance between us, and I think it was called Juliana.

I wanted Alice and I think she wanted me, but it was too soon. She was loyal to her mistress, and she did not want to think of me as a traitor to love, and no more did I.

We slept well that night and so did our little palfrey, it seemed, since she whinnied to see us next day when we went round to say good morning, and gave a little clog-dance of impatience to be off. As we said goodbye to Hugues, our host, after our breakfast of bread and ham and ale, he remembered something, or pretended to do so.

'There was this jongleur fellow, decent bloke, left a message for a Master Bertold which he said I was to give you. When you're in Rouen, look him up. He is at the Rose Tavern on Fish Street. You'll find it by the smell.'

'Of fish or roses?'

'You'll have to work that one out.'

We said our goodbyes, collected Blackberry, and started once more on our way. I was struck again by the network of news and information that seemed to run from inn to inn and included the odd wise woman. Their number somehow seemed only to involve decent people, good sorts; pleasants not peasants, according to Alice. That is the true class division of the world.

I was discovering that Alice had a wry kind of humour which charmed me as much as, if not even more than, her other attractions, and yet I had vowed never to love anyone but Juliana. Alice would respect me for that. Better perhaps to say nothing. It is one of the things one learns.

After an hour or so on the road, we caught our first sight of Rouen. I had never seen a really big town, a city indeed, with a huge cathedral towering above it. Twenty thousand chimneys added their smoke to the morning clouds. Alice told me her mother's family came from a place called Les Andelys nearby. Her mother knew the city and had told her stories of it, but Alice herself had never been there.

'However shall we find our way?' she exclaimed. 'All those streets and all those people. What do they all do?'

Secretly I rather agreed with her, but I did not want to show lack of worldliness.

'It is a collection of villages, just like Les Andelys. We will start by getting to know one of them and then we will get to know the next, and so on. It is an adventure.'

Alice looked doubtful.

'I have had enough adventure in the last few days,' she said. 'I would like a little ordinariness and home cooking. What are we going to do for money?'

'I will find work,' I told her, with a confidence I did not exactly feel, though I did have some faith in the league of jongleurs, pedlars and innkeepers that had served us none too badly so far; I had faith in my friend Eliphas.

311

We rode on. Our first impression as we entered the town was of the smells of woodsmoke, horse-shit, cooking and baking, and blood and guts from the slaughterhouse. There was the salty smell of the tidal river which I would get to know so much better, of wine lees and ale and cider, and kitchen waste running down the kennels in the middle of the cobbled streets, mixing with urine thrown from windows. And as we followed our instructions from the innkeeper at Le Neubourg, there was fish; a most pervasive smell, not unlike urine, but quite different.

No one paid attention to us as we rode in through the city gates. And then I thought again about that. There was surreptitious movement in the turrets by the south gate and I could feel eyes on my back.

'At home they would be asking where we came from and what we were after by now,' she said. 'They all seem so busy here.'

'It is the city way,' I said, knowingly. 'Here it is we who have to speak first.'

I addressed a man carrying a sack of what looked like kale.

'Fish Street?' I asked him.

'Next on the right,' he grunted and moved on.

The overpowering aroma as we rode forward told us we had arrived. Fish Street ran along the docks and a fine street it was for every manner of catch the sea could throw at you. We dismounted and I tied our palfrey to a post at the corner of a warehouse. It was my first sight of salt water. We walked along the harbourside, where the tidal Seine lapped the greasy wall, inspecting the baskets. There was cod, there was hake, there was haddock and halibut, and mackerel fresh as a rainbow, there was pilchard and John Dory, pollock and flounder; there was herring which made me think of the grim castellan Harenc; there was prawn and crab and lobster and squid, and even a bucket of seahorses which Alice wanted to buy and throw back in the water.

'I wouldn't be surprised to find a mermaid here,' she told me, 'sitting on a basket and waiting for a buyer. There's just about everything else.'

We found the inn that the innkeeper Hugues had told us about, and discovered my friend the jongleur Eliphas sitting outside in the mild evening air, drinking a stoup of ale.

'What kept you?' he asked. 'I expected you yesterday. But the ale is good so there has been no discomfort. And this is Mademoiselle ...?'

'Alice,' I told him.

'Ah yes. Very pleased to make your acquaintance, Mistress Alice. Our friend Bertold has excellent taste...'

'In travelling companions. Thank you,' she told him. 'Your friend is very civil,' she said to me.

I could see she was pleased with him. We had got off to a good start. I bought a jug of wine, and we sat down with Eliphas on the fish-quay in the mild late afternoon watching the sun dip below the rooftops. Mist was already gathering in the meadows across the river.

'Your system of messages is very efficient, Eliphas,' I said. 'And we must thank you for it. It would have been hard to know where to go and what to do after we left Breteuil.'

'The barons don't like it,' he told me, smiling. 'They have their own way of communicating and it is nowhere as good as ours. Likewise the priests. They would prefer us to be ignorant and therefore more controllable. The Duke, of course, has his own system which is excellent. He has spies everywhere.'

I launched into the story of our adventures, the blinding, mutilation and death of the Comtesse's two daughters, and how that had precipitated the feud between the Comtesse and her father. It was clear to me that Eliphas knew most of it already.

'It is a terrible tale,' he said. 'Only a man of stone could do that to his grand-children. What was the Comte thinking of to blind the Castellan's son?'

'The Comte is a fool and a drunkard, but he thinks he is clever. The worst sort of fool. The Comtesse is as far above him as the cathedral here is above the shambles.'

'It is the sort of story one could make a play about,' said Eliphas.

'If the Duke heard you were doing that,' I told him, 'you would not be playing for very long.'

Alice had been sitting patiently, almost in a reverie, looking out across the boats bobbing gentle in the river's little swirls and eddies. She was thinking of her childhood by the sea.

'I saw a merman once,' she said. 'They caught him out at sea and put him in the harbour with nets to stop him escaping. The priests wanted him to confess that he was a devil, but one day he escaped and swam out to sea.'

'Wise fish,' said Eliphas. 'If he'd confessed, they'd have killed him. That's if they hadn't killed him already.'

'Is Eliphas your real name?' Alice asked him.

'What is real?' he replied with a smile.

'No ... really ...' she insisted.

'It is real, in so far as I am known by it, but I was not christened with it. It is a Jewish name although I am not Jewish. It is a name of secrets and of mysteries, it is Talmudic, magic one might say, and that is my trade.'

I could see Alice was tired after the cumulative exertions of our escape from the castle along with another day's travel, and Eliphas noted it too.

'Before you tell me of your adventures,' he said, 'we must find you your lodgings which I have taken the liberty of reserving for you. It is a short distant from the fish market, but I think you will like the house.'

'Will it smell of fish?' asked Alice, cautiously.

'Hark at Little Miss Fancy-pants,' he smiled. 'No, it will not smell of fish except on Fridays. The landlady is an old friend of mine and a good woman. Name of Berthe. It will smell of sweet herbs for that is Berthe's trade. She is an apothecary.'

'I never heard of a woman apothecary,' I said.

'Well, you have now,' said Eliphas.

'I think it is a good trade for a woman,' said Alice. 'I hope she may teach me some of her learning.'

We walked down a couple of streets, built out on a curve of the river bank beyond the harbour, until we came to a house built right out, almost on top of the water, with a private jetty in front of it. A smell of some spice I knew but could not immediately name came from a sack a man was dragging up from a small hulk moored to the little wharf.

'Here it is; your new home,' said Eliphas.

'It's lovely,' said Alice. 'Not so much as a kipper. What is that smell?'

'It is grains of paradise,' said the man over his shoulder, carrying the sack to a little warehouse that stood beside jetty.

Of course I knew it by its Latin name of *grani paradisii*; the mention made Juliana and her wardrobe come back to me, and my eyes pricked.

'It is said to fall from the trees in Eden, and they gather it from the rivers that run out of paradise – or Africa as it is commonly called,' Eliphas told her. 'Very good in spiced wine and cooked fruit.'

He took us round to the front door in the street, and knocked. A plump, smiling woman appeared.

'Well, if it isn't my favourite magician and the two travellers he's spirited away from the cruel wars,' she said. 'Come in, my dears. You must be tired.'

She held the door wide open and we stepped inside, but Eliphas held up a hand.

'I'll see you tomorrow,' he said. 'You find your rooms, and get acquainted with the place. Time enough to talk then.'

We protested, but his mind was made up. Berthe took us upstairs and showed us a bedroom and a sitting room at the top of the house that looked south over the river. She seemed to take it for granted that we would be sharing a bedroom. I could see that Alice was not entirely sure about it, but was too polite and tired to demur.

'Best view in Rouen,' she told us, and we believed her. 'Now, when you've made yourself at home, come down for a cup of wine and a little stew I've had on the hob simmering all day. Lovely and tender that'll be. I'll leave you now and see you in half an hour.'

Alice and I looked at each other.

'How are your feet?' I asked her.

315

She had rather fine feet, actually. In fact, as I may have indicated before, the *tout ensemble* was altogether to my liking. As I thought that, a sudden vision of Juliana crossed my mind again. 'Feet pretty good. How are yours?'' she asked.

'They feel as if we've landed on them,' I told her.

We sat on the bed looking out at the river and the watermeadows beyond.

'I should like to draw that,' she said.

'You draw in colour too?'

'Yes, my mother taught me and her father taught her when she was a girl. His brother worked on manuscripts at Bayeux Abbey.'

I thought it was time to broach the awkward subject. 'How do you feel about sharing with me?' I asked.

She evaded my question with another. 'What did you think of me at Breteuil?'

'Well, you were very much Juliana's right hand. One of her ladies. You kept apart from the rest of the castle. It's a man's world, all that soldiering…'

'By heaven,' she broke in with some passion, 'it was boring at Breteuil until you came along. Of course I knew what you and the Comtesse got up to. I've told you that already.'

'And you didn't mind?'

She was suddenly fierce.

'Of course I minded – I was half in love with her myself – but at least it was interesting. Do you still love her?'

This put me on the spot. I did not want to tell her a lie because I loved her, but to admit that I loved another would provoke, at the least, annoyance. To delay would be to multiply suspicion.

'I am glad that I loved her,' I said, 'because love is like anything else. It needs practice. If I had loved you first, you would have got all my awkwardness and roughness.'

'I like a little roughness.'

She was teasing me.

'I meant the gaucheries, the unmannerliness …' I told her.

'I know what you mean ... but you haven't answered my question...'

She was too wise to pursue it. I had not known many women, but I knew that she was a rare girl. I kissed her and told her that I loved her.

I knew it was not the same with Alice as with Juliana. I loved them both but Juliana was already a wife and I was her pastime and, yes, perhaps also her passion. With Alice it could only be serious. A kiss could lead on, and on at last to marriage.

Alice sensed something of my thoughts for she surprised me with what she said next.

'I will sleep with you but I will not make love with you. It is too soon.'

I was content. I had to be. I thought that she would change her mind. We went downstairs and found Berthe who led us to a fragrant room where a table was laid, and sat us down, putting before us trencher laden with the finest beef stew you ever tasted, cooked in ale and divinely seasoned with herbs.

She poured out wine for us and left until we had finished. She then cleared away the plates, offered us apple-cake – equally delicious – poured more wine and sat down to talk.

'Where did you meet Eliphas?' she asked.

'In a village called Verneuil. There was a fair going on and he had a stand there. A priest wanted him arrested, and by good fortune I was able to help him.'

'Priests,' sniffed Berthe disdainfully. 'God's spies, I call them. They're just sneaks, if you ask me. They inform on you to God.'

'And God doesn't need them because He can see everything,' said Alice, entering into the spirit of the thing.

I felt sorry for the priests, having lived for many years among them.

'God can see everything, but He cannot do everything, because that would be breaking the rules of his game. He sent His son to set us right and that was stretching them. Now the priests have to do the best they can, sometimes not very well.'

I could see our hostess was not entirely convinced, but Alice was sensitive enough to steer us away from the subject.

'What made you interested in herbs and spices?' she asked Berthe.

'My father was an apothecary and he met this old man, a seaman he was, who sailed everywhere in his hulk. He told him stories about spices that came from faraway places, and father paid him to bring him samples back with names of the merchants and the places they came from. Tyre and Constantinople and Carthage and Odessa and the Atlas Mountains … I just carry on his work and expand my frontiers when can … I never stop working, that is the trouble. I need help.'

'I would really like to learn about it all,' said Alice, quick as a flash spotting the opportunity. 'Perhaps I could help you. I can draw, you know. That might be a way of telling people what the herbs look like, where they are grown and what they are good for. We could put a wonderful sign up too…'

Berthe's face became quite flushed with pleasure.

'Well,' she said, 'that could be a very good idea. Let's see how you take to Rouen and whether you want to stay here.'

'Good idea,' I said, 'and now if you don't mind we will go up to bed. I am falling asleep as I speak, In fact I can't remember what I just said.'

'Be off with you then,' said Berthe. 'It's a pleasure to have you both in the house.'

Alice undressed in the other room, and came back in a simple nightdress. She put a bolster down the middle of the bed, but she gave me a kiss and held my hand as we settled down on the pillows. I desired the girl, but in all honour, and with the knowledge of Juliana still fresh upon me, in my mind and in my heart, I would do nothing to destroy her trust. We slept like dormice, and woke to a blue sky and a blazing sun streaming in through a half-open shutter and tickling our eyelids.

'I like seeing you when I wake up,' Alice said.

LV

Eliphas came in just as were about to sit down to breakfast. Berthe made him take a seat to share our cold chicken and bread, washed down with a mug of ale.

'We have to decide what you are going to do,' he told us.

'Alice is going to help me,' said Berthe.

She had clearly decided on this course in the night.

'That sounds a good idea,' said Eliphas, 'and what about Bertold? I believe there is work for a fish porter.'

Alice looked shaken.

'Fish?' She shuddered.

'You don't like fish?' he asked her.

'Not all the time.'

'Yes, it would be all the time. But I was only joking.'

'I would do it,' I told him. 'If necessary.'

'But I am told you have an introduction to Master Haimo, the butcher?'

'That I have, from the Comte de Breteuil's marshal. Apparently, Master Haimo is a provisioner for the Duke's army.'

'Is meat better than fish?' queried Alice.

I could see she pictured me coming home dripping with blood and stinking of sweetbreads.

'I don't think Master Haimo has a special need for a meat porter,' said Eliphas. 'There are plenty of lusty men in Rouen. No, I think the Comte's marshal had something else in mind.'

'Well, that is fine,' I told him. 'So long as Master Haimo has it in mind as well.'

'Master Haimo has much on his mind, that is for sure, but I am sure there will be room for you. I will take you to see him when you have finished your breakfast.'

'Do you know everyone, as well as everything?' I asked him.

'That pretty well covers it,' said Berthe, smiling at him.

I wondered whether there was something between them. She was a handsome woman and a clever one. As for Eliphas, he looked different every time you saw him, he was lightly built, of indeterminate age, with an expressive face, a pointy inquisitive nose, and dark hair; you couldn't really tell what age he was, but he had the gift of making a woman smile which is better than a good leg and well-chiselled features.

'I know that people like to listen to stories and they like to laugh. There can be wisdom in a jest and there's many a fool that wears a frown. But I have also looked into things that are more secret.'

'What things?' asked Alice.

'How to change my shape, become a boy, a woman, a fish, walk on fire, cast runes, read entrails, speak languages that have never been heard. There are books I have read that would make your hair stand on end.'

'They would too,' said Berthe. 'I have seen them.'

'But you have not read them?' Eliphas asked anxiously. 'It would not be good for you to do that.'

'I have kept them in the house for you. That was enough. There seemed to be voices talking that I could not quite hear. They are not the sort of books you want to open.'

'I thought you were a jongleur,' I said to Eliphas. 'And now you are a magus.'

'One thing leads to another,' he said. 'I feel at the moment that we are standing on the edge of something bad, something that is slowly gathering shape and weight. Something, in fact, that started at Breteuil and was begun by a fool in a drunken fit.'

'If I stay in this house with Berthe's wonderful cooking, I shall be gathering shape and weight myself,' I said, foolishly.

I did not want Alice to be alarmed, although in a way, I sensed that she might be stronger than me when the Duke's men came knocking at the door. God only knew where the Duke's spies were.

'I shall say no more now, but we will speak of it in due course,' said Eliphas. 'It is good that you should know what is happening. Great matters start with small beginnings. A nail from a horse's hoof, a glass of Burgundy too much ... princes have fallen for less.'

He seemed to be talking to himself about some vision or dream we could not share.

'Don't worry,' he said, seeing our bemused faces. 'It will all become plain in due course. Meanwhile, let's get down to some butchery. Come with me, young master.'

I turned to see if Alice wanted to come, but she fanned her face.

'I am not too fond of shambles,' she said. 'I would really like to stay with Berthe and learn about her herbs, if she'll have me.'

'That she will,' said Berthe.

Once outside the house, Eliphas and I turned right and walked down a little lane towards a crooked street that ran beside the river. It seemed a popular thoroughfare. It was full of people and carts, horses and the occasional donkey. Wagon-loads of barrels trundled by, holding salted fish, pork, ale, and wine, all drawn by those big, sturdy horses of Perche which gave me a sudden pang of homesickness.

'Have you ever been to the back of a butcher's shop?' Eliphas asked.

'Not really. And not much to the front of one, either.'

'Animals with their clothes off look surprisingly human, I always think. There is something shocking about flesh without its skin on – which of course you can see after a battle. That is like a butcher's shop. Do you think you have a stomach for the trade?'

'Butchery or soldiering?' I asked.

He laughed.

'I will do either if I am put to it. If you were to ask me which I would prefer, I would say neither, but I am not in the business of preference. I need to make a living,' I told him.

'She is a fine girl, your Alice. She might have the gift, you know.'

'The gift?'

'She sees things other people don't.'

I thought about that.

'Yes,' I agreed. 'Perhaps she does.'

We walked on. These last three summers had been unusually warm, with drought and failing crops. Some folk had talked of this being a precursor of the end of the world. People are all too ready to seize on such things. It had to be said, though, that this summer, at last, after the recent spell of stormy weather, seemed to be setting fair. The sun was hot on our faces.

'They're planting a vineyard near Chartres,' Eliphas said. 'Never been one in Normandy before, not since the Romans. There's a thing.'

'Haven't they got enough wine in this country?'

'In France they have, but not in Normandy. The Duke likes to keep the two countries separate, but King Louis likes to keep them together. That's what all the fighting's about. The Duke won't pay homage to the King, but at the same time he wants the King to recognise William, his son, as his successor. And the King won't do that until the Duke pays him homage.'

'It sounds like an impasse.'

'Impasse is the word. Look out!'

He grabbed me by the shoulder and thrust me roughly out of the way of a cart that veered aside to avoid another wagon. I had not got the hang of these crowded streets yet.

'You have to go about this town like a soldier,' he said. 'As if you're expecting an ambush. And of course you might get one of those too. Or a cut-throat after your purse…'

I was somewhat alarmed at his words. What kind of place had I brought Alice to?

'Tell me about the butcher,' I asked. 'Why should he want help from the likes of me?'

'You would think a butcher would be a big jolly man, wouldn't you?' he said. 'All jowls and whiskers. But not Haimo. He's a little, thin fellow, always looks worried. But he's the best butcher in Rouen, the Duke's butcher and all. Henry will have no one else.'

'I'm not sure I want to see the Duke,' I suggested.

'Oh that's all right. You'll be out the back.'

'The back?'

I had visions of myself sawing enormous carcasses in half and pulling out giblets from horrific cavernous bellies in a room that smelt of gore. There had to be some alternative employment in a town like this. Eliphas saw my look of revulsion and laughed.

'Relax,' he said. 'I do not see you in the charnel house. And here we are now. This is Meat Street.'

It was a broad street and he was right. It was full of butcher's shops, and the kennel running down the centre of the street ran red. The smell as we progressed down the road was strong, a mixture of fresh blood, ripe flesh and over-ripe flesh.

'The smell of the battlefield,' said Eliphas. 'You'll see.'

Dogs scurried earnestly about like businessmen engaged in some important transaction, momentarily indignant at a kick, but on the instant referring back to the transaction in hand.

'At the back,' said Eliphas, 'behind the shops there is a smaller lane where the beasts come to be killed. The customers prefer the killing to be done out of sight. Besides, the poor beasts shit a lot.'

'Is that where I'll be?'

'Let's talk to Haimo and see what he says.'

We stopped at a shop bigger and better appointed than the rest, its wares well displayed. A small, worried man in a butcher's apron was sitting at a counter inspecting a bundle of small sticks, with a look of despair.

'Haimo,' Eliphas cried. 'Cheer up, my old friend. See, I have brought you Master Bertold.'

The little man's face showed an expression of almost comical depression.

'He is not a butcher? He does not look like a butcher. The Marshal at Breteuil sent me word of a man who might be of use to me, but I took him to mean a butcher. Anyway, the only man who could help me now is a man who can do my accounts, tell me how much I buy, at what a cost, and how much I sell and how much I make. The English soldiers come by and they want meat. They say, the quartermaster or the provisioner will pay, and then they go. What can I do? They are the Duke's soldiers...'

'I know what soldiers are like. Everything has to be on credit, always it is someone else who will pay, someone coming quartermastering along behind. Except he never comes unless you seek him out of the woodwork, or surprise him on board when he's going back to England,' said Eliphas.

'I am in debt because of my accounts. My cursed accounts ... and my man Roger has taken ill and cannot help me. I am a butcher, Eliphas, not a money man, but I soon won't even be a butcher.'

'You are going to be a rich butcher, Haimo, and Master Bertold is the man who is going to see to it,' said Eliphas.

He made his excuses and said he had errands to do and people to see in town, and left Haimo and me to explore each other's possibilities.

The little butcher opened a cupboard door and out tumbled a clatter of sticks, all of the same size. He picked them up, wearing an air of puzzlement and mortification as though they were the architects of his misfortune.

'What are these sticks that you are looking at?' I asked him, though I had seen such things before and knew their purpose.

'Why, they are the accounting sticks with a notch for every transaction. But my man Roger has had trouble with his eyes, and can no longer work. I believe he has put the notches in the wrong place. Do you understand these things, young man?' he asked, addressing me.

I had noted the sticks at Breteuil in the steward's room, and Juliana and I had spoken to slimy Odo about them. Everyone used the sticks and notches. I was back for a moment in old Saul's room at the abbey, saying goodbye. 'More useful than a bag of gold or a bright sword by your side,' he had said, and now I knew he wasn't wrong.

'I understand accounts, but not how you have been using them,' I told Haimo. 'If you explain your business to me, I will sort out your sticks. And then I can give you a better system using figures, written on slate or vellum, showing what comes in, what goes out and who owes you what. All very simple. I can do that for you if you have, perhaps, a room upstairs where I can work...'

He clutched at me as if he were a drowning man and I a piece of cork.

I had found myself a job. No, that is wrong. My friends Saul at the abbey, the Marshal at Breteuil and Eliphas the jongleur had found a job for me. My only annoyance was at how little I was able at the moment to pay them back.

The little butcher led me upstairs to a small room overlooking the shop – rather than giving me a view of the back where the animals were killed, I am glad to say – not that I am usually squeamish, but there is something defenceless about a poor beast being led to the slaughter that reminds me of the way we ourselves meet our fate: more roundabout than the road to the abattoir, but just as inevitable, and we are helpless and dumb to the end. It is too near the truth and God himself must look away sometimes when the suffering grows too much, but that's another story – or rather another part of this one. I believe some of us shit before we die too, especially if we are strung up on the scaffold.

Haimo described to me how he bought the beasts, what they cost to keep, and what the shop and its staff cost to run. I told him I would need slate and vellum, chalk and ink.

'What do you need with all this?' he asked. 'You are not writing a monkish history.'

'Slate is fine for day-to-day accounting,' I told him, 'but if you want a portrait of your affairs which slowly grows and provides you at the year's end with everything you need to run a successful business, the slate must be copied on to vellum.'

'You have done this before?' he asked, suspiciously.

I could not blame him for it. I could ruin the man if my theory was marsh-gas and my sums thistledown. I am ashamed to report, at this point, I lied.

'Indeed, I worked at the Abbey of Saint-Sulpice,' I told him. 'I was taught by an old Jewish brother who had learnt his art from the Arabs. The abbey was not of course a business, but we were there to make what money seemed fair, and then to spend it on good and holy works.'

I didn't actually say that I had worked on the Arabic numeral system at the abbey, but I caused him to believe that I had. Indeed, I was so convinced of its efficacy, I almost convinced myself that we had done so. I remember saying to Saul at one point, before he cautioned discretion, that the system he showed me was too good to keep in a monastery.

The butcher, at any rate, was impressed.

'They're clever, the Arabians, so I've heard,' said the butcher, 'even if they do let the beasts bleed their blood out, and they don't eat pigs. The pig, to my mind, is the usefullest beast. Very affectionate and curious, and makes a lovely sausage.'

Haimo seemed reassured by my experience, organised a table and chair for me, and a cupboard to keep the records, and agreed that I should start next day at a weekly rate that I thought almost princely.

I walked back towards the house, bursting with my good news. At least Alice and I could pay for ourselves in this huge town. I was told that there were at least forty thousand people living in Rouen, a number so vast you could hardly imagine them all in one place – which indeed they seemed to be whenever you walked the streets.

Eliphas reappeared and led me to an alehouse, The Old Barge. The girl behind the bar seemed to know him – as everyone did – and directed us to a table in the courtyard.

'Anything to eat, masters?' she asked. 'Got a lovely brawn or pig's head if you fancy.'

'We'll just drink our ale for a while, Yvonne, thank you.'

'What do they do in Rouen?' I asked him. 'Apart from fish and meat...'

'They send wine and wheat to England and they get tin and wool back. They make clothes, and lace. They go to church if

326

they have to – which they mostly do. They drink. They dance. They fuck. They prefer the Duke to King Louis because he gives them what he makes them believe is an easier time with fewer taxes. They like my shows so they are people of good taste. The women like to dress well and walk in the main street on Sundays. That is about it, really. The river is their *raison d'être*. It defines the place. There is something a little spooky about it, if you ask me – the town, I mean. It feels very old and there are funny little corners where you could disappear if you weren't careful. Tables can walk and chairs can run in Rouen, and not only when your back is turned.'

'And dishes run away with spoons,' I suggested.

Eliphas did not look put out, but I apologized, thinking I had gone too far. I knew he did not say these things lightly, for magic was his profession.

'Indeed,' he told me. 'Much stranger things than that have happened here.'

'We shall be careful,' I said. 'What about the Duke? Will he be looking for us?'

'Not at the moment, anyway. He has more pressing things to do. The word is, Juliana and Eustace are of a common mind at least for the moment – their enemy is the Duke. Mutual hatred has done what love could never do. It has brought them together. What she is doing, I know not.'

'She will not be idle long,' I said. 'She will be hatching something.'

'Meanwhile,' he continued, 'Comte Eustace joined forces with Richer de l'Aigle and they plundered and burnt houses at Verneusses. But the Duke's general, Ralph the Red, saw them off. Meanwhile, the Duke is looking to make peace with a rather more powerful enemy. He is concluding arrangements with the Comte of Anjou for the marriage of his own son, Prince William, to Anjou's daughter.'

My mind quickened at that. The last time I had seen Prince William he was screwing his half-sister; but I wasn't going to say anything about that, even among friends. It was the sort of thing that could cost you your head, or worse.

'Anjou has caused a lot of trouble for Henry,' I said. 'The wedding is going to happen in a couple of months or so, and it'll mean another of the Duke's problems is taken care of. And once Anjou's on board, a lot of the smaller ones will come too. Of course, Fat King Louis is not best pleased and keeps nibbling at the borders and making little feints and stabs like a bad swordsman, but there's nothing much he can do.'

'What is the girl's name?' I asked him.

'Matilda, like every other girl in Normandy.'

Eliphas finished his ale, rose to his feet and held out a hand.

'And now,' he said. 'I must leave for Caen where I have an entertainment to organise. They have their annual Ascension Fair, and they want a play about Daedalus who people thought was a god along with Icarus his son. God ends the play by showing that only He can make his son rise up to heaven – but even the son must plunge to Hell before he can do it.'

'I should like to see that,' I said.

'And so you shall one day, but for now you must go home and see to your beautiful Alice who is a special girl. She has the mark of grace and you must take care of her.'

I promised him that I would. There was no chance of seeing Juliana again and having my boat of fidelity rocked once more. How lucky I was to have known and been known by these two women!

'If you have been invited to the Prince's wedding to Matilda of Anjou at Lisieux, you may catch my entertainment afterwards in the château. I have not been instructed yet but I am sure to be.'

'What will you do?'

'Oh, jokes and tricks and playing with fire. They like that in Normandy.'

I thanked him for all his help, for introducing me to Haimo the butcher of Rouen and finding us a home. I wondered whether to offer him money, but I decided against it and I was glad I did. What he said next convinced me.

'There is a kind of destiny about you, Bertold, whether you know it or not. Remember that. You cannot help yourself or turn aside. The cards will fall as they do because they have fallen already. I always like to help Destiny if I can. She can be curiously grateful. Look after yourself – and Alice, especially Alice.'

What kind of man was this who seemed to know everything? You may well ask, and I ask it too, after everything that has happened. Where did he come from?

'This is the place for news,' he continued, 'it all comes here from wagoners, travellers, soldiers, and folk like me. Listen in, and be careful.'

He turned, moved out through the tavern and passed through the crowd like melting butter. I waved as he went though he did not see me, and I felt all at once bereft as though I had lost a trusted friend and guide, although come to think of it I hardly knew the fellow. He knew me, however, and I had found that comforting. Now I was alone again and had to make my own way. For a moment or two I felt the town to be an unfriendly place, full of cantering tables, galloping tallboys, and lumpen citizens.

I was not cast down for long, though. The sun shone, the crowd was good-humoured that morning, I had a job, and a beautiful girl was waiting for me at home. What was more, I had the curious feeling that I was in the right place at the right time, doing what I should be doing.

I walked home along the river, the late afternoon sun bouncing about on the water while the men unloading wool at the docks cursed its heat as it squeezed them dry as lemons. I reached home to find no Berthe in the house, a smell of thyme and nutmeg in the kitchen, and Alice lying on our bed completely naked in the heat of the afternoon, trying to catch the faintest breeze from the window.

She hastily covered herself when I entered the room, and I apologized for so rudely entering.

'It wasn't rude,' she said, still covered, 'and I should not cover myself when you enter. It was just an instinct of castle and manor-house life. I want you to see me naked. This is our paradise up here. I have nothing to hide.'

'Eliphas was right,' I said. 'You are full of surprises and wonders. He has gone to Caen and sends his special goodbye to you. You seem to be high in his good books – as you are in mine.'

'Stop making speeches,' she said, uncovering herself again, 'and take your clothes off.'

There seemed no reason not to, and indeed there were urgent arguments that I should. We lay for a little while together, feeling the heat disturbing the air – it passed for breeze. And then I began with her hand. The hand was cool, and I felt it with mine that was hotter. I ran my finger over it, tracing the shape of it, the fingers, pressing my hand upon it, turning the hand over so that it lay palm upwards, pressing the palm, pinching the fingers and kneading the mound that lay beneath the thumb. It doesn't sound much, but I tell you it excited the hell out of me. We spoke not a word. And then I began to run my hand up her arm to one of the anterooms of secrecy, the inside of her elbow. I kissed the place as though it were the final secret. It was fragrant, slightly salty. She was breathing a little more quickly now, and trembling slightly.

Alice, naked, smelt of milk and walnuts and wild honey, not the domestic kind.

I ran my fingers very lightly up towards that other private place, the curve where her arm joined her body. I followed my fingers with my mouth. Under her arm, the hair was very fine and light, which I took to be an indication of other things below, exciting for that reason. I explored that hidden place as though it were the most amorous region which laymen could only dream about.

My hand pursued its exploration and next it traced the line of her collar-bone and up towards her neck, which I kissed and felt her start and give a little sound as I burrowed softly and puckered at the skin. Her mouth was open and her breathing was quicker now.

My hand started the journey south. This had all been overture. It encountered the first slope of her breast, a gentle swelling under milk-white skin, very slightly veined. It drifted round, to the side, and under, and the hand which followed the finger, held the breast as if it were a dove. Then the finger touched the centre which transformed at my intrusion into a dark berry of flesh which made her gasp, and I gasped with her. My other hand now followed and they held these gifts with the reverence of Caspar, Melchior and Balthasar (if that is not blasphemous, which it is), squeezing and toying with the fruit as if they would pick it. Solemn things which turn a beggar into a king.

My mouth could no longer be denied its turn, and I sucked at her breast as we bartered pleasure and discovery in the strange commerce of love. And now my hand continued the path down, finding first a little concave buttonhole which occasioned a diversion, more soft skin below that and finally the fine, dark, silky hair again which I had met at the top of her arm. Then I felt my finger slide not just outside the girl, but into Alice, and I clutched at her and bent down and kissed her, drinking in the love of her, sweeter than roses, and kissing her on the mouth at last with the taste of all three mouths upon us. And even as we did that, I was within her, pushing, riding, until with a weird shriek which Eliphas could have used for one of his demonic shows, the thing was done and we were joined together for ever, or at least as long as we were allowed. No, I do not mean that condition in which women have some kind of convulsion and seize the man's member while he is still inside her with a grip like a vice. That was not Alice's way. I meant that she and I were indissolubly each other's. I was young, I was callow, I was selfish, I was puffed up, I had a high opinion of myself, in short I was a bastard – but all of that was excused and moderated and mitigated because we loved each other.

We lay there, looking at each other, looking at the ceiling, saying nothing, feeling everything. I thought then, as I think now, that each time you make love to a different woman it is like making love for the first time unless you are a fool and then it is the same again and again and again like fucking in hell. I had never made love to Juliana like that. With Juliana it was worship – which is to say a Eucharist though I blaspheme to write it – but with Alice it was a love between equals.

An idea came into my head which I wondered whether to express to her.

'Did you ever lie with Juliana?' I asked.

She looked at me, and smiled.

I was quickened once again, more if possible, than ever.

Finally there was a knock at the door.

'Are you all right? Anything you need?'

It was Berthe back from her errands. Alice and I looked at each other.

'Perfectly all right, thank you,' we said together, not meaning to speak in unison.

We giggled and Berthe laughed.

'Supper will be ready in about an hour. Come down when you like.'

I don't think I had ever been – or ever would be – happier.

Well, not since I first slept with Juliana. But that was different, as I say.

LVI

The next weeks and months passed in happiness with Alice in the house of Berthe, and with hard work with Haimo in the butcher's shop and yard. I was learning the butchery trade, a necessity for any accountant in that business, for if you have no experience of the trade you can never understand the finer points of making a profit. I am glad to say that Master Haimo found me a willing pupil and, more and more, a creator of ideas to improve the flow of cash.

There were certain obstacles to smooth running. Chief of which was the credit that he had allowed to build up when dealing with the comtes and the Duke's generals and their stewards, and most of all with the Duke himself.

The aristocrats could never be bothered to deal with affairs that they thought below their dignity – although they consumed money as happily as anyone, and they shat and fucked and ate and drank and fed their ambitions as well as any common man or serf. The stewards who were often siphoning money into their own pockets were only too happy to let the accounting drift – and in the past it had become a tradition with Haimo's clients since his accounts were in such a pickle. As for the Duke, he was the worst of the lot, but one had to tread carefully with him. A word and all that trade and commission and prestige could pass to a rival butcher, and it would not just be the Duke's business that was lost, but that of all the nobs and bobs that liked to travel in his wake.

I taught the men in the shop and the buyers in the field, as well as those who received the beasts in the big shed at the back where the slaughtering took place – indeed all of the employees of Haimo who indented, sold or purchased – the basic 0 to 10 number of the Arabic numerology. Each had his slates on which he marked his trade, and at the end of the day I received them all, checked them over, and entered them in my ledger of vellum.

333

Some of the staff were too idle or truculent to learn the new method, none more so than a big bovine brute called Luc, who I suspected had a little trade going of his own and who refused to adapt to the new regime. I spoke to Haimo about him, and he indicated that he too had had his doubts about the man.

'You are going to have to leave if you won't learn what all the others have found not too difficult,' I told Luc.

'We did all right before you came,' he said.

'Yes, and you nearly drove poor Haimo into debt,' I told him.

'You come from nowhere and start telling us what to do. It ain't right,' he said.

'It is right, if you are doing wrong,' I replied.

His face darkened. He was a lout and no doubt he could be dangerous. Indeed I had a moment of unease when I thought of how precarious our situation in Rouen was, as strangers quite possibly sought by the Duke's spies, but there was no turning back. I told him that his job with Haimo was over.

'You're going to regret this,' he said. 'You see if you don't.'

'You want a fight, then? I'll wrestle with you if you like. We can fight it out in the street.'

I was quite happy to do it for, though he was a little bigger than me, he did not look like a fit man – too many visits propping up the ale-house.

'Nah,' he said, 'I'm not going to fight you now. But you watch your back. I won't be far behind.'

'The coward's way! If I see you there,' I said, 'I'll throw you into the river.'

We glared at each other and he skulked out. I gave it little thought, being used to looking after myself, though there were odd moments when I thought I was being followed as I went back home to Alice late at night, after sitting up over the accounts. But in a town like Rouen there are always latecomers, drinkers and lovers scuttling about their various businesses.

We were happy in those days. It wasn't our home but we were together. The one thing I could not entirely get used to was the butchery business itself. I was brought up in the country where they kill for food, and it is no small business to feed a castle of some hundred or more people. But at Mortagne, or indeed Breteuil, the killing was done to feed people whom I knew, a sort of domestic necessity, and it would happen on certain days and seasons of the year and then it would be over: regrettable for the animal, perhaps, but it meant juicy stews and steaks and sausages – not to mention hams, faggots, brains, liver, lights and chitterlings – for us. And the meat days were punctuated by fish on Fridays and quite possibly on Mondays and Wednesdays too. In Haimo's yard, it was meat every day, all day. It smelt of blood. You could taste it in the air when the soldiers came by and they were hungry. (Killing people does seem good for the appetite.)

No one butchered better in Rouen than Haimo; and his shop was a masterpiece of presentation. I wondered if Eliphas had helped him in this matter and asked Haimo if it was so and he replied that indeed it was. Eliphas knows how to show, how to catch the eye and make the fingers itch to part with silver pennies whether on a stage-set or a shop-front. He could pull a rabbit out of a hat, a canary out of a soldier's nose, a snake out of a jerkin, an angel out of heaven or a great *contrefilet* of beef ready for the Mayor's cook Agathe (than whom none is more subtle and exquisite at the spit or, come to that, at spitting). After all this killing, and totting it up and noting it down, and walking round the premises to see that no one was snitching a little bit of meat without permission – there were some fourteen men working for us, more if you counted the drovers and the fodder-men who looked after beasts if they had to be kept at the yard overnight (the place made the animals nervous so we tried to avoid that, but it sometimes had to be) – at the end of the day, I would come home exhausted and ready for a pint of wine and a good supper. Anything but giblets.

Rouen, as I have mentioned, is more assailed with smells than anywhere I have lived, but spilt blood in quantity is the smell you can least get used to. It clings like the spirits of the unhappy dead. Thank heaven my home here, strewn with herbs and odorous with spices and Alice herself, was a haven of fragrance.

To lift my head beyond my happy daily horizon, I followed the activities and exploits, which I gleaned, here and there and in The Barge, of the Duke and his friends and enemies. Amaury was still making trouble, apparently. No surprises there. News reached us too, confirming Eliphas's earlier forecast, of Prince William the Atheling's wedding which was to be at the end of the month.

'Poor old William,' I said to Alice. 'He's going to find it difficult being married to another Matilda, while the one he really likes is his half-sister!'

Alice looked as though she were sucking a sloe. I had told her about my discovery in the barn at Mortagne (enjoining her to secrecy), and I had been mildly surprised at her reaction. Incest was not a rarity, though scarcely something you would want to make public, but I have noticed that some women who are the most joyful in their lovemaking are in other respects the most prudish.

People in Rouen, anyway, knew nothing of such princely goings-on and approved of the match because a royal wedding was bound to mean some kind of celebration in the town. It was rumoured that the new drink of beer rather than ale, made with hops for better keeping, might even run from the city fountains.

'And a fat lot of good that will do for my trade,' said the landlord of The Barge, as I sat with Haimo later, discussing the day's trade.

I am glad to say that little Haimo was a changed man. With all the financial worry removed, he was making a profit at last, but he drank his hoppy beer thoughtfully; it was plain there was something on his mind.

'What's the matter, Haimo? Things going too well?' I asked.

'No, no,' he said. 'I was thinking about how I could reward you.'

'You pay me well enough,' I said.

'Yes, but … what will happen when you go? It has been worrying me.'

'I am not going anywhere,' I told him. 'I have a good job, Alice is happy. She and Berthe have built up quite a trade with their herbs and spices, and their pharmacopoeia.'

It was true. Alice and Berthe got on very well together, and I had been able to teach Alice something of my medical knowledge derived from Brother Paul. People had started to come to them for cures for their ailments, and so their business had also grown, although there had been mutterings from the local doctors.

'I want to offer you a share of my business,' said Haimo. 'Would a quarter share be of interest?'

I was at a loss. I didn't want to offend or even disappoint the man, but I had never seen myself as a butcher. I had rather hoped to become a nobleman although I knew that was a hard climb like the cliffs of Falaise.

'I am much honoured,' I told him, 'but I had no great plans to spend my life in Rouen – which I would have to do if I accepted your kind offer.'

'Not kind,' he said. 'Mere prudence on my part.'

'Your prudent offer,' I said, laughing. 'But I should speak to my wife about her wishes for she is a strong woman.'

I called Alice 'my wife' to avoid confusion. We were strangers in town, and nobody would be any the wiser. I had spoken to Alice previously about being called Mistress in Rouen and she said she was easy. Maybe one day, she said, but I sensed she would have liked to have been married, after all, and I felt bad about it.

'Speak to your wife, of course,' said Haimo. 'There are worse places to spend your life than Rouen.'

I did talk to Alice that evening, and she was on the whole keen on the idea. She enjoyed working with Berthe and dispensing their pharmacopeia. It was the education she had always felt she lacked. So I came back to Haimo next day and said I was still uncertain, which I was; I had never intended myself, as I say, for a life of butchery. You may think the accountant is able to keep his hands clean, but there were always the little crises in the yard and in the shop when someone was ill or there was a panic or someone forgot that an important customer was coming, and who should step into the breach but the accountant? I sniffed the smell and I heard the lowing of frightened beasts and I thought of my father the Comte de Perche and how low a butcher would seem to him – and then I thought of my mother who would have said what a fine profession is the butcher's, just as good as a vintner if not better, and they are always round, jolly and fat – except of course Haimo. And then I thought of Juliana and what she would think – but I put that thought out of my mind because her life had moved on and so had mine.

At that point Haimo increased the offer to half his business, and I accepted. There is no point in being an underling.

So the weeks rolled on like the Rouen river, though to a less foreseeable conclusion. Alice wanted to show me where William the Conqueror had died, so one day we took cheese and sausage and bread and a flask of wine, and walked up a hill to the west of the city to the church of St Gervase. We ate our food close by, looking down on the great bulk of the town and the winding web of the river, trying to spot Berthe's house. Here, at the church and its buildings, William had spent his last months in terrible pain from his stomach ('I hope this sausage is all right,' I said) giving away money for the good of his soul to churches and abbeys he had founded or burnt.

'Wouldn't it have been better not to have burnt the churches and saved the money?' Alice suggested.

'Better for his stomach. He wouldn't have had the pain of guilt and regret. But not so good for the Church.'

Just at the moment a great bell boomed its answer from the Cathedral of St Mary, announcing the service of Nones. We looked at each other and laughed, it was so prompt on its cue.

'That same bell was what woke the Conqueror just before he died,' she told me. 'My mother heard all about it in Barfleur because the English use it as their port for home. He had a painful death, but it was worse after he died. His children

338

deserted him. His eldest son Robert had just struck a deal with the King of France. Rufus had gone to England. Henry was over in London and Winchester making sure of the cash his father had left him; and no one was here to take charge. The richer men dashed off to look after their property and the poorer ones looted the royal lodgings. They had a chaotic service in Rouen but apparently he had to be buried in Caen. Then they could not find anyone to pay for taking him by sea to Caen, so there was another delay. Finally, a nobody knight called Herlouin, a friend of my grandfather's, said he would pay for it himself. So the great man was taken by slow boat to Caen. By that time the corpse was beginning to go off. They had another service in Caen and, when they came to bury him in the Cathedral, he had swelled so much they couldn't fit him in the sandstone tomb. They pushed and pulled and finally the Conqueror burst.'

'That's one way of clearing a church,' I said. 'I'm glad we finished that sausage. What a way to go.'

'*Sic transit gloria mundi.*'

'Ah, you speak Latin?'

'The little girls used to teach me,' she said. 'So pass the glories of the world. They said it was one of your favourite lines.'

LVII

Prince William and Matilda of Anjou were finally married, as forecast, and the fountains in Rouen still coursed obstinately with water. People who didn't depend on the fountains for refreshment raised their cups and wished the couple long life and more legitimate children than the Duke had managed, and all the time Alice's story of the great Conqueror's death and funeral rang in my ears. If he had known he would end like that, would he have changed his life in any way? How fragile was the present, how uncertain the future.

It was particularly the wagoners, driving from all over the dukedom and beyond, who carried news to Rouen. Soldiers tended to be more taciturn and brusque, bargees coarser, travellers more secretive though sometimes sensational. There were still the strolling players and musicians, but wagoners led a lonely, ruminative life, jolting along, passing through and coming back again, bearing goods and freight, inwards and outwards, and carrying news like pollen in their coats. They heard it all, and to them it was all snippets but to me every snippet fitted into the picture of the Duke and what he was, and what he was trying to do – and, yes, what his daughter Juliana might be trying to do, for I had no reason to believe that she had given up, and imagined that her dearest wish was still to destroy him.

We heard at The Barge that the Duke had won a great battle with the French under King Louis at Brémule, only just failing to capture the King himself. The townsfolk were very excited, hoping (in vain as it turned out) for the fountains to run with beer. They lived in a state of suspended optimism for this phenomenon, though it had never occurred and no one could ever see how it might be achieved.

Only a few weeks after that, there was more news from the wagoners. Amaury de Montfort had inveigled the French king, who was feeling humiliated as well he might, to join him in attacking Breteuil, now held by the Duke's man Ralph de Gael. Once more, they had been beaten back by Henry's trusted general from England, Ralph the Red.

LVIII

All through the early autumn of that Year of Our Lord 1119, Alice and I and Berthe made ourselves snug in the low-beamed house with its gaps stuffed with wattle to keep out the draughts, and Juliana kept popping into my head like a sudden scent half-caught as someone passes in the street. Juliana – what was she doing, how was she feeling, did she still think of me? What would she make of me now, knee deep in blood as I tried to help a struggling slaughterer, clutching a cleaver for him over a half dead heifer?

Juliana, I thought, my first love whom I have betrayed. 'Come again, sweet love, to me,' I warbled when no one could hear, high in my counting-house. It's hard to put out thoughts that come into your head. And here, and in the shambles, thinking of her, I was betraying Alice too whom I loved beyond reason and who had the gift of knowing what I was thinking. She had the gift of quietness, of only saying what needed to be said. No wonder Juliana had liked her. I felt the luckiest of men at times, and at others, the most accursed.

Our eyrie at the top of the house, which had been hot enough to cook bread in during the heat of summer, became cool then cold under the roof, but it was the tribute we paid for the privacy the top floor gave us. Privacy! Now there's a thing you don't get in a castle. The only time you get to be by yourself is in bed – and sometimes not even then when you find yourself bundled up with a snorting, hairy knight on important visitor days.

Harvest-time came and went. Michaelmas spelt the beginning of the slaughtering season for pigs, the carcass that most of all resembles the human body. There was salting and smoking to be done, and curing too. The whole town was pig for a fortnight. And then we moved on to the season of game and, of course, venison. And all at once it was All Souls Night, with players in the town making the dead walk, and All Saints when the Archangel Michael trounces the forces of darkness and clears up the drunks. I had looked to see Eliphas in town at this time, but he failed to show up. Some prince or baron was no doubt commanding him. Some silly comte ... or comtesse ... and there she was again: Juliana, my lost love, cause of so much happiness, and the reverse, whom I can never quite shake off.

Late autumn was windy and wet with floods, terrible gales and the river over its banks. Floods everywhere; never seen such weather; the world must be coming to an end, said the locals. It's all because of your sins, said the churchmen. Meanwhile, the Pope came to Rheims for a Council, and King Louis complained about Duke Henry. Our Archbishop of Rouen represented Henry's case, but was booed and drowned out by supporters of Louis. The Duke then went to see the Pope himself when he moved to Gisors, and a fair old bollocking the Pope gave him, all about kicking out his brother the Duke Robert, and not paying homage to King Louis – not that Henry couldn't take a bollocking and give back when he chose. Henry said his brother Robert had ruled over chaos and he, Henry, was all for homage to be paid to the French king – but he wanted it done by his son William. And so it went on. We heard all about it from the landlord who'd been told it by a wagoner from Rheims who knew one of the pages. He reckoned Henry might finally be getting what he wanted: peace in Normandy with him on top, and his son William confirmed as his successor. That last bit was what Henry coveted most of all, having himself attained the royal seat by some unorthodox and even (some said) unlawful routes.

This history, you see, is not just about Bertold and Juliana, or Bertold and Alice. Well, it *is* of course about both Juliana and Alice, but it is also very much about Duke Henry because he is, in a way – as Eliphas would say – a leading player. If he wins, Normandy wins. That is what a good king or duke does for his people – and Henry was good in that way. If he loses, it is his tragedy and ours. As a family man, he has two little tragedies already. As a king, he is still Beauclerc.

Two things made me give special attention to the wagoners' next report. One was that that shit Amaury de Montfort had finally made peace with the Duke. Henry had given him, in the end, the county of Évreux minus the castle. Amaury had accepted with his usual bad grace. The news made me grind my teeth. Why is it that the undeserving so often triumph in this world? It leaves virtue without a leg to stand on.

The other special nugget of news was that Eustace of Breteuil and his wife Juliana, the Duke's daughter, had approached the Duke – unbidden and unheralded, barefoot – as penitents. The Duke was apparently amazed at their outrageous behaviour, but Eustace grovelled suitably as only a truculent drunkard can. Juliana as a penitent, however, did not ring true to me. I could not believe she would do that in sackcloth weeds and a state of undress. Apart from anything else, she had always been someone who delighted in her clothes.

Anyway, apparently her half-brother Richard had put in a good word for her, and the Duke forgave them, so good relations were re-established. Juliana was told to go back to the castle of Pacy, while Eustace was ordered to accompany the Duke on his rounds. Henry intended to visit Rouen before moving on to Caen and this indeed he did, riding with his entourage, through the city gates a week later.

Alice and I decided to keep indoors during the duration of the Duke's visit to the town, for if Eustace saw me he would certainly point me out to his liege, and then there would be knocking on the door, and the men in hard helmets would take us away. However, I could not refrain from creeping out one day with my hood over my face, and peeking at the ducal party as they rode past. The Duke looked like iron, hard as a helmet, while Eustace slouched in his saddle: the man seemed to have shrivelled; he was all used up. It reminded me of a knitted toy I had had as a child which slowly lost its stuffing. The Duke must have given him a hard time, as he could. Perhaps the man had even stopped drinking.

Soon the ducal party moved on. Henry could never stay long, there was always something doing.

LIX

Christmas approached, and the butcher and I were busier than ever. Soldiers were coming past in companies heading for England, wanting food, and their quartermasters not wanting to pay. We had the odd set-to with the rank and file, I can tell you, and the arrogance of some of the knights – less well-born than me, drawling at me to feed the men or else – took my breath away. But I bit my tongue and said nothing, fixing my thoughts on the profit, as Haimo advised.

At last it was Christmas itself. How different from our Christmas last year with all the regalia of a great castle! This Christmas in Rouen was rather more private, more *sotto voce* as Brother Paul used to say, but we loved it for that, only I could not help thinking of the little girls and indeed of Juliana.

On Christmas morning, I gave Alice a new cloak trimmed with fur and some new shoes from the best shoemaker in Rouen. Alice and Berthe and I attended Mass at the Cathedral with Haimo (he was a widower and lived alone). Then we had a feast at Berthe's: goose and pork pies and venison patties and cakes and marchpane and ginger puddings and pressed cinnamon wafers, washed down with flagons of the best Burgundy Haimo could find. Haimo was invited to dinners given by some of the burgesses in their halls, since he was an important trader in the city, and we went with him. I had anticipated a quiet time over the twelve days of Christmas, but Alice and I hardly had a day to ourselves.

At one of these civic parties, a Twelfth Night Feast, in the Fishmongers Hall, Alice and I had a slight contretemps with an over-inquisitive priest, some canon of the Cathedral who proceeded to ask us when and where we had been married, and whether we had any document to show for it. Grossly impolite and impertinent at someone else's party, but there it was, priests are like that and think they can do anything. He hit on the idea of asking Alice first, and then me, which church we were married in, when we were separated from one another. And of course, being unprepared – which we should not have been – we gave different answers.

Luckily the priest became inebriated and we were able to escape, but I reckoned he had us marked down. There could have been trouble, ecclesiastical courts, and all sorts. Alice and I would have our story right next time. The priests are everywhere, snouts in the trough, eyes in the back of their heads, and hands in your pockets (if you're lucky).

You didn't have to be a priest to notice that Haimo and Berthe were getting on well; indeed the little butcher actually appeared to be putting on weight, while Berthe seemed to be losing it.

At last, Christmas was over and the slaughtering started again, a burst of activity before Lent. January had been milder than usual, and windy, but February turned bitterly cold. The river half froze over again at the part where a lagoon forms against the southern shore, and a boy looking for his dog was drowned when he tried to walk on it. There were celebrations on Shrove Tuesday and then most of the men at Haimo's were laid off for the duration. The whole quarter of the town by the river inhaled an extra Lenten whiff of fish. I took the books home to Berthe's kitchen where I could work on them in the warmth. I finished them one dark day in February and took them back to Haimo in his room at the butchery. He loved it there even when nothing was happening.

'Haimo,' I said, 'you have made a decent profit. It would have been bigger if we'd done this sooner.'

'But you weren't here sooner,'

'That is true. More's the pity. Even so, you should buy yourself new clothes. A prosperous man needs to look prosperous. You are a walking exemplar for your business.'

'Our business,' he corrected me.

'Indeed.'

'So you should buy some new clothes too.'

The old boy was growing quite skittish.

Something that looked like spring came at last with a bluster of wind and a tremble of daffodils. A hulk capsized downriver and bales of cloth were washed ashore as far up as Les Andelys. Houses up and down put out their rugs to air and stretched out their sheets gaily on clothes-lines across the alleys. There was, as there always is, a sense of refreshment and new beginnings.

Before Easter came, something occurred that made the Duke angry. We heard all about it from another wagoner who had come from Caen where the Duke was quartering. Henry had had a long-standing quarrel with his Archbishop of York, the man called Thurstan, who would not agree to being ranked lower than the Archbishop of Canterbury, and exiled him from England. The Archbishop was now trudging around France, long in the face, and making trouble. The Pope's decision was that Henry, on pain of excommunication, had to let him go back to England, and the Pope was insisting on a meeting between the Duke and his Legate. This whole matter of Normandy, the Duke's homage to the King of France, the Archbishop's return to England, Prince William's succession, and the submission of the barons still opposed to Henry, was coming to a head.

It didn't mean much to most people, to whom the price of bread is more important than a battle, but of course I was interested. Alice and I talked about it, and our feeling was that our own position would be better if the Duke was a happy man. I was still on the list of those who had stood against him at Breteuil, officially an enemy. I could not forget that short sojourn I had spent in the dungeon at Ivry. It could happen again, without warning, without reason. As for Alice, she was a deserter; she had run away from her mistress who happened to be the Duke's daughter. Juliana, now reconciled to her father could say anything if she chose: that Alice had stolen silver, was living immorally; anything. Alice too could find herself on a bed of straw in a hard place. If the Duke could do that to his own brother, who still lay prisoner in a castle, who knows what he could do to a passing irritation. He could crush us like fruit flies.

It was Easter, late this year, when the killing started again (well, it started before Easter so that we should have enough meat for the Easter rush), and after that the year rolled forward in a familiar butcher's trundle, for I realised with some shock that we had been in Rouen a full twelve months and could almost consider ourselves Rouennais.

We went to Mass on Good Friday, and again on Easter Day – twice. There were plenty of eyes and mouths to tell on you if you didn't in Rouen.

At Ascension-tide, there was great excitement upriver at Vernon, a dozen miles or so away. The Pope's legate, Cardinal Cuno, had arrived to see the Duke, and they were joined by Archbishop Thurstan, stubborn old josser that he was. Some said it was a snub to Rouen that the bigwigs didn't meet in the town, but others said Henry was uncertain of big crowds – Rouen was the second biggest city after Lyon in the whole of France, not counting Paris – and you could never quite tell how safe the town might be for great people in that jostling throng. Perhaps they were nervous of the Jews. There were six thousand of them in Rouen, nearly a sixth of the city. The Jews always added an unstable, exotic element, rather in the way old Saul had done at Saint-Sulpice.

At all events, Henry and Cuno met in Vernon, and Henry was forced to agree to take his old mule of an Archbishop, Thurstan, back to England in the near future. We sent them up some meat by boat because Henry insisted on Haimo's provision and learned the news from the landlord of a snug little tavern, The Water Rat, in Vernon. He told us Henry could not go back to England without first agreeing peace with Louis, who could then accept homage from Prince William (which was dear to Henry's heart), so Henry had to agree to the Archbishop's return. Back in England, he had previously given an oath to the Archbishop of Canterbury that Thurstan of York would not return until he agreed to submit to Canterbury. It just showed how proud, selfish and stubborn these spiritual princes could be – just as bad, in fact, as the lords temporal who couldn't keep their sacred promises.

Funnily enough, it was the troublesome Thurstan who proved clever at finding ways through the thickets of Norman negotiation. He got King Louis to agree to the idea of Prince William paying homage not to Louis himself, because he had previously made an oath to the deposed Duke Robert, but to Louis' son – a small boy, almost a baby.

'Nothing so strange about that,' said King Louis the Fat. 'Do we not pay homage at Christmas to an infant?'

So Henry got what he wanted: his son recognised as the future Duke of Normandy; the French King on speaking terms with him; and the unruly barons no longer with a powerful figure to give them support. The only fly in the unguent was having his troublesome Archbishop Thurstan in England again, but he would be in York where he belonged, far from London, with orders not to come down and fight with Canterbury until it suited his king to call him.

'So what?' said the jolly fat landlord of The Old Barge. 'They'll all be fighting again next year.'

'If you ask me, they want their heads knocking together,' said the barmaid.

'What does it matter?' asked Berthe, as we sat round the table at home. 'They're just like a lot of children.'

'This will be going on for weeks,' said Haimo. 'Talk talk talk. But what would they all do if they didn't have such things to waste their time on?'

'They'd be rushing out of their castles and killing everyone,' said Alice. 'So it's just as well they have…'

The negotiations did indeed go on for weeks, then months. In the meantime, many of the Norman Comtes who had been at odds with Henry saw the writing on the wall and opted for peace. If the King of France was going to stop fighting Henry, they could hardly keep the trouble going by themselves. Meanwhile, the King accepted Henry's son as rightful inheritor of Normandy, and Prince William performed homage to Louis's son, one heir to another, as had been negotiated.

At this point even people like the Comte of Flanders – a dyed in the wool opponent of Henry's along with Stephen, Comte of Aumale – threw in the towel, and the son of the erstwhile duke, Robert, gave up his years-long quest to avenge his father and secure himself the dukedom, even though the King of France had made an oath that he would help him. Luckily for Louis, the Pope or his delegate absolved him from his promise. It was too bad for Henry's nephew, son of the erstwhile duke, but that is the way of princes and of Popes.

And all the while, as the Church and the nobs chopped up the kingdom, we chopped up the animals, but at least we were honest about it. The beasts came in and the yard ran red and the hunks of meat, cleverly cut and creatively presented, were sold to peer and peasant alike, and we became rich because Haimo was the best butcher in Rouen and I was the best accountant.

My method was simple – a little money out, a lot of money in. Simple arithmetic, and firm on credit. I had not gone into those devices and ingenuities of money-making that we heard people in Italy were practising – maybe they needed them in the business of crusading and banking and usury, I could not tell. For butchery, what we made with honest trading and Arabic numerals was money enough.

It was still not exactly the life I had seen myself leading, but you can't have everything, can you, or else you would become spoilt and unpleasant to know. One consequence of our success, rather sadly, was that Alice and I were seeing less of each other. She was sad about it too, but she worked until late, dealing with the sick who came to Berthe's door, and I came home tired after a day at the butchery – and so it continued. We loved each other just as much, and spoke of marriage when things had quietened down a little, but somehow it didn't seem to matter. We belonged to each other anyway. I tried to encourage her to draw a line and see those who came late, on the following day, but she shook her dark head. She had the healer's art and, if she could help them, that is what she did. It was what she had been waiting for all those years – that and me, she told me. The next day may never happen, she used to say, so when it was late and we made love it was as if there were no tomorrow.

She was, unfortunately, too good at her art, for one day in September when the stubble stood in the fields like the bristles on a badly shaved Norseman, her skill came to the attention of the town authorities and in the end, the Mayor sent for her to attend his mayoral hall. Two constables escorted her, and Berthe and I walked at some distance behind. Doors opened, a crowd flocked in and I flocked with them. Alice looked as beautiful as ever – not downcast, but determined – and the Mayor looked ugly; fat with a downward mouth and a nose beginning to show incipient rosacea. I do not know how I looked but I felt terrible.

They soon discovered she was not a native Rouennaise at all. The Mayor supervised proceedings from his great seat (one great seat on top of another because he had a fat arse), while a man in a black gown, some kind of advocate-cleric, conducted the enquiry. I thought I recognised him.

'So who are you?'

'I am Alice Blouet.'

'Where do you come from?'

'Breteuil.'

'Breteuil? Are you sure?'

'Of course I am sure. Where do you come from?'

'Do not be impertinent with me or it will be the worse for you.'

'I do not know who you are. It is hard to be impertinent to someone one does not know. I ask the question so that I may be better acquainted.'

'I am asking the questions. Do not chop logic with me.'

Be nice, Alice, I implored inwardly. Be sweet. You know you can be.

'Breteuil was the seat of the Duke's enemy, Eustace. Are you too an enemy?'

'I was one of the Comtesse's ladies. She is the daughter of the Duke.'

There was an indrawing of breath from the crowd and even the inquisitor paused to digest the news. It did not seem to make him more friendly.

'And why did you leave?'

'The Duke and she had a quarrel. I did not wish to take sides. I decided to leave because I heard how kind and hospitable were the people of Rouen, where I might find people who would benefit from my knowledge of medicinal herbs and spices.'

'How are we to know you are not a witch, expelled from the Comtesse's court for dark practices? Witches too are good at healing those who they love – and harming those whom they don't. We have a witness who says you have given him cramps and blains. There is a black cat in your house. He says it is your familiar.'

It was time for me to speak up.

'This is all a mistake,' I said smoothly. 'I am sure we can clear this up.'

'And you, sir, who are you?'

'I am Master Haimo the butcher's tally-man.'

'Oh, we have heard of you. We were coming for you. Haimo is an honest man but you have tricked him with your craft. You employ ciphers to do tricks with his accounting. You use the round sign which is the sign of Anti-Christ. You charm the maids with your a-*conting*.'

He tittered at his own joke and a few toadies tittered with him. Someone in the crowd said:

'Arrest him so he can play no more tricks.'

I thought it was Luc, the butcher's shopkeeper whom I had sacked. While I was pondering that, I found two stout constables holding my arms.

'You, sir,' said the inquisitor. 'Stand in the witness box. This woman, Alice Blouet, is your wife?'

'Yes. And I protest at my arrest. I thought the people of Rouen were fair-minded folk who do not like to see people arrested on trumped-up charges.'

'Silence. Answer the questions or it will be the worse for you. No one knows you here. You may be a spy.'

Alice spoke up at this point. 'Let go of his arms or it will be the worse for you.'

The inquisitor became enraged. 'I have warned you, madam...'

He started to raise his arm at her.

'You do that and you're a dead man,' I told him.

'Oh dear me,' a silky voice interposed. 'All squabbling like children.'

I peered into the throng of churchmen, and saw a movement at the back. The throng parted and a tall fellow, white-faced, high-voiced and portly as a eunuch, walked forward.

'I am the Pope's Enquirer,' he told me. 'I travel with Cardinal Cuno. I am sent to examine, for instance, the question of the large Jewish population of this city; their influence on the behaviour, belief and morals of the populace.'

'Many of them come from Spain, I believe, bringing new ideas in medicine, mathematics and *rerum naturae*,' I said, mindful of my old mentor at the monastery. 'Surely the town could do with some of that.'

'New wine in old bottles, tally-man, and you are a Latiner, I see. Never a good idea. We are told also of new people, strangers in our midst, who muddy faith with a spirit of rational or intellectual enquiry derived from the pagan fathers, followers of Abelard in Paris who profess a quasi-heretical belief in Modernism, Realism, Conceptualism, and isms beyond whatnot, and we know what happened to *him*.'

'He had his bollocks chopped off,' shouted a voice from the crowd.

'Indeed he did, as I shall have yours if there are any more interruptions. There are others in Northern France, I have heard,' he continued, 'who begin to postulate the duality of the Creation, They believe that God created the spiritual world and the Devil created the physical one. They begin to wander about, these people, telling others of their heresies and suborning them to join their corrupt faith. There are others too, just a few as yet,

355

but they will spread like evil weeds, who have the impertinence to say that love is a sacrament, and defile love's name. These are troubled times when people wander about. It is quite possible that you two strangers may be such wandering people. Tell me about yourselves.'

'We have told you,' I said to him. 'We are who we are. We come from Breteuil, before that I lived at Mortagne. Alice comes originally from Barfleur where the Duke changes into the English King and sails for Southampton. We have found shelter and work here in Rouen. Shall it be said there is no welcome here in Rouen for strangers who can work? You all started here once, or your fathers or your great-great-grandfathers did, arriving here one day. There is a wall around the city, but there are gates in it. People come and go. We came. We stayed. We love the city.'

'As for heretical belief,' Alice chimed in, 'we leave all that to churchmen. Our religion is our fathers' religion. We do not hold with sectarianism or secret meetings. We do not like trouble. We give unto Caesar that which is Caesar's and to God that which is God's. Our Lord never said we should give it to the Church, though.'

There was a considerable cheer from some of the onlookers furthest away from the constables when she said that, but I knew she had made a mistake. It does not do to make the Church look foolish. You must always be very pussy with churchmen. They want their money. Where would they be without it?

'They seem like rascals to me,' said the representative of Pope Callixtus the Second, who seemed as interested in heresy as the Pope was in investiture. 'Talmudic numbers learnt from Jews. Potions to increase desire in young maidens and old men. Unnatural powers and bestial persuasions! She is from the south-west, almost Brittany, and should not be here; a Breton witch and a spy for our Duke's enemies, the De Montforts. Throw them into prison. Their presence in Rouen is like a pestilence ... Take them away, constables, and put them in the darkest cells where they may consort with the darkness that they preach.'

'Shall we put them together, my lord?' asked one of the guards.

'By no means. They will commit acts of darkness together. We have no record that they are indeed married. They may well be adulterers and commit fornications which offend all true Christians. Away with them to separate cells and feed them on hard commons. I will find out the truth from them and what goes on in their minds if I have to put a gimlet in their skulls so I may look inside.'

Alice and I cast sorrowful glances on each other and I tried to include some measure of confidence that this was only a temporary setback, but I am afraid it was a weak show for I felt nothing but dejection and concern. How were we to get out of this pickle? I knew the fault was mine, for had I not sacked the idle and reprehensible Luc, and had he not warned that he would get his own back? I should have been more cautious, not so full of myself and my new broom.

So now here we were, laid low by that malicious sneak, and under suspicion of crimes which, if proved, would follow us to the gallows or worse. I doubted whether Alice, sweet girl though she was, would ever forgive me. How she must wish she had never set eyes on me, and could be back in the castle playing games with the ladies!

We were led out of the mayor's building and taken through the streets to the castle, accompanied by the whistles of tosspots, ostlers and carmen. There we were shown to our rooms, by which I mean we were roughly thrust into the dungeon, and allotted cells at opposite ends of that dismal place. It was damp and it was dark. In fact, the dungeon at Ivry was like a palace compared with this one.

The gaoler was a huge man with an enormous tongue too big for his enormous mouth and a fist the size of a ham. He showed it to me when I started to call out to Alice to tell me how she was, and whether the room was to her liking.

'This,' he said, proffering his great ham, 'this is what you must answer to. Only this isn't Alice, it's ... do you know what its name is?'

'Malice,' I said.

He seemed rather put out. I had taken the jest from his enormous mouth.

'Yes, it fucking is, you tosspot and bottle-fucker. Malice is my name too. Stay on the right side of me and I'll try not to hurt you too much. Stay on the wrong side of me and...'

'You'll try harder.'

He gave me such a slap across the face that my whole head seemed to turn round on its base like John the Baptist's in a saucer.

'Oof,' I said, involuntarily.

'That is the kind of conversation I like,' he said. 'Not too scholarly and disputatious. And for your information, your tart can't hear you. We put her round the corner in the royal suite.'

'Take her some water, please,' I asked.

'Water's in the morning,' said the gaoler. 'You'll be calling for a tapster next and a mutton pie. Lights out now, and no talking or I'll come and fuck you both about.'

He blew out the smoking lamp that illuminated the ghastly place and lumbered off to a warm cubby-hole somewhere. We were left alone in the darkness with our damp straw, our thoughts and our thirst.

Gaolers must have mothers, I thought, so why is it that gaolers all seemed to come out of the same relentless womb? Is there some monstrous universal gaoler-mother like a queen bee or ant who eats gaoler-jelly and produces endless gaoler replicas? Or do they put on their foul mouths and their evil masks like uniforms when they come to work? Are they really pussycats at home, cuddling their wives and showing their girlfriends every kind of gallantry and instructing their children in playing Hunt the Prisoner?

I must have slept, though how I knew not in that vile circumstance, but in the morning I woke to the sound of distant voices. One I recognised as the gaoler's. The other, though heard at a distance, had a curious familiarity to it. It was a woman's voice. I heard the chink of coins and perceived that the gaoler's tone had imperceptibly softened into acquiescence. Somebody, in short, was bribing the gaoler. A light approached.

'Lady to see you, fuck-face,' said the gaoler.

And then I saw the lantern's beams lighting up the face of Juliana, love of my life – correction, former love of my life – who now stood beside the gaoler beyond the bars of my cage.

'Good morning, Latiner,' she said. 'How is it with you?'

LX

Questions jostled in my mind and jumbled at my lips. I opened my mouth, but no sound came.

'It's all right,' she said. 'Don't goggle. It's me.'

She turned to the gaoler.

'Thank you, Turgis. You can go now. We will use your room. A jug of wine, if you please.'

Turgis! What a name! Imagine being called Turgis. Dogs would come up to you and sniff your bottom.

Turgis bowed and withdrew. Good dog, Turgis. We moved down the passageway and opened the door to the gaoler's chamber. It smelt too much of Turgis so we kept the door open for a while. There was a fire inside which was pleasant, and a table around which were set two chairs.

'How did you get here? How did you know I was in prison?' I asked her. 'When did you …?' The questions tumbled out.

'I arrived at Vernon with my father who is in conclave with Cardinal Cuno. He told me you were here. His spies are everywhere because he likes to know everything. It is the secret of his rule. I asked him where you were and he found you. Alice too. How is she?'

'Very well. Until she came here.'

'I'm sorry to do this to you. There seemed no other way to have a private talk.'

'A private talk? You mean *you* had us arrested?'

'Prison is a fine place to talk. I could not guarantee such privacy anywhere else. We could make love if you like. Here on the straw.'

I shook my head.

'Only joking,' she said.

'And you could do this?' I gestured at our surroundings.

'Of course. I am the daughter of the Duke with whom I have made a rapprochement. I can do many things.'

The gaoler appeared again, bearing wine and two cups.

'Do you wish me to pour the wine, Comtesse, your Extremiousness?' he asked, like an elephant trying to dance.

'No, thank you. Leave us now, Turgis.'

She seemed to find an irresponsible delight in repeating his name.

'Madame,' he bowed, tripped on his own feet, and left.

She poured wine and I drank thirstily. It had been a dry night.

'It strikes me that you are the witch. You are the cunning woman. You are Madame Eliphas.'

'I have to be, for what I have in mind.'

'And Eustace? Where is he? What has he in mind?'

'Oh, Burgundy and claret, cinnamon and cloves. He's drinking somewhere. My father ordered him to give up for a bit. He became almost human with his cunning little eyes swivelling about. But now he's off again.'

'And your father?'

'He has bits of business to finish up and then he's off with his precious son, and his court and his generals, back to England for Christmas.'

I felt I should tell her about Alice.

'Alice and I ...' I started.

She raised a hand. 'It's all right. I know. Eliphas the jongleur told me, or maybe my father. I don't blame you.'

'But I still love you,' I said. 'I love you both.'

'You do not have to choose,' she said. 'It's not a competition. To be honest, since my girls died, I lost interest in all that. I am not sure that I am capable of love any more. All I can feel is rage. Oh, how it burns, Bertold! Feel ... feel my heart here.'

She guided my hand to her breast and it did indeed seem near incandescent, or I did.

'I want you to do something for me.'

'Anything,' I cried, excusing her disgraceful guile in putting us in prison.

This was the effect she had. I wish you had known her.

'I am glad you say that – because what I am asking of you is a lot.'

'Anything,' I replied if a trifle less enthusiastically.

'You know that I have made a humiliating submission to my father?'

'I had heard that. Eustace too.'

'I grovelled, Latiner. Eustace too – but he is finished. He is good for nothing. My father knows that.'

'And what does he know of you?'

'He knows nothing of me. He thinks I am tamed as well as shamed. He does not know that I cannot rest, I cannot sleep...'

'Alice has a draught that can help you.'

'You understand nothing,' she said angrily. 'What a fool I was to love you.'

It was the first time she had ever used the word love in my direction. I noticed, as she spoke, that I desired her more than ever. She had that effect on me.

'What do you mean?' I asked. 'What is it that afflicts you?

'I cannot rest until my daughters are avenged. And when I sleep thcy haunt me because I have done nothing.'

'This is wild talk,' I said to her. 'The last thing they would want is revenge. They were gentle girls. You cannot put right a wrong by committing another.'

'My mind is made up,' she said. 'Will you help me or not?'

That put me on the spot. I was aware as I stood in the dungeon that I was not in a good negotiating position, but I thought that the power of love would prevail, and that she still wished me well.

'I see you pause,' she said.

'I pause,' I told her, 'because the man on whom you want your revenge is the Duke, and though I have some quarrels with him, I have saved his life and that ties me to him. I am not sure that I want him harmed again.'

'I do not have it in mind to harm him personally. I have no poisons, nor hired assassins, no daggers under my robe. His person is not in the line of my bowshot.'

'Well, then,' I said, 'let's hear what you intend to do. But first, can we not go out of this vile place, somewhere where I can see the day? And even before that we must rescue poor Alice.'

Juliana shook her head. 'I cannot do that,' she said. 'We have to speak in secret, unobserved. The gaoler will not talk. He knows what will happen to him if he does, but I do not wish others to see us. I intend to strike at the very heart of my father, at everything that he holds dear.'

'And what is that?'

'His son, my half-brother, William the Atheling.'

'You are mad, Juliana. You cannot do that. And how would you do it if you could? The Duke won't let you near him with your crossbow. And I'm not going to do it.'

'I'm not expecting you to shoot him or to stab him. It has to be something a bit more subtle than that.'

'A subtle killing?'

'Yes. I have the beginnings of a plan.'

'The beginnings?'

'You have not much time. The Duke leaves for England at the end of November. So you have little more than eight weeks, if that.'

'What do you mean … *I* have?'

'It will be enough. I am thinking of the sea.'

'I'm not. Cold at this time of year.'

'So much the better.'

There was something different about her, now I came to look at her closely: her natural grace was a little strained; she seemed intent, fixed, as one who has found religion. The grief over her daughters' death must have tipped her very near the brink. I had thought she was exaggerating when she talked of something dying in her, but now I realised that words could not convey her lust for revenge.

'Some have found the sea very restful,' I said. 'You should talk to Alice. She comes from Barfleur. She knows sea things. I think her father has shares in a hulk.'

'I know she comes from Barfleur. But no, I am not going to the seaside. You are going to Barfleur.'

'I am not a sea person,' I told her.

'You are going to meet a shipbuilder called Thomas FitzStephen. Remember that name. His father provided the fleet for my grandfather, the Conqueror, when he invaded England. He loves our family. He will of course have no idea of your purpose.'

'And what is my purpose?'

'I am nearly there. It will be delivered when it is ready.'

She spoke of it as though it were a monstrous birth.

'I have no knowledge of the sea,' I told her again. 'Nor love of it either. I do not swim well.'

'Well enough for the lake at Breteuil, I recall.'

We had once swum naked together in a little nook of the lake, hidden by trees. I could not believe I was standing, now, in an oozy dungeon, talking to that same woman whom I had loved to distraction but who was now, it seemed to me, completely mad.

'The *White Ship* – which is to be the fastest ship afloat with all the newest refinements – will be offered to my father when he sails for England at the end of November, two months from now. I happen to know Henry has already made his arrangements, but FitzStephen does not know that, nor will he until he offers the ship to my father for his pleasure and convenience when he arrives a day or two before he intends to embark.'

'I still do not understand.'

'You are very slow, Latiner. My father, feeling sorry for FitzStephen, will then accept it on behalf of his son since a vessel has already been reserved for the Duke's personal service. The Prince will of course be delighted with the new ship. All the young generals and staff officers and the ladies of the court will want to come with him. He will try to race his father because that is the sort of prince he is. All the better for you.'

'I am afraid I am still in the dark.'

365

'That is good at this stage. That is as far as we need to go.'

'Yes, but hold on. If it were remotely possible that I should do what you ask – whatever it is – I see one enormous problem.'

'Only one?' She was laughing at me in that way she had.

'Only one to start with, but it's big. I am not going to be involved: I am unacquainted with the sea; I am scared of your father.'

'Ah.'

'I am glad you say ah. This is a cock-eyed scheme, wherever it's leading, and you must forget you ever told me about it. Put it out of your head, Juliana.'

'Listen to me, Latiner.'

I was taken aback by the ferocity in her voice. She was a tigress, she was a panther, there was a wildness that I could not name. It had to be madness. And yet she had already put a great deal of thought into her scheme. I could see that. Whatever it was, it involved the Prince's whole court, putting to sea, in a ship that she had commissioned...

So why would she do it?

The realization dawned on me – and it seemed that I stood on a floor liquefying under my feet – that she meant something to happen to the ship ... No, more, that she meant to sink the ship with everyone on board.

I gazed at her open-mouthed. She was still the Juliana I had loved. What a vengeance that would be! No one would say her daughters' deaths – their murder – had passed unnoticed. The Sultan Suleiman, a monster hated all over Europe for his recent massacre of thousands in Antioch, would have been hard put to it to do better. The flower of Norman chivalry and English aristocracy, a cluster of royal brothers and sisters, a welter of cousins, the pride of the Norman army and of the fleet, all to go down in one calamity.

I gasped at the scale of it. I did not ask her if that was exactly what she meant, I knew it, just as I knew the woman who was speaking to me.

366

'You're not seriously expecting me to do this? To sink a big ship? I wouldn't know where to start.'

'I am not asking you to do this, Latiner. I am telling you.'

'You can't make me.' I said again, rather weakly.

She laughed. And then she had me really worried.

'Oh, but I can.'

'You can take a horse to water but you can't make him drink – especially if it's sea water,' I said, jesting feebly in the face of what seemed to be an impending *force majeure*.

'You will drink if I tell you to.'

I decided to ignore the threat.

'And how will I find time to go to Barfleur when I am working with Haimo?' I said, lightly.

'You will ask your butcher friend if you may train up an assistant who can look after things while you take the opportunity, for instance, of visiting your brother who lives nearby.'

'I...'

'And don't tell me you don't have a brother, because I know – I am convinced – that you will find you have. Or maybe you could look up Alice's family on some urgent pretext. We know she comes from those parts. I forget nothing that may be useful, Latiner.'

She was half-amused, half-angry.

'And don't pretend you won't be able to find someone who can follow your strange Arabian mathematical methods,' she continued.

An idea struck me.

'Alice could look after the books, I suppose. I have explained my ways to her.'

'Alice will not do it. Butchering? What a horrible idea for a girl! I have other plans for Alice. When you have trained your assistant, you will go to Barfleur on a matter of business, that is the best excuse, Haimo will like that. You will take up lodgings and make yourself known to Master Thomas FitzStephen, the shipwright. I have told him about you. I have said you and your partner Haimo are thinking of investing in shipping – he is always short of money because his ships are too good. I have said you are a merchant, a necessary man. He will show you the harbour and the coast nearby. He will lend you a boat so you can explore for yourself. I shall contact you again when you are there. It is no good flapping your hands at me. I have arranged it all.'

She was talking about some fantasy in which I was never going to be part. I have always disliked the idea of the sea – it's a slopping, peevish kind of place. Why couldn't she find some mariner or fisherman to do her dirty work?

'Are you paying attention?' she asked, noting my general air of resistance.

'I am not good on the water – or in it for that matter,' I said again. 'I don't think bastards like the water.'

'You were perfectly good on the lake at Breteuil. You will come to like the sea.'

'I don't think so.'

'You prefer that you and Alice should stay in prison?'

'You wouldn't do that?'

'Try me.'

She was smiling at me, teasing me, desirable as ever, in a green dress that showed off her admirable bosom. I knew just how sweetly she smelt under that dress. If I said yes, she might let the bastard Bertold fuck her now, here on the straw.

'Look, Juliana, I love you very much – I will always love you – but you have to find someone else to do this.'

'You are the only one for me,' she said.

And the bastard was entranced yet again by her big green eyes and her wide smile. Who would have thought anyone could be so pretty and so mad!

'I won't do it,' I said. 'And there is Alice to consider anyway.'

'I was afraid you would say that, though you have often told me you would do anything for me.'

'I would. Almost.'

'What a wide gap there is between a true knight and an almost true knight. Which brings me on to a subject which I had hoped I would not have to raise. You see, I have taken Alice hostage.'

I felt the earth shaking as when a massive breaker hits the headland – something which I had not seen, but I was beginning to imagine. All this talk of water was getting to me.

'You have what?' I shrieked.

'Hostage,' she repeated, 'hostage to your good behaviour. If you succeed, you shall have her back, more beautiful than ever, and you yourself will be richer by one thousand pounds. If you do not, she will be put to death.'

'You can't do that.'

'You keep telling me what I can and cannot do. It is tiresome, Latiner. I can do what I want. I can very easily have Alice killed. Or blinded, if you prefer, with the tip of her dear little nose cut off.'

'I do not see how you can joke about that sort of thing.'

'I am not joking.'

I let that sink in.

'I just want her back.'

'Then you must do what I ask.'

I thought about it. There seemed very little choice. I was impressed, as ever, by Juliana's spirit and determination, but she was too fierce, she shone too brightly, I was being burnt against her flame. How I longed to see Alice again!

'And how can I possibly explain my presence in Barfleur, or even on the ship? The Duke thinks of me as an enemy.'

'I have seen to that. You saved his life, remember.'

It was true. He could hardly execute me after that.

'You will be on board to collect money owing to you and Haimo,' she continued. 'The Duke's army is hungry and eats prodigiously, especially so near Christmas. When better to collect your money than on board? They can't escape and many of them will be feeling queasy and therefore offer less resistance to a creditor.'

'You seem to have thought of everything,' I said.

'Not quite. There are still bits of the puzzle to be worked on. But you are right. I have thought of nearly everything. What do you think I have been doing for the last year and a half?'

All that show, forming up to her father barefoot in rags, as a penitent, had been a masquerade. She had probably got Eliphas to direct the performance. All that time, she had been stirring a slow pot of revenge. What a woman she was! Even while I hated her for taking Alice, I felt the power Juliana had over me. She pulled me as the moon does the sea.

If only the action could have been on land I would have been more easily reconciled. But on water! I fell in the river once and when it closed over my head, I knew I was going to die. How small I felt in that liquid land. My breath came out like marbles. Still, you know a bastard does not sink; he swims – someone pulled me out. There was a lesson there somewhere.

My mind was now in turmoil. There was threat, there was alarm, there was love, there was honour. That shaft of hers about a true knight – better aimed than when she fired at her father – had struck home. And she could not mean what she had said about Alice being a hostage. She would surely not play the hostage game with me of all people.

And then I thought: there are still two months to go. Much can happen in that time. Nearer the hour, there will be opportunities to turn back, to change her mind.

I made a decision.

'I'll go to Barfleur,' I said. 'If that is what I have to do, but I cannot be responsible for something whose end I do not know. You must answer to God and man on my behalf.'

'Oh I will, Latiner, I will.'

'And I should like Alice back at once.'

'I am afraid that can't be arranged. She is already far from here. Quite safe, I can assure you. She sends her love. Yes. I am impressed. I always thought Alice rather self-contained, quite cool indeed, but she wept when she told me to tell you she loved you. And look, now you are doing it too.'

'Bastards do not weep,' I told her, weeping. 'She is a healer and you are a killer.'

370

'I am quite jealous. But I am finished with all of that. It's a nunnery for me when this story's done.'

'It will be a loss,' I said.

'All life is a loss,' she told me. 'We start losing the moment we are born.'

A darkness crossed over her like the shadow of a bird. I could see now the etchings of grief on her face.

'And now we must get you out of this place and back to Haimo who is expecting you with your noughts and crosses to help him cope with the Christmas rush. And I must go with the Duke my father to Gisors where he has a final conference with Cardinal Cuno, settling the issue – as if it mattered – of when Archbishop Thurstan returns to England before he himself journeys west again to Vernon, Rouen, and Barfleur, and finally to England where he looks forward to being joined by his son and court. I cannot, alas, join him this Christmas as I have been too long absent from my husband. From whom, of course, a too long absence is never enough.'

'You won't ... harm her, will you?'

'Who, Latiner?'

'Alice, of course.'

'Certainly not. But Latiner...'

'What?'

'You have eight weeks to prepare. You will not fail me, will you?'

It was a statement not a question.

'I will kill you,' I told her, 'if I do not have Alice back safely when I have done what you ask – whether your project succeeds or no.'

'Agreed,' she said, smiling. 'What is love but a little death? Another glass of wine?'

LXI

I found Haimo in my office fiddling around with tally-sticks. He might as well have been sticking them into his hair.

'I turn my back and you're back to your old habits,' I said.

He rose from the table and embraced me. He had been informed of my imprisonment, but not exactly why I had fallen foul of the law. It was not considered a disgrace in Rouen, he told me, to be arrested on some religious pretext, so he hadn't worried too much about having a partner who had tasted the Archbishop's hospitality. What did worry him were his books: neither he nor anyone else he knew in butchery had a grip on my new system. I confess I had mainly followed Brother Paul's advice and kept the secret close but there was one lad in the shop, one Bernard, whom I had started to instruct in my system of tallying against such a day. However, it was too soon, the lad was not ready yet, so Haimo had fallen back on his old method of accountancy and his affairs had already started to degenerate into a butcher's muddle.

I took him over to The Barge and bought him ale. I needed time to think.

'I was expecting you earlier,' he told me over a mug of the landlord's best. 'We heard that a noble person had seen to your release. Everyone likes a well-connected partner. Good for business. Who was he?'

'I am not at liberty to say, alas.'

'I understand.' He touched his nose. 'What did they get you for?'

'Mistaken identity. They thought I was someone else who had been a follower of Abelard, or an Adamite.'

'What's an Adamite?'

'Someone who thinks a fuck is the same as the Eucharist.'

'Fuck me!' he whistled.

'That would be a Eucharist.'

373

He laughed. 'Well, I'm not surprised they banged you up if they thought you did that.'

'I was shopped,' I told him. 'Alice too, but she's out of prison. She has had to go home, her mother is ill.'

'I am sorry for that. Who would do that, though? Denounce you both?'

Juliana had masterminded the whole thing. It hadn't been Luc after all. She had used him and I couldn't blame him if she had; she was impossible to resist.

'I don't know. I thought it might have been Luc, whom we sacked, but I don't know. You never know who's lurking in the shadows with a knife, do you?'

One thing at a time, I thought. I will tell him of my visit to the seaside tomorrow, though not, of course, of the purpose behind it. I was embarking now on a litany of deception, and the idea did not please me. My next duty was to go home and face Berthe, who had lost a friend as well as a workmate. I found her in her kitchen with a barrel of nutmegs which she was putting out into portions for her shop. I told her that Alice would not be coming back for a while, and of course I lied.

'Her mother is ill,' I said. 'When we got out of prison she had to go straight home. The family steward collected her.'

'Poor Alice,' she replied. 'She is such a lovely girl. Too good for you.'

She smiled when she said it but I know that is what she thought. I was not constant enough. I was afraid she could sense there was something I was not telling her.

'Much too good for a bastard,' I agreed.

She looked serious. 'You shouldn't go on about being a bastard, you know. Half the population of Rouen are bastards.'

'I know,' I told her. 'But, you see, I could have been a Comte if my father had been married to my mother. Bastard matters when you are brought up in a castle.'

'But then you might not have been born at all,' she said.

In the light of my conversation with Juliana, it perhaps would have been better if I had not.

'Alice will come back,' I told her. 'Alice is going to be all right.'

It was easy to say, but if Juliana were to be believed something bad was going to have to happen before that promise could be fulfilled.

'I might have to go away,' I told her, 'in a few days for some time – a couple of months. Haimo and I are thinking about setting up a shipping business.'

She nodded. I knew she could see through me, but what could I do? We are often crueller to our friends than to our enemies.

'Look after Haimo while I'm away. I don't want him slipping back into bad habits and growing thin,' I urged her.

She cheered up a little at that. I knew she would find him an easier subject for her concern.

I set to work next morning putting the accounts in order, and in a couple of days they were tidy again. I called in the lad Bernard, who knew the business and seemed to have an aptitude for the new figures. For a few more days I gave him a brisk course in accounting until I was satisfied he had the thing well in his head. In fact, the lad had quite a genius for it. I told him I might have to go away for a while and he expressed confidence in the opportunity – a confidence that I thought well-placed.

'You could go far,' I told Bernard, 'and maybe even further than that.'

He swore he would not let me down, and I told him I knew he would not.

Then I went down to Haimo.

'I have an idea we might learn something from the fishery trade,' I said to him. Juliana's idea of giving business as an excuse was obviously much better than a hypothetical brother. How well she had researched my situation! I could talk Haimo into all manner of implausibilities now he trusted me so much.

'But I'd need to go down to the coast to look around. Barfleur, for instance. Would you mind if I went for a month? I have trained Bernard, who is quite as good as me, to muddle up the books while I'm away.'

He laughed, but his brow was wrinkling.

'Fishery?' he asked. 'It's quite a different matter.'

'Did I say fishery? I meant shipping.'

'Shipping?'

'Shipping feed, shipping fish, shipping cattle, shipping pigs. That sort of thing.'

'Where to?'

'To and fro. It's just an idea, Haimo. Like my ideas about accounting. It might work. We would be rich. I need to have a look around, do some calculations, then we can talk about it.'

He gave in because he trusted me, poor man, and indeed I had made him more money than he had ever possessed.

'Don't worry about the accounts,' I told him. 'Bernard is already better than me. He's quick and he has a talent for figures. Go easy on him and he will do you – both of us – proud.'

He looked thoughtful.

'Fishery's a dirty business,' he told me. 'Let me think about it. Fish doesn't keep as well as beef or venison. And the supply is less certain…'

'Not fishery, Haimo. Shipping.'

I didn't like to tell him not to think too hard because the project wasn't going to happen, but I mumbled something reassuring.

LXII

Taking a sackful of clothes and necessaries, I picked up the palfrey Blackberry from the stables where I kept her, mounted up, and made for the west, wishing I had my darling Alice behind me again. I was aiming for the little town of Pont L'Éveque. It was a long ride, and I could have stopped earlier at Pont-Audemer, but there was an abbey there I had been told about where you could find a good supper which included a special cheese they made, and a decent bed for the night. I like a good abbey. It reminds me of simpler times in my life. And the cheese was excellent: soft and creamy and not too sticky.

There is a virtue in excellence in whatever form it comes. I know what you are thinking: my separation and predicament had not taken away my appetite. But to that I would answer: to face untold challenges, one has to keep one's strength up, and you don't want a diminished hero, do you?

Next day, I rode on to Caen, not as big a town as Rouen, but, I thought, more handsome: plenty of those honey-grey buildings, especially the castle, a huge affair built by the Duke's father William. I found lodging at The Turk's Head and a kiss from the landlord's daughter which made him bristle, but there you are, you have to take it with good grace when it is politely offered.

Onward to Bayeux and then, following the river Aure, to Carentan where it rained and I stayed in a fleapit doss-house and spent a miserable night scratching; and then finally through Carentan which has five roads leading out of it. I took the muddy one to Barfleur. A long road it is, and by the time we reached Barfleur, Blackberry and I were weary. You come over the long, slow, gently undulating Normandy terrain to Sainte-Mère-Église and on to a funny little place called Quettehou. Now if that is not a Breton name I do not know what is; the prosecutor back in Rouen made a snide remark about Alice's homeland, and he was right about the Bretons, but not about sweet Alice, a bastard's curse on him. Here you glimpse at last the ocean. Before you actually come to the water, though, there is an uneasy flatness to traverse. Poor Blackberry hated it. The terrain, even the road, is full of rocks interposed with coarse grass which occasional sheep nibble with disfavour, in the manner of dowagers taking rhubarb pills.

When the land can hold up no further, it sinks, as though exhausted with the effort of being dry, into beaches, but the rocks persist, washed by a chilly tide, sitting in the sand like prunes in custard.

Alice had told me a little about Barfleur though on the whole she had not been happy there. Her father had died and her mother had married again, a man whom she had not liked – another drunkard. It had not been a joyful house. At any rate, since this was to be the town from which I was to launch my desperate venture, I decided to make up my own mind about it.

I found it a low place at first.

I do not mean its morals or its women – which are after all often the same thing – because where would men be if women didn't have morals? I mean Barfleur's physical setting, its appearance, the way it presents itself to the newcomer's gaze, is low – low like the fields that surround it; low, as if it were sitting at the foot of cliffs which for some reason had been removed.

Duke Henry would have seen it many times, since it was his main port of departure for England. I wondered what he made of it, if he made anything at all, or if he just passed through.

In Barfleur, you keep going back to the sea. The sea is what it is all about. Sea in its incarnate form of fish is the underlying presentation to the nose with all manner of gradations building on top of it: fish near the fish dock, where the great flapping turbots and halibuts are passed out of the boats to hands on shore and then laid out on slabs for the trade, where the fish-smell gathers strength; the aroma migrates to the kitchen where the cook fillets and carves, mashes and pulps, roasts and simmers and the smokery exhales; and thence it graduates to the dining room and finally to the piss-house where it all flows back to the sea. Each time, at every stage, leaving a little bit of itself to cling and dry, adding to the fragrance of Barfleur that gently attaches itself like burdock to your clothes as you pass through the town. There is the smell of wood too, of course, out here near the boats, and the pitch and paint which keeps out the water. And nearer the edge of town, grass and rock and small, salty, seaside cows, which have a smell of their own. There is also the seashore smell: half land half sea; part man, part fish; sand and water and foam, dead starfish and sandhoppers, and the occasional dead bird teeming with life. And then there is the smell of sea rain...

The smell of a place is how you remember it. If you bottled the smell of Barfleur and held it under my nose a hundred miles from the place, I would be back there on the instant and tell you what was going on at the jetty and in the town. I would sit with you in the tavern and we would drink wine and talk about the power of the nose and the smell of the sea.

There are low headlands around Barfleur, which poke granite fingers brusquely into the ocean. Further out to sea there are more rocks. Sometimes there are boats on the horizon, avoiding the rocks. Sometimes the ships even come into Barfleur – trading hulks and cogs and carracks and even warships – where a big jetty of honey-grey stone protects the harbour from the worst of the north wind, and all manner of shacks and store-houses fringe the seafront. There is a semi-permanent population of fishing boats: some bigger, with sails, for venturing out beyond the bay into the treacherous waters of the British sea; some sturdy little rowing boats for tending to the lobster pots and crabberies at the tip of the headland.

The town itself is not large, maybe six hundred souls, though it swells to twice its normal size and more when the soldiers come through. Then its habitual ebb and flow is disturbed by hoarse commands and rough requirements for food and drink, and beds, beds, beds for the night. Kitchens spring up and the landlord of The Seabass (named after the town's crest) sets out trestle tables and benches for the soldiery, and the girls wash their hair and put on their dresses. Ale flows, fiddlers play and fights break out. The church of St Nicholas sometimes has to serve as a dormitory for large contingents, this the priest enjoys, for he can make a charge and claim from the general or lord in command, and energetically does so.

The lords and officers eat with the mayor or the squire, or take over one of the other Barfleur inns – The Jolly Sailor or The Lobster Pot – and use it as their mess. Some of the quartermasters even commandeer space from the boatyard if the weather is bad. Otherwise, the men under their captains, sergeants and lancepesades have to live under canvas.

The houses in Barfleur are mostly wattle and daub, except those of the more prosperous citizens, for which they have started to use the light, honey-grey stone of Caen. The church of St Nicholas itself is newly built of the same material to the familiar form of square tower, chancel, choir and nave. They are already talking of enlargement.

I give you all this information, gleaned from various sources in the first week of my stay, because it forms an important background to the watery crisis of my tale, but the one thing I have not dwelt upon is the shipbuilding tradition of the place. It had a reputation then – and quite possibly now – for building the best ships anywhere. Perhaps it stemmed from the Norse traditions of the people. After all, it was only two hundred years since Rolf the Ganger arrived with his ferocious blond- and red-haired hordes and took over vast swathes of the French King's land, having the cheek to call the result Normandy. They did not do that in England. There is nowhere called Normandy there that I know of, but here they set up a whole country, and we've been bloody-minded ever since. The point I am making is that the Norsemen knew how to build a ship better than anyone, and they went to Vinland far across the ocean and to the edge of the world to prove it.

I chose The Seabass as my base in the town soon after I arrived, mainly because it looked cleaner than the other inns, and was furthest from the jetty, which means that it gets fewer military visitors. The room they showed me was at the top of the house which reminded me of the rooms I had shared in Rouen with my darling Alice, whom I missed more every day.

There I set up my temporary home. I placed a piece of rich, curious blue cloth, inlaid with real gold, that Alice had found in the market, on the wall opposite my bed so that I could look at it and think of her. That was better. She called it a favour such as a lady gives her knight, and I always had it about me. There was also my medicine chest and a small volume of leather-bound vellum, with mysterious illustrations featuring the secrets of perfect proportion, which Saul had given me in the monastery. These I placed in the oaken chest which, along with a chair and the bed, furnished the room. There was a simple lock for the chest whose key I kept about my person.

Having completed my domestic arrangements, I was now ready for the next stage of my tour of Barfleur. I did not call on Thomas FitzStephen, shipbuilder, immediately. I wanted to do a little more research first, but it was hard to ignore his shipyard. It towered above all the other buildings on the seafront. Noises of sawing and hammering came from it, curls of smoke or steam danced from the roof, and tradesmen arrived with supplies of wood and sea-coal. A slipway connected the building with the sea which licked at it eagerly as if in anticipation.

Everyone in the town seemed to treat the building and what went on there with respect, and there was much talk in the inns of the great ship that had recently been completed. It was to be launched the following week for its trials, attended by much excitement as well as civic dignity.

After a few days, I decided that I had reconnoitred the town and its environs enough. It was time to visit Master Stephen and his white wonder-ship. There had been an influx of soldiers the previous day, a small advance party, which had sailed with the early morning tide. They had left on the jetty, as usual, the things they did not want to take home: tattered canvas and broken pegs; split shoes; splintered arrows; stinking pieces of dried meat which even the seagulls didn't want. People from the town crept out and gathered them up after the soldiers had left – everything was useful – the dried meat made useful bait.

I picked my way through the mess, setting my course for the great shed that covered part of the shipyard. There was a house beside it on the jetty, which seemed to serve as an office, and I addressed myself to the front door. Getting no answer, I advanced on the shed itself. Sounds of polishing grew louder as I approached and the smell of wood, varnish and paint tickled my nose. I knocked at a half-open door in the side of the building and, treating that as a formality performed, let myself in.

I was at once aware of something enormous towering above me – vast, white, beautiful. It was like a goddess. I had never seen anything built in wood that was so big. I stood there in extreme awe, gazing upwards, lost in reverence, sniffing the strangely elating smell of paint and varnish, the waft of worked wood and the frankincense of resin. I was looking at the underbelly of the *White Ship*. It was like the roof of a cathedral.

She was clinker-built like a proper Viking ship – and indeed like the little boat we had rowed on the lake at Breteuil – plank laid over plank so the side has a slightly serrated appearance. And it curved in the most seductive way imaginable as its flanks bellied out and then tucked in to meet the keel-board, which ran like a perineum down the whole long line of the ship. As I wandered reverently, back and forth, I started to try and quantify this goddess. There seemed to be no one about, so I paced the length of her from stern to prow and hip to hip. I measured it as a shade more than a hundred and forty feet long and over thirty feet across.

I reached across and patted her, and she felt good.

'You are the most beautiful thing I ever saw in my life.' I said.

And she answered back:

'And who m-m-might you be, master?'

I turned and saw a man with blue eyes and curly, snow-white hair that seemed to fizz with energy, who must have been in his late forties. He wore a shipwright's leather jerkin and a hard, driven, slightly ironic expression. Here was another person in the grip of some passion. His slight stammer seemed a product of this energy rather than any diffidence. He couldn't get the words out fast enough. Words were a waste of time.

'Master Thomas FitzStephen?' I said.

'That is the one. And you?'

'The Comtesse de Breteuil suggested that I talk to you.'

He did not immediately take me up on my reference to Juliana.

'You like m-m-my *White Ship*?'

'I do indeed. I should die happy if I had built anything as lovely.'

'That is my problem, master. She is too lovely. I don't want to let her go. And that is of course absurd.'

'I should feel the same. There is one thing that perplexes me, though.'

'What is that?'

'There is a contraption around the stern that I do not recognise. It breaks the fine sweep of the vessel.'

'That is a rudder.'

'I do not know the word.'

'It is the new way. Forget the old clumsy steering oar over the starboard side. The ships in future, all ships – though it may take some time – are going to have rudders: more efficient, safer for the helmsman, less prone to failure, more conducive to speed. There is less drag on the ship's progress through the water. An oar dangling over the side is always bound to set up resistance. It will break on rocks and shallows...'

'Where did this idea come from? Did you invent it?'

'It is an ancient invention, the Arabs used it and the Romans before them, although they both used bindings to lash the rudder to the hull. We prefer a wooden stern-post to which we attach the rings holding the rudder to the ship. Having gone to the trouble of building the fastest ship afloat, I was not going to fob her off with an old-fashioned steer-board. When we go on

383

board, I will show you how we m-m-move the rudder with a tiller.'

He spoke about the vessel as though he lived for it, as though it were his mistress. It was a passion I could share though I did not think it was altogether healthy. The man's pale face spoke of tension, of snatched meals and sleepless nights.

'I know who you are,' he said. 'The Comtesse Juliana sent word. You want to learn about the sea and you might be interested in a merchant ship for carrying livestock; what we call a hulk.'

'I might,' I said. 'A hulk. More than one, very likely.'

I grasped his hand. 'I am Bertold FitzRotrou.'

'Thomas FitzStephen,' he declared. 'I can sell you a hulk, but wouldn't you rather own part of the *White Ship*?'

'Is part of her for sale?' I asked.

The man's quest for perfection had cost him dear. There was a tremor in his voice. He wouldn't sell one nail of the *White Ship* unless he had to.

'A small part,' he said. 'And as to which part? You choose.'

'If I had that opportunity,' I told him, 'I would put my money on the rudder.'

He laughed rather more immoderately than I would have thought my suggestion merited. I could not tell whether he was serious about his strange offer. It seemed, more than ever, that this was a man under considerable strain. He was of medium height, but wiry build, and he had an odd, intense expression – maybe he was not eating enough, or was drinking too much.

'I don't believe I have seen a painted ship before,' I told him. ?'

'It is not strictly necessary for a ship to be of a colour,' he told me. 'Normally varnish will be sufficient. Coloured paint m-m-made with oil is only for special ships that will be used by royalty or suchlike. A king's barge will be painted where a m-m-merchant's hulk will be varnished wood. The *White Ship* was always going to be a swan, not a brown duck. Come with me.'

Gripping a ladder which was positioned up the side of the ship, he shinned up it like a squirrel. I followed rather more laboriously. At the top, I climbed over the vessel's painted side down some steps that he had set up, and found myself on a vast deck along which lay a sturdy mast, not yet in its vertical position because of the proximity of the roof. At each end of the ship, there was some shelter in the form of two small covered spaces, below a raised deck reached by stairs. On either side of the central gangway were rows of benches, built into the fabric of the vessel so that they were completely immovable.

My guide now paused by the mast, which he said would be fitted when the vessel was launched. It would hold a square-rigged sail bigger than any that had so far been considered manageable. I said that I thought ships had oarsmen to propel them.

'Indeed they do. I am coming to that. But first let me show you the tiller since you have expressed interest in the invention.'

He led me up to the stern of the ship and showed me where the helmsman would stand, upon a platform or little deck, what he called a castle, providing a shelter for those below, but yielding a clear view for the helmsman above the crowd of passengers and oarsmen. The tiller itself, the most important part of the ship, was a stout piece of wood which projected out through a wide hole in the after-board into the rudder post itself.

'Try it,' he said, 'You'll find it sweet as a honey-apple.'

It was true. The thing was perfectly engineered, and it needed to be: its components were essentially heavy, for the ship was enormous, but like all good creations, it appeared easy. A child could have steered that vessel. Only a truly vicious man could willingly destroy such a huge and perfect work.

'So how does it function?' I asked. 'I put the oar-thing over to the left and ...?'

'Tiller hard a-port,' he corrected me.

'We put the tiller over to port, and the ship goes to the left ... to port.'

'No no no,' the man was quite agitated. 'You put the tiller over to port and the ship goes to starboard. You must think of the tiller as the other end of the rudder. The rudder impedes the

385

water on whichever side you turn it, and the ship goes in the direction of the impediment.'

'How very perverse of it,' I cried. 'There must be confusion.'

The man became quite vexed.

'Not at all,' he exclaimed. 'Only for a dunce.'

'How many people can you take on the *White Ship*?' I asked him quickly.

'Three hundred,' he said. 'Three hundred and fifty at a pinch.'

'It could take a whole regiment!' I exclaimed. 'You could begin an invasion with a ship like this.'

'Come,' he said, 'let me take you to the power-house of the vessel.'

He led me down from the castle again, to the huge floor of the ship. Here there were holes in the sides of the vessel made for the insertion of great oars which were lying stacked down the centre aisle, some shorter, some longer. I asked the reason for this.

'You see the benches here along the gangway are slightly athwart. Each bench holds two m-m-men, the one further away has the longer oar, the one nearer has the shorter. That way we can fit more oarsmen to the ship without over-crowding the passengers.'

On the floor, in front of each slanting bench, were small adjustable chocks for the oarsmen to put their feet on, to help take the strain. Thomas was proud of this because he said no one else had ever provided such an aid to the business of pulling on an oar. It was yet another thing that would add extra speed.

'The *White Ship* will fly across the sea like an angel.' he said. 'There has never been a passenger boat or cargo boat that could chase a warship. Now we can outrun anyone. Bring on the pirates!'

'And how many oarsmen will help her do it?' I asked.

'Twenty-five each side,' he said. 'That is the optimum for the vessel's s-s-size and s-s-sail power. In one week's time we will take her out for her trial and you will see her fly. We will have fifteen a side for the first trial which will be quite enough. I am waiting for some m-m-more oarsmen from Caen. If everything goes according to plan, I will then be in a position to offer my ship to the King of England, our Lord Duke.'

'To give it to him?' I asked.

A look of dismay crossed the shipwright's face,

'Oh dear no. Everyone gives him things. He doesn't want another ship. He wants an experience. He wants the wind on his face and the spray curving away on either side, and the North Star above and the ship quivering like a greyhound. I can't *give* anyone the *White Ship*, it is mine. I can lend it to him whenever he wants it to convey him to Southampton for the start of his Christmas holiday. That is what a true man can do. I would be a toady if I gave it to him. What I want from him, and I have a golden mark to give him for the honour, for the fief, is the office of Comptroller of the King's Ships, which my father Stephen had before me. He put together the fleet for the invasion of England, you know.'

'Really?' I said, politely. She had said he would tell me about it.

'Do you think I should give the *White Ship* to him?' he asked, suddenly anxious. 'Would you, if it were yours?'

I probably would, as it happened, if there were advantage in it, because I am that kind of person, but I had never built a ship.

'No,' I told him, poor bastard, 'definitely not.'

'She is a wonderful woman, his daughter,' he said suddenly. 'I built the *White Ship* for her, you know.'

So that was the connection. She had visited him. He was in love with her, poor fellow. How many more were there like him, like me? Had she ... given them favours too? Was there nothing she would not do in pursuit of her revenge?

The more I saw of this enormous vessel, the less likely did Juliana's plan seem to be capable of success. It was huge, unsinkable. Barfleur was a working port full of professional sailors who knew what they were doing. They were the ones she should talk to. It was the height of optimism for her to come to me for advice on any kind of naval operation. Surely something would turn up and this whole thing would turn out to be a wild goose chase, a madness cooked up at full moon? Common sense was on my side, but I couldn't quite manage to dislodge the small cold toad that had taken up residence in the pit of my stomach.

I shivered. Someone had walked on my grave, or I had walked on someone else's. I was glad to be wearing my sheepskin coat, gift of the good Haimo. Perhaps after all I was I was beginning to feel the cold in the shipyard. It was a relief when FitzStephen took me down to his office and poured me some wine. Thin stuff, I'm afraid – I had been spoiled by Juliana at Breteuil and by Berthe at Rouen – however, I gave no sign of the shock to my mouth, and gulped it down with a will as he continued to speak about his ship as though she were a living being. There you are, I called it she. I was beginning to catch the fever myself.

I asked him if I could come on what he called the trial. He seemed pleased.

'As long as you keep out of the way.' he told me. 'I will only have half the oarsmen at this stage, but that will be fast enough.'

I did not ask if he was rationing the trial for some professional reason or because it would cost him more. I suspected the latter. He needed Juliana's money. I questioned him about the oarsmen – were they bondsmen or prisoners?

'No, no, not slaves as the Arabs use,' he protested. 'Do not call them that or they will walk out. They are skilled professionals and very touchy about it; well paid too, and always asking for m-m-more.'

'Meanwhile,' I said, 'I will think about your offer of shares in the *White Ship*. I will have to talk to my partner the butcher of Rouen, and of course to the Comtesse.'

And then he said something that shook me.

'The Comtesse said you might want to borrow a small rowing boat to take round the harbour. To get your sea-legs,' he said.

I could hear Juliana ratcheting up her plan.

'Sea-legs ...? Yes...'

I tried to sound enthusiastic. What were sea-legs? They sounded fishy to me. At any rate, I had to go along with it.

'You can have *Perrine*,' he told me, further adding to my confusion.

'Perrine?'

Was he offering me an inducement that was not purely financial? He didn't seem that kind of man. 'Ah. Yes. Yes, of course. *Perrine*.'

'Or *Delphine*. Two little boats. Can you row?'

'Yes.'

I didn't like to say 'on a lake'. I was charmed to discover a *Perrine* again. I had been strangely homesick for Breteuil recently

'Don't go beyond the harbour after high water. There's a hell of a tide here especially at the spring. It will take you out to the Quilleboeuf in no time.'

'The Quilleboeuf?'

It was not a name I had heard before.

'Bloody great rock, sharp as a needle, about a mile out to sea from here, but not so far from the cape out yonder on the left. Taken down a good few ships in the last ten years. It's a shortcut, see. Saves a half an hour on the run to Southampton. You just have to know what you're doing.'

It was as I had feared. This sea business was not for the timid. I had walked out onto the headland to the north of the town, and watched the waves crashing onto the rocks, and the ominous ripples in the water where currents stirred like crocodiloes. I had seen the tide come in with hunger written all over its fat face, greedy for the day when at last it would overwhelm the whole of the land but now drooling for the flotsam that lay on the margin of sea and sand. I had seen the tide go out, hurrying its prey of bladderwrack and dead dogs, with many an eddy and ripple of ooziness, out onto the broad ocean for Poseidon's breakfast. I did not want to be on that bill of fare.

I had seen, years ago, on one of my expeditions from the abbey, a corpse lying bloated on the river strand, and wondered what it felt like to drown with nothing but the gulls overhead and the burble of water in your ears. No, thank you very much, Juliana. And yet, somewhere, she had Alice in her power, to do what she wanted with her, until I brought home the bacon. If I only could find some way to do what she wanted without killing anyone … It was. I was sure, simply a matter of time before the answer struck me; but every day that passed, the toad was growing bigger.

Lost in thought, I missed something the shipwright had said. He was looking at me expectantly.

'My wife is dead,' the fellow was saying, 'but I could rattle something up.'

He was asking me to sup with him. It sounded horrible, but I knew the man wanted to talk, and it was my job to see that he trusted me. Stick close to the man, Juliana had said.

'Fish and cabbage … that suit you?'

'Why don't you come up to the inn and we could have supper there,' I suggested. 'They actually have a good cook. And judging by the smell, they may have got hold of some venison. An English lord brought some of it along for a farewell feast before his party embarked for England, and then they all fell ill with what they'd had the night before in Carentan, and didn't eat it.'

'Oh, well, that sounds like a good idea,' he said.

The thought of him cooking up a fish supper in his lonely cottage filled me with horror and an unfamiliar instinct of compassion. Poor old wifeless FitzStephen. He didn't have lovely Alice waiting for him at the end of the day. But then, I thought, neither did I; nor might I ever have. I arranged to meet FitzStephen at the inn shortly after dusk, and walked back to The Seabass, unusually depressed. This thing was not going as I expected.

The evening passed, pleasantly enough. Warmed by good wine and venison pie, the shipwright became quite cheery and regaled me with many a nautical yarn. There were races, there were shipwrecks, there were mermaids and there were manatees; there were great storms and high tides sweeping onto the land, there was a hulk full of bullion which was wrecked on Barfleur Point, but no one had ever been able to find the gold, though many had drowned in the attempt; there was a child, hiding in a boat, which was swept out to sea and ended up in Cornwall!

'So what's your game?' he said suddenly, surprising me by turning his icy blue eyes hard on me.

'I cannot tell you that,' I told him, recovering as best I could, and hiding behind Juliana. 'You know what she's like. I am her man.'

'It's all right,' he exclaimed, clapping me on the back, 'I confess I was just testing you. I like a man who can keep a secret, but the fact is, I know about it already. She has taken a share in the *White Ship*, and reserved it for its maiden voyage. She wishes me to make a show of offering it to the Duke, as a courtesy, for his voyage to England, but we know that in fact he has already made his arrangements. No, what she really wants to do is to offer it to her brother the Prince for his use and his Court's – it will be her wedding gift, she says. The fastest ship afloat! It is just the kind of thing he likes. He will take wagers on the time it takes to reach Southampton. He will race after the Duke's ship – built by some rascal in Honfleur – and overtake it. When he has won his wagers, he will be told of her gift, so it must be our secret until then. He loves to win a wager. She tells me she has sent you as her officer to see that everything goes according to plan. It will take quite a weight off my back, I can tell you. So there you are. Glad I got that off my chest! The Duke's spies are everywhere so this has to be between ourselves and no one else. The Comtesse is explicit about that. She wishes the whole thing to be a complete surprise, especially her share in it. She sent you to find out if my ship is as good as I say it is. And that is what I am going to show you when we do the trial ...'

His throat must have been dry after his confession. We drank a further toast or two or more to the *White Ship* and the Comtesse Juliana, so that when I took to my bed I was less worried than I should have been. She had primed the man perfectly for me to do my job. Everything was falling into place. All that was needed now was my get-out clause.

I woke to a grey morning and the cry of gulls which sounded like the souls of the damned, and understood that I was being shoe-horned into something that fitted far too tightly.

LXIII

Warm in my sheepskin coat again next day – the best for cold weather you could ever wear, Haimo had said, although it smelt a bit – I took out *Perrine*, a business-like little rowing boat, tubbier than the one on Breteuil lake, with two oars from under the seat and FitzStephen sitting in the stern to see how I handled her. The sun had come out and Haimo's coat became uncomfortably hot, so I took it off and laid it on a thwart. We went up and down the harbour a couple of times. It was high water, mill-pond calm, and I fared none too badly, feathering the oars like a ferryman, so there was hardly a splash. At last, FitzStephen declared himself satisfied, and I put him out on the jetty.

'If you go beyond the harbour wall,' he said as a parting shot, 'remember that it's coming up to high water now. You only want to be out there for half an hour. If you're out there much longer, you won't be able to come back.'

'Ever?' I asked, thinking he was trying to scare me.

'Well, you could come back with the returning tide this afternoon. Or you could find yourself halfway to Guernsey. And then you'd have to pray for good weather, and I'd have to come and get you.'

'How far is Guernsey?'

'About twenty miles'

'That's a lot of sea.'

'Oh, it is that.'

He was a funny, fussy old fart, I thought.

I paddled around for a while as he stood watching me, then he turned on his heel and walked back into his office. I rowed out beyond the jetty where the water moved with hardly a ripple. I rowed towards the point that lies off to the right of the harbour where I had stood a few days before looking at the tide nibbling the rocks. I didn't want to seem to be a landlubber, so I rowed around a bit more, thinking of my beloved Alice and

393

missing her more than I ever thought I could miss anyone. Then I came back, tied *Perrine* up where I had found her, and did some walking around the town while I encouraged the idea that was forming in my head to take shape. What I needed was a plan of action. At the least it would be a fall-back position if she were ever to chide me for lack of dedication. It would show her that I meant business. She had given me my role. I had to sink the *White Ship*. Now all I had to do was work out how it might be achieved. It didn't mean that I would actually have to do it. After an hour's pacing about, I thought I had it. I would practise my oarsmanship for an hour or two maybe for three or four days in a similar manner, and then embark on an adventure. I recalled my friend the Marshal telling me that battles are only won after thorough reconnaissance. I thought I might go and take a closer look at the rock with the funny name, and try to take some kind of reckoning as to where exactly it was and how I might find it, first by day and then perhaps by night. I didn't like the sea, but the idea of Alice languishing in captivity urged me forwards. Wasn't that her favour that I had hung in my room?

I thought too of Juliana and the bond there had been between us, that was still between us, though I considered she had behaved badly, taking Alice hostage; it was insupportable, it smacked of jealousy. And her plan for revenge on her father smacked of worse than that – but then she had been pushed. Those poor girls of hers. Surely they would never have wanted me to be plotting the death of others? How many had FitzStephen said would be on board? Three hundred? No, the very idea was anathema. The girls had been such gentle creatures...

These unhappy images filled my mind as I walked about the old town with its smell of fish and the sea and the tar and the tackle. I found myself walking down a lane going out of town, such as Alice had described to me when I had asked her about her home.

'An old grange,' she had said. 'Low roofs and sagging windows and a fire going straight up through the ceiling. They call it a manor, and it has some fields and a wood. But my stepfather never did much to it. It was damp and the rain came in if the wind blew from the east. I had a room with a window from which I could see the sea. I dreamt of riding away on a ship to England and starting a new life. And what did I do? I rode away on an old palfrey halfway across Normandy to a cold castle ruled by another unhappy man. There were cowslips in the garden in spring and roses everywhere in summer, and smoked fish for supper. That's what I remember about Barfleur.'

And there it was before me, or something very like it!

I looked at the sagging roof and the roses in the garden, and there was one white rose left, in perfect bloom, and I thought it was Alice, and the house was Alice's, and I wept for her. Whatever it was I had to do, it would be done without fail. There was smoke coming out of the centre of the roof, but I did not go in. What could I say?

'I am lying with your daughter who is at the moment in the hands of a she-devil who would not hesitate to kill her if it served her purpose.'

It would not be well received, and the drunkard would huff and puff into his beer.

LXIV

I cannot impress upon you enough the oddity of those initial days at Barfleur before the final act could unfold. It seemed as though I were half at play, and half in the midst of a trap whose mechanism had been set and from which there was no escape; a disaster that could overtake me as well as everyone around me. I tried my best to persuade myself of the first. There was no point in becoming nervous so early in the matter. A hundred and one things might happen to prevent the necessity of fulfilling my promise. But at the back of my mind there was always a moment when a sudden word or memory would send a cold toad of terror down to sit somewhere under my belly-button. Perhaps indeed it never completely went away. But I was young, and even the condemned man eats a hearty breakfast.

Next day, and the day after, and the day after the day after that, I went down to the harbour in my sheepskin coat, untied *Perrine*, and we rowed about, out beyond the harbour wall when the tide was right – and on the last day when it was *almost* right...

Perhaps I was impatient, but it is also easy to misjudge the time, especially in a new place. The church bells rang, it seemed to me, at odd times. The fishermen would have told me the time just by looking at the water, but they were out fishing. I was simply not sufficiently experienced in the sea, that was the long and short of it. I intended to wait until the tide was almost out when the water would slacken, and then row out to the rock, but meanwhile I thought I would take a turn outside the harbour while the water was at its height, before the tidal race had started.

Out I rowed, out and about in the wide bay. The flood tide had been higher than usual, someone had said something about a spring tide, but this had not really registered with me. The October sun shone and the water licked the boat, it was very calm, and my thoughts were far away. I mused over the events of the past two years and the people I had met: Juliana and Alice, the little girls Marie and Pippi, my little palfrey Blackberry, the witch Mother Merle, my mother, my father, that dreadful half-brother of mine, Fulk with his hopeless love, Eustace the Bad, the Duke and his intransigent barons, FitzStephen and his passion for his white ship ... So many people. What did they think they were doing? They thought they had freedom to choose their way, but weren't they really like the flotsam in the river at Rouen, carried away like bugs on a branch; scurrying to the left, hurrying to the right while all the time the hungry waves of the wide ocean were waiting to gobble them up...

I did not like these thoughts, and I shook myself and lifted my head to look around me. The water had been so still, but now there were little waves.

Something was happening that had not happened before on my outings in *Perrine*: the water had started to go out it struck me, rather forcibly, that I had better row back. The quay was not where it had been when I left it. Rowing back, however, was now a problem: the water seemed stiffer. Stupidly, I caught one oar in the air as I rowed harder, and I fell backwards into the bottom of the boat, bumping the back of my head.

I must have been out for a few moments and lay there like a gaffed pollock. When I regained my seat, I could see FitzbloodyStephen had come out of his office and was laughing. At least I thought that was what he was doing, because he was jumping up and down and gesticulating. He, too, seemed to be diminishing. I bent to the oars, but it didn't seem to make much difference. There was no doubt about it. The shoreline was getting smaller. I was going out to sea.

The water was moving with more urgency out here. A slight breeze was coming in from the north-west and the tide was flowing out against it. My little boat bobbled about in it, and I bobbled with it. Of course I tried and tried to row back to the harbour; I am not an idiot. Well, yes, you probably think I am, because I had been warned about the tide. I just thought I could do it. Nobody likes to be thought a loon; I didn't want FitzStephen to go back to Juliana with an adverse report.

The fact was, I could make no impression on the flow of the water, indeed all I was doing was exhausting myself. I gave up and leaned panting on my oars. The rocky point where I had walked yesterday drifted past. One or two outlying rocks drifted past as well. I turned the boat round and look back at the jetty. FitzStephen had disappeared. A small group of rocks eased by on the right hand side – sorry, starboard – and then a big jagged bun of stone on the port.

Oh well, I thought, he'll come and get me. He's gone to round up some men and they'll have a bigger boat with more oars which will cut cleanly through the water. He won't let me just float away … Will he?

And then I thought: Barfleur is a busy harbour, there will be ships coming in, fishing boats, they will give me a tow.

I turned back to look at the sea. There was nothing; it seemed endless. One or two seagulls swopped low over me, hoping that I might split a fish and toss it overboard, but they soon turned away, crying disgustedly. A bigger wave rocked the boat and I was gripped by panic. The shore was half a mile away. There was just half an inch or so of planking between me and drowning. This was how it was going to end. Next stop Guernsey. If I was lucky.

I closed my eyes and said a few prayers, regretting my past wickedness and thinking of my mother, then of Alice who I would never see again.

Perrine and I drifted on, she oblivious to the danger we were in, mounting the little seas with a certain dash while I was almost insensate with alarm. There is a fear some people feel about being in wide open spaces. I had never had it before, but the broad bosom of the sea was having that effect on me now.

I perceived a shape in the water ahead of me. I thought for a moment it might be a distant vessel, but on closer observation it turned out to be another, bigger rock around which the water eddied and sparkled. This must be the Quilleboeuf about which I had heard from FitzStephen. A plan formed in my mind to land on the rock – it was the only thing that would keep me from being swept out – and then, at low water, the tide could bring me in again.

As I approached the rock, which proved indeed to be a bloody great thing, mostly under water when I neared it, dark as a sea monster, I started to row against the current with all my strength so that when my boat hit it would be a gentle contact. On what I judged to be the south side, I noticed what seemed like a little inlet, and I aimed for the safety of this enclosed space. Just before we touched, I shipped the oars, tied *Perrine*'s painter around my wrist, and when the contact came – a hard rumbling scrape – I scrambled out over the stern and plunged onto the slippery barnacled stone. I was almost submerged by salt water, and bumped my leg, cracked my funny bone, nearly lost *Perrine*, swallowed a quartful of water, and at length found myself sitting on my rocky island above the waves, lord of one followed by six zero acres of ocean.

The tide hurried past. *Perrine* jostled uncomfortably on the low rock beside her. I pulled her round to face the flow, so that the tide held her straight, keeping her in position between the two shoulders of the inlet.

I sat and surveyed the scene. All around was sea. Behind me lay a clear route to England. To my right, only half a mile away, was the rocky shore of the Raz de Barfleur, to my left was the open water of the Baie de Seine, in front of me was the way back to Barfleur, a matter of a mile. The tide would cease in five hours or so. I was quite safe on my island. I caught a glimpse of the bottom now, sand and rocks, about ten feet or more below. FitzStephen had told me that the tide hereabouts was famous for its rise and fall. Twenty-five and a half feet, he had said. That was half a foot higher than Honfleur and a foot higher than Cherbourg. The man seemed to take pride in his bastard tides. All I knew was that this blob of rock was going to end up twenty-five feet high, from low tide mark to summit. It was going to be substantial – high as a house – before the tide started coming in again. At the flood, however, for all the rock's size, its top poked, as I had found, only a few feet above the water.

Since there was nothing for it but to sit it out and wait for the tide to turn, I made myself as comfortable as I could (which was hardly at all), drew my sheepskin coat about me, and set myself to thinking of my plan of action. I could hardly be in a better place to contemplate it. I put the moral dilemma aside for one moment and tried to treat what was manifestly the most horrible crime as an academic project. Yes, a part of me still thought at this stage that there was precious little chance of Juliana's mad scheme ever happening. That is what I still told myself.

If a ship were to come this way in darkness at just past high water on the ebb tide, the rock could doubtless be avoided if you had a good pilot and a hawk-eyed look-out, and even then you could not be sure. But what about navigating to *hit* the rock at night, what would you do if that were your game?

There would be help from the current and the stars, so long as the stars were not covered by cloud and you knew which star to steer by. In fact, as the rock was due north of Barfleur harbour, it would be the Pole Star. That was simple enough. I would have to watch the weather, and do a reconnaissance under cover of darkness. Come to that, perhaps I could put a white marker on it, using one of the fishermen's buoys, and could steer for it – that was assuming I could get hold of that rudder thing old FitzStephen was so pleased about, and was free to use it at the critical moment.

Alternatively, there were various ways of scuppering a ship other than driving it onto a rock, and I imagined myself performing them. I could stove in a plank of the ship below the waterline before she sailed, assuming I had the requisite equipment and would not be seen or heard while I was using it. Or perhaps the application of a rather large gimlet might do the trick, not perhaps the most unobtrusive thing to take on board – or else I could bore a hole in the hull beforehand (if I could bring myself to desecrate a thing of such beauty), cover it with wax, and then unstop it once we were under way. It would be slow to admit the ocean and could be caulked in no time by a passing sailor, but it had been known to work.

When I considered all these other stratagems, though, I concluded there was nothing quite so clever at sinking a ship as a good, simple rock like this big fellow I was now sitting on. He had the makings of tragedy written all over him, and no questions asked.

I patted the rock as if he were a horse. I tried to be insouciant, making an entertainment of my reconnaissance, for there is no point in being a jelly-boy nor yet a hang dog, but I was overcome once again by the most dismal foreboding. It is a large matter to sink a vessel full of people, and it weighed on me, not that it was going to happen, you understand, because something would come up, I was sure of it. Yet, I could not see how Juliana's plan could be averted. She had it all – and me – worked out like the machinery of Fate itself.

Sitting on the rock in the sunshine now, looking out at the prospect in front of me – the distance from the land, the hungriness of the sea – I tried to imagine a shipwreck at night: darkness would add terror, confusion, isolation; the water would be icy cold; there would be no hope, no help, nothing but the sudden realisation that this was the end, often considered, never expected. There would be noise and commotion, of course, but the whole thing would be far enough from land for it to be mistaken for seabirds, or not be heard at all. It was something that I could never, in my right mind, wish on my worst enemy. On Comte Eustace, if he were on board, or Amaury de Montfort? I decided not to answer that.

Clouds came up and the sun went in. I was cold now, even with my sheepskin coat on, though not as cold as I would have been without it – six hours is a long time when you are sitting on a wet rock in the middle of the sea. A small crab, lodged in a little rock-pool, had appeared. The creature regarded me with an impassive eye and started nibbling at my toe. I lifted my foot up but the creature hung on. I put my foot back in the water. The crab returned to its feast.

No ships or boats came by, though I saw some beating about in the distance. I had been told by FitzStephen that it was considered prudent to approach the harbour with a strong incoming flood, so it seemed we were all waiting for the tide to turn, and a long wait it was. It had been high water at nine that morning and it would be low at around three. The crab grew tired of his nibbling and I grew tired of waiting. It was the cold, and the fear of what I had to do, and the intrinsic uncertainty of the sea that really took the spirit out of me. It might be that I would have stories to tell Alice, or Juliana – or my grandchildren whoever they might be – at some later date, over a roaring fire with a glass of sack in my hand. Then, I would cut a fine figure as I told of my exploits, but now I was a sad creature. I huddled in the no-shelter of the rock. I was wet, the sun was hidden by a further sequence of clouds, and the wind was not a drying wind; it was a wind that simply tickled the wet and made it feel wetter.

More crabs appeared and I noticed one or two shrimps. There were a few mussels on the rock and a selection of limpets. At one stage, I saw several small fish and, further out, a shoal of what might have been pilchards, which surfaced and dived. I set two of the crabs to have a race, but they went in opposite directions. Out in the dark water under a ledge of rock, something big moved that I thought might be a lobster – and indeed, I saw that it was when it emerged a little way from its shelter, driven perhaps by curiosity, or indignation at my encroachment of its habitat. We eyed each other. Lobsters are scavengers, and doubtless it was wondering whether I might be dead. I felt cold enough to be.

'You shall have feast enough before the month is out,' I told it.

Mollified perhaps, it withdrew. Patience is everything in the sea.

I was by now beyond cold. Grateful though I was for the sheepskin coat, it had become sodden through my various flounderings. Exercise was virtually impossible. I grew thirsty, but there was nothing I could do about that. Slowly, slow as the shadow on a dial, the water subsided. As I fell to ruminating on my two ladies and the entwining of our fates, all precipitated by that oaf of a comte, the contemptible self-pleased drunkard who is no longer Lord of Breteuil (and serve him right), I had rashly untied *Perrine*'s painter from my wrist – it was beginning to chafe – and my hand must have slackened and unclenched. I came to my senses just in time to see her starting to bob away. I plunged into the water, soaking myself anew, and grabbed the painter as she floated past the island, scarcely preserving my hold on an overhang of rock as I pulled her in.

I tied the painter in a knot once more around my wrist, and lost myself in thought again, imagining myself back at Breteuil, living again that beautiful, distressful dream.

At last, I noticed the pace of the water began to slacken. My island was now, as I guessed, thirty paces round. I was told later that you could walk on sand here at a really low spring tide. The breeze dropped. The chafing of the sea subsided. The sun came out again.

It had become a perfect late autumn day. I was beginning to warm up now so I waited a little longer, stretching out in the sun; there was no point in going until the tide had really turned, and I confess I was a little nervous about the reception I would get. Soon, the backward quirk of a ripple or two and an eddy curling under the brown wriggle of a seaweed, told me it was time. I steadied myself and, holding each of *Perrine*'s generous sides, I scrambled onto the seat, and pushed off. The boat held steady in the water for a moment, and then turned obediently towards the shore.

'What the hell did you think you were d-d-doing?' said FitzStephen, I thought rather ungraciously, twenty minutes later, when I finally made it back, carried sweetly with hardly more than a gesture at rowing home on the incoming flood.

'I got caught by the tide.'

'I warned you about that.'

'No you didn't.'

'How can I work with you if you do not listen? You will have to go. You are a danger to us all.'

'You thought I had gone to Guernsey, didn't you?'

'Yes. And I wasn't going to come and look for you. I'm not taking the *White Ship* out before her trials.'

'Don't you want to know what I did?'

'No.' The man was sulking.

'I landed on the rock.'

'The rock? Which rock?'

'The Quilleboeuf.'

'You're joking.'

'I scrambled out and held on to *Perrine*. Then we sat and waited.'

'Impossible.'

I could see he was impressed.

'Well, I never heard of that before. I can see you can handle a boat,' he said, 'and a rock. You had better come inside and get warm.'

Somehow my misadventure had turned into an advantage.

LXV

The trials and testing of the *White Ship* were due to start in a week's time, but first we had to have the launching ceremony, a tradition at Barfleur. FitzStephen invited me to attend, as long as I kept out of the way.

Thirty ruffians from Caen – they looked like jailbirds, but I was told they were regular oarsmen – turned up the day before with a mountainous keeper who was to be the galley-master. They had all rowed before under various captains, most of them piratical ones by the look of them.

It was considered good luck to splash a jugful of wine across the bows and for someone to christen the vessel. There was no titled lady in residence in the town, so we used the prettiest girl we could find, Lisette, the barmaid at The Seabass.

A crowd gathered for the launching: fishermen and foragers and quartermasters from the armies; and publicans and sinners like me. The priest turned up too, because priests never like to be kept out of things, and a couple of friars who happened to be passing. There was rumour that there would be wine later.

Lisette grasped the jug of wine and cracked it across the lovely blonde prow of the vessel. 'I name this ship the *White Ship*. May God bless her,' she cried.

Then the priest said a prayer, and the two friars said two more prayers, and Lisette kissed everyone, and the great ship slid into the water, causing a big wave to form that nearly pulled over the men who were holding the ropes. There was more cheering when she was finally tied up at the jetty and FitzStephen declared her ready for action. Then it started raining and we all went back to the inn.

The following week, we all formed up again on the jetty for the first day of the trial. FitzStephen had explained to me that they do not normally trial a ship, they just put her in the water and if she doesn't sink, they sail her, but this was a special ship – a ship for a king: everything had to work perfectly.

The *White Ship* was trim and taking in no water. She sat there easily in the harbour, like a seabird. The oarsmen – looking surprisingly fresh considering the amount they had been putting away the night before – were first on board followed by their enormous galley-master who, with a practised eye, allotted each man his particular place.

'It is a great s-s-skill,' FitzStephen whispered, excitedly, 'the ordering of the rowers. You don't just sit them down any way. This Sigebert is the best galley-master I know. He could drive his crew across dry land if I told him to.'

'He looks as if he could scull the ship single-handed,' I replied.

We walked on board. The rest of FitzStephen's crew was assembled – some forty useful-looking men, most of them sailors, but interspersed with carpenters and fitters. He addressed them and I could see the respect he commanded. He did not suffer fools gladly. He told them to look sharp and do their duty. It would be their honour to take the highest in the land as passengers.

Finally, telling me to stick close to him, he took the tiller. His foreman cast off, the sail was raised, and we were away. Soon the regular chanting of the galley-master, calling the time for the oarsmen, could be heard above the mutter of the sails and we were moving through the water at speed. You could feel the power of her as she sliced through the water, making for the open sea beyond the Raz de Barfleur.

'The ship is incredibly fast,' I said to FitzStephen, caught up in the excitement of the moment. He let me take the helm, and I felt her quiver under me. It really was the most beautiful ship; more than mere wood, she was like a racehorse. She trembled to go faster.

'We are only using half the complement of oarsmen,' he said. 'It is safer to take things slowly as we try her out. We will sail close to the wind, we will sail *into* the wind, we will turn fast about, we will run with the wind behind us at more speed, we will sail on a lee shore, we will manoeuvre, we will stop and start again, we will run with tide and outstrip the incoming flood; we will practise every eventuality, and only when I am confident will I offer her to the Duke.'

And so we tried her, that day and thereafter, on fair days and foul days, sometimes with me at the helm under his watchful eye, when great waves curled around the prow and the spray punched our faces, back and forth, round the Sound, across the Bay, starting and stopping, taking the wind side on and fully behind us, defying it with our oars. One day we even ventured as far as Alderney, this time with a full complement of oarsmen so that I felt the ship almost take to the air she was so quick through the water. The craftsmen tinkered with the ship when we returned, making little alterations which they first discussed with FitzStephen, and then addressed far into the night so that the vessel was ready for her trial next day. We lived with the smell of wood and paint, of sailcloth and sweat – for the men below decks were less fresh than a fish and twice as smelly.

FitzStephen addressed the galley-master on this issue for, said he, we shall be taking gentlefolk and fair ladies who must not be offended with rank odours. They were instructed to wash under the pump both before and after each voyage, which instruction indeed occasioned some muttering. The galley-master was so impressed next morning, he called in his daughters for a sample ride, and both young women expressed themselves well satisfied, especially at the sight of all those brawny midriffs.

Finally, at the end of the first ten days in November, the shipwright declared that he was happy.

'I have word,' he said, 'that the Duke is now at Gisors, talking to the Pope's legate and concluding business there. He will shortly leave Gisors and make his way slowly, with his oldest friends and advisers, across Normandy to Barfleur. He should arrive here by the twenty-fifth of the month. Then let our business begin! I shall surely be the happiest man alive.'

He would also, with any luck, be able to pay off some of his creditors. His accounts were in a fearful muddle, and I had tried to make some sense out of his tangled affairs. I had seen some of the figures that he was in hock for, and I was nervous for him, but if the Duke smiled on the *White Ship* there was no doubt that all would be well. It was a gamble, but it would surely be worth it.

LXVI

All I had to do now was ask a fisherman for a buoy and somehow attach it to the Quilleboeuf rock one night. Finding the buoy was easy for anyone with a little money. I located an old man called Jérôme who had given up fishing because of his back. He was only too happy to make a little cash, and he had a big, white, corky buoy with thirty-five feet of rope and a weight to attach it to the seabed. I told him I was after lobsters, and he tried to sell me his boat, but *Perrine* was all I needed – *Perrine*, and a calm night with a good moon, if possible.

I waited three nights and there was cloud, and then there was rain, and then there was a strong wind so the sea was too rough.

A week later, the weather turned mild and calm. The wind dropped, the clouds dissipated, and it was near low tide at around nine o'clock when most honest people were in bed.

I crept out of the inn and made my way to the lean-to where the old fisherman kept the buoy and the tackle. Taking them up soundlessly, I went down to the jetty and placed the cargo in *Perrine*. I climbed into the boat, when a drunk came lurching by with a skinful of wine. The last thing I wanted was discovery, even by a drunk, so I crouched low over the buoy, embracing it like a bosom friend until the disturbance had gone. And then I set off under the harbour lights, muffling the sound of my oars as best I could. It was all quite different at night. As I pulled away from the mooring on the jetty, past the *White Ship*, pale as a ghost, and the company of all the vessels in the harbour, I felt scared. Yes, I must admit it; who knows what monsters lurk in the deep? *Perrine* was stout, but she was a little boat; you could tip her up in a second, broadside to a stiff sea or a leviathan. But none of that was going to happen.

As I pulled away from the harbour, I entered something like a waking dream – sea flat as a looking-glass, moon on the wane but still plenty of it, making a moonpath right up to *Perrine*, light bouncing off the water from the moon and a million stars. Far away a bell was tolling, solemnly. *Perrine* swam gently down the current, the lights on shore passing like ships. It was only for a few moments but I had a feeling of mysterious and universal union, and then it was over. I rested on my oars and took a draught from a flask of wine I had brought with me in case I became marooned – or thirsty.

Enough of mysticism, I said to myself sternly, there is a job to be done, and I will never see Alice again unless I do it. To start with: how was I going to find the rock? I could row around for ever and get hopelessly lost.

I knew that the current had previously taken me almost directly to the Quilleboeuf without any navigation necessary on my part. Indeed I had been told that the current here flows due north, which was why the Quilleboeuf was so dangerous to shipping. Follow the Pole Star too closely and you hit the rock; I had been told that many times by the old salts and sailors of Barfleur.

All I had to do was drift and paddle, drift and paddle, and in ten minutes I would turn *Perrine*'s bow towards the shore, keep a close look-out for the rock over the stern, and hope to see it somewhere in the vast and silent dark. No, don't be a funk, I *would* see it.

There was a sudden splash over towards the starboard, or was it the port – harder to tell when you're facing the wrong way. I have always, as I say, had this slight problem with left and right. Oh, I know where they are intellectually when I have time to think, but in emergency I sometimes get it wrong. Anyway, there was a splash and it momentarily spooked me. What would splash like that unless it was a shark or giant squid? I began to form the impression that I was not alone; someone was following me in a small dark boat, a shape I could almost see, I was certain of it, over there to my right, yes, right...

I felt a slight bump and there I was, dead on target, nuzzling up to the Quilleboeuf Rock which loomed like a mountain in the dark. It seemed I couldn't miss it – which was good augury for the main event if it ever came. I tell you, I chucked the weighted buoy over the side as near as I could get to the rock, and rowed hell for leather for home. As I rowed, I could see the lovely buoy bobbing about gamely in the water only five feet from the rock, and looking for all the world like an innocent lobster pot marker, possibly too catch the very lobster I had spoken to a few days before. Everything was going to be all right.

And thus, like a child who believes that if he shuts his eyes, he will be invisible, I laid my plans. No one saw me when I tied up at the jetty behind the big ships. No one noticed me enter the inn. I was just in time to catch a cup or two of wine and a kiss (nothing more) from Lisette before I went to bed. Job finished, all done and dusted.

LXVII

The Duke arrived with his entourage on the twenty-fourth of November. It had been a dry week and we saw the dust rising from the hill long before the procession appeared, as the party marched down between the banks to the flat meadows that lay between the slope and the town. Then we saw the guard itself, and at the same time the sun came out; there must have been five hundred people at least, and they made a brave sight with their banners, and the glint of steel as lances and swords shimmered in the light.

Trumpets sounded, and an answering call came from an advance party already in Barfleur. The soldiers finally marched into town and formed up on the square overlooking the jetty, staring out at the vessels that would take them to England. Another ship would appear on the flood tide today and moor on the jetty beside the *White Ship*. This was the *Pelican* from Honfleur – we knew that the Duke had chosen her because the Mayor of Honfleur had let it be known that he was upset: he did not understand why the Duke preferred to sail for England from Barfleur; it was something of a slur on the loyalty and efficiency of Honfleur as a port. If the Duke had to do such a thing, it at least rewarded Honfleur's dedication and service if he sailed in a Honfleur vessel.

The reason for the Duke's choice of Barfleur was really quite simple. Barfleur was the nearest port to Southampton and saved an extra thirty minutes of sailing, and nobody wanted to spend longer at sea than they had to. However, the Duke never liked to cause unnecessary antagonism (though he did not mind in the least when it *was* necessary), and so he had instructed the mayor of Honfleur to send his best ship to take him home for Christmas.

And so he made his entry into Barfleur with his soldiers and his courtiers and his hangers-on, with the clanking of metal and hoofing of steeds, with trumpets and hoarse commands and quartermasters scuttling about, the whole host smelling of dust, mud, horses, sweat and steel. He had with him trusted older friends – William de Tancarville, Comte Theobald of Blois, Othuer FitzCount, William Bigod, and Gisulf, his scribe – as well as two of his best captains, Gilbert of Exmes and Ralph the Red of Pont-Erchenfray, and his own Chaplain, Bishop Roger of Coutances. There were also some hundred elite archers, dark men redolent of yew and leather, from Wales (where they still castrate forfeited prisoners), and beefy, red-faced foot-soldiers from England.

If anyone was going to drown the next day, it would not be this lot, so I felt I could look them in the eye. They seemed like hard men and pretty good, average ruffians. It was going to be a noisy night.

The men fell out and were allotted sleeping quarters in the great hall of the town, and in certain barns set aside for the purpose. There was feasting because they were going home and Christmas was coming, and of course there was drinking too. Everyone was in a good mood because the Duke himself was smiling; it had been a successful season and much had been accomplished.

The harbour was by now full of vessels bobbing and creaking at the quayside, riggings twittering in the southerly wind. The *Pelican*, a fine capacious vessel, rode easily at her moorings and was already being loaded with some of the Duke's baggage and impedimenta, but the pride of all the fair vessels was the *White Ship* which floated like a swan and was the centre of general attention. I saw FitzStephen standing in a corner thinking he was unobserved, gloating over her like a father seeing his daughter dressed as a bride.

This same day, I received a package from my lad at Haimo's in Rouen setting out the sum owing by Prince William and his men for meat, and by Ralph the Red who was ever extravagant (in battle as in bed, it was said). This would give me legitimacy in the eyes of anyone, even the Duke himself, to come aboard whichever ship I chose. It was while I was walking by the jetty looking at the bustle of lading and the men coming and going, that I was prodded sharply in the back by someone coming at me from my unguarded quarter. I whirled round because you can never trust a place where soldiers are waiting. They are a raw and brutal breed and would as soon knife as look at you. But it was the Duke himself, large as life and twice as impressive. A couple of very large soldiers stood at a discreet distance behind him.

He stood there, a man in the full flush of his maturity: four square; *barbu* as the French say; black and ruddy with too much campaigning in sun and rain; dangerous, with eyes that never stopped roving. No wonder he had had more children out of wedlock than any other King of England. He could spot a pretty girl a mile off and a traitor too, some said. To say I was disconcerted is to say too little.

'Ha,' he said. 'I thought it was you. I never forget a face. And I don't like yours. Latiner, isn't it? Last time I saw you, you were taking up arms against me.'

'I was defending your daughter, sire.'

'You were encouraging her in her insurrection.'

'Hardly that, sire. You had just as good as killed her children.'

That brought him up short. I could see he was weighing up whether to have me arrested or just taken away and killed, but the truth of what I had said struck home. He rubbed his brow, looking suddenly more human.

'It was a terrible thing,' he muttered. 'That fool of a Eustace. Who would have thought he would do a thing like that?'

'I was their tutor. They did not deserve a fate like that. It was brave of them to die.'

'It is done now, Latiner. We must move on. I pardon you for fighting against me, but what are you doing here? Hardly teaching Latin to the shipbuilders. Come on, man. The Duke must know everything.'

His big, black beard with its red, whiskery ends wagged as he admonished me. His eyes flickered over me like a lizard's tongue.

417

'I am working for Haimo, butcher of Rouen. He is owed money, sire, by one of your generals and by the Prince. He has asked me to collect it from the paymaster.'

'He arrives tomorrow, and sails with the Prince. You had better beard him then.'

A secretary appeared and asked for the Duke's signature – a confirmation charter for the Abbey of Cerisy had to be signed and sent off.

'I must go,' the Duke said to me. 'Get your money tomorrow. Don't let them fob you off. And thank you for looking after my grand-daughters, though I'm not sure I should thank you for looking after their mother...'

I could hardly believe I had heard the last sentence. He appeared to be in an extraordinarily genial mood. He turned to go, then paused.

'If you ever feel like coming to England,' he said, 'come and see me sometime. I am sure we could find you a manor or something.'

For an absurd moment, I was grateful and rather tempted I could see myself with an English manor. I had heard that Sussex was very pleasant. Alice could come over. And then I thought: all this is going to change. And if the story gets out, and they catch me, I won't just be hanged.

LXVIII

There was revelry in the town that night, and I was glad that I was away from it all at the top of the house. I bolted the door, as I knew there would be those below looking for a place to sleep or bed a wench.

Now the moment was so close at hand, I was concerned that I had had no word from Juliana and then, late at night, there was a scrabbling outside and a sealed parchment was pushed under my door. I ran to it, of course, undid the bolt and looked out, ran down the stairs and peered around, but I could see no one I recognised. When I returned a captain had slipped into my room and was fornicating with the lovely barmaid, which was a great disappointment to me. I had thought she was made for better things. I hustled them out, still almost joined together like dogs, and read the manuscript at leisure.

My dearest Bertold,

I wonder if you realise how much I miss you and think about you. You are my very best man. There has been no other to come near – indeed I have had almost no other if you don't count a nice tutor I had back in Abingdon where my mother lived. I have always had a weakness for tutors.

I stopped reading for a moment. She wrote so exactly the way she talked, I felt she was with me again and that we were walking in the herb garden at Breteuil. I sniffed the parchment she wrote on and it smelt of her – rose, jasmine, candied orange, orris root, *grani paradisii*. I was in love again; realised indeed that I had never stopped loving her.

What I want you to do is this – and I know you will not fail me, for mine is a good plan and I have spent months upon it, working out every detail. FitzStephen, who is not privy to the

419

plan but owes me a favour, will arrange that Prince William and his party sail in the White Ship. There will be wine of course. There is always wine where William's party goes. The first thing you must do is make sure there is a little cockle boat tied to the stern. That is what you will make your escape in. Do not forget this. I want you alive, not a pale corpse with your eyes pecked out by the crabs and your white body draped with bladderwrack.

The King and his Court will leave harbour first, an hour or so before the Prince's party.

When you are on board William will want to race the King and get to Southampton before him, you must encourage him in that. It is the kind of young man he is, always on the dash, rather tedious, to be honest, and horribly spoilt.

When you are on board, as I say, I want you to follow FitzStephen closely. Go where he goes, do what he does. He will be steering the ship unless there is some urgent reason why his attention is called for elsewhere, and we will not let that happen. It will be up to you to prompt the Prince to see that the ship takes the short cut, heading off the King who will be on the longer, safer course. You will make sure that the White Ship holds the course that takes her near the Quilleboeuf Rock whose acquaintance I hear you have made quite intimately, clever boy. When you are very near, and the passengers, by then, stupid with wine – they are not going to survive anyway, so why worry? – you will hit FitzStephen over the head, or tumble him over the side. Don't be squeamish, he is going to die anyway. Take the tiller and steer straight into the rock. At the speed you will be travelling, it should be quite enough for the vessel to go down.

However, as it sinks, you will be in your little boat, pulling away. Do not linger, Bertold, or think with pity on those who drown. They have reached their adult life and have been lucky – luckier than Marie and Philippine who never had that chance. And, after all, my father has killed more in battle than you will drown in a shipwreck.

As I read on, the cold-blooded scheme to kill three hundred passengers and crew, which had seemed to me like a distant plan, a suggestion, a hypothesis – something that happened to other people – became disgustingly real. I heard the screams, the crash of stout wood on stone, the surge of water, the panic, the pandemonium. It horrified – it appalled – me. But I was caught up with this woman, and with Alice whom she held hostage, so what could I do? Tell the Duke that his daughter was plotting to murder his heir, his two other bastard sons and three bastard daughters, not to mention five of his best bastard generals and seven of his bastard barons? No thank you, master parson.

Juliana had spies here, she had learned that from her father. The boat I thought I had seen in the darkness was doubtless not a phantasm. They had been watching me. I should have thought of that. Not that it mattered; I liked the feeling that she had master-minded everything. Although, now I thought about it, there was actually one other thing she hadn't considered – or maybe had decided not to mention – and that was how was I going to row the dinghy to shore against the tide? I knew that the day and time for embarkation had been chosen to coincide with a late-evening high water and the tide about to flood. Was I too going to be swept out to sea along with all the flotsam? Well, I would have to cross that bridge when I came to it, or simply take refuge again on that bloody rock as the waters subsided. I comforted myself with the thought that such considerations were the least of my worries at the moment, though not much comfort it was.

She concluded the note with a vague promise about a reward:

Do this last thing for me, and I shall make sure you are never short of gold, honour or the love of one who holds your life more precious than her own.

J

No, I had to go ahead with her plan, and somehow find a way to circumvent it, but in such a way that Alice would be returned unscathed. Though I would always love Juliana, Alice was the woman who could make me happy. She never gave me hard things to do. She had her own mind, but she didn't hold it against me. One thing I knew: Juliana would find out if I failed to carry out her orders, and kill Alice anyway.

There was something else, which I discovered next morning when I woke up. Someone had slipped another note for me under the door. At first I thought it must be more instructions from Juliana, ever one to build a mountain and then put a molehill on top of it, but it was a scrap of a thing written in brown paint or ink and it looked as if it had been smuggled out of a dark place with great care and secrecy.

It simply read: *I am with child. A*

Oh my God! A little bastard, and I had always sworn I wouldn't.

There was a picture of a heart done in more brown paint, wherever that had come from, and then it struck me that it had been drawn in blood which, of course, dries brown. You may imagine what that extra ingredient did to the cook's seething cauldron of emotions that I now experienced.

I breakfasted on a dry crust, small beer and a thousand regrets. I heard that the Duke was up betimes and from the doorway of The Seabass, I could see that FitzStephen was too, poor man. Indeed they were both poor men – for one was to drown and the other was to have his fondest hope and cherished dream most cruelly removed from him and dissolved in water.

I threw my crust at a seagull and went to the harbour to walk beside the shipwright as he led the Duke towards the jetty. It was my instruction to be close to the man, and I might as well start as I meant to go on. The nightmare was over. I had woken up and it was real.

'Thank you, Master Shipwright,' I heard the Duke say as I approached the group standing at the harbourside, mindful of instructions to stay close. 'I do indeed recall that it was your father who supplied the ships to take my father to England for his conquest of the country. I believe he was rewarded with a manor or two in England for his pains.'

I approached closer. My God, but the Duke was an impressive man; you could not help but admire him. No wonder he had bred all those bastards. He could instil fear, but at the same time, I believe it could also be a kind of love. All those bastards were not bred out of duty or fear. They were bred because the fine, and even the not-so-fine, Saxon ladies were in love with him. There is nothing so impressive as majesty when it is worn well, and this man knew how to wear it; it came naturally to him, as some men appear to advantage in sackcloth while others look lumpen in ermine. And the other thing about majesty is, the more you exercise it, the bigger it grows.

I trembled even to be considering the breaking of this great man's world.

'He was rewarded indeed, sire,' said FitzStephen, 'the manors are still in my possession. They lie in the county called Berkshire, I believe. My uncle still lives there and manages the estate.'

'But meanwhile you continue your calling here. Very good. I see you have a fine ship riding in the harbour here. They call it the *White Ship*. Ah,' the Duke continued, observing my arrival, 'you again, Latiner? You do seem to crop up everywhere, don't you?'

'Yes, sire. My own mother called me Too Much Too Soon.'

'Ha,' the King laughed, shortly.

'A very fine ship,' said FitzStephen, eagerly. 'I have put everything I know into her. Come this way, if you please, sir.'

He led us back a little from the jetty's edge where we could have a better view of the whole vessel. FitzStephen then started to explain how he had started working on the ship well over a year before and what he had put into it. I had thought the Duke would be impatient, but he showed, as so often, a keen interest in minutiae, especially if they had a military usefulness.

'Everything I know and more is in there,' FitzStephen continued. 'There are certain new contrivances that I have learned about in my travels to the Roman Sea and in voyages I have made to Sweden. Knees and beams passing through the planking give the hull strength, as do riveted and clenched fastenings. We have small decked areas fore and aft, castles as we call them now, which provide shelter below and indeed useful platforms for archers on top. And on the stern, as you will see, she does not have a steerboard or rudder of the Norse kind. For such a large ship, I have preferred a tiller and rudder attached to a stern post at the back. The steerboard is a clumsy thing in a big ship, and this ship is big, sire, but she handles like a thoroughbred. The Romans used tillers, sir, so do the Arabs, and we begin to see them now on heavy hulks. They are the way forward. A sternpost compromises the shape of the old Norse ship, it's true. But we have taken certain measures so the *White Ship* runs through the sea like a sword. With a ship like this you could rule the seas. Would you like to come aboard, sire?'

'I should be interested, FitzStephen, and indeed I must know more but now is not the time. I see you have an excellent vessel which we can learn much from, but my son will be here soon and we have a busy day ahead ...'

But FitzStephen was bursting to impart something. He was steaming like a kettle.

'I should like to offer the *White Ship* to you, sire. To take you to England today. It is truly a royal ship and...'

The Duke raised his hand.

'No, no, FitzStephen. I have made other arrangements. If I do not use the Honfleur ship, the mayor will have a seizure and the Comte d'Honfleur will start burning my castles.'

The Duke was trying to be tactful; quite an effort for him, but he was doing it. FitzStephen tried another tack.

'May I ask for my father's position then, sire, the fief that my father was given, to provide ships for the royal service. I have money to purchase the honour – see, sire, one mark of gold.'

The wretched FitzStephen dangled a purse at the Duke who you could see was tempted. Gold was short in the royal coffers.

'Well, honest FitzStephen, I agree to your request for the fief, but I must tell you my decision is made for this particular voyage. Next time, I shall doubtless be very much obliged to you.'

'But you m-m-must, sir. Anything else would be...'

'No one says must to the Duke.'

FitzStephen saw he had gone too far.

'I am sorry, sire. My enthusiasm ... I am only anxious for your state, your dignity.'

'I leave in the *Pelican* this evening just after high water tonight. Half of my baggage train is loaded already. I cannot go back on my word; I have made a contract with Honfleur. It is fitting that the King should be seen to keep his promises.'

I knew that better than anyone, except perhaps Juliana.

'Sire. The *Pelican* is a fine ship, and my colleague of Honfleur is a clever man. But surely as King of England you should arrive in a ship that dazzles all eyes; you cannot creep home in an old slop-bucket.'

'By the wounds of Christ, FitzStephen, you go too far! I do not creep anywhere.'

'I think what he means is, by comparison, sire,' I said, in appeasement. 'You cannot blame a man for being too proud of his creation.'

'Nor do I, Latiner, nor do I.'

It had been a good performance by FitzStephen. He already knew the Duke was spoken for in terms of travel arrangements but he had led him well along the path. It was my turn now.

'Perhaps, sir, the Prince would like to consider...'

'Yes, indeed, good thinking, Latiner. As I was about to say, FitzStephen, what we shall do is this. The Prince – who has this month received not just King Louis's approval and authority as my heir, but also the Pope's benediction – the Prince and his brother Richard and their party shall have your excellent *White Ship* to take them to England where we may inspect it at greater length. How many can it hold?'

'She, sir.'

The shipwright was too shocked by the casual impersonal pronoun to consider even the impoliteness of correcting a king.

'How many can *she* hold?'

He was in a good mood today.

'Three hundred and fifty at a pinch.'

'We do not want a pinch,' said the Duke.

'There will be no pinching, sire,' I put in. 'Unless there are ladies on board.'

The Duke threw me a sardonic glance.

'I know about you, Latiner,' he said. 'Why is it that good women like little shits such as you?'

I spoke without thinking. 'I follow the example of my betters, sire.'

I saw FitzStephen quail and I was about to take cover myself, when the Duke roared with laughter.

'If you ever need a job as a jester, boy, let me know. My fellow's got piles and can't crack a joke any more. Can't even crack a turd.'

And then, turning on his heel, he said 'That's settled then. I will speak to the Prince myself.'

'Well,' I said to FitzStephen, 'you got what you wanted. The Duke values his son more than he does himself. I would say you have the better bargain.'

'I don't like that little shit,' FitzStephen replied. 'I've heard one or two things about him.'

'And so have I,' I told him, breaking my rule of discretion, 'and seen them too.'

That little cry of love I had heard in the barn at Mortagne seemed a hundred years ago now. I had a pang of homesickness for a moment. I could smell the place, and wished I had not got myself into these deep waters. But for me, for all of us, it seemed there was no way out. We were all caught in Juliana's net, my new little bastard-to-be included – unless, of course, I somehow escaped the doom I could see closing in upon me, survived, and returned in time to marry Alice. That would be a fine thing, but the future was too dark for me to read.

LXIX

From this time on, it seemed to me that a gathering darkness lay over me. I walked in the shadow of death. There was nothing I could do to stop the course of events that I had set in motion, and for which I would everlastingly be cursed if I was successful in my enterprise – and indeed if I wasn't, by those who valued morality and justice. I was a soul in the antechambers of hell, whose door is always open.

The Prince and his party arrived late. He had stopped for a two o'clock dinner in Quettehou (he had a taste for pancakes as his father had a lust for lampreys) and did not enter Barfleur until seven. He marched to a very different drum from the martial beat of his father. The armour had come off and the ladies were in attendance, as well as some of the most dashing of the younger generals; silk and furs prevailed. There was music in their entourage, pipes and little castanets, timbrels, tambourines and fiddlers. A fool travelled with them, a creature hardly bigger than a football. I got wafts of perfume from the ladies – orris and jasmine, oranges, lemongrass and sandalwood – mingling incongruously with notes of dust and steel, horse sweat and human sweat, and fatigue (that has a smell of its own) which accompanied the elite soldiers arriving with the Prince. In spite of their exertions, they marched with a certain swagger. You couldn't blame them; fighting was over and they felt they had won. It was time for pleasure. The only exception was the prince's half-brother Richard, one of his father's most trusted officers, who wore a somewhat rueful expression. Richard was a bastard like me, and a rueful expression is something that bastards wear. Rue is a herb that bastards eat. I was sorry that he was going to have to drown. They were all going to have to drown.

One particular coxcomb, loud among the riders, caught my attention. I looked closer and saw, to my horror, that it was my half-brother Robert, now a knight. I made a note to try and avoid him, but my heart bled for my father, since if I were successful, the loathsome youth was going to have to drown. Worse, if he died, the likelihood was that my father would make me Comte, and what sort of person would I be then? I would be a murderer. Well, I was going to be a murderer anyway, but I would be a worse sort of murderer, a murderer for common advantage and I didn't like that, but still I saw no way out.

I thought that I caught a glimpse of Eliphas in the throng. It was the sort of glittering company he would sometimes be found in, but I could not be sure it was he, nor did I have the time to search. I badly wanted to speak to him. It was terrible for me now to see the people who must die.

The Prince had already enjoyed a hearty dinner, and a light supper now sufficed, as he did not want to wait around. His father, who had been irritated at the lateness of his coming, now greeted him affectionately, although his son displayed what I thought was scant respect, indeed impatience. The Duke then showed him the ship he was to sail in, the *White Ship*, which rode high at the jetty.

'Look, William,' he cried, 'you will be riding a swan like Jupiter himself!'

This seemed to be to the lad's grunted satisfaction, though he grumbled at the time it would take to re-load all his provisions and supplies. The bar in The Three Horseshoes was cleared for the comfort of the ladies of the court including my pretty little stepmother Matilda, Comtesse de Perche, who affected not to recognise me. Maybe she didn't. The word was that she was in love. Was she to die too? I looked at all these people and I thought: if they knew what I am intending to do, they would turn on me and rend me in pieces.

Wine was called for, and provided by the Duke, in what I thought considerable if not immoderate quantity. Hogsheads from Burgundy appeared (the Duke of Burgundy was something of an ally of Henry's since he too had trouble with the King of France). I was surprised at the Duke for unleashing such a supply for the prince just before a sea voyage. I also noticed that some of it was making its way not just to the passengers but to the sailors, notorious for glugging and grogging. I would have called it rash, but the man was besotted with his son, and would do anything to win a smile. A party atmosphere began to make itself felt among the *White Ship* party; the girls giggled hectically, the men started singing and I noticed a player's stall had been set up. I wondered again if it was Eliphas, but I could not get across to investigate.

At length the Duke was satisfied that his own ship was properly stowed and ready to sail (I noticed that their captain had forbidden *his* men to drink the wine). The King's Court and his men boarded her and the last farewells were made. I noted that some of those mighty men of valour, Gilbert of Exmes and Ralph the Red among them, along with William Bigod and a man I had marked as another Latiner, Gisulf the Scribe, were not after all travelling with the Duke, but were waiting to join the Prince's party.

It was a starlit night, but with just a thin crescent moon and the clarity of frost about it; not so dark you couldn't see some distance ahead. There was a slight evening breeze from the east, firm but not brisk, driving towards Barfleur Point on the port side. Although the tide was still just on the flood, the wind in the sail coupled with the efforts of the oarsmen would more than compensate for the pace of the water. It was time for the Duke to leave for his other country.

'Look after my son,' the Duke enjoined FitzStephen.

'I will, sire.'

'You had better. If anything happens to him in your damned ship, I'll string you up from that mast myself.'

He smiled, like the mouthpiece of a steel helmet, to make FitzStephen see that he was serious. The water behind him was as black as his beard, tinged with red, from the embers of the fires around.

'And you, Latiner? What are you waiting around for? You're surely not going to England?'

'As I told you, sire. I am here to collect money that is owing to the butcher of Rouen.'

'You don't look like a butcher. You look like a Latiner. Spit it out, man. The real reason! You have the look of a man carrying something close.'

I did not like the way his questions were leading. He surely did not suspect me of a plot, though he would have good reason if he did. I reminded myself that he suspected everybody, all the time. It was his way. I repeated my excuse.

'I shall be debt-collecting, sire. For butcher Haimo. I look after his accounts.'

'Why, so you do. I had heard something of that. You have so many talents, Latiner. Schoolmaster, wrestler, sailor, accountant, ladies' man ... but always the bastard. Tell the Prince to pay. He can afford it.'

I nearly reminded him that his own father was a bastard, but I held my tongue for I had quite enough adversity for him that evening.

'As for not looking like a butcher, sire. My coat is made from our own sheepskins. Do I look the part now?'

I unfolded the sheepskin coat that I had brought along against the cold, and put it on. He wrinkled his nose.

'I'd put the coat on after you are on board. They won't let you on the *White Ship* looking like that. And smelling. Oof!'

He turned and stepped up onto the *Pelican* where one of the twins, famous for their disputation in front of the Pope, William (or was it Waleran?) Beaumont was politely waiting to assist the Duke should he require it. FitzStephen and his men on the jetty pushed the ship off, the wind filled her sail, and the oars poked out of her sides like the legs of a centipede and began to move in long, rhythmic strokes. Her lights twinkled and faded in the darkness, and then she was gone. It was a calm night and her master knew the course well. She would be in Southampton in less than five hours.

I stood for a while in the quietness as the water licked up onto the jetty. The flood tide has a different smell from the ebb which carries all away.

LXX

Another of the Duke's hogsheads of wine had been broached. FitzStephen – taut and nervous, his dreams near to fulfilment – made himself known to the Prince, and the young man thrust a cup of wine into his hands. More soon followed it. I do not think the shipwright was used to strong wine, or he would have stopped his sailors drinking.

I walked about, trying to recognise some of the passengers. Someone pointed out Rabel de Tancarville, son of the King's chamberlain. He was a steady-looking young man, who seemed a little on edge, as he talked to a serious William Bigod. I noticed another bigwig, Richard, Earl of Chester, with his wife, who looked nervous. Apart from the Bishop of Coutances who kept lifting his eyes to heaven – perhaps because he was breaking wind or seasick already or both – these were about the only sober people in view, and I included in that category two monks from the Abbey of Tiron and the Archdeacon of Hereford, who were laughing at something that could well have been a dirty joke. The devil was afoot that night and putting his shite in good men's mouths. Gilbert of Exmes and Ralph the Red may have been excellent generals, but they were well away now. Even Richard, the Prince's half-brother, was flushed and garrulous, pressing himself upon one of the young ladies in a manner more befitting a melee.

There was one man who caught my eye who was not drinking. I asked FitzStephen who he was and he told me his name was William of Pirou, a sometime royal steward – not a race of men I usually liked for they were full of guile at the expense of their betters and cruel or exacting to those beneath them. He was a pale-faced man, of middle height, lean but sinewy, ideal for disappearing in a crowd. He seemed to have some intent of purpose on his face, but what it was I could not discern. He was a man to watch: always smiling a little as though at some incipient jest; never laughing – as though he had

431

a knife about his cloak. There were one or two rough-looking knights, more like scullions, I thought, who did not seem to fit in with the fine company, but then neither did I. It did cross my mind to wonder what they might be doing on board, but I had other things to think about.

The crowd had now surged out onto the jetty. The lading of the ship was finished, and it was almost time to be away. FitzStephen lurched up and murmured something in my ear.

'I beg your pardon?' I said.

It had sounded like a cryptic word, a password. Why would he say a password to me? Was there some kind of plot – another one? In that hour of urgency and suspense, it seemed to me that anything was possible. I cocked an ear more closely.

'Ofnanour,' he slurred.

'Ofnanour?' I questioned.

''S nearly high water,' he explained.

I was only temporarily relieved. I sincerely hoped FitzStephen was going to cock the whole thing up by being too drunk to step on board.

'Shall I go and tell the Prince?' I asked him.

'Yes, get 'em on board. I'll tell the M-m-mate.'

The mate was a square-shaped, bearded, elderly seaman with a rolling gait, called Roger, whom FitzStephen trusted, but who didn't know how to treat princes and courtiers. The last time I had seen him he'd been sticking his beak into a pint pot. I set off to locate the Prince who alone could give the order to embark. I found myself charged now with a strange energy and confidence. I knew what had to be done. All directions were leading towards it. I found the Prince with his arm round the waist of his half-sister, the Lady Matilda. They were laughing immoderately at some sally by Gisulf the Scribe who evidently fancied himself as a wit. All around him the party hummed and buzzed, I recognised William of Rhuddlan, drinking with the two sons of Ivo Grandmesnil, and William Bigod – pointed out to me earlier as important nobs by FitzStephen. The girls with them were screeching and cackling. It was all very regrettable, not my idea of princessly behaviour, and I felt we were embarking on a ship of fools, such as may not return. Out in the harbour, masts wagged like the tongues of gossips. I had the feeling, I'm sure you know it, that all this had happened before.

'The Captain begs your pardon and says he thinks it is time to get the party on board, sire,' I told the Prince.

'The Captain does not give the orders, fellow. I give the orders.'

'Yes, sire. But if I may say so, the tide gives the orders. I don't know if you have heard of King Canute and his problem.'

'Who are you, fellow?'

'Wait a minute,' said the Comtesse, 'don't I know you from somewhere?'

She was breathtakingly beautiful in that Saxon way, thick blonde hair, delicate features like an angel, her cheeks slightly pinker than usual from the wine. I had grown a beard since she last saw me.

'I don't think so, my lady,' I mumbled, turning my head away from her, towards the Prince. 'The Captain has enlisted my services, sire, to help get everyone on board.'

'Who are you, fellow?' he asked again.

'Well, sire, in fact I am the butcher of Rouen's counting-man, and I have come to collect money owing to him by your court for six months past.'

'Go away, little man,' he said, and I wanted to strike him.

'Your father said you would pay, sire,' I told him. 'I have the bill with me here.'

I offered it to him, but he half turned away.

Gisulf the Scribe intervened. 'Better do what he suggests, sire,' he said. 'There'll only be trouble when you come back next year. You know how the Duke likes to play fair.'

'I'll sort it out later, on board, or we'll never get home for Christmas,' the Prince complained petulantly.'

This gave me my opportunity.

'Very well, sire. I shall attend you later. But what you say about getting home … this is the fastest ship afloat, sire. So you'll be all right for Christmas, I believe,'

433

It was a feeble pretext but it caught his attention. The Prince loved speed.

'Fast, is she? Faster than the *Pelican*?'

'I should say so. But you won't catch her up.'

'Who says so?'

'I do. I'll wager you can't. She's way ahead of us now.'

'I'll wager we can,' he cried. 'We'll have some sport on this dull ocean. How much?'

'Well, I didn't really mean …'

'How much?'

'All right, then. Half of what you owe,' I told him. 'Five hundred silver pennies.'

I knew Haimo would never agree to such a thing.

'You're on, butcher.' he said. 'Call FitzStephen. Where is the fellow?'

'Sire,' said the shipwright, appearing at our side.

'This fellow says we can't catch the king. I say we can. There's fifty silver pennies for you if we do.'

'Thank you, sire.'

The Prince had sailed this route several times before and knew the options.

'We'll take the shortcut,' he said.

FitzStephen blanched. The shortcut was not what he wanted to take at speed on an almost moonless night.

'But, sire …' he protested. 'I don't think your father would wish...'

'No buts,' cried the Prince. 'The matter is settled.'

There was no way out for FitzStephen. He could hardly claim that he wasn't fit to sail when he had been plied with drink by the Prince himself. The honour of his ship was at stake as well as his own reputation. Besides, he needed the money. The Prince strutted impatiently behind us.

'I didn't know you could take a shortcut,' I said. 'That's unfair.'

'Your bad luck,' he giggled.

He was hooked now.

434

'All aboard,' shouted the Prince. 'By the blood of Christ, we will catch him.'

He was using his father's favourite oath. He'd be trying on his crown next; and he was cuckolding my father with his own half-sister. Now that is not very nice. Tell me, who was the real bastard there?

He turned away to continue his conversation with his sweetheart, and I thanked the man Gisulf, noting his ink-stained hand, and trying not think how the sea would wash it clean.

A mad scramble to board the *White Ship* was not what FitzStephen had in mind, but eventually a captain of the guard and the coxswain of the crew managed to fill the vessel in a half-orderly manner, putting the ladies under the protection of the fore and aft castles with the men ranged along the length of the vessel beside the oarsmen. 'Wine!' called the Prince. 'Bring on the wine.'

Another hogshead was heaved on board. With hogsheads, military equipment and this great company on board, even the great *White Ship* was a little lower in the water than her captain would have liked, but he had boasted that she could take anything, and he could not demur.

No sooner had we got them on board, than a party of priests from the local abbey turned up to bless the voyage.

'Silence,' shouted the Bishop of Coutances, and everyone stopped to listen.

The monks did some solemn chanting and then their leader started praying in a loud rather nasal voice, making the sign of the Cross in the direction of the ship, and saying:

'*O pater omnipotens, oramus nunc pro nave candida et pro principe Guglielmo et illi qui cum principe navigant, tene omnes in tutamine, domine, salve et...*'

By coincidence, one of the attendant crows that hopped about the harbour all day looking for scraps and vying with the gulls, was up late tonight, for they had learnt to salvage scraps from the crowd, and gave a loud 'cawwww' at that moment, or else it was a wit among the passengers. It came from the direction of the Prince himself. There was a great guffaw from Ralph the Red and someone, whom I could not see, shouted:

'Go away, you sad old crows. We have wine and good company here. We don't want all your mopping and mowing and pax vobiscuits. Be off with you! Cawww.'

The voice sounded very much like my half-brother's.

There was a gasp from some – you didn't go around insulting priests like that because you never knew who they would report you to, even God, and there were a few who abstained – but most of the party took up the cry:

'Go away, you old black crows. Caw, caw, caw …'

'This is a disgrace,' remonstrated the Bishop, until someone knocked his mitre off into the crowd.

In the end the little party of monks scuttled back to re-group in the church with many a dark backward look, calling down retribution. It did not augur well. I took advantage of the general outburst of mirth, and the aftermath of mirth, and more mirth after that to tie my little *Perrine* (who I had already positioned nearby) to the stern rail of the *White Ship*, tucking her away so that she bobbed quietly in the shadow, unobserved.

Just at that moment, I felt a hand plucking at my sleeve. It was Eliphas.

'What are you up to?' he asked me.

I had to tell someone the truth.

'I am going to wreck the *White Ship*,' I told him. 'The lady Juliana has taken my wife Alice, who is with child, and she threatens her with death if I do not do what she demands. She will have revenge on her father for what happened to her daughters.'

He looked grave, but not surprised.

'How will you do it?' he asked.

'I will try to see the ship is driven onto the Quilleboeuf Rock.'

'I heard as much,' he said.

'No one is supposed to know. From whom did you hear it?'

'The Lady Juliana,' he said.

'And you are here to try and stop me?'

'I am here to try and help you. I think a lesser man would be breaking up at this stage. You must embark now and let destiny take its course. The wreck may happen, or it may not happen. It may both happen and not happen at the same time. You have to be there, and the decision will be made. Be easy on yourself. What can I do to help?'

'I have to find the rock,' I said. 'If I cannot find the rock, I cannot make the wreck.'

It sounded like gibberish to me. What was I saying? The whole thing was unreal.

'What have you done so far?'

'I have left a buoy near the rock to mark it, but it is dark.'

'I think you will find there is more light than you imagine,' he told me, putting his hand on my head. 'Good luck. I am sure we shall meet again.'

It was extraordinary the effect he had on me; I was altogether relieved by our short conversation and indeed his presence, and I felt the pressure leave my head where he had touched it. He turned and lifted up his arms over the ship as if to bless it, in a gesture that seemed to me ancient, futile and at the same time important. It was almost time to go.

Just at that moment, a disturbance broke out, and I looked over to see several people leaving the ship. One of them was the Duke's nephew, Stephen, Comte of Mortain, who clutched his stomach, white-faced. Another was an ambitious little shit called William of Roumare who was notoriously plotting for his mother's lands, the honour of Bolingbroke. He too was smiling about something with his obsequious steward, Robert de Sauqueville, two bad apples if you ask me.

'The party's got too big for 'em, too much booze, too much parlez-vous,' said the old mate, appearing beside us, waiting to step aboard before they cast off. 'Either that or they got wind of something. That prince, he shouldn't ha' laughed at them holy brothers. They can call the wind, you know, curl the currents and draw the rocks. As for twins, sailors don't like a twin on board. It's unwholesome, so they chuck 'em out. They'd chuck out the ladies if they could because they're bad luck and all on a ship.'

As Comte Stephen passed by on the jetty, he groaned and clutched his stomach again, almost as if he were acting, glancing at us sidelong. Roumare was next to leave, still laughing at some secret joke. One or two others followed. I felt something of the mate's superstitious alarm and also something that was more of men's making. I glanced up at the ship and saw the steward, Pirou, make a gesture that was directed at Roumare who had glanced slyly back at him. I recalled that the man who had been horribly executed for plotting the Duke's death had also been a royal steward. The air seemed all at once full of menace and dark contrivance. It puzzled me, of course, because I was meant to be the figure of ill omen, providing frissons for anyone with a sense of impending doom who cared to be watching. Something was going on that Juliana for all her planning had not foreseen.

The marine guards, drunk too, were singing now, a dirty version of '*Il était une bergère*' which I had always thought was a nursery rhyme.

'Stephen of Mortain pretends he has the squitters, but he's a canny devil,' Eliphas said. 'I wouldn't stay on a boat sailed by a bunch of drunkards. Maybe he thinks if the Prince goes down, he'll be the next king.'

'The King has a daughter,' I said. 'Matilda would be next in line.'

'Yes, but…'

'Hey, you, jongleur,' called a voice from the ship, 'come on board. You can entertain us as we go and join our Christmas revels in Winchester. You have not seen a revel until you have seen an English revel. What do you say?'

I stupidly thought: what an opportunity for Eliphas! And then, recalling what I had to do, I decided it was not. I did not want to drown the player, even though he would doubtless go down with a jest on his lips, and I would have liked to have known what it would be.

'Alas, sire,' he called up, 'my father is ill and you know what fathers are at Christmas. They want you near them.'

'Too bad,' the voice called down, 'we have better plays in England anyway.' It was, I think, the most graceless remark I have ever heard, from prince or commoner. The man who said it, whom I had been trying not to recognise, was my half-brother, my father's son. I smiled at Eliphas and raised my eyebrows. He laughed.

'I am sure you will think of that,' he said, 'when the time comes.'

I did not dare ask him what he meant. He was the kind of man you would trust with your life, but he could be damnably enigmatic. I was starting to shiver with suppressed tension and the imminence of action.

The old mate was signalling to me now to get on board. Eliphas grasped my hand and told me he hoped to see me soon. They were already pushing off as I sprang onto the deck. Just for an instant, I glimpsed not one but a pair of dinghies bobbing at the stern. What the hell was the extra one doing there – and who was it for?

Eliphas waved from the jetty and I returned the wave, wishing I could have had him with me, but it was not part of Juliana's design which had so far been precise in its planning and accurate in its forecast. The breeze filled the sail with a cracking, bellying sound, background to the hoarse injunctions of the coxswain to his crew. It was even colder now, still clear of clouds, the moon no more than an apostrophe, the stars pinpricks through which shone the glory of Heaven. The Pole Star showed the way, straight ahead, to the Quilleboeuf Rock.

'Row, you devils, row. In … out … in … out …' called the Prince. 'We have to catch the King, helmsman. I have a wager to win. Take the shorter route.'

His cry was taken up by the younger members of his party, my stepmother among them.

'Row, row, row,' they cried. 'In … out … in … out…'

'There's a purse of silver for you, coxswain, if we catch them,' cried the Prince.

And the coxswain, nothing loath, urged the crew on, bellowing imprecations, exhortations and commands.

I saw FitzStephen give the helm to one of his underlings, and step forward, down off the helmsman's castle, to speak to William. I edged closer to hear what he was saying.

'I am not sure the shortcut is a good idea, sire.'

'If I say it is a good idea, it is a good idea. Are you not confident in your vessel, helmsman, or in your powers of navigation?'

I could see FitzStephen nerving himself to say that he had taken more ships out of this harbour than he, the Prince, had had hot dinners, but tipsy though he was, he controlled himself. He did know these shores, this sea, and there was none to equal him.

'Of course I am, sire. If that is what you want, we will do it. But I should point out that there are rocks out there, and risks, sire.'

'I say pish to your rocks and risks. What do I care for such things? We have beaten the French King. He is the rock we have fought and broken. What else is there to fear?'

The Prince, flushed with excitement as well as the King's good Burgundy, strode up and down the line of oarsmen.

'Put your backs into it, you rogues. Three silver pennies for each of you if we reach Southampton before the King.'

The men were warming to him. Maybe he wasn't such a bad lad after all, but I was not going to feel sorry for him. We were caught up, all of us, by the spinning spider of destiny.

'Row row, row,' sang the courtiers and the captains. 'In … out …' The oarsmen bent to it with a will, too much so to my way of thinking for they would be exhausted mid-Channel, before they reached England. But of course they were not going to reach England.

Somewhere in Normandy, Alice was alone, afraid, and carrying my child. How I longed to be with her now. I had to do what had to be done; all I could do was try and save her. The

Quilleboeuf Rock was only a mile out. We would be there in less than ten minutes.

'Why are you on this ship, peasant?' asked a truculent young blade asked me, looking askance at my coat.

I recognised him as Geoffrey de l'Aigle as he stumbled into me, splashing wine on my sheepskin.

'To take some money off you, peasant,' I told him.

No one in a sheepskin coat had spoken to him like that before. His jaw dropped.

'Wha' wha' wha' ...' he gibbered. 'Who d'you think you're talking to?'

I walked on towards the stern, weaving my way between groups of drunken soldiers and courtiers, to where FitzStephen stood, swaying to the movement of the good ship alcohol. I noticed that his coxswain, a man to trust, was now on the stern castle, holding the tiller. For a moment, I saw the fellow Pirou in front of me, sidling through the crowd, stopping now and then to exchange a word but always moving on.

'Hey, fellow,' said a young lady, 'you have a bu ... bu ... colic look. And a ...' she approached nearer, 'fwaaahh smell. If we stood you by the sail, you could drive the ship forward on smell alone. Hey, William. Smell power could win battles for you. Just send in the men with smellskin coats.'

'*Bonne idée*, Comtesse. You can campaign with us anytime. In fact, we could have a little campaign of our own tonight.'

'And you a married man!'

'My wife is only twelve years old so it doesn't count.'

Drunkards surged up and down the middle of the ship, sometimes falling over the oarsmen who swore at them. I turned and tried to look forwards over the bow, cursing FitzStephen's innovation of a little castle at each end for I could not see ahead from where I was standing, flat in the belly of the ship. The water gleamed sleekly, dappled with icy flecks of foam. I leant over, felt it and shuddered. We were moving like a boulder down a mountain with tremendous, headlong, irresistible speed.

Row, row, row.

A girl smiled at me, she must only have been seventeen or so.

'They laugh at a sheepskin coat,' she said, 'but you'll be the one laughing before this cold night is out.'

I didn't really have the time to stay, but what she was saying was important.

'Would you like it?' I asked her. 'It smells a bit, but it's better than goosebumps.'

'I am fine,' she said. 'I have a fur trimming to my cloak. You just look rather sweet in it.'

'What is your name?' I asked her.

'Hélène,' she said. 'I am the daughter of Ralph the Red.'

'I think you have saved my life,' I told her.

'I don't understand …'she started to say.

I held up my hand in a gesture as if to say I should like to talk more, but I simply can't just now. But it wasn't my life she had saved. It was her own life and the life of everyone on board. I could not go through with it now, even for Alice and her baby; she would not want me to. This Hélène was like the righteous man in the story of Sodom. Someone good and kind and unassuming whom I could not kill; possibly one of those angels whom we entertain unawares.

I started to move as fast as I could back to the castle in the stern where the coxswain stood holding the tiller, legs braced, his eyes straining into the night. It was hard finding a way through that milling crowd as it swayed to the movement of the vessel. The *White Ship* was saved, though. I didn't need to hurry. I turned to look forward again, to see if I could discern the Quilleboeuf ahead. Yes, and there it was, slightly, but safely, over to port, a little spray from wavelets fretting around its top, the water around it almost luminous. No sign of my buoy, though – now why would that be? That was a minor issue, however; the main thing was, the *White Ship* was safe. I felt an immense surge of relief.

Just at that moment, as I struggled to reach the coxswain, and as everyone turned towards a blast of music from the horns and a burst of cheering that erupted from somewhere up front, I saw the dull flash of something metallic moving fast against a patch of starlit sky – a bar or rod of some kind. It was wielded by the man Pirou and landed on the burly coxswain's skull with a crack I could almost feel. Even as the man collapsed, he was gathered in Pirou's arms and swiftly heaved over the stern into the water. Pirou himself grasped the tiller and, as I scrambled up the steps to the castle, I saw the unmistakable shape of the Quilleboeuf Rock, much closer ahead of us now, and only very slightly to port. The moon must have had more strength than I had reckoned for there was definitely a ring of light around the rock. For some reason, I thought of Eliphas. It was quite evident to me that Pirou was steering for the rock deliberately. He was doing my dirty work for me, work that I myself had now decided to reject. That must be his little boat bobbing along beside *Perrine,* in which he planned to make his getaway. So that was why someone had removed my buoy, doubtless thinking it was there to warn rather than lure! There had been more than one plot in the offing that night. That was why Stephen of Mortain had left the ship before she sailed! Diarrhoea my left foot! Or was it that Roumare fellow, hand in grudge with Pirou?

'No,' I shouted furiously, crazedly at Pirou. 'Go right ... starboard ... away from the rock.'

Of course there was no chance that he would do so.

Seizing the metal bar again, and keeping one hand on the tiller, he lashed out at me, and missed. People were looking at us now. I grasped the bar with both hands and prised it from his grasp to give him some of his own medicine. I swung, the vessel lurched, and I caught him on the shoulder – a glancing blow, but it still hurt him. He launched himself at me and we wrestled on the floor of the castle. He had chosen the wrong man to wrestle with, though. I put him in a lock and threw him down the stairs. A sack of carrots would have landed better, and the stuffing was knocked out of him. He was at least out of the way for the moment.

I grasped the tiller. Everyone could see the tip of the rock now, flecked with foam, about thirty yards ahead on the left. People were shouting at me:

'Hard a-starboard or you'll have us all drowned!'

I knew what to do now.

Pirou, had resurfaced sooner than I expected and now, sporting a bloody head, even he seemed to have caught the general frenzy. He fought like a madman with me to put his hand once again upon the tiller, and I fought as madly to restrain him.

'Hard a-port,' he shouted.

'Hard a-starboard!' shouted the mate, starting to clamber up the stairs, gasping for breath.

I was overcome with a stupid confusion, forgetting everything FitzStephen had tried to teach me. Did I push the tiller right to go right? Was that what hard a-starboard meant? Why was I, a landlubber, in this stupid position, in charge of three hundred people?

I had time for only one move and I made the wrong one. I pushed the tiller hard over to the right and Pirou, hurt though he was, clapped his hands.

And then the *White Ship* struck. It was as if the very earth had cracked.

We hit the rock with a great, coarse, rending wooden cry of pain. I had fulfilled my promise to Juliana perfectly, and Alice and I were free.

For a moment, there was silence from all the people on board, disbelief, and then commotion and fear spreading like an instant disease. For a start, there was a great deal of very cold water. The mate and I struggled through the panicking crowd to try and see what the damage was – it might be possible to staunch the hole and limp back to shore – but the ship was holed below the waterline, planks were shattered and there was no warp on earth could repair that wound.

I started sloshing about the boat, apologizing.

'I'm sorry,' I kept saying. 'Hard a-starboard.'

'Are we sinking?'

'What can we do?'

'Will they send someone from the shore?'

'We're all going to die!'

'Christ have mercy!'

And so on. I was so overwhelmed by guilt, shame, and confusion I did not think of my own danger.

While the general confusion reigned, I noticed the Prince's personal guard, appointed by the King himself, men of fierce loyalty and military presence of mind, scouring the ship for anything that might float. They quickly located *Perrine* and brought her round to the side. I knew what had happened to the other little boat; Pirou must have scrambled into it and was sculling home even now. He would not get far against that tide, not with that wounded paw.

I was still in a state of shock. I could not believe that I had been responsible for this disaster, and yet here they all were, spluttering around like goldfish in the remnants of a broken bowl.

The ship was sinking lower in the water and beginning to list. Stability wasn't helped by too many people trying to climb up onto the castles to get away from the danger. The bow was now under water, lodged precariously on ledges of the rock, and slipping. There were already people in the sea, some swimming, others floundering; no one could last long in that cold. The little boat with the Prince and four men aboard, including the Prince's half-brother, Richard, was already some twenty yards away.

It was just at that point that a piteous voice cried out:

'William … don't leave me…'

It was my little stepmother, the lovely Comtesse de Perche, calling more in love than fear.

The Prince, on hearing her voice, immediately ordered his oarsmen to row back and collect her. The guard demurred. I could see them arguing against it. It was obvious what would happen if they obeyed, but the Prince was insistent, I will say that for him. He loved that girl to the end. So they rowed back.

When they reached the side of the ship she stepped on board, but as they turned the boat to row away again, a myriad hands like the tentacles of a great octopus, reached up out of the water and clung to the side of the little skiff ... And of course my brave little *Perrine* turned on her side. Then they were all in the water: Prince, Comtesse, and the bravest of the brave.

I saw William clutch the little Comtesse to him and they sank together, beyond the reach of his tutor Othuer, who had leapt from the ship to succour him. I made the sign of the Cross and prayed that God would not punish them for I knew more about the impossibility of love than I had when I first saw them.

It was all at once borne upon me that I now had no escape plan for myself. *Perrine* was gone. The ship quivered, slid down a little more, the mast cracked and toppled over the side in a welter of sail and sheets. It was time to leave. I saw a spar floating nearby. I huddled my coat about me and jumped into the water. I tried to call out for someone to join me on my spar, but the cold took my voice away.

At this point, the weight of the people in the ship's castles – proud innovation of FitzStephen – made the ship capsize. The whole party was flung into the sea. The air was full of the despairing cries of drowning men and women, sounding like seabirds. I looked around desperately for the little girl who had smiled at me, because I wanted to save her for being so nice, but I could see her nowhere.

'Hélène! Hélène!'

I tried to paddle round the ship as I called her, but it began to slide off the rock and with shocking speed disappeared into the ocean, almost carrying me with it. The whole thing was so completely unreal that I could not believe it had happened. People were drowning all around me. A bedraggled wretch swam up and asked if he could share my spar.

'Yes, peasant,' I said, smiling to show I welcomed the company.

It was the same proud young baron who had insulted my sheepskin coat.

'This is a terrible thing,' he said. 'The King will never recover.'

'I'm not sure any of us will.'

I was finding, to my surprise, that my coat which now gathered itself up around me on the surface like a skirt, actually helped me to float. Perhaps, I thought, with its fatty skin, it would even help to keep me warm. It did not help to keep me dry though, and the cold – fatty skin or not – soon penetrated to the very marrow. Our spar was drifting on the ebb, away from the rock. There had been a moment when I wondered whether to repeat my late survival stratagem of sitting on the Quilleboeuf, but I saw there was someone there already, looking very disinclined to be removed. And when I looked again there was a fight. And when I looked once more there was no one on it at all. It was, anyway, too far from me now.

I stayed where I was with my companion beside me, hanging onto the spar. We exchanged names and some little information. Bodies floated past us, some alive and feebly struggling, others white and still, here a beautiful woman, there one of the King's Guard, there the jester rolled up like a woodlouse on a half-full hogshead. Among these motionless bodies, I perceived the Prince again, yielded up by the water and torn from the arms of his love, in the embrace now of his bastard half-brother, the great general Richard who must have found him, momentarily buoyed up by the bubbles in his clothes. I wondered for a moment whether to try to collect the Prince and anchor him to the spar, and I questioned my companion as to whether it should be done.

'Let him be,' said Geoffrey. 'The King will not thank you for bringing his son back dead. In fact he will secretly hate you for it. Better to let the waters take him and yield him up on the shore if fate wills it.'

The Prince and his brother sank under the water as I watched. It entered my mind now, slowly, because the cold made everything slow, that Juliana had hedged her bets. She had not completely trusted me. The other party had been there on her command...

'What fools we were,' exclaimed Geoffrey, 'and how the wheel of fortune turns. I fear I will not last the night, Bertold. I feel the cold entering my heart. Will you tell my father that I loved and honoured him to the end, if you survive?'

'I will. But I am certain you will endure. I will make you endure.'

My companion shook his head.

'I will try, I promise. I am not anxious to die out here. But it is cold. It is so cold. This night has been like the end of the world.'

The effort of speaking had exhausted him and he sank back against the spar. There was a slight commotion not far off, as though someone were swimming inexpertly towards us. Then, poor FitzStephen appeared out of the gloom, splashing like a dog, a sad woebegone figure whose dream had been broken and who still could not get the words out fast enough …

'I have l … l … lost the Prince. Is he a … l … l … live?'

'He is dead,' I told him. 'We saw him go.'

'I have lost everything, I cannot live now,' he said, and put his head down, under the water, where he stayed.

Slowly, as the chill tightened its grip on us, the last desperate sounds abated and the bodies floating past became infrequent. Hours must have passed; we were numb with cold and half dead with shock and exhaustion. I tried to stay awake because I knew if I did not, I would never wake up again. I kept shaking Geoffrey to try to keep him with me, but I could see he was not in good shape. And so we drifted until there was no vestige left of the *White Ship* and the three hundred people on board, only Geoffrey de L'Aigle and I, the bastard FitzRotrou, heir now to the county of Perche and feeling no better for it.

LXXI

I was losing the sense of cold now, and a kind of sleep enfolded me. I was no longer afraid, and still I floated on. I passed out again, and remained in a kind of stupor, falling in and out of consciousness, a half-world or threshold which must have persisted for some time. In that sort of state, you begin to lose the person you are – or were – and I was not sorry to lose myself completely; it seemed an encumbrance.

'Bertold! Bertold!'

Who was that?

I opened my eyes and a man's face filled my vision – young, distraught, exhausted, deathly pale, at the end of his tether. I was surprised to find it was this man who was shaking me and shouting a name.

'Thank God,' he cried, 'you are still alive'.

I looked beyond and around him and saw an endless vista of cold, dark sea, punctuated by an occasional lump of rock. I looked down and saw that we two were crudely fastened, by the boy's golden cloak, to a spar big enough to cling to but not to sustain our weight. One or two pieces of wood were floating nearby along with other cumbersome, bobbing objects, which I saw were bodies; the dead coming back to us for company.

I could not feel my own body any more, but I found there was something thick and familiar around me, pliable and ice-cold, helping me float. Very slowly, like an old mill-wheel in a slack stream, my brain turned. Ah yes. It was my sheepskin coat, which they had all mocked me for when I came aboard, the courtiers and the pretty girls. And I remembered who I was and how I came to be here.

I was Bertold, the account-keeper of Haimo Labouchère, the King's butcher of Rouen, on an errand to collect debts before their owners could run away to England. My companion was Geoffrey de l'Aigle, son of the powerful Comte of Vexin and Earl of Lincoln, one of Duke Henry's generals in Normandy.

And we were in the sea, about two miles off Barfleur, our vessel – the fastest and newest and safest in Christendom – having struck a rock and sunk in ten minutes, leaving just the two of us from a total of more than three hundred people on board.

Just at that moment, I saw Geoffrey's head fall forward into the water. He had spent what little strength he had trying to save me. I found a new reserve of energy and redoubled my efforts to keep Geoffrey awake, telling him jokes, making him sing, repeating old stories, telling him how I got into all this, even the bits about Juliana's revenge. His response was sluggish.

'You have to try harder, Geoffrey. You must have told jokes in your father's hall. What gave the sieve a hernia?'

But his head fell forward on his chest, until I beat him on the shoulder.

'Wake up, you silly bugger. Geoffrey!' I cried, resorting to the same tactics he had employed, slapping him on the cheeks, pulling him up in the water.

He opened his eyes, it seemed with an enormous effort, the lids heavy as portcullises.

I stopped, it was kinder to let him die. And then all at once, he said:

'Fish supper.'

I thought about it for a while. That was not what gave the sieve a hernia. I must say that my own responses were beginning to slow right down again.

'When we get home,' I told him, humouring the poor boy.

'We are,' he said, and gave me the most beautiful smile. Then his hands lost their grip on the spar and he started to sink.

'Geoffrey,' I cried. 'Geoffrey!'

'You will tell him, won't you?' he said. 'My father …'

'I will tell him.'

He tried to smile, and then he just started to slip away into the water, sliding through my arms. He was the son of a powerful count and I was a bastard, working as a book-keeper for a butcher, but I wept as though he had been my own brother.

With all my remaining strength, I hung on to him and tried to haul him back, but I was too weak and the sea was too hungry. He was dead; I let go and he sank like a sword. I wept until I could weep no more and I had salted the whole sea. I wept more for him than for all the dead people I had sailed with who now lay scattered over the deep, and I thought of the wickedness of Juliana who had killed so many people in her pursuit of revenge.

'Happy now?' I called.

I was not altogether surprised to receive a distant answering cry; anything was possible, it seemed to me, in this night of madness. My state of exhaustion and shock made me ready to admit anything natural or supernatural, a hulk or cog from Barfleur or the imp Merle in a foggy cloud.

'Happy now?'

Something struck me on the head – a floating spar, a cask lifted by a wave – and I must have passed out for some moments. It was good there where I was and I hung on to it ... until I woke from comfortable oblivion to the cheerless light of dawn and the outrageous smell of salt water, which hits you like a brick when it means to kill you. I was still *in* the water, but with someone slapping my face. It crossed my mind that this was like being born again, something I didn't want to be doing..

'Wake up, wake up,' someone was shouting in a funny voice.

My God, I *was* being born again. It was true, I felt like crying. Slowly I took in the scene around me.

The sea was full of bodies again. Currents, which had scattered the dead, had now twirled them back again in some kind of *contredanse macabre*. It was a ghastly sight for the fishermen who had appeared out of the morning mist, crossing themselves and making exclamations of horror and pity.

'Poor souls!'

'Oh my God!'

'Christ have mercy!'

They had seen me as a floating corpse among all the other dead, this one in an old sheepskin coat – and then someone noticed a faint movement. It made them realise that maybe I was still alive, and with rough attentiveness, they lifted me up as though I were a halibut and put me in the bottom of a smack, along with five crabs – maybe one was my old friend from the Quillleboeuf rock – a lobster and ten pilchards and a load of mackerel. And that is how I came, shivering uncontrollably, once more to Barfleur.

LXXII

I had been convinced, when I'd thought about it before, that in the event of my survival, Alice would be waiting for me on the shore. I imagined that Juliana would have brought her to me in a gesture of gratitude – but Alice was not there. I did have the feeling, though, that she was waiting for me somewhere. I needed to get back and find her, and meet the bump that was my child. But I was barely alive.

Soon a congregation of lately arrived, rearguard soldiers and lords who had not sailed, along with local officials, started to gather about me like gulls, and surveyed my huddled figure as the fishermen debated what to do with me. Finally, they took me to the harbourmaster's office and laid me upon the floor against a cupboard. I promised to reward my rescuers when I was sufficiently recovered. Someone produced a blanket. Someone else found some strong wine and tipped it down my throat.

Stephen of Mortain, the King's nephew – a tall, pale-faced man whose drooping moustaches gave him a mournful expression – made the first move. He seemed to have recovered miraculously from his diarrhoea, and swooped upon me accusingly as I lay and shivered. I was the only survivor of the wreck and therefore, by implication, the perpetrator – a logical assumption which happened to be true. As I blurted out my tale, however, leaving out all mention of the fight with Pirou (he might have been Stephen's man, and then where would I be?), it seemed that he changed his view. I had a perfect reason for being on board: money for my boss. I was clearly a simple fellow. I had survived because I was dressed in the uniform of my trade. The reason for the wreck was what I was gulping now – strong wine and too much of it. There was nothing for it, he said, but I must go to England and tell the King.

They allowed me to sleep most of the day, then at last they woke me up, and I crawled to my room at the inn for some respectable clothes. Lisette insisted that I have a bath, which was the best thing she could have done. My stiff, pale limbs unbent and regained some colour in the warm water. I changed into more respectable clothes, persuaded her with silver pennies to keep my room for me, had a huge supper, and then took a thick coat the landlord provided (not as warm as my sheepskin), and my own sullen carcass out onto the jetty to catch the evening boat for Southampton with Stephen and a couple of minor lords. He made me feel like a piece of questionable luggage.

Again, it was a clear, calm evening. They preferred to sail on such a night for the stars made navigation easier. Stephen and a couple of lords sailed with me. It was my first visit to England and we arrived, as dawn was breaking, in Southampton – not much of a place at that hour. We transferred to horses and by evening we were at the King's palace in Winchester. A reaction to my previous night's ordeal had set in and I was already dog-tired.

Half-dead though I was, I dreaded the confrontation with Henry, knowing he would be suspicious of me and my lone survival, and I was given little time to settle my story. I was ushered into a hall full of nervous-looking lords and courtiers, and I braced myself for a meeting that I knew could be disastrous. I was grateful that at that point Stephen resisted the suggestion of a lord called Robert d'Oilly who spoke in the slight quacking dialect they use here, so I only caught the gist of it – that I should report immediately to the King. I was dead on my feet. It seemed to me that we were all players in some kind of mummer's charade in which we had our allotted and ludicrous parts.

'It would surely be better,' Stephen said, 'if this terrible news were broken by someone he loves, but for whom his natural delicacy would mitigate any anger he might feel at this calamity.'

'Terrible news, terrible news,' said the courtiers.

Stephen, at least, spoke proper French, but he had ever a politician's way of talking. We were in a parlement of birds, and he was the heron, always waiting.

'Who then?' quacked d'Oilly.

'Who then?' asked others, looking about dazedly like chickens. 'Who then? Who then?'

You could see they were all scared of the King, as I was. I looked from one to another of these old birds with Norman names who lived in England – William de Mohun, Robert de Lacy, Bishop Roger of Salisbury, and so on – and I said to myself, we make better lords in Normandy. I was careful, however, to look subservient. I wanted to scatter corn for them.

'Why not you?' another wise owl asked Stephen. 'You're supposed to be his favourite.'

'Not I! He would doubtless blame me for the whole affair. You tell him, Tancarville. You yourself have lost a son in the shipwreck.'

Poor man. I did not know young Tancarville, but perhaps I might have recognised him if he walked in now with seaweed in his hair.

'No, no. I am already quite overcome. What about you, de Lacy?'

'No, I fear I have almost lost my voice.'

'William Bigod, now, he is a straight-talking man…'

'But where is he?'

'He's drowned.'

'Ah.'

At last Theobald, Comte de Blois, Stephen's brother and a better general, an energetic cock-robin of a man, suggested a little boy, son of one of the courtiers. This child of six or seven years of age was, at times of ease and relaxation, a favourite of the King's and made him smile. Surely Henry would not be angry with him!

The barons and courtiers, the whole lot of them, rose as one, swooped around the room, and settled on this proposal, which I thought disgusting and showed how low England had fallen.

Tired though I was, I put my hand up and volunteered myself again, but they looked at me as though I were a sea-urchin.

The small boy, Robin – who reminded me, and perhaps the King, for a sad moment of Roger, the Castellan of Ivry's little chaffinch – was briefed by me, by the barons and by Stephen himself, and was finally considered to have got the drift of the disaster. At first he thought it was a fine game, but as I told the story his eyes grew bigger and his mouth turned down.

'Everybody dwowned?' he asked. 'Even the fine lady?'

'Everybody. And the Prince too,' I told him. 'That is what you must tell the King. They went straight down. No one was saved except me, and I am a nobody.'

He didn't want to do it, indeed his mother came and made a fuss, but the barons over-ruled her. They would have rolled the little fledgling along to the King with their beaks, and his mother as well, if they had thought it would help. It might have done too, because she was a good-looking woman.

When he had taken in what he could, and repeated his message to everyone's satisfaction, he was ushered into the throne room, all by himself, where the King was at work, at a table, with a map of Normandy in front of him drawn up by the Brother Cartographer of Saint-Sulpice, a man with terrible piles. Comte Stephen kept the door ajar and we jostled for position behind him, squawking and muttering. The King was sitting at his table.

'Ah, Robin,' he said, 'I am afraid I am too busy to talk at the moment. Come back a little later.'

But Robin did not go. The King was puzzled; a little impatient, as he can be.

'I am busy, Robin. Come back later.'

Robin kept standing there. The King raised his voice.

'Robin. Later.'

Robin burst into tears.

'I am sorry, Robin, but really ... What is the matter with you?'

Robin forgot his careful briefing and blurted everything out.

'It is the *White Ship*, sire. She is wrecked. Prince William and your generals and your daughters, everyone is dwowned!'

At that point, the King folded his wings and fell forward in a fit. He had to be helped to a private room where he drank a great deal of strong wine and ate nothing, not even a lamprey. He kept to this room and spoke to no one, it was said, for a week. Some said he never smiled again.

The boy Robin had inadvertently saved me from the King's questions, and the barons thereafter completely ignored my existence in that way they have – I had been given quarters near the scullions – so I took the opportunity of the King's affliction, and returned to Normandy by stealth to find temporary accommodation in the Abbey of Saint-Sulpice.

I had seen Juliana's revenge complete and a mighty king brought to his knees, and I felt disgusted with myself. I had been responsible for killing three hundred people, and I couldn't even go to Confession because what priest these days could keep a confession like that to himself?

LXXIII

This is where the accountant should draw the line.

The King is in debit to the tune of that thing he prized the most: an heir, a boy just married, on the verge of manhood. He has also lost two bastard daughters and a bastard son who was also a good general. In fact the loss of his generals seems to have hit him almost as hard as that of his son. He has lost a host of good men, a dozen pretty girls and possibly a couple of mistresses.

I am in debit to the King. He will find out that I survived and will come after me, even though I once saved his life. Some will say that I, the bastard FitzRotrou, sabotaged the *White Ship* so that my half-brother, heir to the Comte de Perche, should die and the bastard inherit. I don't think the King will believe that, but he will feel that my presence at Barfleur was more than coincidence. What he will do is anyone's guess, but I wouldn't like to be in my shoes when he works it out.

Juliana is in debit to the tune of two daughters and a husband she never loved and, you might say, a lover she never husbanded.

Eustace will, of course, be blamed for having started it all. In addition to that, he too is in debit to the tune of a spouse and two daughters, and his reputation.

The Castellan of Ivry is in debit of a son's eyes and the goodwill of all who read my writings.

The town of Barfleur is in debit because the Duke will never use the place again.

Today I learned, through a letter delivered to the abbey, that I am also in debit of a father. This grieves me more than ever I could have thought possible. He died three weeks ago. They sent for me, but did not know where I was. The word was I had been drowned.

It is not all debit, however.

On the credit side, Alice and our child (not yet born) are now at Mortagne. Alerted by a message from Juliana, my father summoned Alice to await me at his castle. Her note says that she sat with my father – it was an impostume in his chest – until the end. I am indebted to her for that. When I assume the title of Comte de Perche, she will be my Comtesse. Perche is a useful county to the Duke.

My partner, or rather ex-partner Haimo, is also in credit – not just because his books are in order, but because he has a wife now – Berthe, of course. I could see where that was leading. I have urged him to sell the business, buy Berthe a rich manor, and get the lad Bertrand – now rewarded by Haimo – to destroy my accountancy system. The religious authorities seem to have taken against the Arabic ciphers and the lewd concept of zero.

But enough of accountancy.

Juliana is in neither credit nor debit, she is in a nunnery. It is better not to say where, but I thought of her a great deal as I completed my History. 'When we have to part, think of me as dead,' she told me once. Even so, and in spite of promises made and anticipations of regret, I discovered where she was. It would be invidious for me to tell you how I found her, but I did, with difficulty and the help of Eliphas.

LXXIV

After a prolonged sojourn in my old abbey of Saint-Sulpice where I was well received by Brother Paul, and restored in body and mostly in mind, I rode once more to Rouen to say farewell to Haimo and Berthe, and to settle my affairs with the butcher. Berthe was with child upon which I congratulated them both. Here at their house I found Eliphas again who put me on the path to Juliana. I told him that my purpose was to speak with her one last time before I closed my account and headed for Mortagne.

He approved of my plan but said I would find her changed. 'She looks much the same but she is different. It is like speaking to someone who has gone through the gate.'

I had no idea what he meant by that but I resolved to find out.

The convent was only a slight detour from the road that led to Perche, and twenty miles or so from the abbey at Saint-Sulpice itself. As I rode Blackberry down the hill to the town of Chambois, set beside the stripling river Dives, I could see the buildings just beyond the town, set on a little eminence. I wasted no time in the town dawdling at the inn, though I could have done with a draught of beer, fatigued as I was from my ride. I wanted to press on for Mortagne where my future lay, but I had to put the past to rest.

I handed Blackberry to the nunnery's stable-boy and made my way back again to the front gate and the porter. The Sisters had employed a large man for that role. He and his dog growled at me as I entered his lodge. 'What do you want?' he asked. 'Do you have an invitation?'

'In a way,' I told him.

He didn't seem happy with that, so I tried to explain that the Duke's daughter would like to see me, and that I would tell her father if any jumped-up nunnery porter got in the way.

He rose slowly as if being hoisted by some invisible but neglected device, and went into the main body of the building. He was gone for a little while. The dog – a mastiff cross – looked at me as if I were some kind of felonious chop.

Finally, the man returned.

'You are to come with me,' he said. 'And no funny tricks. Sister will see you now.'

We walked across the front courtyard and entered into a kind of vestibule. A nun appeared from behind a grille.

'You want to speak to Sister Juliana,' she said.

'Yes.'

'She will see you for quarter of an hour. That is all.'

It was more than I had feared and less than I wished, but I was incandescent with excitement. I was in love with someone else, I knew that and she knew that, but I still felt like a foolish swain with a heart too big for my ribs at the prospect of seeing Juliana again.

There was the sound of a latch, a door opening behind me, I turned, and she was there; my own, my love. They had not dressed her as a nun because she had not yet taken her vows. She wore a simple grey dress. Her hair was up. She took my hand and we walked out into the garden.

She looked paler and, I have to say, older than I remembered. That was good; anything to make me want her less – but it didn't. She had always been slim, but now she was thin and there was sadness in her eyes. That, I felt, would never change; it was resident. And there was resignation too. Although a king's daughter, she had been dealt a hard hand. It sounds like treason to say it, but I thought I noticed a silver strand in the golden hair.

'Come away, Juliana,' I whispered. 'You shouldn't be here.'

'Come away to what? Come away with you? I think not. My life is over. That is what I want it to be. The meal is over, it is time to digest and reflect. And then, I think, a sleep.'

'I love you.'

There you are. I blurted it out like a schoolboy.

'I know you do, but love is really not enough. Love is just the scent of the flower. It attracts the bee who goes tumbling around in the pollen. What a thing is love, says Bertold the Bee!'

There were plenty of them out here, tumbling with the lavender.

'But, of course, it is just an addictive aroma,' she continued, 'a preface to something absolutely basic and rather crude. If you turn it into something else, you're missing the point. It's not a nice smell at all. It's marsh-gas, and the next thing you know, you're in the marsh, up to your neck.'

Did she really believe what she was saying? Indeed, had she ever really loved me? I didn't want to ask her. It seemed so callow.

'Did you ever really love me?' I asked.

'Of course I did.'

'Well, then, let's leave now and go away together.'

'You are forgetting something.'

I knew what I was forgetting: Alice. I had never felt more wretched. How hard it is to seem a hero to oneself – and yet we are meant to be the heroes of our own lives.

'What happened to Eustace?' I asked.

'Oh, he's around. I think someone cut his balls off.'

'Was that you?'

'Probably.'

I thought: I am going to kill myself if I stay here much longer.

'I'm sorry,' she said.

'I'm sorry too.'

Neither of us wanted to mention her little girls. I thought of them and felt the tears welling up. Funny, isn't it, how we have no control over our tear ducts. They are rather like the penis in that respect.

Neither of us mentioned the three hundred people who had died. I understood now what Eliphas had meant about passing the gate.

'Five minutes to go,' said the nun, coming out with an hour-glass, and then going out again.

'Let me know how you're getting on,' I said.

'You too.'

We both knew we wouldn't.

'It was bad of you to kidnap Alice,' I said.

'I didn't kidnap her. I just said that I had.'

'So why didn't she come and find me?'

'I needed her.'

'You kidnapped her.'

'In a way, yes. Alice is very fond of me.'

I thought of that little conversation I had had with Alice on the bed in Berthe's house.

'She's very fond of me too,' I told her.

'As I am. We all seem to have trouble with that.' The ghost of a smile lit up her face for an instant.

'I had better go,' I said.

'Yes. Look out for my father. He'll be coming round asking questions.'

'Yes. You too.'

The old nun reappeared and made shooing gestures.

'I think it would be best if you didn't come back,' Juliana said to me.

'Yes.'

'I love you.'

'I love you too.'

'Goodbye, my dearest, sweetest heart,' she said. She had never called me that before. She kissed me on the cheek, and held me close for a long moment. And that was how it ended. It was time to leave for home.

Post scriptum

I have written, long after the event and in the interests of truth and of history, this account of the proceedings leading up to the wreck of the *White Ship*, and my part in them, as I have seen my old friend Vitalis scribbling away with his ecclesiastical history in the Abbey of Saint-Évroult. I will not trouble you with my own subsequent history. It has had its share of sun and shadow, which is the portion of mankind.

Vitalis will doubtless have written his account of the wreck even as I have written mine. They will be very different, but mine is the true one because I was on the ship. That is why it is important for you to have the story from me, as it happened – not a reported event, but a confessional statement. I have written it, of course, in Latin since it is the *lingua franca* of the educated and will always be understood when our rough dialect has rotted into gibberish.

My history is written on vellum, and I will place it in a sealed container made of lead, the construction and concealment of which I have entrusted to my old friend Eliphas whose hermetic secrets and mysterious arts could not be put to better use.

I have asked him to place it somewhere in the demesne of the Abbey of Saint-Sulpice where it will not be found in many a hundred years – for it would be death to myself and others if it were opened in our lifetimes. I will not ask him where he puts it. Perhaps it will never be found, but I believe the truth will out, and the very earth itself will bear it upwards until it comes up like a thorn in the skin, at last, to the wonder and pity of the world.

History and Guesswork

History is the bones of this story; guesswork and romance are the flesh and the blood.

In terms of history, much of the tale is based on fact – so far as we can retrieve accuracy from events that occurred nine hundred years ago. We have a kind of feeling that the people who lived at that time were not really flesh and blood, but moved in a series of Anglo-Norman attitudes, rather as in the Bayeux tapestry, in a life of great discomfort and semi-barbarism. Nothing could be further from the truth. They were as alive as we are, possibly more so; life was shorter, but the earth was closer, the water colder and the sky nearer. We are prepared to allow that the Tudors, for instance, were proper living people because they were able to tell us so much more about themselves – but the fact that we know less about the men and women of the twelfth century makes them, in a way, even more interesting.

We do have a very good guide in the form of a monk called Orderic Vitalis, a man from Gloucestershire who moved over to the Abbey of Saint-Évroult in Normandy on which my Abbey of Saint-Sulpice is loosely based. He wrote an exhaustive *Ecclesiastical History* covering the years this story deals with, and considerably beyond them on either side. He had two names. Orderic was English, but the monks could not pronounce that in Normandy so they called him Vitalis. Using him and one of two others of his kind, plus a certain amount of intelligent guesswork, we can piece together what happened after the *White Ship* went down.

When Bertold was brought back to shore, one of the first people to speak to him was probably Stephen, Comte of Mortain, Henry's nephew and one of his two possible heirs. Henry's daughter Matilda, of course, was in direct line to the throne, but there had already been rumblings and rumours that some of the barons would not accept a woman – a tendency that

Stephen of course did his best to encourage. It is interesting to note that Stephen, along with one or two others, got off the *White Ship* just before it sailed. Stephen's reason at the time was indeed diarrhoea, a plausible if somewhat uncourtly excuse, though he may well have had other ones.

We do know that the consequence of the vacuum left by the death of the sole male heir, was (after King Henry died in 1135) nineteen years of civil war between Stephen, the King's nephew, and Matilda, the King's daughter. What happened to Bertold, history does not relate. He was on the ship and was the sole survivor. Whether he was the butcher's accountant or a bastard is entirely open to question, but Juliana, Comtesse de Breteuil, did indeed enter a nunnery where she lived quietly until she died. Of her estranged husband Eustace there is no record. I have quite possibly traduced the man – but there seems little doubt that it was he who ordered the putting out of the Castellan's son's eyes. We know that the two little girls were blinded and disfigured by the Castellan (delivered by their grandfather, the Duke, who was holding them) in revenge for his son's blinding. What happened to them subsequently is unknown.

In terms of historical accuracy, I have tried to be as authentic as I could in relation to everyday life, table manners and so forth, and have immersed myself duly in contemporary reference and research...

One can always do more but research can be a monster that devours the creative impulse. You use what you need and you try to avoid too many people saying 'but that wasn't invented until three centuries later'. Yes, in some respects I have followed the novelist's desire to embroider and on the whole I incline to the Sir Walter Scott or even Shakespearian school of historical writing.

I must freely confess that the current Chateau de Breteuil bears no relationship to the Breteuil of my story. It is in a different place and dates, I believe, from the seventeenth century. It is a very handsome building, but anyone making a pilgrimage to it will be disappointed if they hope to catch a whiff of the matters narrated here.

There are some mouldering remains of the original version near the town of Breteuil, but I must admit that I have been geographically and architecturally promiscuous. I have re-designed my Chateau of Breteuil to suit the telling just as I have done with Breteuil town itself as it was in 1118, and the various other towns and cities that Bertold passes through. I have allotted lakes where there may have been none and abbeys where they did not exist, *et cetera* and so forth, but time has played tricks with geography too.

I have absolutely no evidence that Prince William and his half-sister Matilda were having an affair – except we do know that she, above all the people on board, was the person for whom he turned his little boat back – and with whom he drowned

In short, there is a great deal of historical fact in the book, much supposition, but few downright lies.

A Note on Alcohol

It was, if not discovered, at least developed by the Arabs who used it for perfumes and possibly medical purposes. I have not been able to ascertain if it was taken as medicine – though later writers have praised it for 'puffing away ventosity' and 'preventing the bellye from womblying' and so forth. The influence of Arab knowledge was notable in many areas as it spread upwards from Spain in the eleventh and succeeding centuries, especially via the Jews, some of whom had converted to Christianity. It suited my purpose for alcohol to make an appearance in the story, and though it may be hard to prove it was around at that time, it is also hard to disprove. The same might be said for the appearance of Arabic numerals and the marvellous concept of 0. Now physicists tell us that nothing is full of particles popping in and popping out, a bubbling vacuum pregnant with latency. That is how a novel is, before it is written.

Acknowledgments

I must acknowledge with grateful thanks all manner of people who have helped me, and who cannot be held responsible for some of my more flagrant leaps of imagination or ignorance. The historian whose work has held me together and provided the 'skeleton' for my fleshing out of a story, and sometimes the framework of my narrative where it deals with the troubles Duke Henry had to face in Normandy, is Professor Judith Green. Her indispensable book *Henry I: King of England and Duke of Normandy* has been constantly beside me from start to finish as I have embarked on this journey. And indeed it was on the pages of that history that I found embedded the seeds of what I have taken to be the dark flower of Juliana's fearful revenge. I heartily recommend it to anyone who wants to know more about this intriguing king and his times. Any historical *bêtises* in my narrative are down to me and certainly not to her.

I must also gratefully acknowledge the scholarship, patience and kindness of Dr Linsey Hunter who has read and re-read the manuscript for me, and spent far more time than she should have done as a busy academic herself, hunting down and listing my historical howlers and suggesting ameliorations. Any mistakes that remain, I say again, are all my fault or pig-headedness and *cannot* be laid at her door.

I should also give grateful thanks across the years to Orderic Vitalis, the twelfth-century monk from Gloucestershire who spent most of his life in Normandy. His *Ecclesiastical History* is the main source of contemporary information on King Henry's struggles in Normandy, and on the wreck of the *White Ship*. Thanks are due also to William of Malmesbury who gives us the poignant detail of the prince's half-sister calling to him from the sinking ship as he is rowed away. I am most grateful to Trinity College, Oxford, for protractedly lending me the copy of Orderic's *Ecclesiastical History*. I have had further reference and inspiration from Robert Bartlett's *England under the*

Norman and Angevin Kings, and more mid-mediaeval information and indeed encouragement from Ben Lake, also of Trinity College, Oxford. On the naval side, Dr Ian Friel has given me invaluable help with his knowledge of the history of ships and in particular (for my purposes) of twelfth century shipbuilding. There is not much doubt that the *White Ship* was a standard Viking-type ship with square sail and oars, and a steerboard on the starboard side. The fact that I have decided to make FitzStephen, my shipwright, into an innovator who has introduced a rudder and vestigial castles to his ship is entirely my own vision or mulishness. It is possible that such innovation occurred, but there is no wreck or visual confirmation of such innovations until they appear on town seals more than fifty years after the wreck, also on the Kalmar boat, found in a drained castle moat in Sweden, in the thirteenth century. That is not to say that they could not have happened. The Arabs used rudders and so, on occasion, did the Romans. I liked the idea of my shipwright, a man of whom we know next to nothing, being an innovator obsessed with making a special ship. So I have flown against expert opinion – but sometimes innovations happen that way too. I though it made the shipwright a more interesting character. After all, there must have been something about the *White Ship* for everyone to have been so excited about it – even before it sank. I am told it was not unusual to paint royal ships, but a white ship must have looked especially mystic and wonderful.

Finally, but not least, I would like to express my enormous gratitude to Francis Bennett for his support and encouragement, to my agent Laura Morris for her belief, experience, wisdom and good advice, and to my patient and creative and long-suffering editor Rebecca Lloyd as well as Penny Hunter, Bethan James and everyone involved at Accent Press.

Difficile est longam subito deponere amorem. Catullus

It is hard, after a long and great love, suddenly to say goodbye.

THE INVADER SERIES

Edward Ruadh
BUTLER

SWORDLAND